LINEAGE

FATE: BOOK 1

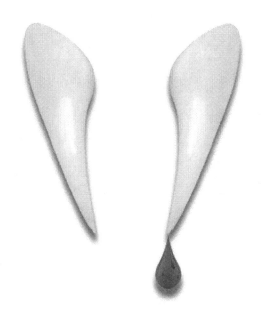

BY
DAVID S. SHOCKLEY II

LINEAGE
Fate: Book 1

HAPPY THANKSGIVING!

- LOVE

ANNA & EMMA

Emma & Anna

For Mary,
Thank you for dreaming with me!

Love, Dave

CONTENTS

PREFACE

"Accept the things to which fate binds you, and love
the people with whom fate brings you together,
but do so with all your heart."

Marcus Aurelius

"When I start movin', you see a blur.
Get hooked on me baby, there ain't no cure.
I've always been able to laugh at fate.
Two brown eyes filled with hate."

The Ramones

~

Jack ducked under a low-hanging branch and caught a virgin spiderweb in the face for his efforts.

"Apologies..." he mumbled while pulling the ghostlike silk from his eyebrows and hair. He reached back towards the tree and returned a tiny green spider to her original perch. She wasted no time in beginning construction on a new web for the night, and Jack imagined the little creature grumbling under her breath as she spun away. It made him chuckle.

He was only seconds from the mountain's summit now. The sun had vanished just below the horizon, and the constant stream of visitors visiting the boulders overlooking the valley below had ceased. The small mountaintop was a popular one, and for good reasons. The view from its peak was spectacular, and the ascent, while strenuous, was brief. Several stars sparkled to life, and a cool, sweet-scented breeze danced into being. The air smelled of honeysuckle, pine, and granite, all of which had spent too long baking away in the day's oppressive heat. The enchanting aroma permeated everything.

Jack found his usual spot, cleared away a small trace of pollen, and sat down. The stone beneath him was still warm, and would remain so for most of the evening. This was the eleventh night in a row he had visited this exact spot on the mountain. Eleven nights, without fail.

And all of them had been too early.

He knew that. He even chided himself over it nightly. Yet he couldn't convince himself to wait...and tonight was different.

1

Tonight could be *the* night! And if not, if things progressed as he hoped, tomorrow *would* be. So Jack had come early, evening after evening. He was far too nervous not too. Nervous, and somewhat giddy—a feeling he'd learned to appreciate again, even enjoy. Jack's heart skipped a beat, a dizzy feeling stirred in his stomach, and he smiled.

His family would object, of course. He was acting irrationally; in fact, what he was doing was even somewhat irresponsible. Even Jack acknowledged these things. But he was powerless under the circumstances. He could no more resist returning to this location, on this night, than the stars could resist shining above. So he'd kept his little escapades a secret. Covert travels that would, he hoped, prove worth the inevitable pain and suffering which would follow. If Jack was right, tonight or tomorrow night would be the night he'd been anticipating for an entire year. Very soon, if he was lucky, would mark the beginning of a new adventure for him. A new life. A new...

...there it was again.

Jack bolted to his feet, turned a complete circle, and examined his surroundings. He half-expected to see one of his family members, but he was still alone. The shadows below, the dark ridges beyond, and the forest behind him yielded no clues. No strange sounds, no exotic eyes peering back at him, no alien smells. He was alone. Except he wasn't. Not really.

For the eleventh night in a row now, Jack was certain he was being watched.

1

Michael took a final sip of his wine. It had been a nice wine, as the label had promised, full of colorful notes like cherry, chocolate, and cinnamon. Perfect for dinner, especially red meat. The irony in that made Michael chuckle, but he would much rather be drinking a good cider. There was a small convenience store about twenty minutes from the house, but there was an amazing cidery even closer. Bold Rock Cidery had been through a major renovation recently, and while Michael hadn't yet taken the time to see all of the improvements, he had enjoyed quite a bit of their product. The idea of flying over, breaking into their storeroom, and absconding with a little selection flashed across his mind before disappearing. On any other night he'd have already done so, but tonight, he settled for the wine.

Tonight, Michael was studying someone.

Just over two miles away stood Humpback Rock, a massive greenstone outcropping near the peak of Humpback Mountain. It rose about three thousand feet in elevation and was an extremely popular hike due to its proximity to an easily accessible entrance to the Blue Ridge Parkway—and multiples colleges all within an hour's drive, which ushered in droves of day hikers and selfie sticks. It wasn't unusual to see dozens of hikers on the trail leading up to the summit and picnicking atop the rocks, especially on the weekend.

What *was* unusual, though, was seeing someone atop the rocks at night.

The hike itself, though strenuous at times, wasn't a difficult one. It was short. Then again, the elevation gain was considerable for the average person, and while the trail was well marked, there were quite a few places where you could twist an ankle or take a nasty spill if you weren't paying attention. So to see someone out on the rocks at night was unusual...not unheard of, but strange.

Beyond that, what made the man Michael was studying even more peculiar was that this was the second week in a row he had appeared on the summit of Humpback just after sundown. The mysterious figure always always arrived at the same time, sat in the same spot, and always stayed for the night, only leaving when the sun began to peek over the horizon (for which Michael was thankful). These were all strange behaviors, but nothing too weird, really; just someone with a penchant for sitting in the wild, alone, at night. Admittedly, the view was quite magical from there, particularly the stars.

What was most puzzling, though, was that Michael could never discern where the man came from, or how he left. There was a parking lot at the bottom of the rocks that was clearly visible from where Michael sat watching. There was never a car to mark the man's arrival, nor his departure. He wasn't driving there, and no one was dropping him off and picking him back up. He could have been hiking in from somewhere, but Michael never saw him on the trails once he left the rocks. There was a small campground at Humpback, but there were no tents visible right now, and there hadn't been for the better part of the summer. It was just too hot for the average camper. For all Michael could tell, the man just magically appeared, spent the night sitting on the rocks overlooking the valley below, and then disappeared—only to repeat the process the next night.

2

Vampires are exceptionally good at seeing long distances, and they are unmatched in their abilities to see at night. At least, Michael guessed as much; he honestly had no clue. In fact, he was the only vampire he knew at present. He had only ever known a single other vampire, and even that was just long enough to learn her name, Elizabeth, that she'd been responsible for turning him, and to explain to him the very basics of what he was now. And basic it was: she'd told him what not to do in order not to die, and that he would need blood to survive. Oh, and that he was practically immortal outside of the few ways it was possible for him to perish now. And that had been it! Off she'd gone, leaving behind a very confused, very frightened, and very naïve 21-year-old. So to say that Michael didn't know one way or the other if vampires were unmatched in their nocturnal visual acuity wouldn't have been too far from the truth.

So to think that a couple of miles off, sitting on an isolated cliff face in the middle of the woods, might be another vampire…well, that intrigued Michael. The idea that this lone figure might be another being like him wasn't outside of the realm of possibility. It was unlikely, but unlikely didn't mean impossible. It would certainly account for the man's strange abilities to appear and disappear. It also checked the box of never arriving before sunset and always leaving before sunrise.

Michael had spent the better part of his observation time just trying to build up the courage to pay the man a visit.

5

He didn't really have many friends these days. He didn't have any, to be honest. Friendship was now a complicated issue, and Michael had thought it wise to avoid extraneous complicated matters. He had enough to deal with. By avoiding relationships, Michael had inadvertently turned himself into somewhat of an introvert, which was unnatural for him. He'd become a hermit in his little fortress on the mountain. He hadn't been like that *before,* especially after losing his family. When that had happened, he'd surrounded himself with friends, daily, hourly even, doing his best to make more on an almost weekly basis. Doing so helped bury the pain of the loss he'd endured. But then entered the vampire Elizabeth, and things had changed for him, irrecoverably so—and not long after that, friends became a luxury Michael didn't think he could afford.

Nanook and Thorn wagged their tails as Michael sat his now empty bottle of courage on the banister, pulled back his dark hair into a ponytail, and stood up. He wobbled just a little. Sometimes courage comes with a price.

"Not right now, guys. We'll go for a walk when...well, when I get back, I promise."

At the word "walk," both dogs began to prance and bounce around. Michael smiled and rubbed each dog's head.

"I won't be long," he said. "I hope."

Michael looked down to his yard below, and then out over the dark forest leading to Humpback.

"Go...just go...go, go, go...."

"I'm drunk."

"You're buzzed. Tipsy, at best...now go!"

Michael took a deep breath, concentrated for a moment, took two long strides, and leapt over the balcony railing. He soared into the cool summer breeze, taking large gulps of fresh air in an effort to clear his head.

"Yep...I'm drunk."

He hovered there for a moment, took a few more deep breaths, and oriented himself about twenty feet above the treetops. Michael then turned and made straight for Humpback Rock. As he flew, he decided it was best to approach the man from further back along the trail—from enough of a distance to intentionally make himself known, so as not to spook the stranger.

When Michael was close enough, he hovered in the dark a moment, checked that the stranger had not moved, and descended through the treetops onto the trail below. This section of mountain was well traveled but not well-groomed. An average person might be able to navigate it in the dark, but a vampire? Well, it wasn't a problem. There was a nice breeze which rustled the leaves overhead just so, and carried with it more scents of the season, especially the honeysuckle. Deer were everywhere, and raccoons scurried about in search of something to steal. Two possum, a black bear, and several snakes meandered through the woods, paying Michael little to no mind. They were night creatures like him, and most seemed to understand he meant them no harm. They simply studied their nocturnal kindred for a moment or so, and then carried on about their business.

As he hiked on, Michael guessed he was now two, possibly three minutes from the summit at his current speed. A speed that had slowed often as he stopped and proceeded to fight an overwhelming urge to leap back into the night air and race back to the security of his home. This was proving more difficult than Michael had guessed, and the liquid courage was wearing off.

"Come on. Just go talk to him. Easy. Simple. Just go say hi."

Michael began to hum a little tune, snap a few branches underfoot, and generally attempt to appear as anything other than a highly skilled nocturnal predator. It also helped calm his nerves. This was easy! Right? And he wasn't threatening! Right? He was singing a tune from *The Lion King;* how dangerous could he be?

"You suck at this; you know that, right? Hakuna matata, my ass."

The path leveled out, and the trees parted beneath a brilliant starlit sky. A warm breeze drifted up from the valley below, whistling through the many pine needles overhead. An owl called out, a bat dove into the shadows, and a....

"Why are you here, vampire?"

Michael let out a yelp, tripped over a jagged rock, and sprawled hard onto the dirt path. "Jesus!"

The stranger he'd been watching these past few weeks stepped out onto the trail from where Michael had just been. He'd blended so well with the shadows that Michael hadn't even sensed the man, much less seen, heard, or even smelled him.

"Why are you here, vampire? And why have you been watching me for so many nights?"

Michael scrambled back a foot or two and began to get up until the man stepped closer. Michael held up a hand. "Look, I apologize if I frightened you—"

"You did not," the man said. With that, he produced a large blueish blade seemingly out of nowhere. The path and trees surrounding the two were bathed in a deep cobalt light. "I will ask you a final time, vampire. Why are you here? Why have you been watching me?"

Michael inched backwards in the dirt and twigs, raising

both hands. "Look, look, I'm not here to hurt you. I, I just wanted to talk, to chat, you know, say hi! I'm not looking for a fight! Again, I apologize if—"

The man stepped forward and held the point of the blade to Michael's throat. He stood there like that for several seconds before his eyes narrowed and he cocked his head to the side. "To chat."

Michael had been holding his breath. "YES! Yes, dammit! To chat! That's it! I...I saw you sitting out here, night after night, and—"

"Say hi...."

"What? YES! Say hi! Chat! Be fucking neighborly and shit!"

The man studied Michael a second more, his brow furrowed, and then he nodded. "And you are in fact, a vampire, yes?"

"What? Yes! I mean.... Aren't—"

"Interesting. Apology accepted."

"Inter...apology what?"

"You are telling the truth. Apology accepted," the man said, and slid the blade behind him. It vanished, the path fell back into shadow, and he extended a hand.

Michael blinked several times in an effort to regain some of his night vision. The stranger continued to stand there, hand extended. Michael exhaled, rubbed his eyes, and accepted the gesture. "Thank you."

The man nodded and pulled Michael to his feat with ease. "You are welcome."

The two stood there for a moment, neither saying a word. Michael shifted his footing while the stranger looked poised to say something, only to stop, and then start the process over again. This lasted long enough to summon a palpable shroud of unease around the two.

The stranger finally managed to clear his throat. "Do you mind if we carry on this...this *chat* back at the overlook?"

"Sure, sure."

Michael dusted himself off and followed the stranger towards the cliff face above. When he was able to shake off some of the embarrassment and jitters, he noticed the man was dressed a bit, well, oddly. His clothes looked different, alien, sort of...*off*. The shirt resembled silk, but wasn't; it was heavier, yet still retained that silky sheen. The pants appeared to be dark brown leather, but again, like the shirt, a little different. And the blade, the sword, the fucking real-life lightsaber or whatever that damned thing was, had vanished. It wasn't just hidden; it was gone. The man's shirt was tight enough that it was obvious he wasn't concealing a weapon beneath it, and the weapon certainly wasn't tucked into his pants. It was just...gone. The stranger also wore calf-high boots, black and covered in intricate forest green embroidery, with his pants tucked neatly inside. Again, no blade hid there, either.

The trees and dirt gave way to stone, and the peak of Humpback Rock appeared before them. A short scramble over several boulders, and the two were surrounded by literally tons of granite. When they reached the edge of the cliff face, the man took up his usual seat and motioned for Michael to join him on a stone several feet to his right. Michael sat down and was about to speak when his new acquaintance raised a hand signaling him to wait. They sat for a full minute like that, then the stranger cocked his head to the side for a moment, took a deep breath, and sighed.

"I apologize. I thought I heard someone below. Only deer."

Michael stared out over the dark woods. He could neither hear nor see any deer within the shadows from this side of the mountain. He redirected his attention back to the stranger, who was studying him back.

"I, uh...I don't mean to be rude or anything. But um, how did you know I was watching you? And uh, that I was, you know, a...a vampire, too? I mean, I can't tell if you're...."

"Too?"

"I mean, you're a...you know," Michael motioned to the man and then back to himself several times. "A, uh...well, you know, a...." This time he took a deep breath, sighed, and cleared his throat. "Aren't you a vampire?"

The man smiled and let out a small laugh. "No."

3

Michael was confused. Confused, and now frightened. If this man wasn't a vampire, how the hell did he know he'd been watched these past several nights? Observed from over two miles away, no less! If he'd been a vampire, he'd likely have seen Michael, wouldn't he? Michael had spied him easily enough. And wouldn't he have sensed something? Michael had been able to tell if someone was watching him for years now.

"Soooo...." Michael started, and then stopped. He cleared his throat and offered the stranger a small apologetic grin. "Sorry, gimme a sec."

The man nodded.

Michael's heart was racing, injecting a low, disconcerting rhythm deep into his ears and through the back of his throat. If this guy wasn't a vampire, how did he even know that they were real? Or that Michael was one of them? All of that, combined with being ambushed on the trail—something Michael had no idea how the stranger managed—the casual ease with which the man called him a vampire, and the disappearing, real-life Star Wars prop? Well, it all gave Michael a sick feeling.

"So you're not a...a umm... a vampire, then? But, how did you know that I was? Or that vampires...you know, that, that well, they, we—me—we actually exist?"

The stranger looked over Michael for a moment, his eyes narrowing, his smile growing. "You are not very old, are you?"

"What?"

"And you do not travel between, do you?"

"Travel where?"

"I'm sorry. I am being rude. I am just...well, I am very surprised to meet you. My name is Jack, and you are?"

"Michael."

"Well, Michael, I do not mean to be so direct. What I meant was, you are young, are you not?"

"Well no, not really. I'm forty-nine."

"Hundred?"

"What? No, no, no...I'm only...forty-nine hundred? Vampires get that old?"

"You don't know?

"I don't know *what* the hell is going on right now, man," Michael said.

Jack smiled. "I've heard rumors that some vampires live much longer than forty-nine hundred years."

Michael shook his head. "Soo...." He stopped. "I..." he started, and stopped again. He was at a loss.

"I apologize, Michael. What I meant to infer was, you appear to be too young to be capable of sensing other vampires just yet. Considering what I have read, I understand that your kind's appearance changes very little over the years. So I was uncertain of how old you actually were, you understand. And to be honest, I have very little firsthand knowledge of your kind. In fact, I have none whatsoever. Please forgive me. I am honored, privileged even, to meet you, and I meant no offense. I beg of your pardon."

Michael was shaking his head. "None taken?"

Jack nodded and sighed, visibly relieved. "So if you thought

I was another vampire, that means you have no understanding of what I am, then?"

"Well, you're not…I mean, I know you're different, man! I know that much at least. No uh, no offense."

Jack cocked his head to the side again. "None taken. You do not travel between realms, do you?"

Michael laughed this time. "Man, I don't even know what the hell that means, much less know if I do or don't travel to and from wherever you're talking about! You're not from around here, are you? I mean, you're not like anyone I've ever met."

Jack laughed, too. "No, no I would expect not." He stood, straightened his shirt, ran a hand through his hair, and bowed formally. "I am faerie. It is my pleasure to meet you. Well, meet you again, as it were."

"Umm," Michael started, and stopped again.

"Fey? Fey folk."

Michael remained silent.

"Hulder? Elven? Elvish?"

Michael's eyes widened. "ELF! You're an elf!"

Jack smiled and nodded.

"Wait, you're an elf? Like a…like an elf, elf?"

"I am not certain of what an elf-elf is, but yes, I am an elf."

"Like," Michael paused. "So you're an elf. Like, *Lord of the Rings* kinda elf? Santa's elves and whatnot?"

Jack laughed long and hard, collapsing back to his usual seat. Several tears even rolled down his cheeks. Michael felt his own cheeks flush, but Jack's amusement with Michael was somewhat comforting at least. The man seemed genuinely amused.

"No, Michael, not like Santa's elves."

Michael grinned and chuckled a little. "Sorry, I...." His voice faded, and his cheeks burned.

Jack smiled. "Though, to be honest, I can see the similarities. Santa, while an elf himself, does not employ other elves; the stories get that wrong on almost every occasion. He does, however, utilize gnomes and pixies; they help him quite a bit, especially when it comes to the chimneys. I, however, am Elvish. We are a much older race than the pixies and gnomes Saint Nicholas employs."

"SANTA CLAUS IS FUCKING REAL!?"

Jack began to laugh again, this time much louder, and he toppled backwards from his seat. New tears glistened on his cheeks. "I like you, Michael!" the elf said from his back while wiping his face. "I like you very much! But unfortunately, no. Santa is not real. I was just...making a little joke, smoothing the ground between us, as it were." Jack pulled himself back into a sitting position. "The chimneys of the worlds are safe from magical, gift-bearing beings," he added, and wiped away another tear.

Michael was one hundred percent positive that his face was actually on fire now. "Ahh," he managed, and took another deep breath. This was NOT how he had expected tonight to go. Not at all! "How did you know that I was a vampire, though?"

Jack regained his composure, cleared his throat, and wiped away several more tears. "When you first began watching me, I felt it. It was something new, yet simultaneously, it was a familiar feeling in a bizarre fashion. I've never sensed a vampire before, so the feeling was very strong when it occurred. Strong, yet...alien in a rather confusing way. A rare thing shines so much brighter, would you not agree?"

"Rare?"

Jack looked confused. "I am sorry, I do not follow you."

"You said rare, so there, what, there aren't a lot of us, where you're from, then? Of vampires?"

Jack's smile faded away. "I am sorry, no, not any longer. Not there, nor here, I am afraid."

"Here?" Michael's mind was spinning faster now. "Did they like, die out? Or...?"

Jack sighed and stared out into the night. "Your keeper, did they not tell you these things?"

"Keeper? I, I don't understand. You mean the vampire who turned me?"

"Turned, yes; turned, sired, made or created you. Your mentor. Did they not tell you these things?"

Michael shook his head and fell silent.

"I am sorry," Jack said. He then made a small motion with his hand, and the air seemed to cool just a bit.

Michael nodded, took a deep breath, and tossed his hands in the air. "So yeah, umm, no, she didn't tell me much at all, really. She told me what I was, that no, it wasn't a joke, that it was important to be kept a secret, that I could be killed but not easily. Stuff like: stay away from sunlight, drink blood when I feel "thirsty," quote un-quote. Avoid killing people when I *did* drink. That I would be able to fly one day. Like, actually take flight. I'd have stronger senses. Be able to kinda control people. And to keep my new reality a secret or "someone," more quotes, that *someone* would find me, find me and then kill me. She really drove that one home. That if I exposed myself, someone would just show up and straight up murder me! Then she just—poof! Gone! Like she'd just told me what the day's specials were and would be back in a minute if I had anymore questions! Just like that. Poof! Gone! I never saw her again, and believe me when I tell you that I looked! Like, I looked for years. You know what really made it really real, though? Like, drove it home? That morning? After the whole "welcome to vampirism" talk? When the sun came up, I caught on fire, man! Like, I literally exploded into flames in my bedroom. Don't ask how, but I managed to get into my shower and flip it on before passing out. Woke up after it got dark, soaked, cold, naked minus my shoes, water still running, and my shower curtain nothing but melted plastic on the bathroom floor." Michael took a deep breath as he finished and looked over to Jack. The elf sat there, his eyes wide, his mouth open. "So yeah, man! That's me."

Jack was quiet for a moment more, his brow furrowed. "That is...that is very...that was cruel. Cruel, and very unusual."

Michael laughed. "You're not kidding!"

"What was her name? Was she decent enough to provide that?"

"'Said her name was Elizabeth."

Jack's eyes narrowed again. "Well, that is something, at least."

"You were saying there weren't many of us left?" Michael asked. "So what, like, what happened? I have so many questions."

"I am sure you do, Michael. I honestly wish I could answer all of them for you, but I do not know what happened exactly. I only know that vampires everywhere winked nearly out of existence seemingly overnight. One moment they were there, and then the next, they were not. Most of them, anyway. There are rumors that some still live. I am told that the event was very strange, very sad. It happened before I was born."

"You mean like, like where you're from *and* here as well?"

Jack nodded. "To the best of my understanding. Vampires everywhere simply, well, they vanished."

"And vampires are…" Michael paused. "Well, vampires were just like, common knowledge over, umm…over where you're from? Not just, you know…well, over here they're just imaginary creatures, man! Fictional—or at least, that's what most people think. Hell, it's what I thought!"

"Yes. Where I am from, vampires are just as real as any other race. I am sorry that I do not know much more about them, or what happened."

Michael sighed and leaned back on the rocks. "Dammit."

"I am sorry to upset you, Michael. Shall we discuss something less, less painful? What brings you here, for instance? And how did you discover me?"

Michael stared into sky above. The stars were always so beautiful now. Especially since he'd become a vampire. There were so many more than he ever remembered seeing before; millions more, in fact. They comforted him. And right now, sitting next to what appeared to be an elf and learning that he was practically alone in the world as a vampire, he needed the comfort.

"Are you all right, Michael? I am sorry to be the bearer of such news."

"Yeah, yeah, I'm okay. Thanks, Jack. I was just, I was…you know what, I don't know what I was thinking, or hoping really. It's just been so damned long, and I've had to learn so many things on my own. I was just, just hoping to finally get some answers, you know? It's hard to explain."

"No, no, it makes perfect sense. And you have my sympathies."

The two sat there for a bit, neither saying anything. A full moon climbed over the horizon, chasing away some of the stars, but replacing them with something just as magnificent. The air was so clear, and the lack of any other light pollution made the silver orb appear close enough to touch.

Michael cleared his throat. "So I first spotted you about two weeks ago...."

4

Jack nodded. "That is about the time I felt something,"

"So you could, what? You could sense me watching you?"

Jack nodded again. "Of course."

Michael shook his head and continued, "Oooookay. So I had just woken up, and the dogs were whining and begging for a walk. They do that all the time when I first get up. Anyway, I figured I'd take them out on the trails. We were up on the deck, ready to head down, and I think I stopped to tie my boot or something. When I did, I glanced over in this direction."

"Here, towards the Emerald Seat?"

"The what?"

"Apologies, that is what I have always heard it called, the Emerald Seat. When the sun sets just right, the green flash illuminates it for the evening; hence the name Emerald Seat."

"The green what?"

"The green...I am sorry, I did not mean to interrupt you. Please go on."

"You're not a fan of contractions, are you?"

"Contractions? Oh! Informal speech? I'm. You're. I've. You've. Is that what you mean?"

"Yeah, man, you just don't seem to use them. You sound, I dunno, you sound almost as nervous as I do."

Jack smiled. "In my culture, informal speech is to be used only with friends and family, and never with—well, apologies, but...strangers."

Michael nodded. "Ahh, right. Umm, okay. Sorry, I just kept noticing the way you speak, and I... You know what? What were we talking about? The green seat and the green flash?"

Jack chuckled. "I had interrupted you. Rudely, I might add. You were telling me about the first time you noticed my presence here."

"Right, so um, yeah, I looked over here to the uh, what did you call it?"

"Emerald Seat."

"...the Emerald Seat, right. We call this place Humpback, by the way."

"Humpback? I prefer Emerald Seat, if I am honest."

"Yeah, now that you mention it, I do, too. Humpback doesn't exactly convey the message "beautiful," does it?"

"No, not at all. Unless you consider an unfortunate physiological condition beautiful, that is."

"I know, right? Anyway, Humpback, sorry, the Emerald Seat always looks so amazing this time of year. You know, these gray rocks jutting out of a sea of green. It's really a nice sight in the evenings. Anyway, I remember seeing you sitting here, and that was kinda it. I didn't think much more about it. You were just some hiker admiring the stars. I walked the dogs for a couple of hours, did a little work on one of the trails—I'm a trail angel, and—"

"A trail angel?"

"Yeah, it's part of trail magic."

"You know magic?"

"Well, no, it's...lemme come back to that."

"Of course. Again, my apologies. It seems we both have quite a lot of questions for one another."

"Right? Um, anyway, when I got back, I fed the dogs, grabbed a cider, and walked out onto the deck. What made me look back over here, I have no idea, but I did, and *when* I did, there you were! Still just sitting here. Honestly, I thought maybe time had gotten away from you, and you'd just decided it was safer to stay up there for the night instead of risking a bad ankle sprain or a break by going back down in the dark. Maybe you hadn't brought a flashlight or something? I dunno. Anyway, that was it, really. At least until the next night, when you showed up again. One minute the rocks were empty, the next, well, there you were again! That's when I started paying more attention."

Jack nodded and looked in the direction of Michael's home. "I wonder why I never saw you."

"Can you see like me? I mean, I can see pretty far. Can *you* see that far?"

"To the dwelling you just described? Yes. Actually it is the only one with a sitting area facing this direction for quite a distance."

"Quite a distance? How far *can* you see?"

"With my eyes? Quite a distance. I can see as far as the land allows, anyway. I can not see beyond the horizon with them."

"Your eyes...what do you mean by that?"

"Well, I can see much further with my mind. It is like seeing where you *want* to see instead of simply where you *can* see. Do you understand?"

"I don't think so, not really."

"Well, how far can you see clearly, right now, right here?"

Michael looked back towards his house and as far beyond it as he could before things lost color and began to get blurry. About a mile or two further, a small parking area sat at a trailhead to another hike.

"I guess maybe, two and a half, three miles? I can see a parking area not far beyond my house."

Jack turned and gazed in that direction. "The clearing beside the painted road? All right. So, imagine looking there, and then at the extent of your sight, using your mind to travel further and further along, seeing not with your eyes, but with your mind. Does that illustrate the point a bit more?"

"I think so?"

"Good. You mentioned magic earlier. Trail magic, to be precise. What is trail magic, and what did you mean by you being an angel?"

"Ahh! Trail magic!" Michael began to tell Jack everything he knew about being a trail angel on the Appalachian Trail, and then stopped himself mid-sentence.

Jack glanced up at the sudden silence. "Are you all right?"

"You know, I just thought of something. We just met, what, a few minutes ago? Not only that, but I just found out you're an elf, like, there are other supernatural beings besides myself, and I just told someone that I'm a vampire for the first time... IN MY LIFE! I mean"—Michael waved his hands at Jack—"an ELF! I'm talking to an elf! You don't know how weird that is to me!"

"I think I—"

"...and with all of that, you would think I'd be a bit more

cautious, you know, a bit reserved, but NOPE! Here we are talking like old friends, and I'm blabbering on and on and on about literally everything! I was about to explain obscure hiking culture to you, as if a vampire and an elf, sitting on top of a rock in the middle of the woods, in the middle of the night, was as normal as, I don't know, whatever is like, really, really normal! I mean...just listen to me!"

"Yes, I see where—"

"And you know what I think? I think this must feel an AWFUL lot like what someone under my thrall goes through when I have to use it!"

The two sat staring at one another for a moment, and Jack raised his hand as if to ask permission to speak. "If you would permit me...?"

Michael nodded, but he did stand up and take a step back.

"You are correct, Michael. I have woven a sort of...how did you describe it?"

"Thrall? I dunno, I looked that up or saw it in a movie or something. I don't know what to call it. It's like hypnosis."

"Well, thrall would not be inaccurate. Regardless, yes, I did cast a small—*thrall*—as it were. But not in order to take advantage of you, and nothing quite as powerful as what a vampire can cast or do with his or her ability."

"Soooo, what does that mean? Am I under your control? Did you hypnotize me?"

"No, no, no...what I did was simply assure you. Or reassure you, on a subconscious level as it were. I let you know that you need not worry about speaking with me—to tell your inner self that you could be comfortable around me. We call it a glimmer or glimmering."

"So it's like a thrall."

24

"Well, in a way, yes. But in a way, no. From what I understand, by casting a thrall, vampires can compel their subjects to do certain things, even if those things go against the subject's very nature, or might lead to their own harm or even their demise. They, vampires that is, can also force a subject to tell the truth, even if, again, that is something that might lead to their personal harm or the harm of others. It is a very natural ability for a vampire. With glimmering, certain faerie can use it to do a variety of things, but one thing it can not accomplish is forcing a being to act out, or to do anything they would not otherwise already wish to do. We certainly cannot compel a subject to tell us something they would not already wish to reveal naturally. Well, not without utilizing quite a bit of forbidden magic—and to do that, one would break several of our most cherished and honored laws. The act would be virtually unforgivable. Does that make sense?"

"I think so. Maybe? I'm not really sure."

Jack continued. "With glimmering, what I did for you—it is important to note that, by the way, I did that FOR you—I simply allowed you to be comfortable with me. I could sense your unease, but I could also sense your honesty and your sincere wish to connect. I knew you meant no harm. So I simply allowed you to...be comfortable. I apologize if I overstepped my bounds; I meant no offense, I assure you."

"How do I know you're not lying to me? Like, this sounds really similar to what a thrall can do, and I can tell people to believe anything I want them to believe. And they do, man, seriously! I once had a guy convinced he could...you know what? Never mind, forget that. How do I know you're not lying to me?"

"Well, you might have noticed that you are feeling a bit more worried now, yes? A bit more reserved, uncertain, afraid even, yes?"

"...I wouldn't really say afraid. You know, I'm not...not scared or anything,"

Jack's eyes narrowed. "Mm-hmm. Good. But you are nervous, uncertain. This is because as soon as I realized that you were uncomfortable with the knowledge I had cast a glimmering, I removed it at once. I did this so you could understand why. One thing I cannot do is lie. It is faerie law. And to prove that everything I am saying is true, I invite you to thrall me and ask me yourself!"

"You don't lie? That's exactly what a liar would say!"

"Yes, yes it is. Again, that is why I invite you to cast your thrall on me. Ask me anything, but be sure to ask me if what I just told you was, in fact, the truth."

Michael just stood there. Silent.

Jack stood as well, and when Michael stepped backwards, Jack held up his hands.

"Michael, I'm not lying to you. You're in no danger, and I'd very much like to be your friend."

This time, Michael cocked his head to the side. "You just..." He paused for a moment. "You just used, like, three contractions in a row."

Jack smiled. "Informal speech."

"Right!"

"...with those we consider friends or family."

"So you, you're saying we're friends."

"I'd certainly like to consider us as such, Michael. Even if we're very newly acquainted."

Michael started to speak and found a rather uncomfortable and embarrassing lump at the back of his throat.

Jack lowered his hands. "If that is all right with you?"

Michael nodded. "Yeah, I uh, yeah..." he said and cleared his throat. "I umm, yeah man, that would be, uh, that would be cool."

"*Cool.*"

"Yeah, cool man, umm..." Michael's voice faded into silence.

"We were discussing our abilities to influence others?" Jack said. "And I'd invited you to cast your thrall on me?"

Michael nodded and considered what Jack was saying for a moment. He *did* feel different now. Certainly more nervous. And he had felt at ease just moments before. More than just a bit, even—Michael had become a rambling, walking-talking-prologue for the stranger he'd just met. So yes, he'd been a bit *relaxed*. At least, before Jack said he'd removed the whatever-he-called-it from him. It had been a pleasant feeling, not at all disconcerting. Like having a couple of beers when surrounded by strangers. But he was still a bit shocked at just *how* comfortable he'd felt. He had literally just plopped down and opened right up to a complete stranger who not only acknowledged that he was an imaginary "creature of the night," but also appeared to have zero concern about it whatsoever. AND, that stranger professed to be something that, until Michael had become a vampire, would have never believed possible, not outside of fiction, anyway. Jack, the real-life elf, even had a magical disappearing sword! He'd even ambushed Michael —snuck up behind him as if it were no more difficult than performing a simple magic trick to a captivated audience of sleepy five-year-olds. Michael hadn't been surprised or caught off guard like that in decades; not since he'd been turned, anyway. Not even close. Even his dogs, who could stalk prey with the best of them, couldn't sneak up on Michael or surprise him.

"Michael? Are you all right?"

Michael cleared his throat again. "Yeah, so…so you want me to use my thrall or whatever it is on you?"

Jack smiled. "Yes, if it would make you more comfortable. Especially since it will allow you the chance to ask me anything you'd like, and discern for yourself whether or not I am indeed lying to you."

Michael thought about that for a second. If Jack *was* lying to him, he could *easily* force him to speak the truth. Then again, he was an elf, or so he said. And if he was an elf, some magical being Michael had only ever read about or seen in fictional stories and films, who was to say he couldn't resist a thrall, or even manipulate it? What if he could just pretend to be under Michael's influence? But he'd be able to tell, wouldn't he? Michael had influenced people before with his ability, and he'd known immediately if they were resistant, or outright resisting him. It was rare, but it did happen.

"And you won't try and stop me? Or somehow…I dunno, trick me?"

"I'm not sure I could, if I'm honest. But I promise you Michael, I will not attempt to resist you. Again, I'm not sure I could if I wished to. That being said, would you give me your word that you will not to harm me in any way?"

"Harm you?" Michael asked. "I don't want to hurt you."

"Thank you."

Michael began to speak and again found himself at a loss for words tonight. His hands were shaking now.

"I'm not lying to you, Michael," Jack said. "You must trust me in this. You seem a genuinely honorable soul, so please believe me when I tell you: you can ask me anything you like."

Michael nodded. "Well, I appreciate the sentiment. But you'll understand if I just, well, make sure for myself."

Jack smiled. "If I were you, I would most certainly do the same."

Michael nodded to the elf again and began to concentrate. It always felt like he was gathering his will, his determination, and then balling it up in a nice, neat little sphere within his mind. It was the same sensation he used to fly. It appeared as a little, mental, silver orb, and sparkled like a miniature disco ball deep in his imagination. Once he had it, the feeling was similar to tossing someone something, like you might do with the car keys or the remote control. He cast his little thrall-ball towards Jack, and waited. The effect was usually instant, or close enough to it. Michael was always able to see it take hold in his target's eyes—as if the silver globe he conjured took root in their mind and shone forth from deep within, causing their eyes almost to glow, to sparkle. It was an invisible effect to anyone other than Michael, and perhaps other vampires, but on that point, he wasn't certain. He'd never been able to ask another vampire if they could actually see or sense if someone was thralled, but he'd been around other humans, who never seemed to notice their friends' eyes shining like that.

Jack's eyes didn't sparkle. They didn't even glitter for a moment. Nothing. They remained just as blue and as clear as they had from the minute the two had met.

"That felt a little strange! Like a breeze made of tiny feathers, if I'm honest," Jack said.

Michael sighed. "I'm not sure it took hold."

"Well, by all means, please try again! That was very interesting!"

Michael concentrated again, this time making the silvery sphere just a bit larger, and a bit brighter. He tossed it toward

Jack.

Nothing happened.

After several more attempts, Michael's head was pounding, and the last thrall he tried was damn near the size of a basketball. The effort of "tossing" it towards Jack had Michael not only out of breath, but dizzy enough that he knelt down gasping for air, drops of sweat rolling over his cheeks. Again, nothing. An awkward silence fell over the two.

Jack cleared his throat after a time. "Well, these things happen, Michael. It's nothing to be embarrassed about."

"I'm not..."
  *gasp
"I'm not, embarrassed..."
  *pant
"I'm kind of... annoyed, actually!"

"Yes, I can see that. Perhaps it's a matter of age?"

"You're not helping."

"What I mean is, you are very, very young, after all. I would wager you could cast a thrall on just about anyone you came across outside of, in this case, an elf of my age. I would suspect your ability will increase in strength as you grow older. If it's any consolation, the last one felt like a rather large pillow resting gently on my head!"

"A pillow?"

"A large pillow?"

"I nearly gave myself an aneurism, and it felt like a large pillow?"

Jack smiled. "Well, I hope it convinces you of my sincerity in a small way, at least?"

Michael thought about that for a moment. He did like Jack,

and the elf did seem very sincere. "I've always thought I had a pretty good BS meter, man, and I'll be honest, you don't seem to be setting it off."

"BS?"

"Bullshit."

"Bull...ahh! Well, for that I'm grateful."

"Well, since I can't seem to use my thrall on you, I guess I'll just have to take you at your word. As crazy as this all seems to me, by the way, I'm just gunna trust ya for now."

"And I'll trust you, Michael. Perhaps in time we will both earn the trust we are so freely giving to one another now."

Michael half collapsed, half sat back down on the rocks. "That would be nice."

"Agreed."

"So you keep saying I'm young. How old are you, anyway?"

"As far as I know, I am about four hundred years old. We don't measure time from where I hail as you do here. A day is a day, certainly. We have units of time that are similar to your weeks and seasons, even years, but they do not compliment one another perfectly. Again, to you, I would be nearly four hundred years old."

"You're four hundred years old? You look twenty-eight, maybe twenty-nine, tops!"

"Well, thank you."

"How old do elves get? I mean, I was told I was practically immortal, whatever that really means, but are you, are elves immortal? How long do you live? I mean, naturally, I guess? Can you even die?"

"That's a very good question, really. As far as I know, we,

too, are virtually immortal. We can be killed, much like most living things, though it isn't easy; at least, those who have tried have discovered it to be most difficult at times. Unfortunately, however, it's not impossible. We do age, albeit, the older we get, the less we age physically. The physical aging begins in short order, much like the rate of mortals, or humans as it were, but then the effects slows quite dramatically. My parents are quite old—my mother far older than my father I believe, though she does not often speak of her time before they met. They, too, look as if they are my age, outwardly. The oldest living elf that I am aware of is old enough to remember the first humans. She's spoken of the first trees, and the second moon that used to travel across the sky. A faerie moon."

Michael shook his head. "Wow! What, umm, what happened to that, the uh, the faerie moon?"

"Tales tell of a war, during which elvenkind brought down the faerie moon—creating our lands in the process, but simultaneously wiping out almost all life here."

Michael laughed. "So *you guys* killed the dinosaurs!?"

Jack nodded. "Dinosaurs"—he paused a moment and smiled —"yes! I guess we did. Though not all of them. We saved a great deal of life here before the moon was ripped from the heavens, dinosaurs included."

Michael looked up. "Dude, I was totally kidding! I supposed you guys scored all of the unicorns and dragons too, huh?"

"Yes."

Michael chuckled. "Sure...wait, what?"

Jack laughed. "I do so enjoy chatting with you, Michael. Yes, we saved most of the unicorns and dragons as well as the dinosaurs."

Michael grinned. "Well, I'm glad I can make you laugh. So

your lands, that's where the faeries live?"

"Faeriekind, yes! Our world exists alongside this world. Not part of it, but also not quite separate, either. The two cannot exist without the other's connection, to my knowledge. Where we sit, for instance, exists not only here, but in my world as well. It is a good example of why you and I share a similar language, though somewhat different vocabulary at times. Two realms, separate but also one and the same. By the way, my world, or realm as it were, we call Fae."

"The Fae."

"Or simply, Fae. As you would say Earth, we would say Fae. Earth, earthling. Fae, faerie."

"Ahh."

Jack paused the conversation again and seemed to look and listen to the forest below. He stayed that way for almost a full minute before apologizing.

Michael scanned the woods below as well. He detected nothing out of the ordinary. "What exactly are you looking for?"

Jack sighed and stared into space, the shadow of a minuscule smile appearing at the corners of his mouth. "That is a long story, really. Let's just say, I met someone, and I am eager for them to return."

Michael peered at the elf. "It's a girl, isn't it! Or a guy?"

Jack looked back at Michael and smiled. "Yes, I met a woman here, and I hope to meet her again when she journeys through the area once more."

"Well, do tell! Actually, hang on a second, this sounds like we could use something to drink. Do you like cider?"

"Cider? Apple wine! Yes, very much."

"Well, not quite wine, but...have you ever had the cider that is made near here? Bold Rock?"

"No, I'm afraid not. Is that a type of apple?"

"Bold Rock? No, no, no, it's a...you know what, never mind, just wait here a couple of minutes. I'll be right back."

5

Michael flew as fast as he dared to the cidery. It wasn't that far, so the trip took less than three minutes. He could have flown faster, but at his best speeds, the air tended to rip his clothes to shreds, especially if the wind was up—not to mention that his eyes usually stung for hours after his top speeds if he was without eye protection.

Michael circled the cidery, made sure no one was there, and landed on the storage and shipping building. From there, he made his way to the maintenance hatch he used when paying a visit such as this.

"Elf. I'm sitting in the woods talking to an elf. An elf with a magical sword."

Behind the maintenance hatch stood a ventilation chimney surrounded by four large metal fans. Michael reached in, stopped one of the whirling fans and with his other arm, reached into the shaft and retrieved a magnetic hideaway box. He let go of the blade, the motor stopped protesting, and the fan whirred back to life.

"An elf named Jack."

Michael walked over to the maintenance hatch, opened the hideaway box, retrieved a small brass key, and unlocked the door leading down into the warehouse.

Before he descended into the storage room, Michael shook

his head and laughed. "An elf. I've met an elf." Then he saw the new security cameras below him, all pointed down to the main floor. Michael sighed, took off his t-shirt and tied it around his face like a makeshift mask. He jumped down, retrieved some of his favorite cider from the walk-in refrigerators, left more than enough money to pay for it, walked over to the gigantic whiteboard, and scribbled his usual "mystery note" for the employees to find in the morning,

"Thanks again for the delicious cider!
As usual, this should more than make
up for the cost. Until next time!
B. Hood
P.S. Your new security cameras are very nice!"

Word had gotten around the area that Bold Rock had a secret admirer and, more importantly, a thief of their cider— one who not only broke in and out of the business, but left no trace, and *always* paid or more than paid for what he took. The employees had nicknamed him Bobbin Hood, which Michael now used as his signature after a night raid such as this. It was a fun, mostly harmless game. Michael had needed to thrall one of the employees in order to have a secret master key made, but that was as as far as he'd gone where influencing the staff was concerned.

Michael made his way back to Humpback and landed near Jack. "Sorry if that took too long."

Jack nodded. "Not at all! You're actually quite fast. I'm not so sure I can move at those speeds when flying. Perhaps we can compare some evening!"

"You can fly?"

"In a way, yes. I imagine our abilities in that respect are very similar, though I believe you use more of a force of will, while I require assistance to take flight."

"Assistance? So like, you just kinda, what, cast a spell, or whatever?"

Jack chuckled. "In a way, yes. There are several methods for controlling weight, space, or distance, and this sometimes involves time as well. I take advantage of a talisman to assist me in flight, for instance." He pulled a small silver chain above the collar of his shirt; it sparkled in the moonlight and seemed to shine just a little too bright. "This. Before I could even place this charm over my head, I had to memorize quite a few techniques involved in taking flight. Once I'd managed that, I was able to wear the chain. Now, when I require the ability to distort my weight, or the air, or even the gravity around me—in short, fly—I can summon the lessons I memorized and draw on the energy I poured into the talisman. There are various other techniques one may use for flight, but this just happens to be the one that serves me best. Should I abuse or drain too much of the power stored in this talisman, or one like it, I would need to, how best to put it...recharge it?"

Michael nodded. "I'm not really too sure I understood much of that, but I think I get the gist. Can you fly without the, uh, the magical necklace thingy or whatever?"

"My talisman? I can, though it is very difficult," Jack said. "I would not want to try for very long, or in dangerous conditions. I wouldn't want to try most of my magical abilities without the aid of my talismans, to be honest."

"Gotcha," Michael said. "But uh, yeah, we should test our abilities against each other sometime!"

Jack motioned to Michael's chest. "Your shirt?"

"Oh!" Michael sat down the case of cider, un-wadded the t-shirt he'd crammed under his arm, and pulled it back over his head. "Sorry, I had to use it as a kind of mask," he said, and removed a bottle which had cracked and set it aside. "They pop sometimes when I move too quick. I actually flew too high once, and the whole case exploded on me. That was a mess. Here ya go."

Jack reached out and accepted the bottle from Michael. "Thank you. A mask, you say?"

"Well, yeah, I have to steal the cider sometimes. I guess they installed some security cameras since my last visit. But anyway, they're not open at night this time of year, so it's hard for me to get their cider any other way. So I kinda, well, I break in and take it."

"So you steal from them?"

"Well, kinda. I take the cider, but I always leave money behind. Enough to pay for whatever I take and a little bit more for the employees to buy a pizza or something for lunch."

"So you are a gentlemen thief, a highwayman!"

"I guess so, sure!"

Jack studied the bottle Michael had handed him. "It's been ages since I drank a beverage from here."

"Well, I hope it doesn't disappoint."

The two took long drinks from their respective bottles. Jack's eyes widened, and he inspected his bottle more closely.

Jack shot a glance at Michael. "This is magnificent! What did you call it again? Bold Apple?"

"Bold Rock! They're the ones who make it, and this is my favorite flavor: Granny Smith. Good, huh?"

"Bold Rock! I must remember that. This granny is delicious!"

Michael laughed. "So! You met a girl! Tell me all about her."

Jack finished his cider and motioned to the case. "May I have another?"

"Of course! Have all you want, man."

"Thank you."

Jack accepted another bottle, opened it, and took a long drink. "Yes, I met a girl. Her name is Melissa, and she's from a place called Virginia Beach. I understand it's not far from here."

"Actually, that's where I'm from! It's only about three, three and a half hours from here by car. You can fly it in no time, really."

"You hail from there? Interesting! I met her last year, right here at this spot. Apparently she'd just ended a longstanding relationship."

"Ahhhh...." Michael said, and chuckled.

"Ahh?"

"Nothing, sorry, go on."

"...and apparently, she decided to hike these mountains for a time. That's how we met."

"Yeah? Does she know you're a..." Michael made a vague, all-encompassing motion towards Jack.

"An elf?"

"Yeah."

"Well, not at first. To be honest, it's not something we generally reveal to most mortals—if ever."

"*Buuuut...*"

Jack grinned. "But...well, it's a little embarrassing, actually. You've no doubt heard the term 'love at first sight'?"

Michael chuckled. "So you're a romantic, are ya, Jack?"

The elf grinned and took another sip of cider. "It appears so. It's real though, you know? Love at first sight?"

"Yeah?"

"Very. It's magical in nature."

"So that's why you told her? Told her that you're a, well, an...."

"Elf. It's okay to say that, Michael. You're a vampire, and I'm an elf."

"Okay, sorry. I'm really out of practice with all of"—Michael made broad motions with his hands—"this."

"Meaning?"

"Meaning, I uh, I don't talk to people that often."

"That's unfortunate. I've enjoyed our chat thus far."

"Thanks, man. So, uh, we were talking about, I'm sorry, what's her name again?"

"Melissa."

"Right. So we were talking about Melissa finding out you're an elf."

"Yes. One moment we're having a lovely conversation, she's telling me about her life, and the next, I'm telling her not only who I am, but what, where I am from, and then I'm whisking her off to Fae to show her everything I just described! I never even considered the ramifications."

"Wait, you took her to your, like, your world?"

"Realm, yes. I've struggled with the wisdom behind that decision for the last year, if I'm honest."

"Why? I mean, you make it sound like it wasn't a smart thing to do?"

"Well, there are certain…rules, as it were. Not really laws, but traditions. Generally speaking, one does not bring a mortal into Fae. It so rarely, if ever, turns out well."

"Yeah?"

"There are hosts of reasons, even examples why not to do so. I guess the most common is adjusting. For instance, before you became a vampire, how would you have reacted to someone telling, maybe even showing you an actual vampire or vampires, and then, just like that, you are back in your natural surroundings, your familiar world—only now, you have seen, if only for a moment, a world that exists beside yours, beyond yours, hidden in the shadows? Would you ever look at anything the same way again? Or anyone? How would it affect you? Would you tell others? How could you? What if there were vampires out there that didn't *want* you talking about them, or want you revealing what you saw?"

Michael nodded. "Honestly, man? That's kinda what happened to me, but yeah…I guess that makes sense. Makes a lot of sense, actually."

"There are so, so many more reasons I could go into, but suffice to say, it doesn't ever really end well, and it's something that one just does not do *normally*. Many times it's just not safe. We are referring to a place that is filled with all manner of beings, most of them immortal, and most with magical means. Beings that might be somewhat oblivious to the inherent dangers within the realm they call home. Dangers that might very well prove fatal, or worse to a mortal."

"Worse than fatal?"

"There are far worse fates than death."

Michael sat there for a moment and thought about the idea of a new entirely different world existing beyond the one he'd always known. Not just a race of beings like him living in his world, but a new place, a new reality. It made his head spin and hurt.

"So tell me more! Is she nice? What does she do? You said she's coming back through here?"

Jack took another sip of his cider and smiled. "Yes, apparently. She said she would attempt to return in a year's time. So we made an informal promise to try and meet one another if she did."

"In a year? Well, did she text you? Or call? Did you guys swap info? Why a year?"

"I'm afraid I don't understand."

"Have you talked to her since then?"

"Oh, no. We agreed not to. We simply agreed that if we were meant to meet again, we would both be here, at this exact spot, exactly one year, your time, from then, and we would see where fate took us. I'm not entirely convinced she thought our encounter was real, if I'm honest. I think she might have left not quite trusting her own mind, which is one of the things I was concerned about. But yes, one year. And tonight marks the one-year mark, give or take a few days. I have had trouble keeping track of time here."

Michael frowned. "You're kidding, right? That's like...that's like something out of a movie, man. *An Affair to Remember*? *Sleepless in Seattle*? Sorry, you know what a movie is, right?"

Jack laughed. "Yes Michael, I am familiar with films."

"Ahh, good. But I mean, c'mon, you're not serious, are you? You agreed to wait for a whole year?"

Jack nodded. "I am. Though I'm beginning to wonder if I was acting foolishly."

Michael laughed at that. "Well, you are a romantic. But

we're all fools when it comes to matters of the heart, Jack. All of us! But a year? That's a long time to wait, man. Why a year?"

"Keep in mind, Michael, to an immortal—and you will come to know this as you grow older—but time, the length of a year even, is an incredibly minute span of one's life to wait when love is involved."

"Yeah, you're a romantic, all right! And I still think it's a long time," Michael said, and winked.

Jack laughed and raised his drink. "Romanticism and philosophy aside, I am inclined to agree with you."

Michael laughed. "But seriously, though. You guys haven't talked or anything?"

"I'm afraid not."

"But you think she'll show up here again?"

"I certainly hope so! We spent quite a few days and nights together. It was such a beautiful time. I can tell you that I've never experienced anything like it, not even close. It was...it was magical, for lack of a better, less cliché description."

"So when you guys first met, did she just think you were another hiker? I mean, what were you doing here? Were you, I dunno, were you dressed like"—Michael waved his hand at Jack—"like that?"

Jack looked down at his clothing and chuckled. "Well, yes. But when I heard Melissa approaching, and I heard her singing, I decided I would like to meet her. She had such a beautiful and honest little voice."

"Honest?"

"Yes, I could hear the honesty in her voice."

"I'm not sure I get it."

Jack's brow furrowed. "How best to explain? Have you ever thought you could sense when someone was dishonest? Even if you did not know them, and even if you had just barely spoken with them—you could just feel it? You mentioned your "BS meter" earlier."

"Ahh, I think I see where you're going. So you're saying you can tell if someone is being honest just by the sound of their voice?"

"More that I can sense if a person is honest by nature by the sound of their voice. Not necessarily if they are being honest or dishonest about a particular thing or subject, but as a whole. You, for instance. You come across as an honest person. Very honest, in fact."

"I think I get it. You're saying there's something in the way they talk, or the way they sound."

"Precisely. Where were we? Ahh, my appearance. So I, well, I chose a different appearance. At least outwardly."

"You changed clothes."

Jack laughed. "Yes, in a way," and with that, he snapped his fingers. The shirt he was wearing changed shape and color; it looked almost identical to the t-shirt Michael wore. His pants became jeans, his boots, tennis shoes.

"Oh, my God! That's awesome! Can you do that anytime you want?"

"I can, yes."

"I'd kill to be able to do that."

"Perhaps some day I can teach you."

"You can teach me to—"

Jack motioned for Michael to stop. He cocked his head to

44

one side and bolted to his feet. "She's here!"

Michael scanned the area, looking and listening for whatever Jack had seen or heard. "She's…are you sure? I can't hear or see anyone."

"I'm sure of it!"

Jack stood and remained silent a moment more. Michael noticed that for the first time since they'd met that the elf looked nervous.

"I guess that's fate smiling at you, man!" Michael said in an effort to calm his new friend.

Jack turned and nodded. "Thank you." He hesitated a moment more. "I hate to be—"

"Don't even mention it!" Michael said as he began gathering the empty bottles and what was left of the cider. "I will leave you two to it!"

"Thank you, Michael."

Michael turned to go and stopped, "Look…Jack, I, uh, I really appreciate you talking with me tonight. I…." Michael cleared his throat. "I don't really get a lotta chances to chat with people much anymore. So uh, you know, thanks for that."

Jack made a small bow and extended his hand. "Not at all. It was a pleasure, Michael. And I would be honored to do it again sometime soon. Do I have your permission to call on you?"

"Hell yeah, man! Anytime. And me too, Jack. Seriously, this was…" Michael paused. "…this was fucking crazy weird man, but it was awesome! Thank you."

Jack made a low, very formal bow, and Michael leapt into the air, the remainder of the case of cider tucked beneath one arm. As he leveled out and turned towards home, he looked back at Jack, and called down, "Good luck, man!"

Jack smiled back and nodded.

6

Michael landed on his deck and slid the patio doors open wide. Nanook and Thorn greeted him by jumping, spinning, and slobbering all over the place. Michael nearly dropped what was left of the ciders.

"Easy, easy, easy! We'll go for a walk in a sec, guys. Let me put away the drinks."

"Alexa, turn on the living room lights," Michael said as he headed towards the kitchen. He didn't need the lights, but he felt bad when the dogs were left in the dark for too long each night. Michael proceeded to load what ciders remained into his fridge, took out a large metal thermos, and grabbed a mug from the cabinet closest to him.

"I'll tell you guys what, though," he began while pouring a large mug of fresh blood. "Tonight did NOT go as planned, that's for sure!"

Michael placed the mug in the microwave and set the timer for forty-five seconds.

"Not. At. All."

Thorn and Nanook cocked their heads as if they were curious to learn more. Michael smiled and retrieved a box of dog treats from the cabinet above the stove. He tossed each dog a snack just as the microwave finished warming his own.

"You guys wouldn't believe me if I told you!" he continued, and took a long drink from his mug. "But trust me when I tell you, things got weird!"

The dogs finished their treats and resumed wagging their tails.

"Okay, okay, let's go for a stroll."

Michael finished his blood, rinsed out his mug, placed it in the sink, and walked over to the coat closet. He fished out his small day pack, tossed it over one shoulder, and grabbed the hand axe that hung on the door beside the dog leashes.

Michael looked down at his friends. "You guys are good off leash tonight, yeah? Not gunna go chasing skunks or anything, right?"

Nanook barked, and Thorn just wagged his tail even harder.

"You wag that thing any faster, Thorn, and you're gunna to take off. Seriously though, please—no more skunks."

Michael ruffled the dogs' heads and then led them onto the deck. He glanced towards Humpback but decided not to look too hard. The moon was in a bright mood tonight, so he could have gotten a good look at this Melissa, but he avoided it. It felt like he would be intruding, so he turned his gaze towards the steps and the dogs who were already down and racing off into the trees.

When Michael entered the forest and the cool air hanging there, his mind raced over the evening's events. So there hadn't been another vampire out there in the night. Not even close. That disappointed him, but he was also somewhat relieved, because if it had been, if the mystery person had turned out to be another vampire, well, who knows what might have happened? Maybe that vampire had been told the same things he had? In particular, don't reveal yourself to others?

Nanook dropped a slobbery stick at Michael's feet, and he chuckled. "Okay, okay...." he said, and picked up the chunk of wood and threw it farther down the trail, where both dogs charged after it.

Michael had spent years searching for others like him. He'd read countless books, websites, and anything he could find on the not-so-mythical creatures. He had watched movies, documentaries, and joined several online groups dedicated to paranormal research. He'd even joined a virtual roleplaying group of "Vampire: the Masquerade" fans. It was a great game —basically D&D with vampires—and it had proved somewhat beneficial, much to Michael's amazement. But short of traveling the globe and digging up ancient relics, he found nothing regarding vampires beyond fantasy, power-hungry religious leaders, and paranoid dark-age peasants. So who really knew what might have transpired if Jack had turned out to actually BE a vampire? What we *he* do if another vampire just walked up and introduced him or herself right out of the blue? Would he be excited? Relieved? Afraid? Michael didn't know. Elizabeth *had* warned him that someone would come looking for him if his secret was ever revealed. Someone who would then murder him, apparently.

Thorn barked from somewhere up ahead, and Nanook yipped in response. They were playing, as best Michael could tell. He'd named them after two of the dogs in one of his favorite movies as a kid: *The Lost Boys*. Also, the main character in that flick was named Michael too, and the movie *was* about the coolest vampires to ever grace the screen, so why the hell not?

Michael quoted the movie's tagline: "Sleep all day. Party all night. Never grow old. Never die. It's fun to be a vampire," he said, and continued down the trail.

"If you don't mind being alone."

So he'd met an elf. At least, that's what Jack said he was. And honestly, Michael couldn't think of a reason not to believe him. He'd displayed some pretty amazing abilities, none of which were more impressive than the ability to sneak up him! That alone was pretty stunning. There was also the inescapable feeling that Michael just felt like Jack had been telling the truth. He somehow knew it. He couldn't explain how or why he seemed to know it, but he did. Maybe he'd hit the nail on the head back there when he told Jack that he had a pretty good BS meter, and nothing of what Jack said set it off—nothing at all.

He'd met an elf.

Where did Jack live? Where exactly was this...this Fae he spoke of? Did he have a house? Did he live in a giant tree with a bunch of other elves who baked cookies and crackers all day long? Did he fight goblins and orcs in his spare time? Did he know any hobbits? Was he related to any house-elves? Michael ran these and many more ridiculous questions around in his head while he hiked. He stopped from time to time to clear a downed tree or large branch from the trail. He trimmed back a few thorn-riddled blackberry bushes so hikers could get by unimpeded, or at least with most of their blood still intact. The irony that this was being done by a vampire was not lost on Michael. He also dug up quite a bit of poison ivy and poison oak. He'd discovered years ago that one of the many benefits to being undead also included the immunity to such weeds. You couldn't ask for a better trail angel than a vampire, really.

"Well, maybe an elf."

When the night grew late and the horizon began to glow, Michael turned back for the house. He called out to the dogs, both of whom came charging back towards him. They were used to the routine and knew their way probably better than he did. It had been a long and wonderful night; weird, but wonderful. He'd made a new friend, probably the first one he'd had in many years, and Michael was glad for it. He missed his little "clan" from back in the day. More than missed, actually; he mourned it. It was always him, Dan, Amara, Josh, Jake, and

Eric. They'd all grown up together, minus Amara, but she fit in immediately, and it never stopped her from affirming the fact that she was just one of the guys—more than just one of the guys, really. They all finished each other's sentences, they always seemed to know when the other needed something, and they were always there. *Always*.

Michael never thought that would change...but "always" seems to always find a way of ending.

So it was nice to have someone outside of the four-legged variety to talk face-to-face with again! And if Jack lived as long as Michael, or longer, then Michael didn't have to worry about so many of the things that plagued him with other relationships. The fact he looked exactly the same after twenty-plus years; watching his friends grow sick, or worse, die, while he never even caught so much as a cold, or the occasional seasonal allergy; that everyone he ever loved would die and leave him here alone in the end. None of these things were a concern with a friend like himself, like Jack. It was encouraging.

When the trio returned home, Michael went about the process of locking down the house. He'd had enormous storm shutters installed years ago; they blocked one hundred percent of the daylight, and kept quite a bit of the sound out as well. Over the years, Michael found it more and more difficult to sleep as his other senses seemed to grow stronger, so he had to adapt his surroundings to compensate.

Michael had designed his house with the help of several builders in Charlottesville and Harrisonburg. He'd spent more than two years going over plan after plan and intentionally hiring several different architects to help him create his home. The first company he'd hired did nothing but install the basements and the support structures for the rest of the home. A second company designed and built an additional subterranean structure which connected to the main basement via two different access points. The third and fourth firms had built the main floor, the second floor, and the walk-in attic.

When the entire thing was finished, Michael made the rest of the necessary adjustments and installations himself. There were hidden passages throughout the home. One room was connected to almost every other room if you knew the right secret door to open or the right crawlspace to access. The security systems, of which there were several, were all state-of-the-art, and each professionally installed. Michael could access the cameras and microphones on a myriad of devices in mere seconds should the need arise. If being a vampire did one thing, and did it well, it made one slightly paranoid about security. The idea that exposure to sunlight, if even for a moment, could be fatal instilled a very real sense of importance where security was concerned. Michael had never really forgotten the smell of his burning flesh and the melted shower curtain after his first exposure to sunlight post-vampirism. It had been a sweet smell of crispy bacon and blistering garbage bags which had been left in the sun all day.

When the house was locked down, and the alarms armed, Michael turned on the lights throughout the house. He was too excited, and too much had happened tonight to go to sleep just yet. He collapsed onto his couch and flipped on the television. It was an enormous thing, complete with surround sound and almost every popular game console the market had to offer, and a few that were long since retired. Michael was a video game junkie of the highest caliber, and he played one title or another on a nightly basis. Tonight, though, he just stared at the screensaver when it kicked in, lost in the images and ideas that his mind played for him instead.

"You met an elf."

7

Jack was nervous. In fact, he changed outfits at least a dozen times as Melissa and someone else— another woman, it appeared—made their way up the trail towards the Emerald Seat. He shuffled his feet, paced around the rocks, stammered over what he would say when they arrived, and then repeated the entire process. He also changed his outfit again, because why not?

"You're acting like a child."

The self-admonishment made him smile. He felt like a child again.

The voices were maybe three, four minutes away now, at least based on the speed they were traveling. Jack noted that it was a bit slower than what he considered a normal pace, but shrugged it off. Melissa and her traveling companion were likely fatigued. Not surprising considering the late, or at this point early hour.

"You should have brought something. A gift."

Jack thought about that for a moment, and tried to imagine what might have been an appropriate token for such an occasion.

"Anything would have been better than nothing."

Jack shook his head and uttered a quiet curse. The voices were closer now. The sun was still well below the horizon, but the sky began to glow a soft grayish-pink, and the treetops started taking on a dull green appearance. Maybe he should

53

meet them? Or would that frighten Melissa and whomever she traveled with? Would it seem presumptuous?

The vampire's words echoed in Jack's mind for a moment. *"I will leave you two to it!"*

Jack smiled. He honestly liked Michael and was glad the vampire finally paid him a visit. They certainly had talked quite a bit, and about quite a lot. Jack noted how easily he'd revealed so many things to the vampire. That was a little alarming, even out of character for him. Regardless, he was pleased that the two had met, not to mention surprised! He'd met an actual vampire!

"Hello?"

Jack spun around. There, at the edge of the boulders, stood Melissa. On her left stood another woman, slightly older, a very clear look of surprise washing over her face.

"Melissa! I'm so glad you came!" Jack almost ran to where the two women stood. "May I assist you with your packs?"

Melissa reached out and hugged Jack, planting a soft kiss on his cheek as she did. "Yes, please. We've been hiking for hours now. Jack, this is my sister Becky!"

Becky cleared her throat, and extended a hand. "Nice to meet you, Jack."

"The pleasure is mine."

"I've heard...so‑much‑about‑you," Becky said.

Jack noticed the peculiar way in which she'd said those words. "If I may," he replied, and motioned for Becky's pack as well.

The two women removed their gear, each sighing thankfully as they did. Jack picked up the packs and motioned for the two to join him out on the rocks. Becky noted how little effort he seemed to exert in carrying all of their equipment. Her pack alone must have topped out around forty-five, fifty pounds, and Melissa's couldn't be less than thirty-five or forty. But he just grabbed them, smiled, and led the way out onto Humpback as if they weighed nothing.

"I was really hoping you'd be here," Melissa said as the three sat down.

"And I was hoping you would come!"

The two looked at each other for a long moment, smiling.

Melissa reached over and touched Jack's hand. "So how have you been? What have you been up to? Tell me everything!"

"I could ask you the same."

Becky began rummaging through her pack, and in short order produced a canteen, a small collapsable lantern, and a towel.

"You first," Melissa said.

Not knowing what to say, or where to start if he did know what to say, Jack just began talking. "Well, I just had the most peculiar visit—"

"So my sister says you're an elf!" Becky interrupted. She was now holding a large black knife.

Jack choked.

8

"I'm sorry?" Jack said when he managed to regain his voice.

Melissa shot a look at her sister. "BECKY! What the hell? What did I say!?"

Becky ignored her sister. "Melissa said that you told her you were some kind of elf, that the two of you spent a few days hiking together and you convinced her that you're a, a make-believe magical being!" She accented each of her points by directing the tip of the blade towards Jack.

Jack looked at Melissa, surprised. Melissa just sighed and dropped her head.

"I, umm—"

Becky continued, "So I came along in case *you* actually showed back up! Because my sister is one of the smartest women I've ever known, and it's not like her to fall for something so, so….like this! Now I'm here in case a crazy person she met last year on her little pilgrimage of self-discovery and reflection decided to come back and take advantage of her need for a good rebound fuck!"

Melissa choked back a tear and wiped her nose. "Becky, please, you promised."

Jack stood and straightened his clothes. "I'm afraid I—"

Becky stood as well. "So trust me when I say this, *elf man.*" Her eyes swelled with tears. "I dated a Navy fucking Seal for *five* years! FIVE! This"—she waved the knife in front of her, flipping the blade so she now held it point down, blade out—"this is an Ontario Mark Three. The blade is over six inches long, and I know how to use every single one of them! Now spill! What are you trying pull here?"

Jack had been too distracted at seeing Melissa again to have noticed her sister's weapon. Now that he studied her a bit more, he saw she wore the knife around her waist, where it must have a horizontal sheath on her lower mid-back, as a warrior might wear a blade.

Jack cleared his throat. "I assure you, there is no need for a weapon—"

Becky took a step closer to Jack. "I'll be the judge of...."

Jack snapped his fingers, and a cobalt blue glow appeared just above the trio. Becky, mid-sentence and mid-stride, stopped and looked up at the sudden light. She watched as it cascaded downward, almost like a bedspread would if it billowed up and then settled down over and around you. The scent of flowers and spices flooded the area; potent, pungent aromas. Before, where there had only been stone, now sat plush emerald blankets and sapphire-colored pillows. A bowl of dazzling colored fruit appeared, as did a basket of what looked to be pastries, candies, and chocolates. Three crystal goblets materialized, each filled with a sparkling purple liquid which flashed gold every few seconds. Tiny winged humanoids flittered about, arranging the fruit and sweets while also delivering beautifully colored flowers to every conceivable surface.

"Jack," one of the sprites said, and made a sort of bow in mid-flight.

"Hello, Rose," Jack said, smiling.

"So which one is Melissa?" the sprite asked.

Jack chuckled and nodded at Melissa. "Rose, this is Melissa;

Melissa, this is my very good friend Rose."

Rose curtsied mid-flight and smiled. "A pleasure," the little sprite said. Her voice was so high, so musical, that it was almost hard to hear.

Jack motioned at Becky, who stood in stunned silence. "And this is her sister Becky."

Rose looked at Becky. "Likewise."

Becky barely acknowledged her.

Melissa smiled. "It's nice to meet you, Rose!"

Rose smiled and turned back to Jack. "Your mother was inquiring about you."

"Please tell her I will return home shortly."

Rose nodded again, and set back to arranging the many flowers which had appeared.

One of the sprites, dressed in pink and gold, landed on the face of Becky's blade. Her wings were translucent, and shimmered in every color imaginable. Becky rotated her wrist just a bit so she could better see the tiny visitor. The sprite curtsied, smiled, and fluttered off to continue whatever it was she'd been doing. Where the tiny woman had just stood, minuscule ruby roses began to sprout from the metal blade, while dark green vines crawled down the black face of the knife towards its razor edge.

"Jack," one of the sprites chimed as a farewell, bowed mid-flight, smiled, and then vanished, along with all of the other tiny beings. As soon as the sprites vanished, dozens of gold and silver candles appeared around the newly improved site.

Large, rolling tears spilled from Becky's eyes, and she collapsed to her knees, shaking.

"Your sister told you the truth, Rebecca," Jack said.

Becky tore her eyes from the magical flowers growing on her knife, and looked up. Her mouth opened, but no words came.

Jack made a low, formal bow. "I am indeed elven, and I am at your service."

Melissa began to giggle, while her sister sat there, dumbstruck. "I told you!" she said and knelt down, hugged Becky, and kissed her on the cheek.

Jack smiled. "I must apologize. Tonight has been very strange already, and to be quite honest, I was not thinking clearly when you arrived. I should have sensed your unease long before meeting you, Rebecca."

"B..Becky. It's okay if you...you can call me Becky."

"Becky, yes," Jack continued. "As I was saying, I was quite nervous when you arrived, and again, I had just experienced a very unusual occurrence, then suddenly, here you were, and here I was, and well, here we are now! I apologize if I interrupted you, Becky. But I thought it best to reassure you as quickly as possible, and thereby, I hope at least, assuage you of your fears."

Becky continued to stare at their new surroundings, her mouth agape, her eyes wide. "Sh...sure. So...you're—"

"He's different. Like I told you, Becky," Melissa said. "I also told you not to say anything, but"—she motioned about —"well, we see how *that* turned out!"

Jack smiled. "Again, I do apologize Rebec—ahem, Becky. I should have been paying more attention. Please forgive me."

Becky gave a small nod, picked up one of the plump, crimson cherries, and bit into it. Her gaze drifted out over the edge of the cliff and the treetops far below. Jack cast a small glimmer for her and smiled as he watched the tension in her shoulders and neck fade.

"Jack, would you mind maybe taking a short little walk with me?" Melissa said. "You'll be okay here for a minute, right, Becky?"

"I'm, yeah, I'm fine. You two, uh…." She motioned for her sister and Jack to go on and took another slow bite of her cherry.

"I think she's in shock. At least, a little," Melissa whispered.

"She'll be just fine," Jack said, and offered Melissa his hand.

Melissa stood, and the two walked back towards the trailhead. When they reached the trees, Melissa stopped, grabbed Jack by the shirt, pulled him close, and kissed him. Hard. He kissed her back.

"I've been wanting to do that for a year," Melissa said.

Jack smiled. "I've been *wanting* you to do that for a year."

The two continued down the path, Jack holding Melissa's hand and guiding her through the shadows.

When they reached a small clearing, Melissa stopped. "So there's something I have to tell you."

9

Michael's alarm did not go off. He knew that because it was the first thing he reached for, and it was still early yet; barely 9:00 p.m. He closed his eyes, collapsed back onto his pillow, and tried to drift off again. Ever since meeting Jack, his mind was a whizzing, whirling windmill of ever-revolving questions. It was racing so much, in fact, that he'd slept very little, if at all, in the last three days. He had so many questions, and he desperately wanted to talk to Jack again.

He was just slipping back to sleep when the sound came again. A weird knock, followed by a muffled voice.

Michael crashed back into consciousness and half-stumbled, half-fell to the floor as he struggled out of bed. He brushed his hair from his face and eyes, grabbed his phone, and scrolled to the app controlling his home's security system. The screen glowed to life, and Michael blinked the sleep from his eyes as he cycled through the various cameras.

He saw no one. No one at any of the doors, no one in the driveway, or on the back porch. No one, nothing. He had half-expected a delivery person, or as usual, another pizza guy coming to the wrong house on this weird street. It was a long, twisting, steep road, and the homes were a good ways off of it. That, and GPS sucked up here. There were no deer, no raccoons, and no black bears roaming about—not that he could see, anyway.

Another strange knock, and a muffled voice echoed up from downstairs. Michael rose several inches from the ground and floated towards the bedroom door in complete silence. According the the security cameras, there was no one outside; someone was *in* the house. He scanned the landing and bedroom. The dogs were gone. His heart began to sprint.

Something broke, followed by a faint, "Oops."

Michael glided out onto the landing overlooking the living room. No one was there. He then drifted down the stairs, listening as best he could, holding his breath as he went. None of the lights had been turned on, the television was off, and the storm windows were still closed. So whoever it was down there had to have a flashlight or some other form of night vision; the house was pitch black, which served Michael well. He could see everything. But what about the dogs? Where were his dogs?

When he reached the landing, he sniffed the air. There was *definitely* someone in the house. Another muffled sound floated up from the kitchen. His nerves were tingling now, and whatever amounted for adrenalin in vampires began coursing through Michael's veins. Shivering coils were wrapped tight throughout his body. He would act fast. The intruder would have no chance.

"I appear to have damaged one of your glasses, Michael," a voice said from the black.

Michael froze mid-flight.

"JACK?"

The elf looked up and turned towards Michael. "I am so, so sorry...."

Nanook and Thorn sat at Jack's feet, their tails wagging. They seemed utterly unconcerned that a stranger had ended up in their home while their owner had been fast asleep upstairs.

"Jesus, Jack! What are you doing in here? You realize I could have killed you?"

"I'm sure you could have, my friend! But alas, I am very, very hard to kill, and I desperately need your help. Please Michael, I don't know where else to go."

Michael flipped on the lights and stared at his new friend. He seemed...off. "Are you drunk? You sound drunk."

Jack bent over and picked up a case of Bold Rock cider and set it nearby. Two more cases rested on the counter by the refrigerator. Not only had the elf managed to break into Michael's home, he'd snuck in with three cases of booze! He'd apparently been in the process of pouring two tall glasses when Michael arrived. "I'm afraid I broke this one," Jack said, pointing to one of the glasses. "But I fixed it!" he added with a large grin.

"Jesus, man! You ARE drunk!"

"Yes. And I am so, so sorry for coming here like this, Michael. And for entering your home! I apologize, I sincerely do!" Jack said.

"Okay, okay. It's not a—"

"And we only just met, no less! I am still a stranger to you. A stranger, and I force my way into your domicile uninvited!"

"Jack, it's okay, let me take those," Michael said, walking over to help the elf with the ciders.

Jack continued, "And you were so very kind, and—"

"Don't worry about it, man. Why don't you go have a seat in the living room, and I'll pour these. How did you get in here, anyway?"

"Would you believe the chimney?" Jack asked, and burst into hysterics.

"Ha. Ha."

"No, really, the chimney," the elf replied.

"Seriously, though."

"Sincerely! I entered via the chimney. I am able to, sort of, how best to explain? I can alter my physical self at times, should the occasion call for it."

"Really? I never actually considered the chimney as an access point."

"Well, it certainly is a tight fit! I am deeply sorry, Michael."

"Don't sweat it, man."

"You are very kind, my friend," Jack said.

Michael chuckled. "I don't know about that. But it's pretty clear you need an ear, so I'm here for ya. You sure do like the cider, though, don't you?"

Jack plopped down on the sofa, his back to Michael. He stretched and leaned backwards as far as he could until he was able see into the kitchen, though upside down. "I DO! I left them three gold ingots, in fact!"

"Gold what? Wait, where did you get these?"

"From the Granny building! It's full of it! And no one was there, so I left payment."

"Granny build—you broke into the cidery?!"

"Isn't that what you do?"

"Well, sure, sometimes, but…Jack, they have security cameras all over the place in there now."

"Not to worry, I wasn't seen."

"How do you know that?"

"Magic!"

Michael sighed. "Well, I guess you would know, wouldn't you?"

"I would! And I do!"

Michael shook his head and finished pouring the drinks. He made his way into the living room, Nanook and Thorn not far behind. Michael glared at his furry companions. "Worst guard dogs ever!"

"Don't be cross with them, Michael. I am very adept at handling animals."

"I'm sure you are, Legolas."

"Who?"

"Never mind."

Thorn and Nanook both leapt up onto the couch, Nanook on Jack's left, Thorn on his right. Almost in unison, the two laid down and placed their heads on each of his legs.

Jack smiled. "See?"

Michael nodded and handed Jack a drink. He took a seat in a leather recliner by the fireplace. "Alexa, turn on the living room lights." Smart bulbs all over the ceiling and in some of the lamps came alive. "Alexa, turn on the sunset." At the far corners of the room, separate lights cast a soft orange glow, while others cast a deep red. The effect was, in fact, that of a sunset. Michael had spent hours getting the hues and illumination just right. He missed sunsets, but this helped.

"Oh, that's very pretty," Jack said, looking around the room. "Who is Alexa?"

"She's no one; it's just a smart device. You can connect your lights, or your thermostat, whatever you want. I have my security system connected. She plays my favorite music, or answers questions like: Alexa, when is sunset today?"

From beside the couch, on a small end table, a black, cylindrical object began to glow blue. "Sunset occurs at precisely eight-forty-eight this evening," a female voice replied.

"Alexa, what time is it?"

"The time is now eight-fifty-nine."

"That's wonderful!" Jack said. He smiled for a moment, sighed, and took an enormous drink.

Michale watched Jack drink and noted for the first time how disheveled his friend looked—quite the opposite of their first encounter. "Alexa, open the blinds."

All around the living room, the storm shutters began to rise and disappear into the ceiling. The sun was just below the horizon, but Michael could still feel a slight pain over the surface of his skin. It was at that moment he realized that he was still in his boxer briefs and nothing else.

Jack watched the blinds vanish. "That truly is astounding. It's almost magical!"

"Thanks. I, uh, I love technology. Will you excuse me for a minute? I just realized I'm practically naked."

Jack nodded and took another long drink.

Michael raced up the stairs to get dressed. "By the way," he called down from his bedroom. "How many of those things have you had tonight?"

There was a slight pause followed by some mumbling and then laughter. "Thirty-eight, if I count correctly!"

Michael was halfway into his pants when the elf answered. "JESUS, JACK!" he called down, and fell over.

More laughter from below. "Not to worry, we elves have quite the tolerance for human beverages. I can become lucid any moment I wish to. And I can barely feel a thing."

"Yeah, I bet."

Once dressed, Michael jogged back down the stairs and studied the elf for a moment more after he sat down. Jack not only sounded drunk and looked a mess, but his shoulder-length blond hair was no longer perfectly manicured. His shirt was stained, likely with soot from the chimney, and a small tear was now visible on one of its sleeves. His pants were a bit muddy, with one leg tucked neatly into a boot, while the other was half out.

"Jack, you...you look..." Michael sighed. "Well, you look horrible, if I'm honest, man. What happened up there? Don't tell me your dream girl dumped you or something?"

Jack looked up from his drink. His eyes were watery, and after a second, several tears spilled out of them. "She's dying, Michael. Melissa is dying."

10

Michael's heart sank. He'd just met Jack, and knew next to nothing about the man—the elf, the magical being sitting across from him—but his heart dropped. He might not really know the elf all that well, but he knew what heartache looked like; hell, he'd stared at it every single day in the mirror for years.

"Oh, man. I'm..." Michael said, and shook his head. "I'm sorry, Jack. For real, man, I'm really sorry."

Jack looked up and wiped his eyes. He seemed to sober up in that instant, and he stared intently at Michael.

"Thank you," Jack said. He snapped his fingers, and two more ciders, already open, appeared on the coffee table before him. He took one and handed the other to Michael.

"Thanks, man."

Jack nodded and took a deep breath. "She came back here to tell me. To...to say goodbye."

Michael sighed, and the room fell silent. Michael took a long drink from his cider, his head spinning as he swallowed. Then he took another large drink. "Is there anything, like, is there something that can be done? I mean, like...what—"

"An ailment named sickle cell," Jack said. "Melissa said it became...aggressive? She has already suffered damage to her mind from it, and it, this sickle cell disease, is growing worse despite the treatments."

Jack finished his cider. "That is why she travels at night. I had no idea. Apparently she overheats and fatigues easily; thus, nighttime is preferable for her travels in the wild."

"Fuuuuck," Michael said. He stood up and began pacing the room. "Okay, okay, gimme a second...."

"I have now taught myself everything there is to know about this disease over the last few days," Jack said. "I thought I detected something different about her when she returned. A new cadence to speech, a measured approach to the way she made even the slightest movements. Slower, albeit more determined. And tired; so very tired. Her thoughts and her body seemed so...drained. Rebecca was even carrying most of Melissa's supplies."

"Rebecca?"

"Melissa's sister."

"Her sister?"

"Yes, I apologize. Her sister joined her. Apparently to not only help, but also insure that I was not some charlatan attempting to seduce her sister. Her younger sister. Her *dying* younger sister." Another tear rolled down the elf's cheek and fell from his chin.

"Charlatan?"

"Melissa revealed to her sister who she'd met. What I was."

"Wait, she went back and told her sister that she'd met an elf in the woods?"

"Precisely."

Michael leaned back. "Oooooh."

"Yes. Oooooh."

"So I take it that didn't go over very well, then."

"Not at all. In fact, Rebecca brandished a blade."

"Really?"

"Quite efficiently, in fact. What would you do, what would *any* of us do, if we thought our younger sibling was in possible danger? Or being taken advantage of?"

Michael glanced at a family portrait hanging on his wall. It was of his mother, father, and younger brother. It was taken about three years before they were all killed. "I get it."

Jack looked back up and studied Michael again. "You've lost loved ones?"

Michael tore his gaze from the picture. "How...?" He stopped. He really needed to get used to talking with an elf, with someone who seemed quite capable of reading thoughts, or at least detecting minute displays of emotion. "Yes."

"I'm sorry for your loss, Michael."

"Thanks."

Jack continued. "I assured Rebecca—Becky, that she had nothing to worry about."

"And how'd you go about doing that?"

Jack snapped his fingers again, and before Michael could comprehend what was happening, the room was filled with exotic flowers, candles of all color, dish after dish of fruits, cheeses, pastries, and candies. A soft blue glow blanketed the room, and music played from a source unseen.

Michael tripped over an elaborate pillow which hadn't been there milliseconds before and crashed to the floor. He scrambled back to his feet, stumbled again, caught himself, and stared about the room. "Oh, my God!"

Jack nodded while taking another sip from his bottle.

"So, so, uh...."

"So Becky realized that what her sister had told her was the truth, that there was no predator out in the forest taking advantage of her, and that the stories she told were not manifestations of the illness which had begun infecting her mind."

Michael sat back down and marveled at the fantastical new additions scattered about his living room.

Jack continued. "And before we could get reacquainted, before anything really, Melissa took me aside. That was when she told me. She went on to say there was nothing anyone could do and that she hadn't much time left." Jack's voice cracked. "Becky pleaded for me to help, Michael, to do something, anything, and believe me, I've been thinking of nothing else since hearing the news."

Michael tore his eyes from the room and looked at his new friend. "Well, can you? I mean, is there anything you can do?"

"Nothing that I know of, no. Not really."

"What do you mean, not really? I mean...." Michael motioned about the room. "I mean, you're a, you're an elf! You've got all kinds of magical powers and stuff, right? You can do... things! C'mon!"

Jack nodded and smiled. It was a sad smile. "I have, *stuff*. I can do *things*. I can do many, many things, in fact. But some *things* are far beyond my powers to change, Michael. Far beyond most abilities. Remember, I exist in a world where a thing like this simply doesn't happen; it doesn't occur. Can I mend a bone? Heal a cut? Soothe a burn? Yes, I can help with those things. I, along with others in my world, am very familiar with those issues, and many, many more, in fact. But this? A sickness that, for all I can tell, has never once been mentioned in my world? I have no frame of reference for dealing with it. No one does. It would be akin to me asking doctors

71

here to cure an illness they've never encountered, affecting a being they've rarely, if ever seen, and to do so in short order." Jack sighed. "You must believe that I have spent the last few days looking and researching anything and everything I could find. I have neither slept nor eaten. And I've spoken to almost everyone I know, both here and across the known lands. Even my parents were at a loss and offered no real hope, just further warnings on the dangers of loving a mortal."

Michael was standing again. He started to say something, stopped, tried again, paused, and began pacing about the living room. He kicked one of the pillows aside, where it collided with a bowl of pink apples. "So there's nothing we..." he stopped, and looked over at his new friend, who was already looking back at him.

His heart sank again. "Ohhhhh, shit...."

Jack nodded.

"Oh shit, indeed."

11

Melissa poked a stick at the small fire they'd built and tossed a few more twigs into the dancing flames. The soup was just starting to get warm, and it smelled divine. Freeze-dried or not, the aroma of bacon and cheddar incited quite a bit of rumbling from the sisters' stomachs.

"It's too bad we had to make the fire so small. We'd be eating by now," Melissa said.

"All good things, Smurf."

Melissa grumbled. "This Smurf is getting HANGRY!"

She and Becky had dug a Dakota fire hole. It was fire season, and technically speaking, open-flame fires were prohibited this time of year, so their choice of design was the more responsible option of being irresponsible.

"So tell me again. The water was purple?" Becky said.

"It was! I've never seen anything like it," Melissa said. "The waterfall, the little lake, all of it was purple. Like, grape Kool-Aid kinda purple! Even the plants along the shore were a shade of purple. I didn't see any fish, but I would imagine some of them were purple, too."

"And you swam in it?"

Melissa looked at her sister and grinned. "Naked, even!"

Becky laughed and nudged her little sister. "And that's the

area where you spent most of your time? Why again? Because of others?"

Melissa tossed another small twig into the flames, where it began to burn. "Yeah. Jack said it wasn't normal for us, humans, to travel to his home. Something about tradition, something about being fragile. He said too many humans—he uses humans when he talks about us, about mortals—that too many humans have gone insane there. Or vanished."

"Vanished?"

"Yeah, it's not like here. It's big in a way we don't understand. Even the people who live there can't quite grasp it."

"I don't follow."

"He said there's no end to it, to Fae. Like, okay, so we know our world to be finite in size and scope, right? There's no land here that's not on the planet, the globe, right? What's here is here, and even if it's undiscovered, it's still confined here on Earth, right?"

"Sure."

"So unless we were to leave the planet, there will never be more than what's already here, get it? In effect, travel in a straight line, and eventually, you'll end up right back where you started, in theory, right? Finite."

"Right? I guess?"

"It's not like that there. It's so big, so vast, that Jack's not even sure they live on a planet for lack of a better description. It's like, there's always, always, always more over the horizon. As far as anyone knows, Fae is infinite. Not like here, not finite. So people get lost, or go missing just like here, but there, they might have ended up somewhere that's not just hard to find, but literally...unknown."

Becky shook her head. "Yeah. I don't...I don't get it."

Melissa laughed. "Me either."

Becky had spent the last few days asking hundreds of questions about Jack and her sister's encounter with him—questions she'd asked countless times before over the past several months, but until now, well...she'd never really considered Melissa's answers to be anything more than just fantasy. Becky had never quite figured out how to take Melissa's stories, to be frank. She had wondered if her tales were constructs of her wild imagination. Were they somehow products of the damage her brain had endured after the first series of tiny strokes? Had she met a stranger in the woods who somehow managed to secretly drug her? Becky hadn't known. One thing she'd never considered, though, was the possibility that her sister had been telling her the truth for the last year. Not just a truth she believed to be real, but the God's honest truth.

Becky stood up and stretched her back. "This waiting is driving me crazy!"

"He'll be back."

"You know what I mean, Smurf."

"I know."

Becky had asked Jack about a million questions of her own on that first night. And to his credit, he answered them all with a measure of grace and patience she admired. Becky was sure she'd spent more time talking than even her sister, but to be honest, Becky hadn't really given Melissa much of a chance to speak. Besides, Becky had started in almost immediately on the topic of Jack's powers. Mostly centered around whether or not he could help her little sister. And then, if not, who could? Or what could? Or where could they go for help? And could he take them? Etcetera, etcetera, etcetera. Interrogation wouldn't be too far of a stretch for the way Becky had acted. And she'd spent the last few days regretting her lack of tact and decorum.

"I was kinda harsh on him," Becky said.

"He understood. He even said he would have acted the same way if the roles had been reversed."

"Yeah, but it's been three days, Smurf. You don't think I—"

"No."

Becky grumbled, turned, and crawled into the tent. She retrieved a small green bag and crawled back to the fire. She rummaged through it and produced foil-wrapped Pop-Tarts.

Becky offered the bag to Melissa. "Want one?"

"What flavor?"

"Strawberry."

"Gimme, gimme."

The sisters sat in front of the fire enjoying their Pop-Tarts and passing a mug of lukewarm hot chocolate back and forth.

Melissa took a drink and retrieved a small bug from the cup. She flicked it away and took another sip. "I wish we had some ice."

"I wish we had a pool!"

The two laughed, and Becky rested her head on her sister's shoulder. "Tell me more about the magical fairy planet of fairytales and magical-ness."

Melissa chuckled, and kissed the top of her sister's head. "So I saw a unicorn!"

"Shut the fuck up."

Melissa laughed some more, and Becky joined her.

"I did! Its horn was white and silver. Striped, or swirled, like soft serve ice cream."

"God, I'd kill for some ice cream," Becky said.

"I know, right?"

"Sorry, you were saying...."

"And they're bigger than I ever imagined. Like, a Clydesdale. You know, like a draft horse. HUGE. Its back would have been taller than my head."

"Seriously?"

"They're ginormous. And they have those, you know, those big hairy feet."

"I think that's called feathering."

"How do you know that?"

"Discovery Channel."

"Ahh. Anyway, the one I saw was black, and its feet, the uh, what did you call it?"

"Feathering."

"Yeah, the feathering was orange, like dark orange, almost red. Jack said that's how you can tell the breed, or the lineage. The mothers tend to pass that color on to their foal, while the fathers tend to pass on everything else appearance-wise. But they all have blue eyes, apparently! Like, baby blue. We didn't get close enough to see. Jack says approaching them is really dangerous."

"Dangerous? Why?"

"He said they're really, really picky on who they let near them. Apparently no one rides them anymore."

"So how do you know if they like you?"

"They don't stomp you to death."

Becky sat up. "Seriously? C'mon."

"Yeah, they can kill you."

"That's not very *My Little Pony*-like."

The two burst into gales of laughter, and Becky choked on her Pop-Tart for a moment.

"APPLE-JACK YOUR ASS UP!" Melissa said between giggles.

"Don't! Don't! I have to pee."

The two giggled even harder after that. Both ended up lying on their sides, tears running down their cheeks.

When they'd recovered, Becky noticed Melissa rubbing her temples and wincing.

"Smurf? You okay?"

Melissa looked up. "Yeah, sorry. Just a headache."

"You sure? Did you take your—"

Becky stopped as a small trickle of blood escaped her sister's right nostril. She was reaching for a tissue when the trickle turned into a little crimson river. Melissa cupped her nose, and tears began to spill down her cheeks.

"Oh, Smurf."

Out in the dark, deep in the shadows, one of two figures made a mental note. Now it knew which of the two females was "the sick one." And now it knew which one it was ordered to kill.

12

"Jack, I don't know, man. I don't even know if...if I can!"

"I realize that this is a monumental request, Michael. Please understand that I would never, ever presume to ask something like this of someone, much less a friend."

The word "friend" hung in the air for a moment and sank into Michael's chest...again. It felt good, but it made him nervous all the same.

"I appreciate that, Jack. But, honestly, I'm not sure I can even...I don't know if I *can* turn someone else! I'm not too sure how it actually happened to me!"

"Do you remember much from the night you were...re-born, as it were? Anything beyond what you have already told me?"

Michael shook his head. "Ummm...I don't think so, man. I remember leaving work. The next thing I know I'm back in my little townhouse. Elizabeth is there. She tells me that I'm a damn vampire. Goes on and on about what that means. Yada, yada, yada. Every single time I tried to ask a question, she shut me up. Then she just...left! Like I said. That was it. She just took off, man. I've spent YEARS looking for her, another vampire even, and I found no one. You were the first person I thought MIGHT be another vampire."

"Hmm...." Jack sat his cider down, rubbed each dog's head, and stared off into space.

Michael stood. "I'm going to need something stronger than this," he said while waving his empty bottle around. He made his way into the kitchen and tried to process what he was hearing. He didn't know much about sickle cell, but he knew it wasn't good. He knew it affected mostly African-Americans, and that it was a blood disorder. But that was about it. There was something in there about the shape of the red blood cells, hence the name, but really, that was it.

"Alexa, what is Sickle-Cell Anemia?"

The device beside the couch rattled off a generic definition of the disease as Michael retrieved a bottle of Scotch from one of the kitchen cabinets. He also pulled his thermos of blood from the refrigerator and took long, deep swallows.

"Alexa," Jack began. "How are vampires created?"

Michael chuckled. "I don't think that's gunna—"

"*The film VAMPIRES was released in October 1998.*"

"...work," Michael finished.

"Not quite what I was looking for, Alexa," Jack said.

Michael returned to the living room, placed a glass of Scotch in front of Jack, and the two sat there for a while, neither saying a thing. Nanook and Thorn both fell asleep; their snores were a comforting sound amidst the desperate silence.

"Where are they now?" Michael asked.

"Not far; they are camping at a spot just below the Emerald Seat. Melissa says they must return home soon, however. She requires more of her medication, and it was an effort simply convincing their parents and the doctors to let them take this trip in the first place."

"Ahh. Do they uh, know where you are? Or like...."

"Do they know I'm spending the early evening hours with my friend the vampire, you mean?"

"Well, no," Michael said. "Yeah, kinda."

Jack smiled. "No, I've been almost entirely absent since they arrived. They know that I have been looking for a possible *solution,* as it were."

"Gotcha."

Jack stood despite the grumbles from both dogs, who then continued to snore. He walked over to the windows facing the deck and the forest below.

"They're making soup now," he said.

Michael joined his friend. "You can see them from here?"

"Yes, there, just below the rocks."

Michael studied the trees, and noticed a faint glow. He followed the dancing shadows, which led to a small camp below. Two beautiful women sat there, a single tent behind them. They were laughing about something.

"Which one is Melissa?"

"The one on the right. In the pink."

"She's beautiful. They're both beautiful."

"Yes, they are."

Jack turned to Michael and placed a hand on his shoulder. "I want you to know that I understand the gravity of my request, Michael."

"I know, man. And I *want* to help, I do. I'm jus—I'm not really sure I...I know how? What if I hurt her? What if I do something wrong? I, I don't...."

Jack turned back to the window. "From what I understand, the process is relatively simple, painless even." He stopped and looked at Michael again. "Stop me if you're uncomfortable discussing this further. I will hold no ill will towards you."

Micheal downed the entire glass of Scotch and walked back to his recliner, where he sat. "It's okay, man. How does it work? I only know what I've seen in movies or read in books. And most of the stuff I've seen there, well, who knows if it's accurate."

"Thank you," Jack said. He then turned back to the window and placed a hand on the cool glass. "They're so fragile...."

Jack began talking, telling Michael what he knew of vampires and how one was created.

13

"So I just, drain her? Just, drink her blood, like, *all* of it?"

"Almost, yes. Not quite all of it, but most, yes."

"And then, then she what, she has to drink it all back?"

"Some. If I understand correctly, when a vampire takes in blood, it is absorbed almost instantly into their system. It does not need to be digested as, say, food or drink would. It is simply absorbed directly into the body."

"Absorbed."

"Right, think of your body like a sponge. A sponge that is exceptionally good at absorbing blood. And it does this quickly, almost instantly."

"You realize how unappealing this all sounds, right? Gross, even?"

"Well, aren't most physiological functions a bit, gross, when you really start to pick them apart? I mean, we all shed our skin, we almost all secrete some substance or other, we all—"

"Okay, okay, I get it. Go on, Captain Discovery Channel."

A confused look washed over Jack's face, but he continued. "Right. Once you have ingested blood, almost immediately, in fact, your body converts it into something new! It is no longer blood in the traditional sense. It is a different substance altogether. Think of it as a magnificent fuel—an almost perfect substance that your body uses to operate. And your body is *extremely* efficient at doing this. Hence the reason you require so little blood to function for such extended amounts of time! So how does this apply to vampirism, or the creation of vampires? It seems that in order to become a vampire, one must absorb vampiric blood which has been created via one's *own* blood, i.e., a vampire drinks a large quantity of blood from a subject, leaving very little left at all. Then, said subject ingests the same vampire's new blood in short order. This *new* blood, for lack of a better description, begins converting the new host's body. It can happen no other way. The subject must inject their own newly converted blood from a still-living vampire. And soon, if no adverse reactions occur, every system has been affected, and a new vampire is born."

"No adverse reactions? Like, like what?"

"Well, the literature on that is vague at best, I'm afraid. It seems some humans simply don't react well to the, the change. Some perish during the process."

"Jesus, Jack!"

Jack held up his hands. "Apparently this is rare, though. At least, rare amongst average-aged humans. Reports of these incidents almost always involve the very old, or the very young."

"What about the…" Michael paused. "I'm sorry Jack, but what about the sick?"

Jack nodded. "I thought the same thing. Unfortunately, I found very little documentation on that. I did, however, find several stories of vampires saving humans from illness, or grave injuries by turning them. So there's that at least. But…."

"But?"

"But there are cases that involved the weak, or gravely injured, even ill"—Jack paused for a moment and cleared his throat—"…they do not survive."

"Dammit," Michael said, and began pacing the room again. "Jack, you gotta know something, man. I've, I've only ever fed from someone, like a real live...someone, a few times! And never that much. Seriously. They take more blood at a blood-drive than I need on a semi-regular basis. I mean, I get my supply from the blood bank at the hospital! From a damn refrigerated bag! My freezer downstairs looks like a prop for a fucking horror movie, man!"

Jack nodded. "I can't even begin to understand what this means for you, Michael. But I do know that this is not a trivial request. Especially considering the short amount of time we've known one another. Or the fact you do not even know Melissa personally."

Michael walked over to the picture of his family and stared at it. After a moment, he closed his eyes and sighed. "I killed a man once. Not even a man, really. Kid was barely twenty."

Jack's eyes narrowed.

"He was just some punk with a rich family. But he was also a punk with a record of driving under the influence. DUI's stacked up since he turned sixteen."

"DUI's?" Jack asked.

"Sorry, it's what happens when you get drunk and then operate a vehicle, a uh...a car. You know what a car is?"

Jack nodded. "I am familiar with them, yes. I apologize for interrupting you. Please go on."

"So yeah, if you're an asshole like this kid, you have too much to drink, and then you get behind the wheel of a car. At that point, you're likely going to hurt or kill someone. That would be fine if the person you hurt or killed was you, but most of the time, it's someone else. And that's what this kid did. He murdered my family and passed out at the wheel half a street away.

He also had Mommy and Daddy issues, opulent upbringing, spoiled, always used to getting whatever he wanted. He'd been in and out of trouble for years apparently, juvi—that's like prison for younger people, well, kinda, anyway. So yeah, he coasted through the whole gambit of correctional facilities and substance abuse programs. From what they told me, he'd been sober for thirty days, he had that little coin, or the key-chain, or whatever the fuck they give you to acknowledge it. He actually had that on him when he plowed into my family."

Michael looked up and touched the picture and sighed. "So, yeah, skip ahead about two years. What happened to me, the whole date with a vampire thing happened, and what do you know? I turn on the television one night, and that kid's on the news again. Another DUI, another person hurt, thankfully no one died this time. His dad did what Daddy had always done, and got his son out of serving any real time. And before you know it, the kid's back on the streets."

Michael took a deep breath.

"So I did a little homework. Found out where this punk lived. And I paid him a visit one night. I was going to blind him. Take his eyesight. If no one else would do anything to keep him from getting plastered and getting behind the wheel, well, I was going to. I would certainly make sure he never drove anywhere again at the very least! But when I got there... when I crept into his room, the damn kid was, the damn—"

Michael took several controlled breaths.

"Michael, you do not—"

Michael looked over at Jack and help up a hand. "This little fucker...he'd been drinking again. Bottles and cans all over the room. And there he was, passed out in the middle of it all. Piece of shit was still holding a half empty beer can. I lost it.

Just...lost it. Kid never even knew what hit him. I drank him dry, Jack. Right there in his own bedroom. Drank the little fucker dry. He was cold before I let go of him."

Jack wiped at his eyes. "I am so sorry, Michael."

"I'm not done," Michael said. "I have no memory of what happened after that, Jack. All I do know is that I woke up the following night with nothing but nightmares to tell me what might or might not have happened after I killed that kid. Nightmares like you wouldn't believe.

A week later, reports of missing people started popping up in the news. People I'd been dreaming about, Jack. I'd seen their faces, man, I'd dreamt about them, about..." Michael paused and took several deep, quivering breaths. "Whatever happened to me that night, whatever I did, I've only experienced it that one time. The one time I killed someone. Like... like I became...something else. Someone else. And those missing people? I saw their faces before the reports ever came out, man. Saw 'em in my nightmares. I still see them."

Michael turned back towards Jack, only to find him already standing there beside him. Jack reached out and, to Michael's shock, the elf hugged him. Hugged him hard.

"Forgive me, my friend," Jack said. He let Michael go and walked towards the patio doors.

Michael began to say something, but Jack interrupted.

"I can't remember the last time I was afraid. Honestly. I'm old enough now that one would think I'd experienced fear on countless occasions, but I cannot for the life of me recall the last time I was afraid. Truly terrified. I am afraid now, you understand. Afraid of losing Melissa. And fear does wonderful, horrible, and strange things. I believe it's what convinced me that asking this of you was acceptable. I understand now that it was not. Not at all. I can only ask that you forgive me. I will

87

speak of it no more."

"Jack," Michael said, joining the elf by the glass doors facing Humpback. "Don't apologize. I know what fear is. I know what it can do. I've been holed up here on this mountain for more than two decades. I couldn't tell you the real names of anyone else outside of this room, I sneak in and out of almost everywhere I go—when I even go anywhere ,that is—and I have no friends that aren't covered in fur and walk around on four legs! Present company excluded."

Jack smiled.

Michael continued, "I don't talk to anyone, really. I'm so terrified of making friends that I avoid everyone. The idea that I might have to watch someone I love die again, while I go on and on, haunts me; it's made me into this, this damned hermit! The only reason, and I mean the ONLY reason, I even approached you the other night was because I latched on to the delusion that you might be a vampire, too! Someone like me. Someone I could talk to again. And now I know that was my fear at work. My fear driving me to just reach out, to just talk to someone! So believe me, I understand fear, Jack. I know what it is to be afraid, terrified even. If I could go back in time and save my family, there's nothing I wouldn't do, however frightening, no favor I wouldn't ask...of anyone, Jack. Do you understand?"

Jack looked into Michael's eyes. "I do. Thank you, my friend."

Michael nodded. "I'll make you a deal, man. Let me just, let me just get my head around all of this, if that's okay? Can you give me the night? I just—"

Michael was interrupted as Jack grabbed and hugged him again.

"Thank you," the elf said. The words came out as a whisper.

"It's okay, man. It's okay. We'll figure something out, I promise."

Jack nodded and waved his hand over the living room. The fantastic additions vanished, leaving the space exactly how the night had started. Even the empty bottles were gone.

"I should return to them," Jack said.

Michael nodded. "You know what? Fuck it. Why don't you just bring them back here, man? You know, get the hell out of that tent for a night? I've got plenty of room, and, like, three different showers! You know women and their showers!"

"I thought you lived here alone?"

"Well, yeah, but when I designed the place, I had to think about selling it eventually, ya know? Recoup some of my investment. Hard to sell a place this size with one bathroom."

Jack smiled. "Thank you, Michael. I will certainly mention it to them."

"...and we've got plenty of ciders for the night!" Michael said, and added a wink.

Jack laughed, and Michael gave him a pat on the shoulder.

"Also, how the hell did you sober up so quick? You seemed like, like, smashed thirty minutes ago!"

Jack grinned. "Magic."

14

Jack made his way toward Melissa and Becky. He'd decided to walk so he would have more time to think along the trail. That, and flight took far more concentration than simply walking required, even if it was a dark forest path he navigated. Michael was right; Jack wasn't certain if his new friend could indeed help. And even if Michael did attempt to help, which Jack wasn't positive he would, who could possibly guess what the outcome might be? There was so little literature on vampires, and so few of them remained, that answers to questions like this proved difficult to find. Jack had run into quite a few dead ends during the last few days where the species was concerned, especially when the subject of the mass disappearance came up. It was as if that in the span of less than a year, almost every single vampire just...ceased to exist. If Jack had done his math correctly and was to believe the books he had managed to find on the subject, the strange event had occurred five hundred and forty-three years ago. Just over a hundred or so years before he was born. And while the disappearance was strange, what was even more bizarre was that no one, not even the elves at the time, seemed to know why, or even appeared concerned one way or the other. Jack had seen more concern over the extinction of certain plants than the near disappearance of an entire sentient species.

Of course, he found trace evidence that some had looked into it, but no real answers ever appeared to surface. The common belief was internal strife, almost as if a civil war had

broken out amongst the vampires, resulting in a total collapse of the species—but even that was conjecture. To the best
of Jack's knowledge, there was no documentation of any war.
Nothing whatsoever was written about conflicts prior to the
disappearance, and there had been no signs that anything was
amiss leading up to the moment when the vampires, well,
vanished. Researching sickle cell, a disease Jack had never
even heard of, which only existed in a realm he was unfamil-
iar with, had been far easier than researching vampirism and
vampiric history, even in his own realm.

An owl called out somewhere in the dark, and Jack looked
up. Storm clouds were gathering. Perhaps he should take
Michael up on his offer? The idea of letting Melissa and her
sister spend the night in the rain wasn't a pleasant one, and
the thought of taking them into Fae was risky. He'd already
chanced it once or twice with Melissa, so best not to tempt
Fate again. Fae was no place for mortals on a good day, much
less most other times.

A distant flash of lighting lit the treetops; after it, a low rumble spilled over the mountainside and through the forest. The
storm would make it to the girls before he would at this pace.
He'd have to fly, and he'd have to act quick in order to get them
back to Michael's home before the rain arrived.

Jack leapt into the air and made his way south towards
the Emerald Seat. As he was clearing the trees, a soft whistle
caught his attention, and a sudden searing pain struck him in
the chest. Jack cried out, and crashed through the trees, where
he tumbled back to the forest floor and rolled to a stop. Another whistle, and another scorching pain slammed into his
left leg. Jack let out another cry and looked down. The shaft
of a long red arrow quivered in place just above his knee. He
reached for the pain in his chest, and his fingers found the
broken shaft of the first arrow.

Another whistle, this time closer, and Jack rolled to his

side before the arrow could find its mark. The ground behind him exploded, throwing up dirt, rocks, and a deep green light. The crimson shaft of yet another arrow protruded from the ground where Jack's spine had just been. He was on his feet as a new arrow smashed into a tree behind him with a solid THUNK! Jack held out his hand, and in his grip, a glowing blue sword snapped into existence. He cut two more arrows out of the air and stumbled backwards into a large pine. His chest and leg were on fire. A limb snapped in the dark, and Jack spun as another arrow, much larger than the others, tore threw his shoulder and buried itself into the tree behind him, effectively pinning him in place. Jack cried out in agony.

15

"Damn, I knew it smelled like rain earlier," Becky said.

"You and your nose!" Melissa said. She walked over to her bag and began to unfasten the main straps. "I'll get the tarp if you can dig out the bungees."

"On it."

A flash of light illuminated their little camp for a moment, and both women had to blink away sudden neon shadows.

Becky rubbed her eyes for a second. "Geesh."

"No kidding."

The thunder arrived after that. Low and menacing.

"Still a few miles off," Melissa said.

"I counted five."

"I think I got to six."

The site they had picked was a good one in case of a storm. It rested on the crest of a small hill, so if rain did come, it would roll away from their tent and not into it from any direction. The only problems would come if it rained for more than a day. That would make leaving the site a bit tricky, like a giant slip-and-slide through the leaves and pine needles. But the car wasn't far. They'd make it, but they'd get there covered in mud, cuts, bruises, and forest grime, for sure.

"Think we could make the car before the storm?" Melissa asked.

Becky looked up at the treetops. They swayed back and forth, the leaves rustling at a pretty good frenzy. "I dunno. Probably best not to try. Where's your man, anyway? Maybe he could just magic the rain away!"

Melissa chuckled and pulled out the tarp. "I'm sure he'll be here soon."

"Could get cozy in there with all three of us. Soaking wet. All hot and slippery."

"Ewwww."

Becky laughed.

A gust of wind tore through the camp, carrying shredded leaves, pine needles, and a faint scream.

16

Michael stood on his deck, sipping a new cider and watched Thorn and Nanook below. The dogs were busy sniffing about, each searching for an acceptable spot to do their business. Nanook would instigate a small tussle with Thorn every few seconds, and after a brief bit of bouncing and barking, the two would continue their search for bathroom locations.

"Come on, guys."

A gust of wind kicked up, and all three looked north as a flash of lighting blinked across the sky. A nasty storm was approaching, and it looked to be traveling at a pretty good clip. Michael searched the woods for Jack and failed to spot him. The girls looked to be unpacking a rain tarp.

"Damn Jack, I shoulda gone with you."

Michael was deciding what to do when movement and a bit of heat from the trees caught his attention. Apparently it captured Thorn's as well. The dog began to growl, and just to his left, Nanook's ears had flattened; she crouched and began inching slowly towards the undergrowth at the edge of the lawn. A large figure stepped out, and a crimson red arrow sliced through the air where Michael had been standing a millisecond prior.

The vampire was already moving, and so were the dogs.

The figure in the trees moved fast, much faster than Michael anticipated, and far quicker than a bear could possibly move. And bears didn't use bows and arrows. The figure looked like a man, a giant of a man dressed in a long, dark coat with a deep hood. A second arrow raced past Michael as he flew, this one just stinging his cheek. The shape turned, nocked a new arrow, and aimed towards the closest dog, Thorn. Michael crashed into the intruder and reached for his throat, all before the bottle of cider Michael had been drinking had time to shatter on the paved landing below the deck. The arrow launched, flew wild, and just barely missed Thorn.

Michael lifted the man he'd tackled and pinned him to a tree several feet in the air; bark exploded in all directions, and the hood fell backwards, revealing the man's face. He was massive, easily over seven foot, and at least three hundred, maybe three hundred twenty pounds.

Michael pulled his face close to the stranger's. "Who are you?"

Thorn took a running leap and grabbed the man's right foot, which now dangled several feet from the ground.

Michael loosened his grip on the man's throat just a touch. "I SAID, WHO ARE YOU?"

Nanook whimpered from the yard. Michael turned to see his friend lying on the ground, a crimson arrow protruding from her shoulder. Blood poured from the wound and fanned out on the dog's fur.

"NOOK!"

Michael turned back to the man he now held, and pulled his face even closer. The man's eyes began to bulge in their sockets, and his face contorted in anguish as he tried to breathe. His hair, a deep shade of blue, covered half of his face, and a closely-trimmed beard, also blue, shimmered in the dark. He clawed at Michael's hand now, and gasped. Thorn growled and shook his head, biting further into the stranger's boot.

Nanook whimpered again.

"Too late," Michael said, and crushed the man's throat.

There was a loud pop followed by a sickening crunch, and the man went limp, one eye now a solid red orb. Michael let him fall lifeless to the ground, and he and Thorn raced to Nanook's side.

As he knelt down, a new arrow struck Michael from behind.

17

Jack gasped; he couldn't seem to get enough air, and his vision was beginning to blur. The inside of his head felt as if it were swimming in the dark and barely able to discern which way was up, which way led to air. He gasped again, and a wave of pain ripped at his chest and lungs.

"Leave him," a voice said from the shadows.

A figure, much closer than the voice, shifted from behind a tree. Jack made out enormous shoulders, a long coat with deep hood, and a sleek bow. He wished a flash of lighting would arrive so he could get a better look, but the storm wasn't cooperating, nor were his eyes now.

"He's done," the closest figure said. "For now."

Jack took a breath, coughed, and gasped for more air. "Who?" was all he managed to call out.

Three more shadows moved in the dark. A flash of lighting arrived, and with it, Jack made out nearly a half-dozen figures. All but one were moving away now. This lone figure remained still, however, its head bowed just so. Jack could sense eyes beneath the hood staring directly into his.

"My apologies, elf," the figure called out over the sounds of the approaching storm. "This was no honorable fight."

The voice was male.

Jack smiled, coughed, and spit a large amount of blood onto the ground. "Dren."

The figure looked up at that, and the others stopped moving. One turned back to stare in Jack's direction and whispered something.

"You are all Dren," Jack continued.

What appeared to be the group's leader nodded, and made a low, formal bow. He then removed his hood and drew another arrow from the quiver on his belt. It made a dull humming sound, and tiny flashes of light sparkled along the shaft. The man's hair was a dark shade of blue, with streaks of white. His beard was a similar color, and emitted a faint glimmer.

"You would not shoot..."—Jack gasped for air—"...an unarmed opponent..."—he coughed and spit more blood—"...a fourth time, would you?"

The man grinned, drew back the arrow, aimed, and fired.

18

Michael crashed forward as the arrow slammed into him. He rolled over Nanook in an effort not to crush his wounded friend, and his shoulder erupted in white-hot agony. Something zipped over his head, and Michael flinched. The ground exploded again, throwing green light and dirt into the dark. Nanook whimpered and tried to claw away, blood still flowing from her wound, her back legs motionless, her breathing sharp and labored. Thorn growled loudly, and from Michael's right, a figure turned to face the menacing sound. Michael shot towards the movement and crashed headfirst into another man.

"KILL THE THING!" a voice called out from the dark.

Michael had a good grip at the man's huge neck with his left hand, but his right arm was sluggish. This man was just as massive as the first, and Michael's grip on his throat did not seem to pose a problem for the assailant. A giant hand grabbed at Michael's throat as well, and his attacker reached behind Michael to find the arrow which had struck him. Michael screamed, despite the hand which was crushing his larynx, as his attacker pulled and pushed at the arrow protruding from his back. A flash of lightning illuminated the entire area for a second, and Michael got a better look at who was attacking him and the dogs. There were five altogether—well, four now that Michael had taken care of one of them. All were dressed the same, in identical long, dark coats with hoods, and each sported an immense red longbow. This attacker had similar facial features as the first: a light-skinned complexion and shimmering, sapphire-colored beard. One of the furthest figures was drawing yet another arrow and directing it towards a now-charging Thorn.

Michael yelled, released the man's throat, and rammed his thumb into his attacker' eye, burying it up to the palm. This garnered a reaction from the giant, and the grip on Michael's throat vanished. Michael grabbed the man's waist as best he could with his right arm and bolted straight up into the darkness. Both men howled in pain, and Michael summoned as much force as he could, twisted, and threw the giant back towards the earth in the precise direction of the attacker now aiming a huge arrow at Thorn.

"THORN!" Michael yelled.

Thorn glanced in Michael's direction and sprang to his left, barely avoiding the flailing giant now racing through the air. The sound of an enormous, violent crash followed, and the two shapes tumbled, broken and mangled, into the forest. The last attacker was already drawing an arrow before his accomplices had even rolled to a bloody stop. Michael and Thorn both raced towards him. The figure hesitated just long enough, glancing from Thorn to Michael and back, that Michael had time to close the distance, but not before the man fired.

Michael rolled mid-flight, snatched the arrow from the air, turned it, and rammed the point through the attacker's throat. He grabbed the giant, and amidst chokes and gurgles, Michael snapped his neck.

As the attacker slumped to the ground, an arrow sliced completely through Michael's arm and buried itself in the closest tree. Another flash of green light illuminated the night, and Michael turned to see Thorn ripping at another figure's arm. Michael raced towards the last stranger.

19

Melissa looked up from the tarp now covering half the tent and flapping in the growing wind. "Did you hear that?"

Becky was already looking in the direction of the scream. "Yeah. That was…"

A flash of green light lit the forest again.

"…weird?" Becky finished.

Another explosion of light, again green, strobed across the sky, and the sisters scrambled to secure the rain tarp.

"Owl?"

"Screech owl, maybe."

"It sounded weird."

"Yeah, spooky."

"Does the lighting look—" Melissa started, when a new flash of light, followed by a low rumble, interrupted her.

"Weird, right?" Becky asked.

A gust of wind tore at the tarp, ripping one of the stakes from the ground. Becky dove forward and snatched it before the thing was flung off into the dark. When she looked up, two figures were staring down at her. She let out a yelp and shuffled backwards.

Two enormous men stepped into the small circle of lantern and firelight. Both held large red longbows, arrows at the ready.

"Hello," one of the figures said. At that, both men bowed—one, the larger of the two, far deeper than the other.

"Who the fuck are you?" Becky asked and scrambled to her feet, only to stumble backwards, landing hard on her rear end.

The largest of the two men smiled and held out a hand to help Becky up. "I am called Pine, and this is Trex."

Melissa was already behind Becky, and lifted her up without the aid of the stranger.

"You, ah, you frightened us," Melissa said.

Pine nodded, "And for that I apologize."

Becky made a motion to her chin and nodded to the men. "You guys, uh, you come from a rave or something? Little glitter and techno before you go off hunting?"

Pine smiled and stroked his beard. It glimmered in the light and flashed a bit at his touch. "I'm afraid I don't know what a rave is, so the answer is no."

"Get on with it, Pine," the other man said.

The man who called himself Pine turned and glared at his companion. "You are here to learn, sapling. There is no honor in this, but we can offer civility. Now silence yourself."

Becky pressed on Melissa's thigh with her hand. Melissa glanced down at the touch, then backed up a step; her sister wanted distance between them and the two men.

"I apologize for my companion," Pine said, and looked back to the sisters. "He is young, and we find ourselves facing an unpleasant quandary."

Melissa stepped backwards another pace, never letting go of

her sister's shoulders. "Yeah? What, uh, what's the problem?"

Pine's smile faded, and he sighed. "The problem, child, is sometimes we are forced to do things we would rather not. For those we would rather forget."

Melissa was pulling Becky backwards now.

The other man, Trex, stepped forward at that point and held out a kind of sword, handle first, and offered it to Becky. "Honorable enough for you, Pine?" he asked, glancing at his companion.

Pine dropped his head and sighed again. He removed the arrow he had nocked and tossed it, point first, into the dirt where it stuck, and propped his bow against a tree. He retrieved a new blade from within his coat. It was much smaller than the sword being offered to Becky, only four, maybe five inches in length, and curved at a wicked angle. It was also constructed from what appeared to be red glass, or another type of transparent material. "No, Trex, it is not honorable. But it will have to suffice. Take the sword, girl. I will not kill a defenseless woman."

Melissa began screaming for help.

"He's not coming, child," Trex said. He grinned when he said it.

20

Jack stared at the last arrow which had been shot. Its shaft still quivered just inches from his right hand, the tip buried far into the tree's flesh. The shaft, while crimson like the others, was also transparent for several inches in the middle. Inside this transparent section, brilliantly-colored gems glistened with a sort of light all their own. His attackers had vanished into the night, leaving him there, pinned to the tree.

Jack coughed, and spat more blood onto the ground. He knew what the arrow meant, and he knew what the gems were. They were payment, a sort of compensation for what had just transpired—or more accurately, *how* it had transpired. He grabbed the transparent section of the arrow and watched as the remainder of the shaft, both front and rear, evaporated in a glowing red haze, even the fletching. All that remained were the cylinder and gems Jack held. He took a labored breath, and slid the container into his pocket. He had more pressing issues to deal with.

Jack reached up and snapped the arrow holding him to the tree. When he did, he let out a groan and paused before proceeding with what had to come next. He held the bit of broken arrow up and examined the fletching. Three cobalt blue feathers, each with a single red stripe, glimmered in the low light. He didn't recognize the clan, but he'd certainly find out. Jack leaned forward and pulled himself free from the rest of the shaft. It hurt, and bright fire danced behind his clenched eyelids as he did. When he was free, his knees collapsed, and he crumpled to the earth.

As he lay there, Jack recognized the signs of shock setting in. He was going to pass out if he didn't do something, and soon. The wound at his shoulder, probably the worst of them since the arrow had gone all the way through, was already beginning to heal now that he'd removed himself from it. But there were still two more arrows to deal with: one in his leg, and the other quite possibly buried in his left lung. Jack forced himself to a crawling position and made his way over to the arrow that had missed him. He clawed at the dirt as best he could and managed to pull the arrow free after several minutes. He then examine the head and sighed. Bullet points, not broad headed.

"Oh, thank you," Jack said.

He ripped the arrow from his thigh and stifled a groan. Blood soaked his pants leg before the wound had time to close. He then reached up to the broken shaft protruding from his ribs and probed it with delicate fingers; the pain was immense. It appeared the arrow had missed his ribs, which was a mixed blessing. Good because he wouldn't have to worry about bone fragments and a slower healing time. Bad, because nothing had slowed the arrow and it was now lodged deep into his lung. It would certainly explain the blood he continued to cough up, and the extreme difficulty he had breathing.

Jack wiped away as much blood as he could and gave the arrow a tug. His hand slipped off of the smooth shaft, and a wave of agony flooded over the him. He screamed.

21

Michael held the last man by the throat and pinned him to the ground.

"WHO ARE YOU?"

The man tried to fight back, kicking and punching as best he could. When he tried to throw a leg over Michael's shoulder, the vampire ripped him from the ground.

"This isn't the fucking UFC, asshole," Michael said, and leapt into the air, carrying the giant with him.

The man yelled, and Michael yelled back as he flew higher.

"I think here should do it!" Michael said, looking down. His attacker looked down, too, and gasped. They were easily sixty, seventy feet up.

"No!" the man gasped and grabbed at Michael in an effort to hold on.

Michael was about to say something in response when he saw Nanook. Instead, he just dropped the man. He screamed as he fell, and Michael was already on the ground before the descending figure hit with a sickening thud several feet away. The stranger shrieked a moment or two after that. Michael took note of the man's legs, and when he was confident they wouldn't do him any good for quite some time, he raced over to his fallen friend.

Nanook had managed to drag herself several yards towards the house. Blood had stopped flowing from the wound, and was now trickling from her mouth. Thorn lay by her side, licking softly at one of his friend's ears. He whimpered when Michael arrived.

"Okay, girl, okay, I got you, you're gunna be okay."

Nanook's tail made a feeble wag, and the dog looked at her master through half-closed eyes. Michael began to cry when he reached down and attempted to pick his friend up. Nanook yelped and shuddered badly.

"I can save it," the stranger said.

Michael looked up, his eyes filled with tears and rage. "What?"

The man coughed and moaned; both legs were broken badly. Bones protruded from his pants. "I can, I can save the beast if you let me go."

Michael looked back at Nanook. The dog's breathing was so shallow, and so slow now, that Michael was sure she only had minutes more, if that.

"How?" Michael asked, "How can—"

"You will free me?"

"Yes, motherfucker! How can you save my dog?"

The man sighed with relief and pointed to Michael. "Your blood. You are a vampire. Give the dog some of your blood."

"What?"

The man coughed, and pointed again. "You. YOU can save her with your blood. Let her have some of it. Your blood will mend her wounds. When it does, then you can remove the arrow. Not until then."

Michael looked back down at Nanook. She was shivering now. "Jesus, girl, okay, okay...," Michael said. He bit into his own wrist, and winced as his teeth tore through the skin, tendons, and veins.

Thorn whimpered and looked at Michael, his head cocked to the side. Nanook's eyes were fluttering.

"Okay, girl, okay, drink some of this, okay?" Michael held his wrist up to Nanook's mouth.

Nanook sniffed Michael's wrist, but that was it. She looked up to Michael's eyes as if to ask if he was okay, and then closed them.

"Come on, girl!" Michael said and lifted the dog's head. It was heavy, lifeless. "Come on, sweetie! You gotta drink, okay?"

Michael forced his wrist into Nanook's mouth. Blood poured into it, and out the other side.

"Come on, girl! Please!" Michael was crying now. "Come on, Nook!"

Nanook's breathing returned just a bit, and the dog's tongue licked at her owner's wrist in soft, delicate motions.

"That's it, sweetheart!" Michael said, smiling.

Nanook grew stronger with every swallow, and within seconds, the dog was shifting her weight onto her stomach. Within a minute, she was licking and drinking Michael's blood as if it were nothing more than a spoonful of her favorite peanut butter.

"You see?" the man said.

Michael ignored him. When Nanook stood, so did Thorn, who was now wagging his tail in quick, wild circles. Michael reached for the arrow and pulled. Nanook didn't even register it. In fact, as Michael watched, the wound closed, and the blood covering most of the dog's side and stomach, even around her snout, began to seep into the fur, as if Nanook's coat was absorbing the blood back into her system.

Michael pulled his wrist away, and Nanook reared up, placing her paws on Michael's shoulders, her tail wagging. Her fur was as white as it had been; dirt still clung to it in places, but the blood was gone. The dog acted as if nothing had happened at all, much less as if she'd almost died just moments before.

"Oh, thank God," Michael said, and ruffled the fur on Nanook's head. Even that felt different, softer, almost puppy-like. He smiled and then turned back to the stranger. His smile disappeared.

Nanook and Thorn looked over at the figure as well. They began to growl.

22

Becky tripped on the corner of their tent and sprawled backwards, arms flailing, but she stayed on her feet.

Melissa was screaming Jack's name into the darkness.

The man offering the sword to Becky laughed. "I told you, girl, he is not coming."

"How do you know Jack? What have you done to him?" Melissa asked.

"I think you should be more concerned with yourself at the moment, child," Pine said. At that, he reached over, grabbed the sword Trex held, and tossed it to Becky.

The sword landed at her feet, and Becky let it. She wasn't taking her eyes off of the two men, and her hand was now behind her, grabbing the hilt of her Mark Three. "You fuckers stay the hell away from my sister, or I swear to God—"

Pine lowered his head and closed his eyes. "I promise that no harm will come to your sister. But you...you must take the blade."

"Fuck you and your fucking blade, motherfucker!" Becky shouted back. Tears were beginning to roll down her cheeks.

"Pine," the other man said.

Pine looked up and sighed. "As you wish," he said, and returned his knife back into his coat. "I will make this as painless as possible, I promise," he said and stepped towards the sisters, now unarmed.

Becky didn't hesitate. She lunged forward and struck the man as hard as she could in the throat with the best straight punch she could muster. He was tall, much taller than anyone she'd seen before, so the blow landed a bit off, but it worked. Pine staggered backwards, eyes wide. Becky had surprised him. In fact, from the look on his face, she'd shocked him.

Becky didn't stop there. She stepped hard on the man's lead foot and threw her weight against him. Pine continued backwards, and as he fell, the tendons in his trapped foot snapped. There was an audile pop from inside the man's boot.

Becky had her knife out a second later, and was about to strike down at the man's leg, preferably into his femoral artery, but Pine's foot slid back, staggering her. Any other average-sized adult would have sprawled backwards, and Becky would have been able to keep their trapped foot planted firmly beneath her own weight. From there, she would have buried her knife in her target's leg. Pine was huge, however, and the momentum he gathered was enough to free his foot and almost topple Becky in the process. She sliced down regardless, the blade cutting easily into Pine's leg just below the knee.

Melissa scrambled for the sword lying on the ground and sliced the fingers on her left hand as she fumbled to pick it up as quickly as she could. Trex stood motionless, a look of surprise now evident on his face. Pine rolled backwards and was on his feet in one motion.

Trex moved to intervene.

"Leave her!" Pine said.

Trex stopped and turned towards Melissa, who now held the sword he'd offered Becky.

Becky had regained her balance and was crouched low, her blade now held in a reverse grip, edge out, like she'd been shown on countless occasions.

Pine was smiling now. He made no motion to advance, only reached down to the cut Becky had made below his knee. He winced just a bit, but the smile never left.

"You have been trained," Pine said, and held up a bloodied hand.

"You're damn right, bitch," Becky replied.

Pine nodded and made a small bow. "I apologize for under-estimating you."

"Apology not accepted, asshole!" Melissa said and took another step towards Trex, who was now watching her every move, his eyes glancing from the blade she held and back to her.

"I despise this," Pine said. "I do. There is no honor in any of it. But we are sworn. Do you understand? This *must* happen."

"If you hate this, you're really gunna love what I do to you in a second," Becky said.

Pine reached back under his coat and re-brandished the red blade. It sparkled in the dark. "You do have my respect," he said, and moved towards Becky. The smile was gone.

23

Jack rubbed dirt between his hands, creating a bloody, sticky mud. He re-gripped the arrow shaft protruding from his chest and squeezed. He took as deep of a breath as he could, pulled, and the arrow moved this time. The pain was immense. Jack tried again and felt his entire pectoral muscle flex, as if it were reticent to let the arrow go.

"Come on, Jack."

The shaft moved, and Jack coughed, gritting his teeth as he did. More blood worked its way into his mouth, but with one final effort, he tore the arrow from his chest. The coughs now came in long, raspy waves, blood spattering the ground as they did. Jack sank back down to all fours and rolled over onto his back. From there he attempted to take shallow, controlled, breaths as best he could. His body would heal in a moment or two, and the coughing wasn't helping things move along.

Why had these Dren attacked him? Why were they in this realm? He didn't recognize any of them. Not at all. The Dren clans were notoriously private and remained mostly isolated from anyone outside of their own. Jack didn't know much about them, but he did know they were renowned hunters, trackers, and warriors. They also held a very strict code of honor, especially where single combat was concerned. Aside from that, he knew nearly nothing of their history. He couldn't speak their native tongue, nor read it. He had only met one or two of the Dren in passing, but that was it. He'd read very little about them, and outside of stories, he'd heard even less. They were an old race, but how old, Jack did not know.

A scream echoed over the sound of the wind, and Jack bolted upright. The change in altitude sent his head swimming again, and his vision swam. Another scream brought him around again, and Jack was on his feet without thinking.

"Melissa?"

He bolted into the air towards the girls' location—the location of the screams.

24

Michael walked over to the man he had dropped. As he did, he looked at the other figures strewn about, reached behind him, and yanked at the arrow protruding from his shoulder blade. A wave of agony flooded over him, and the vampire stumbled to one knee before regaining his footing—but Michael continued walking towards the injured man. None of the other assailants moved; all of them seemed to be losing heat rapidly. They were either dead or soon would be. The final man would need medical attention soon, or he would die as well.

Michael stopped and looked down. "Who are you?" he asked while brandishing the bloody arrow like a dagger.

"You said you would let me go."

Michael knelt down and leaned in towards the stranger. He held the tip of the arrow to the man's eye, and motioned for the dogs to stop advancing. Thorn and Nanook both halted, but their growls continued.

"You don't look like you're going anywhere without my help," Michael said. "So if you want it, you'll answer my questions. Who the fuck are you? Why did you attack me?"

The man sat up and reached for one of his legs. He let out a groan and pushed the bone back into the hole it had ripped in his pants. Blood poured out of the fabric.

"Jesus," Michael said.

The stranger then proceeded to do the same with his other

leg. Sickening sounds of bone grinding bone followed, and the man's eyes glossed over.

"You gave me your word that you would allow me to leave if I provided you with the knowledge to save your beast. I owe you nothing else, vampire."

Michael watched as the man began to move his legs. It was impossible.

"You shot my dog," Michael said, and grabbed the man's lapel.

Michael pulled his attacker to his feet and pressed the tip of the arrow against the giant's cheek, just below the eye. He was shocked to see the stranger stand with little effort. Whoever or whatever he was healed fast, faster than even Michael did.

The man placed his hand on the arrow pressing into his cheek and began to lower it. "You gave your word."

A scream echoed out over the treetops, and Michael cocked his head. The stranger heard it, too, looked in the direction from where it came, and then back to Michael. A small smile spread across his lips.

"How many more of you are there?" Michael asked.

The man continued to smile. "You gave me your word."

There was a blur of motion, and Michael tore out the man's throat. The stranger's eyes went wide, and a fountain of blood and air erupted from the wound. Michael rammed the arrow through the stranger's eye and out the back of his skull. The stranger stood there for a second, then collapsed to his knees. Michael nudged him over onto his side, where he moved no more.

"I lied," Michael said, and leapt into the air, racing towards the screams.

25

Trex was airborne before he could register why. Jack had already plunged his sword completely through the Dren's chest, and was in the process of tossing him into the trees, when Becky screamed. Pine dove towards his bow, completely ignoring the girls now.

"Melissa, get away!" Becky shouted.

Instead, Melissa ran *towards* Pine, sword held high above her head.

Jack cast the dying man away and raced towards the larger Dren. Pine was fast, far faster than Jack imagined he could be. An arrow crashed into Jack's shoulder, sending the elf spiraling onto the ground, his sword vanishing.

Melissa swung her sword and barely missed Pine's head as he swatted the blade away with the upper limb of his bow.

"Smurf, no!"

Melissa glanced over her shoulder and dove to her left as Becky ran forward. Pine, already loading a new arrow, deflected Becky's knife hand, grabbed her elbow, and twisted his body, sending Becky flying over his shoulder. A loud snap followed, and Becky shrieked mid-air.

Jack rolled to his feet, ripped the arrow from his shoulder, and raced towards Melissa, who had stumbled to the ground in her effort to dodge Becky.

"Move," the elf said, and picked Melissa up, depositing her

on her feet.

Pine stepped back from Becky, who was now sprawled on her back, cradling her arm, the wind knocked out of her. He nodded, sighed, and threw his bow onto the ground. He turned towards Jack, his hands held in front of him, empty.

"Enough! This is over, elf!" Pine said.

Jack placed his arm in front of Melissa and summoned his sword again. It snapped into existence in his hand, blue light illuminating the dark camp.

"Why?" Jack asked. His eyes were mirrors of rage.

Pine nodded towards Melissa and then at Becky, who was now stumbling to her feet.

"Bounty. But I will acknowledge it no more. There is no honor here."

Becky stood, and limped towards her sister and Jack. She still held her knife, and made a wide berth around her giant assailant.

"These are warriors," Pine said. "Especially *that* one," he added, acknowledging Becky. "I like that one very much," he said, and smiled.

"Fuck you," Becky said between gasps for air, and spat at the Dren.

Pine chuckled. "Yes, I like her very, very much. I will hunt you no more," he said. Pine took a deep breath, then sighed, dropping his gaze to the earth. "...though it likely means my own death."

Jack reached for Becky and pulled her behind him with Melissa. "Who sent you?"

Pine looked up. "*That* I cannot do," Pine said. "You must understand."

"If there is no honor in this, then there is no honor in those who sent you!" Jack said.

The Dren nodded, "Even so. There are—"

Michael crashed into Pine, driving him headfirst to the ground. Broken tree limbs from the vampire's wake crashed and splintered all about the campsite, and the ground shook with the impact. Michael grabbed Pine under the arms and raced back into the sky, where he vanished above the canopy and into the shadows. More limbs and leaves tumbled towards the earth.

Melissa, Becky, and Jack all stared in shock.

26

Michael raced higher and higher, the giant he held clawing at his face and arms. When they reached what Michael figured to be at least two, two hundred and fifty feet, he stopped.

"This is my mountain, asshole!" he shouted, and with a kind of mid-air summersault, he flung the man back towards the ground with as much force as he could muster. "REMEMBER IT!" he shouted at the falling shape.

Michael hovered and watched as the stranger raced towards the rocks, grasping and flailing at the air. A second later, the sound of a violent thump echoed through the forest and back up to Michael. He grimaced, and dove towards Jack and the girls.

Jack was holding Melissa, who in turn knelt beside her sister, who was cradling her arm. Jack had one hand on top of Becky's head, a soft yellow glow pulsing from beneath his palm. Becky was on her knees, her breath coming in long, hard waves, one arm dangling at a strange angle in her lap. Michael noted the increased heat emanating from it. She still held her knife, though, her knuckles white.

Michael stepped towards the group. "You guys okay?"

Becky looked up. "Who...?" was all she managed before her eyes clamped shut and she grimaced.

"A friend," Jack said.

Melissa tore her eyes from Michael and scanned the dark. "Where's the one you hit, Jack?"

"He's gone," the elf said. "He won't be back."

"Yeah, and the one I just took is a friggin' crater at the base of Humpback," Michael said.

"Are there others?" Melissa asked.

"I don't see or sense more," Jack said.

Another flash of lightning and a loud rumble of thunder shook the mountain.

Michael scanned the area. "Yeah, me either. Assholes caught me off guard earlier, but I'm ready for them now." He feigned a smile, but he, too, was hurt, and it was hard to hide the pain screaming at him from almost every inch of his body. Blood covered his clothing.

Jack nodded. "Thank you, Michael."

Becky pitched forward. "I think I'm going to be sick."

Michael was at her side without thinking. "You're going to be okay," he said, and placed one hand on her back and one under her injured arm.

Becky did vomit then, and proceeded to cough for a full minute. It smelled like strawberries, which Michael did not expect. Tears ran down the woman's cheeks, and a long string of mucous dangled from her nose. She vomited again. More strawberries. She never let go of her knife, and Michael never let go of her.

Melissa leaned over her sister and mouthed a "thank you" to Michael, then took over holding her sister. She, too, had tears in her eyes.

Jack extended a hand to Michael, who shook it back. "I am in your debt," the elf said.

"Anytime. You okay? You look like shit, man," Michael replied, motioning to the elf's bloodied and tattered clothes.

"I'm fine," Jack said, and snapped his fingers. Just as before, his clothes were pristine.

"Seriously, you gotta teach me that," Michael said.

Becky spat, winced, and stood with Melissa's help. She looked at Michael, at Jack, back at Michael, wiped her mouth with the back of her knife hand, and grinned. "So who the fuck are you? Like, Boy Wonder?" Her smile grew.

That was all it took. Michael was in love.

27

Michael looked at Jack, glanced at Melissa, and then back at Becky. "I, uh—"

"...he's a good friend," Jack said.

Michael smiled and extended his hand to the girls. "Michael."

Becky wiped the palm of her free hand on the leg of her pants and shook the vampire's hand. Melissa followed suit.

Melissa motioned skywards and nodded at Michael. "So you can fly, too? You're an elf?"

"Umm...."

An immense clap of thunder shook the group, and even Jack jumped.

"Maybe we can all talk back at my place?" Michael asked, and offered an awkward smile. "And we need to do something about your arm." He motioned at Becky.

Becky nodded and looked down. "I've had worse."

"Worse or not, we should retreat somewhere so I may inspect it further," Jack said. "I'm afraid it is probably broken."

Becky laughed and squeezed her eyes shut."Oh, it's broken, all right!"

"All the more reason to hurry," Jack said.

Becky didn't argue; she just nodded.

The rain started then, and it didn't start light. Huge, angry drops crashed through the trees above and began to soak everything.

"I would suggest gathering only what you cannot be without, and let us be on our way," Jack said. He had to raise his voice above the sounds of the rain and growing wind.

"Melissa needs her medicine," Becky said.

Melissa ducked into the tent and began rummaging about. "I got it."

Jack and Michael each grabbed random items. Michael made a silent motion towards Melissa and Jack, and then to himself and Becky. Jack nodded, and the vampire shook his head in agreement.

Michael looked at Becky. "So, I can take you, if uhh, if that's okay?"

"What do you mean?"

"I mean I could—"

"Up there?!? Fly?" Becky asked, wiping rain from her eyes and face.

"Well, yeah, it's, it's a bit of hike back to my place."

Becky looked up again and then back at Michael. "This is so fucking weird, man."

Michael smiled. "Tell me about it."

"You okay, Becky?" Melissa asked.

"I'm okay, Smurf."

"You'll like this part. It's fun. Flying, that is," Melissa said.

Becky glanced over and saw her sister cradled in Jack's arms; she was shivering. Her pack was secured to the elf's back. It looked so small on his broad shoulders, and her sister appeared likewise in his muscular arms. Becky kicked dirt into the fire pit, killing what minuscule flames remained.

"You sure you're okay with this?" Michael asked.

"Why the hell not," Becky said.

Michael smiled and took the woman's pack. He pulled it over his shoulders and had a difficult time adjusting it. He was larger than the elf by a good bit, and the sister's packs were identical. He held out his arms in an awkward, almost childish kind of way. "M'lady?"

Becky laughed and walked over. Michael lifted her with delicate ease, careful not to hurt her arm, or move it any more than needed. Becky still winced, but seemed okay considering. "Let's do this, Super Boy!"

Michael chuckled. "As you wish. Your arm okay?"

"I'm good. Thank you."

Michael nodded and leapt skywards. Jack and Melissa followed just behind.

"Oh. My. God!" Becky yelped, and buried her face in Michael's neck. "Oh my God, oh my God, oh my God."

Michael laughed. "It's okay, I haven't dropped anyone yet! Well, not by accident, anyway!" he said above the racing wind.

The curtains of dark rain kept Becky from seeing much, but she was able to make out the camp below. One of the lanterns still burned bright behind a hazy curtain of raindrops and wind. "Fly a lot of girls around, do you? Air Uber and shit?" she asked through clenched teeth.

Michael chuckled. "Not really. Actually, you're my first!"

"Oh my God, oh my God, oh my God...."

"But I promise not to drop you if you leave me a good rating!"

"Five stars, I promise!"

Michael felt Becky begin to shiver. Her arm had to be killing her; the heat coming off of it was considerable, and he could not only see it, he felt it against his chest. The rain was coming down hard now, and the wind howled as it raced by, so he dared not fly any faster. A bolt of lighting strobed across the horizon, and a clap of thunder echoed over the forest below. Becky jumped, and Michael heard her gasp at the pain it caused.

"We're almost there," he said.

Becky nodded.

When they reached the house, Michael made a soft landing on the deck next to the waiting dogs.

"Sorry, guys!" Michael said. "I'll get you dried off here in a sec, okay?"

Thorn and Nanook wagged.

Michael set Becky down and only let go of her when he was positive she was steady and wouldn't collapse. Thorn and Nanook sniffed up at the new visitor. Jack and Melissa landed a moment later, and Michael slid open the door, motioning everyone in. Becky glanced back over her shoulder and mouthed a 'thank you' to Michael, who smiled and nodded back.

"Guys, this is Thorn," Michael said. "And that one over there, licking Melissa and soaking the floor, that's Nanook. Nook's had a rough night."

Jack slid the door shut and snapped his fingers. Everyone's clothes, including the dog's fur coats, were dry and warm in an instant. A fire sizzled to life in the fireplace, and everyone thanked Jack in turn. Melissa guided Becky to the couch and eased her down, careful not to jostle her injured arm.

"Would you guys excuse us for once second?" Michael asked. He ushered Jack back out into the storm.

When the door closed, Michael sped over to the railing and pointed down through the rain and wind. "There's like four of those same bastards down there. We should move—"

Michael stopped. He wiped the rain from his face and out of his eyes in order to see more clearly. He shook his head at what he saw, or what he didn't see.

There were no signs of the bodies. Nothing. There weren't even footprints that he could detect. Despite the heavy rain now falling, there should have been prints still visible. The impact marks in the earth where Michael had thrown incredibly heavy attackers with as much force as he could muster were also gone. He studied the lawn, searching for the random arrows which had littered the ground. None remained. He looked over his shoulder at the spot where the first arrow fired should have been lodged in the siding. Again, there was nothing there, not even a hole to prove anything had ever been there in the first place. Nothing.

"The Dren remove their fallen, and all traces of combat should the need arise," Jack said as he studied the surrounding forest.

"The who? Who the hell were those guys, Jack?"

"First, I think we should go inside."

"Yeah, but—"

"Michael, they could still be here."

Michael snapped his head towards the night and the dark, storm-cloaked forest beyond. He couldn't see much of anything now; even Humpback was shrouded in shadow and rain. Michael nodded, and both men hurried inside to the warm glow of the living room, soaked yet again.

28

Michael busied himself by securing the house and closing the metal storm shutters. He checked his phone and inspected each of the security cameras, even grabbing an iPad for a larger view. If their attackers could still be out there, the least he could do was keep anyone from seeing into the house, while also making sure he could see out. Michael worried about any attempts to enter the home, but Jack didn't seem as concerned. He said he could "sense" it, whatever that meant, so Michael, Becky, and Melissa chose to trust him.

When Michael was confident the house was locked down, he made an effort to prepare food and drinks. No one was all that interested, but he fumbled and bumbled about making everyone hot cups of tea regardless. He had to do something to calm his nerves—that, and he was in considerable pain, so the act of caring for others kept his mind off of it while his body repaired itself. He was pretty sure several ribs were broken, as well as several fingers. His left wrist was three times its normal size, and his shoulder felt like someone had poured hot concrete inside the joint. He'd be okay after a good day's sleep and a nice helping of O-positive, but at the moment he felt like he'd been hit by a car and then run over by a truck filled with sledgehammers just for added insult.

Michael passed around a bottle of old Vicodin he'd "borrowed" from a hospital a while back. He never needed any, but he had them just in case. Mainly because...why not? It wasn't like he could get addicted, or that they'd kill him. Besides, it got lonely and boring sometimes (a lot). He wasn't above alcohol or other vices to help him cope—and tonight he was glad he had some. Becky took three, while Jack and Melissa passed. Michael chewed up two despite not knowing if they'd do anything for him or not. He grabbed a cider and his iPad and eased himself down on the couch next to Thorn. Even sitting hurt. It hurt very much.

Jack saw to Becky's arm as best he could. Michael couldn't tell exactly what the elf did, but it involved light and some strange sounds. She was moving it again not long afterwords, so whatever the elf did, it seemed to work a little. Michael was sure the drugs helped as well. The sisters snuggled up in the same chair, and Jack retreated to the fire, where he gazed into the flames.

"So who were they, anyway?" Becky asked. She'd directed the question at Michael.

"I have no friggin' clue!" the vampire said. "I've never seen anyone like that."

Becky turned to Jack. "How about you, Keebler?"

Melissa elbowed her sister. "Were they elves, too, Jack?" she asked.

Jack turned and sat down on the hearth. Michael noted how slow the elf was moving, and the slight wince he gave as he tried to relax. "No, they were not elves. Those were Dren. They are a race of Brùnaidh."

Michael shook his head. "Bru-what?"

"Brùnaidh. You might have heard of them being referred to as Brownies in your lore."

"THOSE WERE THE BIGGEST FUCKING BROWNIES I'VE EVER SEEN!" Michael said.

Jack smiled. "That's because you've never seen a Brownie."

"Well, no, but...."

"I'm with him," Becky said, pointing at Michael. "Those were some big-ass Brownies."

Jack chuckled a little. "Much of what you know of faeries is wrong, or at least distorted, usually by the residents of Fae themselves. But yes, those were Brownies, or at least a type of Brownie. They are called Dren."

"Well, why were they after us?" Melissa asked. "The big one, he said something about duty, or a job, or bounty or something."

"THE big one?" Michael asked. "Were yours not all big? Mine were all huge!"

"Well, that is the important question," Jack said. "Why?" He turned to Michael. "Tell us what happened here."

Michael sat forward and glanced at his iPad. He selected the camera facing the rear of his property, where the fight had started. "Umm, let's see. You left to ask the girls if they'd like to stay here tonight—"

"...yes, please," Becky said.

Michael laughed. "Mi casa, su casa."

"Gracias, man."

"No problemo," Michael said, and looked back at Jack. "So yeah, you took off, I grabbed the dogs, went outside to finish my drink while they ran around below, and that's when *they* showed up. Arrows flying everywhere, man, weird green explosions, just insanity. Nanook took an arrow to the shoulder before it was over."

Jack glanced at the dog, a puzzled look on his face.

Michael noticed. "My blood."

132

Jack raised his eyebrows, and a second later he nodded. "Ahhh...."

Michael nodded back. "Yeah, so there were five of them. I killed the first four and tried to get some information from the fifth—"

"You killed *four* of them?" Melissa said.

"I was about to say the same thing," Jack said.

Michael nodded.

"Mr. Bad Ass!" Becky said. She added a wink.

Michael chuckled. It was clear the Vicodin was working on Becky. He rubbed his injured shoulder. "I wish I was a bad ass. They got me, too. Fucking arrows! Who uses bows and arrows anymore?"

Melissa covered her mouth. "Oh my God, they shot you?"

"Oh yeah, few times! Not that they didn't fire off a dozen more attempts."

"Are you okay? You...." Becky stopped.

"I'm fine."

The girls glanced at Jack, who nodded and mouthed that it was okay.

Michael continued. "Anyway, I tried to get some information out of the last one. I'd messed him up pretty good already, but he said he'd tell me how to save Nanook if I'd let him go, and Nanook, well, she was...." He stopped and cleared his throat. "She was bad. Like, really bad, so I agreed."

Melissa looked over at Nook and began probing the dog. Nanook just wagged her tail and nudged the woman's hand from messing with her to resuming rubbing her head.

"She's okay now," Michael said. "Anyway, the guy tells me

to give Nanook some of my blood, I do, and well...." Michael motioned to his dog, who was seemed perfectly content with having her head scratched by Melissa again, and certainly showed no visible signs that she'd been shot by a large arrow.

"Interesting," Jack said. "So you let him go?"

"No."

Jack looked confused. "I thought—"

"He shot my dog, man!"

"Right on, Mr. Wick!" Becky said. She winced when she said it, and rubbed her injured arm.

Michael shot a grin at Becky. "Thank you! And that was it. I heard the screams right around then, and well, you know the rest. What happened to *you*, man?"

"Hang on a second," Melissa said. "You've never heard of these, these Dren either?"

Michael shook his head.

"And you can, well, you can fly too?"

Michael saw where this was going, "Well, I—"

Melissa looked at Nanook. "And you said you what, you gave her some of your, your blood? That was after she'd been hit by the arrow? And now she's fine?"

"Well, yeah, I umm—"

"Yeah, that's a little weird, right?" Becky asked. She looked at Jack. "Does your blood do that, too?"

The elf shook his head. "I am afraid not."

Melissa continued, "...and you live here? Do you live in Fae, too? Are you an elf, also? Or like, a different kind of faerie? You don't seem like—"

"You seem different," Becky said. "And damn young."

Melissa nodded. "Young, yeah, and just, you just seem *different*. Like, well, like us, almost. You don't sound like—"

Michael was getting nervous. "I'm.... So, I—"

Jack stood up. "Ladies, if it is all right with Michael?" he asked, and motioned to the couch. Michael shrugged a kind of *why not?*

Jack nodded back and took a deep breath. "My friend here is not an elf. Nor is he faerie. Michael was once a human, as you are, but Michael is now something different. My friend Michael is a vampire."

The room fell silent for a moment.

"Get the fuck out," Becky said. She was smiling again.

29

"Surprise?" Michael said, and offered the girls an awkward smile.

Melissa pulled her hand away from Nanook. "A vampire?"

Michael nodded.

Melissa shrank back into her sister. "So, vampires are real, too?"

"Right?" Becky said.

Nanook nudged Melissa's elbow.

Michael smiled. "They're real. At least, that's what I've been told! I've only ever met one other. And I don't think Nanook is some kind of K9 vampire creature of the night now," he added with a grin.

Melissa relaxed a little at the humor, and began rubbing the dog's head again, though with a bit more timid motions.

"And most important, Michael is a friend," Jack said.

"Thanks, man," Michael said.

Jack nodded.

"So do you, ya know, do you actually drink blood?" Becky asked. "Like, from people? And how old are you anyway? You look like you'd get ID'd trying to buy a wine cooler! And how —"

Melissa nudged her sister again. Becky made an "oops,

sorry" face.

"I think the Vicodin is working," Becky said. "I'm sorry,"

Michael smiled. "It's okay. Um, first, I do drink blood, but not like what you see in the movies. I actually don't need that much of it, to be honest. I drop in at the hospital a few times a year, and I keep a little supply downstairs in the fridge. What was your first question?"

"How old are you?" Becky asked.

"Oh, right! I'm forty-nine."

Becky grinned. "Cool."

Michael smiled.

A loud clap of thunder shook the house, and the lights blinked.

"Shit, I better grab some candles," Michael said. He stood up with a groan. "Alexa, turn on the lights downstairs."

From the hallway leading off the kitchen, light spilled out from beneath a closed door. "I'll be right back."

"Michael, that's not needed," Jack said.

"No, it's really not a problem. I've got tons for some weird reason."

Jack snapped his fingers, and the room was filled with al-ready-lit candles.

Melissa and Becky gasped.

"Oh, right," Michael said. "Showoff."

Jack smiled. "So where were we? Oh yes, you heard the screams and made your way towards the girls."

Michael nodded.

"I was ambushed not far from them," Jack said. "It appears

we were both attacked simultaneously, or at least close to it. I would also posit that this was intentional."

"They got you, too?" Michael asked.

"Yes. I was—"

Another rumble of thunder sent vibrations through the house, and this time the lights did go out. The candles Jack summoned lit the room, and some even grew brighter when they were plunged into darkness.

"I really need to get a generator," Michael said. He tapped on his iPad. All of the cameras had gone dark.

"Shit."

Jack stood up and limped over to the large windows facing the forest behind the house. The storm shutters were drawn so he couldn't see out. Instead, he placed his hand on the glass and closed his eyes for a moment. "It's a strong storm, but small. It will pass soon enough. And I do not sense any more Dren. In fact, I don't sense *anyone* near us at the moment."

"So you can see the storm?" Michael asked.

Jack opened his eyes and turned back to the room. "More akin to feeling it rather than seeing it."

Becky shook her head, and she also closed her eyes. "This is so weird."

Jack and Michael both chuckled.

"You'll get used to it," Melissa said.

"*I* haven't even gotten used to it yet," Michael said.

This made the girls smile.

"Where were we?" Jack said. "Ah, yes, I was on my way back to both of you"—he motioned to the sisters—"when I heard Melissa scream. At that moment, I took flight and was immediately ambushed. They knew precisely where we all were, which is disconcerting when you consider that I didn't even know where I would be at that moment, much less someone else knowing."

"Why would they be following you?" Melissa asked.

"I was going to ask the same thing," Michael said.

Jack shook his head. "I have no idea. That is what troubles me most. They were clearly there to delay me. They could have killed me outright, as they had multiple opportunities to do so. Yet they did not. Why? They even apologized before leaving. And they left these."

Jack reached into his pocket and retrieved the small glass cylinder containing the glowing gemstones. The room sparkled with shades of red, emerald, sapphire, amber, and a multitude of other wonderful colors. Jack upended the tube onto the coffee table in front of the couch, and everyone leaned in to get a better look. Thorn and Nanook even sniffed the shining stones.

"Oh, my God," Becky said.

Melissa poked her finger at the gems, which sparkled even brighter at her touch. "They're beautiful!"

Michael found the gems hurt his eyes and had to squint when looking at them. "What are they?"

Jack picked up one of the stones and held it above the nearest candle. It was a brilliant sapphire blue in color, nearly as bright as the flame which danced below it. "These are star stones, very rare, priceless, even. I believe the Dren left them as a kind of apology, or payment for what they were doing."

"Apology?" Becky asked. "That fucker was trying to kill me! Who goes off to kill someone and apologizes for it FIRST? That's lazy, make-believe movie magic at BEST!"

Michael nodded. "Yeah. What she said."

Jack shook his head. "I believe the stones were reparations for their actions. It was very, very strange."

"But *why*? Why were they here? They specifically targeted Becky!" Melissa said. "That guy, that, Pine guy, he was after my sister. And it sounds like they did the same thing to Mike. So why? And why didn't they try to kill you, too, Jack?"

Jack stared into the candlelight. "That frightens me most," he said. "The Dren sent at least half a dozen or more attackers for me. So clearly they assessed I would be the most difficult of us to manage. Obviously, they were sorely mistaken thanks to Michael," Jack said, gesturing at the vampire. "And Michael, you counted five attackers, the girls only two. Apparently, they wanted me out of the equation, so the rest could deal with all of you. So yes, why? Why would they do that? Why target you two, especially?" Jack asked. motioning to the sisters.

Michael flew to his feet.

"Elizabeth!" he turned, eyes wide, towards Jack. "Remember what I told you earlier? Elizabeth? The one who turned me? She said someone would come looking for me if I ever told anyone who or what I was! Maybe these were the guys she was talking about?"

"Who's Elizabeth?" Becky asked. "And that still doesn't explain why Melissa and I would be in danger."

Michael looked at Jack. "Maybe they...Jesus, Jack, maybe they thought the girls were...."

The conversation stopped dead, and the room fell silent.

Becky stood up. "Thought we were what, goddammit?"

"Jack?" Melissa asked.

Jack shook his head, "I'm—"

"WHAT?" Becky asked.

Michael cleared his throat. "Vampires. Maybe they thought you guys were vampires, too."

"What? Vampires? That makes no sense!" Melissa said. "Jack?"

Jack remained silent, his brow furrowed.

"Yeah, you said they sent five of those guys after him. FIVE!" Becky said, pointing at Michael. "Just him! And all that came for us were the two, that Pine guy and the other, what was his name, Trax or Truck or some shit. You'd think if they thought we were vampires too, they'd have sent *way* more guys, right? I mean Mike here took out every single one that came after him, AND that big fucker Pine! SIX GUYS!"

Michael and Jack remained quiet.

"RIGHT?" Becky asked.

"And *why* would they think that? Think we were vampires?" Melissa asked.

Jack looked frightened. "This might all be my doing."

Melissa stood and stepped towards Jack. "What? Why? I don't understand."

"I—"

"Son of a bitch...," Michael said. He sat down on the couch hard, his hands on his temples.

Jack looked at Melissa. "I was searching for methods to heal you. To cure you. I thought that perhaps—"

The ceiling exploded and vanished skywards in a violent cacophony of sound and debris.

30

Enormous flashes of green and violet light blinded every-one, while splinters of wood, drywall, and glass filled the air. A monstrous torrent of wind and rain screamed into the room from above, blasting Jack into the air and slamming him against the fireplace. His spine crashed hard into the stone mantle, which exploded with the impact; bits of rock and mortar bounced and skipped in all directions, some embed-ding themselves into the walls.

Michael was flung backwards over the couch and the gra-nite bar separating the kitchen from the living room. He flew headlong into the stainless steel refrigerator, its doors buck-ling inwards with the impact. The appliance struck the back wall, rebounded several feet, and toppled over with Michael wedged inside. Various foods and glass sprayed the air.

Thorn and Nanook were thrown across the room, Thorn crashing into the photo of Michael and his family. There was a loud crunch, and the dog fell to the ground whimpering, shards of glass protruding from his face and side. He tried to stand, and collapsed again. Nanook was sent flying as well, but twisted and landed on her feet, almost gracefully. She raced to Thorn as soon as her paws touched the floor and stood sentinel over him, snarling into the sudden dark.

The sisters were untouched. Not even the blast of air or any of the flying debris seemed to reach them.

The ceiling and everything that had been above it—including the rooms, the attic, and the roof beyond all of that—was gone. Rain fell into the house and began soaking everything. As the storm poured into the home, an enormous head covered in metallic blue scales lowered itself over one of the mangled walls and down into the living room. It snarled, exposing immense, horrifying teeth that glistened in what little light remained. The sound of the snarl reverberated through everything—a low, powerful rumble which shook the floor, walls, and the very air.

It was most definitely a dragon.

The dragon turned, studied Jack, paused, and glanced at Thorn, who growled back and exposed his teeth in kind. The beast ignored the dog, peered into the kitchen at Michael, sniffed once, and retreated back over the broken wall, where it disappeared into the shadows. The monster had completely ignored the two screaming women just feet away.

The rain paused. It didn't end—it just paused, as if the drops simply froze mid-fall and hung about the air like tiny, weightless diamonds. A figure materialized in the center of the room just feet from the two girls. She was dressed head to toe in what appeared to be blue leather streaked with purple veins. She held an enormous, crimson-colored longbow, very similar to the ones the Dren had used earlier, only larger; two arrows were nocked and ready to be fired. The woman was tall, even taller than the men who had attacked them earlier. Her hair was a light shade of sky blue, long, with multiple braids, and it shimmered with a light of its own. Her eyes were a similar color, and her skin, just as the Dren before her, was a soft shade of green.

She looked down at the cowering sisters who now held onto one another, their entire bodies trembling. The woman also glanced at Jack and then into the kitchen where Michael lay.

Both lay still, no longer a threat.

"I am Elm," the woman said, her voice filling the room. It was musical, almost ethereal, but strong. It commanded attention. "I am here to serve you warning, and to honor my fallen."

Becky and Melissa's screams faded away, and they sat there dumbstruck, trembling, and silent.

"You bested my soldiers," Elm said. "For that, I commend you all. Very, very few could claim that accomplishment in any realm. In fact, in all of my time, I have rarely seen it." She knelt down, took Melissa's shivering chin in her hand, and sighed. "This is unfair to you, child. You have my sympathy."

The woman turned to Becky. "Nor is it kind to you." She paused, smiled, and added, "...warrior." Elm then took a deep breath. "Know that I despise this." She was quiet for a moment and then sighed. "But as much as I abhor what must be done, I am sworn."

Becky regained some bit of her composure and sneered back at the woman. "Who the fuck are you people?" Her voice trembled and cracked. "Why are you doing this to us?"

Elm leaned closer to Becky and whispered into her ear. "It is not I who is doing this. Should you survive, think of who might have *sent* me, child. Do you understand?"

Becky spat in the Dren's face, and Elm had her by the throat in an instant. She stood, lifting Becky with ease, her feet dangling several feet from the ground. Melissa shrieked.

Elm drew Becky close. "You and your sister share such a lovely shade of skin. It reminds me of cinnamon, or warm chocolate." She ran her fingers down the side of Becky's cheek, caressing it. "I would hate to see it all removed."

Despite being barely able to breathe, Becky grinned back.

"Try...it...bitch."

Elm laughed. "Pine was right. I see why he spared you." She looked back down at Melissa, then pulled Becky closer so her lips touched Becky's ear. She whispered, "A mother's love is most powerful, young one. It can be dangerous, deadly even, but also foolish. Very, very foolish."

Becky gasped, and clawed at the hand encapsulating her throat. When she failed to pry the enormous grip free, she began to thrash and kick. Elm just stood there, an amused yet somber expression washing over her face.

"PLEASE! PLEASE STOP!" Melissa shouted, and dark blood began pouring from her nostril.

Elm pulled her gaze from Becky and looked down at Melissa; her expression changed to pity, and she dropped Becky, who collapsed, coughing and choking, into Melissa's arms.

Elm wiped away the spittle on her cheek and knelt back down. She reached forward and touched Melissa's cheek in an almost gentle, caring way. "I will allow you a single day, child. One day to make peace with your sister. With your love, the elf. And with the vampire. One day. After that, I will return to take them all."

"Why?" Melissa asked. Tears flowed down her cheeks and mixed with the blood on her chin. "Why are you doing this? I don't understand. We're not vampires!"

Elm sighed. "I know that, child. And it is not I doing this. Think on that. I beg of you, please," she knelt down again, wiped away the traces of blood from Melissa's face, and kissed her forehead in a gentle, almost loving way. "Though I know it is useless, I pray that your friends survive this, I do. And I pray you discover the *real* threat." Her voice was so soft and kind that the juxtaposition between it and the violent energy she exuded was jarring.

145

Elm stood and took a long look around the room. She studied what little she could see of Michael's broken form in particular, her head cocked to the side, her brow furrowed. Then, just as before, she vanished as quickly as she'd arrived. Torrents of rain began falling into the room again.

Melissa cradled her sister and cried as the darkness engulfed them.

31

Jack was the first to regain consciousness. He woke to Melissa stroking his cheek and rubbing the hair from his eyes. He blinked away the cobwebs and water, and as he did, his back exploded with pain. His eyes pinched shut, and he clenched his teeth in an effort not to cry out. A moment later, the wave of agony passed, and he sat forward. When he did, he gasped, clutching at his right side. Several of his ribs were broken; he was sure of it. "Are you...okay?" he asked between still-clenched teeth.

"I'm okay."

Jack looked into Melissa's eyes.

"Really, I'm okay. But you don't move, okay? Jack, please stay still."

Jack looked around as best he could. To his left lay Thorn, a bloodied cloth tied around his ribs. The dog was hurt, but not fatally wounded. Jack could see his aura was still strong. Nanook stood over him, keeping the rain off of her friend as best she could. She licked at his face and head when the water became too thick and rolled into Thorn's half-closed eyes.

Jack coughed. "How....long?"

"Ten, maybe fifteen minutes? Please don't move though, okay?"

Jack touched Melissa's hand and smiled up at her. "I'll be fine."

"Jack, please."

"Melissa, I will be okay. What happened? Is everyone all right?"

"I think so. Becky is looking after Michael; he's breathing, but he's still unconscious. Poor Thorn had some glass in his side, but I got the larger pieces out. I can't see the smaller ones without more light, but they're there, I can feel them. I think some of his ribs are broken. He really needs a vet," Melissa took a deep breath. "There was a monster Jack. A, a...dragon! Like right out of Game of Thrones!" Her breathing quickened, and her hands began to shake. "A dragon! And, a, a Dren, a woman. They tore the house apart, Jack. And she"—Melissa was crying now—"she told us we only had one day. Just one."

Jack shook his head and winced. "A dragon? One day? One day before what?"

Melissa's brow furrowed. "One day before she came back and *took* all of you."

Jack sat up and looked into Melissa's eyes. "Took us? What did she mean?"

Melissa hugged Jack as gently as she could. "She told me to say goodbye to all of you, Jack. Like, like she was going to come back and kill everyone! Even Becky, Jack! She's going to kill my sister!"

Jack worked his way to his feet. "That will not happen, Melissa. I promise you. Where is Michael?"

"In here," Becky called out.

Jack limped towards the kitchen. Michael was still halfway in the now-demolished refrigerator. Blood poured from his scalp, neck, and shoulders. Becky was reaching behind him, probing his spine as best she could without moving him. The task was not easy, and she continued to slip on the rain-soaked floor. The various amounts of food and debris scattered about did not make the job any easier. Neither did her injured arm.

"I can't tell if anything's broken," Becky said. "I just can't be sure."

Michael turned his head. Plastic and glass crunched as he did. "Ouch."

Becky jumped, startled at Michael's sudden voice. "Jesus! Okay, don't move, Michael! You've been hurt. You need to stay still, do you understand?"

Michael opened his eyes. He looked up at Becky, then at Melissa, and finally at Jack. "Am I in the fridge?"

Becky smiled. "Yeah, but don't move, okay? We need to call an ambulance."

Michael smiled. "You're gorgeous, like, really, really, really...really, really, pretty."

Becky laughed, and a tear rolled down her cheek. "Thank you, Michael. Now don't move, okay?"

"So, pretty."

"Michael, I can help you, if I may?" Jack said.

Michael turned his head. "Hi, Jack. You okay?"

"I'm fine, Michael. I'm going to move you, all right? Please don't be alarmed."

"The contractions means he likes me," Michael said, his eyes fluttering shut.

Becky looked up. "I don't think moving him is such a good idea."

Jack placed a hand on Becky's shoulder. "He's going to be fine. But I need to move him so we can get a better look at his injuries. There's no one we can call. Not for him."

Becky nodded and stood up. "Right. Right."

Michael opened his eyes again, raised a finger, and pointed at Melissa. "Your sister is, like, really pretty. Can you tell her that I think she's pretty? I like her smile."

Melissa chuckled. "You can tell her yourself, Michael."

"Okay."

Jack leaned down and placed a hand on the vampire's chest. "Just relax, Michael. I'm going to move you a just a bit."

Michael looked up at Jack. "I'm sorry I called you Legolas earlier."

"It's okay, Michael."

"You're way hotter than Legolas."

"Thank you, Michael. I'm going to move you now, all right?"

Michael nodded and winced. "I think I'm hurt."

Jack closed his eyes, and a soft glow emanated from the palm of the hand he now held to Michael's chest. A moment later, the elf simply lifted his friend up and out of the mangled refrigerator as if he weighed no more than a static-bound balloon attached to the palm of his hand. Jack guided him to the floor, where there was less debris, and set him down to rest.

Michael coughed, and a fountain of blood exploded from his mouth.

"Oh, Jesus!" Becky said, and scrambled around Michael. "Get him on his side."

Jack helped turn Michael over, whereupon the vampire proceeded to choke. Torrents of blood raced across the kitchen floor, where it flooded into the water and debris. Michael began to convulse then, his entire body wracked with spasms.

"A lung?" Melissa asked and looked at her sister. "Something must be torn, maybe his stomach, maybe his esophagus?"

"He needs blood," Jack said.

Becky looked up at the elf. "HE NEEDS A FUCKING HOS-PITAL!"

Jack ignored the woman, summoned a small knife, and sliced deep into his own wrist. Melissa let out a yelp.

"Will that—" Becky started.

Jack shouted down at his friend, "MICHAEL! YOU NEED TO DRINK!" and placed his wrist on the vampire's mouth. Blood poured out around Michael's lips and onto the floor. "Michael, you need to drink, my friend!" Jack said, placing his other hand on Michael's shoulder in an effort to calm him. "Please, my friend."

Michael wrapped his lips around the wound on Jack's wrist, and with his free hand, grabbed hold of the elf's arm. The convulsions slowed and then stopped altogether.

Jack sighed. "Thank you, Michael."

"Is he...is he...?" Becky asked, tears streaming down her face. Melissa hugged her tight.

"He is going to be just fine," Jack said.

The girls crumpled to the floor and waited.

"I promise," Jack added.

Before long, Michael's breathing became steady, rhythmic, constant. Color began to show in his face again, and even in the near pitch-black of the kitchen floor, the vampire looked to be doing better.

Jack snapped his fingers, and more candles appeared. The flames ignored the raindrops that fell into them with a hiss and pop every few seconds, but they never died. Minutes passed, and Michael continued to improve with each.

Becky chuckled. "Go camping, you said! Meet my elf, you said! It will be fun, you said!"

Melissa snorted at that, and the two were soon lost in fits of tears and laughter.

Michael opened his eyes and pulled away from Jack's wrist a moment later.

"You're going to be all right, my friend," Jack said, and patted Michael on the shoulder.

"Thanks, Jack," Michael said. He rolled back over onto his back. "What the hell was that?" he asked, breathing hard.

"We will recount the events for you shortly. For now, rest," the elf said.

Jack stood, limped back out into the living room, and gazed up. The entire house above the main room was gone, simply torn away. Not blown away, or removed with the aid of explosives. The house had been torn apart as if a giant sword had simply swung down and sliced the home to pieces. Two more upstairs rooms on the same wall as the fireplace stood open to the elements, and the chimney which ran between the two rooms had also been sheared away. The room closest to the side of the house was missing a large portion of its outer wall, and a mattress hung over the side, filling with water from the storm above. Wind-driven rain swept in from all angles as the house creaked and moaned with the storm.

Whatever had done this had been powerful, immensely so. But what really worried Jack, more than the sheer ferocity of the event, was knowing he'd never once sensed it coming. Something of this magnitude did not just *happen*, not with the energy and sheer power this had taken. There would have been a build-up of some sort, a charge, something, and Jack should have sensed it long before they were attacked. As it was, he'd sensed nothing at all. Not even the dragon—a beast comprised of almost complete, pure magic.

"Is that my bed?" a voice asked from behind him.

Jack turned to see his friend standing there. "Michael…you need to—"

"Rest, yeah, I get it," the vampire said, still looking up at what little remained of his home.

Jack took a long, slow breath. "I am so very sorry, my friend."

Michael gazed up at where his roof should have been. "With friends like these…." he said, and winked at the elf. "Seriously though, what the hell just happened?"

32

Melissa and Becky trudged off to find a bathroom and more towels, all while being mindful of the now structurally unsound home. Things creaked, popped, and shifted when they were absolutely not meant to. Jack told Michael about the mysterious appearance of Elm and the dragon. Much to the elf's surprise, he took most of the news in stride—most, anyway, but the bit about the dragon. That part he'd asked a quite a few questions about, most of which Jack could not answer —but everything else? Michael just...accepted it. It was as if this bizarre world he had been thrust into over the past few days was nothing short of business as usual. Either the vampire was in shock—which, based on his injuries, he might very well be—or he was far stronger mentally than Jack had suspected. Regardless, Jack admired the vampire's fortitude. In fact, Michael was more concerned about everyone else, much less his house, especially the girls and his dogs.

Michael lifted Thorn and walked over to the rain-soaked couch. The dog was limp and whimpered at being moved; his head sagged towards the floor, and his heat signature was weak.

"Easy, buddy, you're going to be okay. A little vampire V8 and you'll feel right as rai—" Michael looked up at the rain falling into his home. "Yeah, forget that last part. You're going to be just fine, buddy."

Jack held his hand over the dog as they walked, and the same warm light Michael had seen the elf conjure when helping Becky with her arm flooded over Thorn. The dog relaxed in Michael's arms, and his heat signature improved.

"Thanks, man."

Jack nodded. "I wish I could do more."

Each step Michael took, something crunched or snapped under his feet. The couch was soaked, but it was better than the equally drenched hardwood floor. Nanook followed, never once allowing Thorn to be more than a foot or so away. When Michael sat the dog down, Nanook immediately began grooming her friend again.

"He'll be okay, Nook," Michael said, and bit his own wrist again. Thorn was reluctant to lick Michael's wound at first, but once a few drops were down, the dog proceeded with no more qualms.

"Well, that answers some of our questions about your blood and what it is capable of," Jack said.

Michael looked up and nodded. "I just hope it doesn't do anything, like, *weird*, ya know?"

"It doesn't appear to have negatively affected Nanook."

Michael glanced to his other dog, who looked back and wagged her tail despite being soaked to the bone and covered in debris.

"You know what, though?" Michael said. "I feel a little funny. Like...I don't know, I feel like I've had a bunch of caffeine or something. Hyper, almost giddy. Definitely not like I was just rag-dolled into my damn refrigerator, or pin-cushioned by arrows, etcetera, etcetera, etcetera."

"Elven blood, perhaps?" Jack asked.

"Hmm. May-be! You should bottle that shit," Michael said, grinning.

Jack smiled back, but it faded as he looked around. "I'm so

sorry about your home, Michael. I will see to it that you are compensated."

"I'm just glad no one else was really hurt. Present company excluded," he added. He pulled his wrist away from Thorn, who was now standing on the couch, his tail wagging.

Michael rubbed his hand over the dog's fur searching for any glass he might have missed. A few tiny pieces did fall out, but that was all. Just as Nanook before him, the blood coating Thorn's fur vanished, reabsorbed back into the dog's body.

"Three days," Jack said.

"Three days?"

"I guess you never imagined your life would take this sort of turn when you approached me at the Emerald Seat," Jack said. " That was three days ago. I can't imagine all of this from your perspective."

Michael laughed. "Well, it got me out of the house, man. Hell, I'm outside even when I'm inside!" he said, looking up.

Jack smiled. "Are you always so positive, my friend?"

"No. Definitely not. But I do try!"

"That's more than most."

Michael looked at the wreckage surrounding them. "Ya know, I'm no engineer, but I'd say the house looks like it might be leaning a bit. We should get out of here soon, and I need to find a place to wait out the daylight."

Jack nodded. "Agreed. With everything Melissa told me of our latest attacker, I believe the best course of action would involve traveling into Fae."

"Into Fae? You mean, like, to your world or realm or whatever?"

"Yes. I'll explain more later, but I believe we should move in a way Elm would not—"

"...her name was Elm?"

"Yes."

"Wasn't the other guy Pine?"

"I believe so, yes."

"That's weird."

"It's unusual, yes. As I was saying, I believe we should move in a manner Elm would not expect."

"How's that?"

"One would think she anticipates our flight, yes? Fleeing, hiding? She'll be prepared for a hunt."

"That's what I feel like doing right now. I'm all for getting the hell out of here, to be honest, man."

Jack nodded. "What if we fight back?"

"FIGHT BACK? Against that? I don't know about you Jack, but—"

"What are you two talking about?" a voice asked from behind the two.

Michael and Jack turned to see Melissa and Becky coming down the dark hall.

"I believe we should leave. I wish to take you all into Fae," Jack said.

The room was silent. Even the dogs seemed to grow quiet.

"Shouldn't we like, call the police, or the fire department, or something?" Becky asked.

Melissa shook her head. "And tell them what?"

"If they're not already coming, they'll be here soon enough whether we call them or not," Michael said. "I mean, my neighbors are a good hundred yards off or so, but I can't imagine they didn't hear what happened."

Jack pointed skyward. The clouds were parting, and the stars were blinking back. "Not to mention, Michael needs shelter soon, and we all need a place that's safe so we can discuss what should happen next."

"Sorry, this is all just…it's all so fucking weird, you know?" Becky said.

"I imagine so," Jack said. "Regardless, I am able to protect everyone far better in my own surroundings. The fact we were attacked with no warning, no hint of immediate danger, leads me to believe I am somehow weakened here, for lack of a better phrase. I fear I am impaired."

"I didn't sense *that*, that's for sure," Michael said, pointing skyward. "*That* was like a damn bomb went off, and I didn't hear or feel anything before it did. Like, nothing. I should have heard or felt something!"

"What, do you have like a spidey-vampire sense, or whatever?" Becky asked.

"Kinda, yeah," Michael said. "I mean, I can't dodge bullets or anything, but I could probably sense the trigger being pulled, or for instance, a damn arrow flying towards my face!"

Becky grinned. "That's pretty cool."

Michael smiled.

"I don't really…I don't feel so great, guys," Melissa said. She stumbled into the back of the couch and slid towards the floor.

Becky caught her sister before she hit the ground, and was

surprised to see both Jack and Michael at her side in an instant.

"Smurf? Smurf!"

"Okay, we need to get her somewhere warm, somewhere comfortable," Michael said.

Becky looked up, tears in her eyes.

Michael shook his head. "I mean, isn't that what you're supposed to do? Like, hot water or something? Towels and... and...I'm sorry, I'm not very good at this whole...."

Becky reached over and placed a hand on Michael's shoulder. Melissa moaned.

Jack looked at Becky. "If you will permit me?"

Becky nodded, and Jack lifted Melissa in his arms. He walked her over to the couch and placed her on the edge, where she wobbled but began to come to.

"I'm sorry," Melissa said. Her face was pale, and goosebumps sprouted all over her neck, arms, and legs.

Jack cursed under his breath. It was the first time Michael had seen the elf show any emotion outside of general amusement or civility.

A fire erupted in the fireplace again, and nearly a hundred candles appeared all around the destroyed room. The candles were larger than before, and put off far more heat.

"Should I? Like, maybe?" Michael asked.

Jack looked up. "I don't know Michael. I'm..." The elf paused, looked back at Melissa, and then at Becky, who stood behind the couch, tears streaming down her face. "I'm afraid of what could happen."

"Can you help her?" Becky asked. She was looking at Michael.

"I could give her some of my blood, but...."

"But what? Would it help? Like, like what you did for Nanook?"

"I gave some to Thorn, too, when you guys were looking for towels."

Becky looked over at the dogs. They both seemed perfectly healthy—radiant, in fact.

"So will it...can it help?"

Michael shrugged. "I'm sorry, but I have no clue, really. I've never done this sorta stuff before. And not to a—"

Melissa coughed, opened her eyes, and looked up at everyone. "D' we geth home? Is ma' 'kay with you all sleepi' o'er?"

Jack's brow furrowed, and Becky began to sob, though she covered her mouth and tried her best to hide it. "No, Smurf, we're not home yet. You just need some sleep, okay, little girl?"

Melissa smiled and closed her eyes.

"She sounds...that didn't sound—that sounded...Jack?" Michael asked, the panic in his voice growing.

Jack stood and looked at Michael and Becky. "Rebecca. You must know that if Michael does this, if he gives your sister some of his blood, we do not know what might happen. She could—"

"Is there a chance? Is there a chance it might help her? Even a little?"

"Becky," Michael said. "She might get better like Nanook did. Like Thorn did. But, it's...it's how I was...it's kind of like how I became a vampire. I just—"

Melissa began to convulse.

"Smurf?" Becky rushed to pry Melissa's mouth open. Jack tore off his belt and handed it to her. "Smurf! Open your mouth, Smurf! Open your mouth, little girl!"

Becky got the belt into Melissa's mouth just as she clamped down, hard. Everyone heard the sound of her jaw popping; even the dogs whimpered. Nanook put her paw on the woman's leg before Michael ushered her back.

The convulsions slowed after a minute, then stopped. Becky wiped away the frothy drool spilling out onto her sister's chin. Melissa's breathing returned to normal, and after a second, she opened her eyes.

Becky smiled down at her sister. "Smurf?"

Melissa looked at Becky and then around the room. "I don't feel so good, Bec," she said. Tears began to flow then.

"I know, I know," Becky said. "We're going to make it better, okay?"

Becky looked up at Michael and wiped her own tears; she didn't need to say anything. Michael nodded, sat next to Melissa, and bit into his wrist for the third time that night.

33

Michael pulled the door to his basement closed behind him with some effort. The wood creaked and protested as he did, but he needed it closed. He needed to be alone. As soon as he was, his entire body proceeded to shake, and the pain as well as the stress from the evening's events flooded to the forefront of his senses.

"I killed people..."

Before his knees could buckle, Michael limped down the stairs to the basement and made his way to the refrigerator where he kept his supply of blood. He was about to open the door and take what he needed when his legs began to fail in earnest. He turned, found a wall, and slumped down to the floor. He sat there and stared out into the rich blackness.

"...killed a guy I promised could leave..."

The floor here was wet, too. Water seeped into the basement from above and trickled down most of the wall where the stairs were. The aromas of damp carpet and murdered drywall were just starting to permeate the air. The room was pitch black, and Michael found himself wondering why he'd even installed lightbulbs down here in the first place? Much less $65-apiece smart bulbs. Why lights at all? He could see everything just fine; he always could. Maybe he'd done it for the dogs? But that didn't track; they rarely came down here. These were random thoughts, pointless thoughts, but they helped the vampire ease away from the panic which had been building in his mind all evening.

"What are you doing, man?"

His life had not just been turned upside down; it had been badly beaten and irrevocably altered in the span of mere days. What *was* he doing, exactly? He barely even knew Jack. He liked him, sure! He seemed genuinely friendly, and even funny at times, especially when he was drunk. He was good-looking, had a great, albeit strange vocabulary, and besides friendly, he seemed kind—a trait just as important as any other these days. Perhaps even the most important. But in reality, Michael knew very little about him. And faeries? Elves? These new... Dren people trying to kill him? Dragons!? Fucking real-life DRAGONS?

The most exciting thing that had happened to him *last* week was the new season of "Stranger Things" dropping on Netflix! Before that? There *was* no before that. And tonight, tonight he'd almost been killed! And his dogs had been badly hurt. And Melissa? Poor Melissa?

Michael couldn't be sure, but he was almost positive he'd just watched the poor girl have a stroke upstairs. Not only that, her seizure was so violent that Michael was sure he had heard bones crack. And now? Now she had his blood coursing through her veins. It might not be a concoction of hers and his like what he and Jack supposed could turn her, but it was still *his* blood. Who knew what it might do to her? Michael wasn't sure of anything except that he'd never forgive himself if he'd just hurt the already sick girl. For now, she was sleeping; at least she was sleeping. They'd gotten her to drink some of Michael's blood, but not much, less than even the dogs had earlier. And now she rested.

"What are you doing, man? What the hell are you doing?"

Michael shook his head and took several deep, measured breaths. He clenched and unclenched his hands in an effort to get them to stop trembling.

"You killed people."

That was bothering him. Why hadn't it bothered him before? Was it the adrenalin? Was it...was it because of who he was? *What* he was?

"They tried to kill me. They tried to kill my dogs! They came for me! Not the other way around. Fuck 'em."

"Yeah, but what are you doing?"

His life might not amount to much, but it was *his* life, and he controlled everything in it. He'd managed to take control of who he was and of what he was now. He'd made the sacrifices forced upon him, created the routines he followed, and found solace in knowing what each day, week, even month would bring. They would bring *nothing* unless he allowed it.

Another copy of the same picture Thorn had crashed into hung on the wall opposite where Michael now sat. It was literally the only photo he had of his family now, so if a picture hung somewhere of them, that was the one. He stared at his long-dead mother, father, and brother. They smiled out at him, and he smiled back.

His mother, who always sang to him on his birthday and buttered his nose, a ritual she never explained but did without fail.

His father, who read him *The Lord of the Rings* in the hospital when he'd had pneumonia as a child—for two weeks, every single day, without fail. His father, who always encouraged him to try whatever he wanted as long as he learned something if he didn't succeed.

His little brother, who was his best friend, always came
to him for guidance, and always thanked him when Michael
stopped whatever bully-of-the-week decided to test the
waters. His little brother, who'd once come into Michael's
room in high school after Michael had been dumped by the
girl of his dreams and was sobbing into a pillow. He had just
sat down next to Michael and waited. That was it. He had just
waited. And when Michael stopped crying, his little brother
handed him a skateboard, and the two had spent the rest of
the evening hitting a little quarter-pipe ramp they'd built together at the bottom of the driveway. He'd never forgotten
that.

Michael smiled at the picture again and realized why he
was going to go back upstairs. The picture told him that even
though his mind was screaming at him not to go, he would return to the strangers above and even risk his own life to help
them.

Because of family.

Jack was clearly in love with Melissa. Anyone could see it;
you didn't have to know the two at all to feel the connection
between them. So what if they'd apparently only known each
other, or at least BEEN with one another for a short time? It
didn't matter. You could *see* it. Michael could almost smell
whatever it was in the air between them. It had the aroma

of laughter, if that was such a thing. And the sisters certainly loved one another. The way they acted, the way they looked at each other, and the care they displayed towards one another stirred memories of Michael's relationship with his younger brother so long ago.

That was why Michael would go back upstairs. He'd go on this insane, unimaginable adventure, and he'd do whatever he could to help...because of family.

He'd spent decades alone. Sure, maybe twenty-plus years was a drop in the bucket for someone who apparently lived as long as he was rumored to. But to Michael, it was still half of his life. He'd grown accustomed to being alone, but never comfortable with it. He longed for connections, but the fear of them always won out. So he walled himself up, talked (probably too much) to his dogs, left notes for the employees at Bold Rock, and entertained himself online, through books, games, or television. And when he needed money, he stole it. That was something he wasn't proud of, but he didn't lose sleep over it too much, either.

Michael stood, walked over to his supply of blood, took several bags from the dark refrigerator, and made his way back upstairs to his new family.

"If this is what it takes to get you out of the fucking house, then go slay dragons with your elf friend, man!"

34

When Michael reappeared, Melissa was still asleep, Becky at her side. He tried to close the basement door, but the frame had shifted badly when the house was attacked, making it almost impossible. Instead, he left it ajar and turned towards what used to be his living room.

Becky looked up and smiled. She mouthed, "Thank you," and resumed stroking her sister's hair. Michael smiled back and nodded. Melissa did look better. Disheveled, but better. Hell, they all looked disheveled.

"I would assume we need to keep your blood cool, yes?" Jack asked, motioning at the IV bags Michael held.

"Umm, yeah, that would be good."

"I found this," Jack said, holding up a small, blue collapsible cooler. "I put what ice I could salvage from the freezer and, well, the floor in it. Will it suffice for the time being?"

Michael smiled and nodded. "Perfect; thanks, man. You know I don't even remember why I bought this thing?" he mused. He turned the little cooler in his hands. "I've literally never used it."

"Sometimes we unintentionally design our own happenstance."

"Umm, okay? How's uh, how's she doing?"

Jack glanced back towards the living room. "She appears much better and sleeping just fine. I believe we can move her very soon. Thank you again, Michael."

"Don't mention it. But, uh, we should keep a close eye on her, ya know, just in case anything like...*weird* happens."

"Agreed."

Michael packed the blood in the small cooler and placed it on what was left of his now smashed kitchen counter. Thorn and Nanook walked over, sniffed at the container, and looked up at Michael.

Michael knelt down and ruffled the head of each dog. "What's up, guys? You ready for an adventure?"

The dogs cocked their heads in unison, and their tails began to wag. Michael smiled as he looked them over. They seemed fine. They were soaked like everyone else at this point, and their fur was dirty, but otherwise, they were fine. Michael noticed their eyes seemed a little more vibrant, a little more bright, but he didn't think too much of it; it was subtle.

"Michael," Jack said from the living room.

Michael stood and made his way into the living room. Melissa was awake and staring up at everyone.

"How ya feeling, Smurf?" Becky asked.

Melissa sat up and looked around. "Oh, my God. Is everyone okay?"

"We are fine; the important question is, how are *you*?" Jack asked.

Melissa looked at Jack and smiled. "I'm okay. I feel a little... feel a little weird, but I feel fine. Did I faint?"

"You blacked out for a bit," Becky said. "What's the last thing you remember?"

Melissa looked back up at where the ceiling should have

been and then around the room. "There was a, a weird explosion. And then…there was…oh, my God, was there a, a dragon, or did I—"

"You didn't dream that part," Becky said.

"Oh, my God! It was, it was…." She trailed off and sat in silence.

"You okay?" Michael asked. "I can get you some water or something, if you need?"

"She's going to kill all of you," Melissa said. "That, that woman. She said she was going to kill all of you!" Tears began streaming down her cheeks again, and her lips trembled.

Thorn walked over, stuck his head under Melissa's arm, and plopped his head in her lap.

"No. I will not allow that to happen," Jack said. "I promise you. I promise all of you."

Nanook bounded over the back of the couch, and she, too, laid her head on Melissa's lap.

Melissa looked back up at Jack. "What are we going to do?"

"We are going to do what Elm expects the least. We are going to go to her, to Fae. She should not expect me to take the three of you into our realm, even *if* one of our group is a supernatural being. She will know I consider doing so to be a far too dangerous course. Which is why we will take it."

"And then what?" Michael asked.

"And then I will discern why this is happening. Why we have been targeted, and by whom," the elf said.

"You said dangerous, Fae is dangerous. I'm not worried about myself, honestly, but can we"—Michael glanced towards the sisters—"and don't take this the wrong way, please…but can we protect them?"

Jack nodded. "I have an idea on where we can shelter. And yes, it will be dangerous, but I believe we can keep one another safe. It will be difficult, but I see no other alternative."

"I don't know what to do," Becky said, and stood. She made her way to the center of the living room and looked up at the night sky. "I don't understand any of this...."

"I'm afraid I—" Jack said.

"I'm not done," Becky said. She motioned about the room and looked back at the group. "I don't know why this is happening. I don't know what that, that damned monster thing was, a...a, dragon or lizard, or fucking Godzilla! I don't know who that woman was, or how any of this is possible. And I don't know what to do about any of it! But I do know that I won't let my sister suffer any more than she already has. And if that means we have to go somewhere dangerous, then we go somewhere dangerous. And if I see that bitch again, I'm going to kill her."

"I'm so sorry," Melissa said, and began sobbing.

Becky knelt down and kissed her sister on the forehead. "Smurf, I'm not having that, do you understand? I'm not having it, kiddo! None of this is your fault. Do you understand?"

Melissa looked up, and Becky wiped the tears from her sister's face. "Okay."

"Jack, I uh...I need to ask a favor, man," Michael said. "Before we go, I need you to do something."

Jack looked over at Michael and nodded. "Anything."

Michael sighed and looked around. "I need you to burn my house to the ground."

35

"Do what?" Becky asked.

"Michael, no," Melissa said.

"Look, there's like, there's gunna be a million questions about what happened here, and I can't even begin to figure out how I'm gunna answer any of them. Not to mention there are...*things* here, things I can't let anyone find. Things that identify me. The *real* me."

The group remained silent. A pained look moved over Jack's face.

Michael continued, "Look, it's complicated. But if I'm going to go with you, and if I don't know when or even *if* I'm coming back, I need to make sure that when I do, if I do, I'm not walking into something I can't explain to the outside world."

"Are you positive, Michael?" Jack asked.

"I'm sure, man. I just need to grab a couple of things first, and then, yeah, I'm sure. I'm kinda sure. Level the place. Can you do that? Burn it?"

Jack nodded.

Michael sighed. "Okay. I just need to get a couple of things, and then I'm good to go."

Michael turned and made his way upstairs. Melissa and Becky both fought back tears, and Jack swore under his breath. It didn't take long for Michael to return. He held a small, fireproof lockbox. He placed it next to the cooler of blood and turned to his dogs.

"I can't...I mean, I can't leave them here; they have to come."

"I never considered otherwise, my friend," Jack said. "In fact, I am less concerned about them than I am about us. Animals have a way of, how best to explain, of accepting things they might not understand."

Michael sighed. "Great. Plus, they put up a damn good fight earlier. We could use them if things get rough again."

"We need to call our parents," Becky said. "Not that I have any idea of what to tell them!"

"Are your phones in your packs?" Michael asked, and started for the girl's things.

"Yeah, mine's in the black one. Melissa's is dead. Somebody forgot to bring her solar charger," Becky said, elbowing her sister.

Michael grabbed Becky's pack and handed it to her. He noted how careful she was with her injured arm, so he motioned for Jack to follow him into the kitchen while the girls made their call. Jack followed, and the sisters were soon talking to someone on the other end of the line.

Michael lowered his voice. "I think that arm is broken, man, or at least fractured. We'll need to get that looked at, or at the very least make her a sling, or get one, or something."

"Oh, it is certainly broken. I was able to mend the bone, but I agree. She needs to keep it as immobile as possible for now. I will conjure a type of splint."

"You fixed it? Oh, like, you used magic?"

"Yes. I will be able to heal her further once I am rested. The injuries I sustained earlier might not have been life-threatening, but they were severe. Like you, my body heals rapidly, but along with fatigue, my ability to use enchantments is diminished with such events."

Michael and Jack checked on the girls, who were still on the phone.

Michael looked at Jack. "So your magic or whatever, your ability to use it. It's what, it's like tied to your body? Your physical self? It's not just, you know, like something you just conjure up in your head, or snap your fingers, and it happens?"

Jack smiled. "Have you ever been so fatigued that your mind would not function properly? Or even complete the most basic of tasks?"

"Sure."

"Same thing."

"Ahh."

Jack glanced at the small safe Michael had brought down. "Is there anything else you might need before we leave? I'm afraid we need to go very soon. Dawn approaches, and I fear for you, Michael."

Michael looked out at the night sky. He couldn't detect much sunlight yet, but it was coming. "Yeah, I just want to get the dog's harnesses and some food for them."

"Do not concern yourself with food. I will see to it that they, and we, have plenty."

"Okay, cool. Thanks, man."

Jack nodded, then returned to the living room to scoured the wreckage for the glowing gems that had been strewn about. Luckily, they were easy to find in such low light.

Michael walked over to the back door and removed the dogs' harnesses from the wall. The dogs didn't necessarily like the things, especially Thorn, but Michael needed to know he could grab one or both of them if needed. The handles each had made grabbing a quick hold very easy. An owner could even carry a dog by the harness if the situation called for it— even dogs as large as Nanook and Thorn.

"Mom, we're fine, okay?" Melissa said. "We're...yes, Becky has...she has everything, Mom."

"Smurf is fine, Mom," Becky said into the phone as Melissa held it away from her ear. "I'll take good care of her. I always do."

Melissa put the phone back to her ear. "We'll be home soon, and we'll call you guys when we get back, okay? I love you!"

"I love you, too. Tell Dad not to worry, okay? You know how he gets," Becky said. She wiped away a tear when she did.

Melissa shook her head. "Wintergreen. Win-ter-green! It's not far from here, and they have cabins. We're going to treat ourselves for a few nights," Melissa said. "WINTER, Mom! Winter GREEN.... Okay, we'll call you when we get back. Love you!"

Melissa ended the call and wiped away another tear. Becky hugged her.

"Let's see how wobbly you are, okay, Smurf?" Becky said. She held out her hands.

Melissa stood and smiled.

"No dizziness? No oogley-woogley feelings?"

"Nope. I feel pretty good, actually!" Melissa said. She stretched and bounced on the balls of her feet a few times. "I feel great!"

Becky shot a glance towards Michael and Jack, and held her sister's chin in one hand. "Look up."

Melissa proceeded through several of her sister's checks. She was used to them, and even when she told Becky she was fine for the fourth or fifth time, Becky continued her assessment.

"Well, you certainly look better, Smurf," Becky pronounced.

Melissa hugged her sister, and the two turned towards Michael, Jack, and the dogs.

"All right, ramblers, let's get ramblin'!" Becky said. "But first...." She looked at Michael. "Got anymore of those Vicodins, hot stuff?"

36

The flames were everywhere. The group stood at the edge of the lawn and watched the tragedy unfold in silence. Thorn and Nanook looked on from several yards further away, neither keen to be any closer than they had to be.

The entire house was engulfed, but not by normal flames, not by what Michael and the girls had expected to see. The home was shrouded in dark green, almost black fire, and it touched every single surface. The small amount of light the fire produced was by Jack's design so as not to spread, nor attract unwanted attention. He'd asked Michael several more times if he was positive that this is what he wanted, and Michael assured him that it was. Even then, Jack seemed reluctant, almost unwilling to accept his friend's request. Everyone could see the pain it caused him, but the elf did as he was asked.

Michael watched, almost mesmerized, as his home of so many years crumbled and burned. A frozen feather worked its way up his spine, and where it traveled, goosebumps soon followed. He'd loved that home, and more importantly, he loved the secure feeling it provided after so many years living rough after his transformation. The small safe he held contained only the things he could never replace. The photos of his family were saved online, but he still had the original thirty-five millimeter print tucked away in the box. He'd wrapped it in several heavy duty trash bags, and Jack had even done something to it which he assured would not only keep the safe's contents dry, but hidden from anyone but Michael.

Michael cleared his throat after another minute. "So I can just..leave this anywhere, and no one will take it?"

Jack nodded. "No one will even see it or even be able to touch it. Even by accident. Only you can find it."

Michael walked into the woods where Nanook and Thorn sat and placed the safe at the foot of a pine just off the path. When he turned to Jack, the elf nodded and pointed back at the safe. Michael looked again and noticed it seemed somewhat transparent, almost as if it were made of fog, or smoke.

"Only you can see it now. Only you can touch it. It is very secure, I promise you," Jack said.

"That was crazy!" Becky said. "Seriously, you put it down and it just, poof! Gone!"

"Yeah, it looked like you dropped it in a hole or something," Melissa said. "It's still there?"

"Looks like it to me!" Michael said. "But it looks, kinda weird, like a reflection on a dirty window would look."

"I will take Melissa first," Jack said. "We will make sure the Emerald Seat is vacant, and I will return for Becky. Then you follow with Thorn and Nanook," Jack said.

"Wait, we have to go to Humpback?" Michael asked.

"I was about to ask the same thing," Becky said.

Jack nodded. "Yes. One can not reach Fae from just anywhere, not without preparations. And likewise, one cannot return to this realm from just anywhere in Fae. I will explain more once we are safe."

With that, Jack scooped Melissa up in his arms and bolted into the night. Michael and Becky watched as the two vanished over the treetops, then turned back to the burning house.

Becky reached over, put her hand in the crook of Michael's arm, and squeezed. "I know we just met. But I want you to know that I'm really sorry about your home, and that I really appreciate what you're doing for me and my sister. Seriously. Especially what you did for Smurf."

Michael turned to Becky and, for the first time, realized how tall she was. Michael stood 6'3", and Becky must have been at least 5'10" or 5'11". He smiled and turned back to what still stood of his home.

"You're welcome," he said. "Besides, who wouldn't drop everything, set fire to their home, and run off into the night to slay dragons for new friends, right? I mean, c'mon!"

Becky laughed. "Right." She laid her head on Michael's shoulder and couldn't help but notice how muscular it was.

The two stood there for another minute in silence, Michael doing his best to quell the butterflies in his stomach at having a beautiful woman on his arm. He wondered how much of her display towards him was the Vicodin talking, and how much might be the adrenalin and stress. Also, there was a strange effect from whatever it was Jack had done to the home: alongside the bizarre green flames, there rested a peculiar silence. Not only was the fire silent, the house itself was quiet as it toppled in and on itself, crumbling here or there. Complete, total silence.

"You don't, uh…." Becky said.

"Hmm?"

Becky cleared her throat. "Do you remember much after we got to you? After you know, after you hit the fridge?"

"Hmm…not really. The uh, the first thing I remember was Jack's wrist. I remember thinking maybe I'd attacked someone or something. Then it all kind of came back. I don't remember being thrown into the fridge, or the house being torn apart, or anything. One minute we were all talking about Melissa, and how Jack and I were wondering if my blood could help, you know, help cure her, and the next thing I know, I'm on the floor in the kitchen. Why?"

Becky shrugged. "No reason. I was just, I mean—"

"The area is clear, as I expected," Jack said.

Michael and Becky both jumped.

"Jesus, Jack," Michael said, clutching his chest.

"My apologies," the elf said. "Are you ready, Becky?"

Becky nodded, and Jack picked her up, taking care not to jostle her. She wore her own pack this time, and Michael's cooler of blood was secured inside of that. All that remained were the dogs.

"Okay, guys!" Michael said.

Thorn and Nanook walked over to Michael and wagged their tails, expecting a walk.

"See you two shortly," he said to Jack and Becky. "These two have never flown, so gimme a sec."

Jack nodded. "Before we go," he said and motioned to what little remained of the home. There, where what remained of the house burned, an illusion began to shimmer into existence. "This will prevent any unwanted attention, at least until we can come back and restore everything," Jack said.

With that, a strange, opaque image of Michael's house solidified. It was as if nothing had happened at all to the home, much less a dragon ripping it almost in half, and magical flames eating what survived after that.

Jack looked at Michael; the elf looked tired, but he smiled. "We will return, and we *will* rebuild your home," Jack said, and leapt back into the air.

Michael stared at his not-home for another minute, shook his head, and looked down at his dogs. "Well, guys, I can't promise you're going to love this, but I can promise you're going to be okay—okay? I won't drop you."

Michael knelt, cradled each dog under an arm, and stood back up.

"You guys good to go?"

In unison, Thorn and Nanook licked Michael's face.

"Okay, okay. Here we go."

Michael climbed into the air as slow as he dared. When he was above the treetops, he turned, and the three of them looked back at where their home had stood for so many years. The illusion was a good one, but it was still just that, an illusion.

"Fuck."

Michael turned away, spotted Humpback, and proceeded in that direction. Nanook whimpered once, but otherwise seemed fine. Michael wasn't sure, but he would have sworn Thorn was wagging his tail as they sped along. That made Michael smile.

"Guess I'll have to take you guys flying more often?" he said above the wind.

Ahead, Michael could see Jack already on the ground, Melissa and Becky standing close by. He didn't want to go any faster, as the dogs were doing just fine at that moment, and he didn't want to freak them out any more than flying might already be—tails wagging and tongues flopping or not.

Another few moments, and Michael began his descent. When he landed, the dogs both laid down in unison. Melissa crouched next to them and scratched their ears.

"Before I open the door, there are several important things to understand," Jack said. "I will travel through first and make certain the area is safe. If it is, I will return, and bring all of you through simultaneously. If the area is unsafe, we will attempt a new location. I do not wish anyone to be there alone for any amount of time, however short."

"Way to calm everyone's nerves there, Jack," Becky said.

"I apologize," the elf replied. "It is not my intention to alarm you. That being said, Fae is dangerous for humans, and I would not have you harmed any further. Please understand, if I thought there was any other recourse, I would take it. Gladly. This is why I believe Elm will not expect my choice. But before we go, there are a few things you must understand. The rest I will tell you once we are there."

Jack paused, took a breath, and then looked at each person. "Should we encounter anyone, do not speak to them. If you are spoken to, by anyone, or *anything* for that matter, please, I implore you, do *not* reply. Do not touch anything, no matter how innocuous it may seem. Do not stop. Do not pause. Do not leave the group. Stay within arm's reach of one another. If I tell you to run, run. If I tell you to stop, stop. If I tell you to hide, hide. Do not ask why. Do not look for a reason. Do not hesitate. Do as I say, and do it immediately."

Jack paused and then smiled at the group.

"I know how this must sound, and I apologize for my directness. But please believe me when I tell you that I only have your safety and best interests in mind. Once we are safe and somewhere we can rest for the day, I will answer any question you may have, but please, please do as I ask. Is everyone clear?"

"What about them?" Michael asked, indicating the dogs.

"Thorn and Nanook will be perfectly fine. In fact, I am far

less worried about them than I am for you. And by that, I mean, these two will fare perfectly well. Fae is in their nature."

"I don't know what that means man, but I trust ya," Michael said. "You hear that, guys? Just follow Jack here, and you'll be fine." The dogs stood and wagged their tails.

Jack smiled and looked at Melissa and Becky. "Are we ready?"

"Let's do this," Becky said.

Melissa nodded.

"Good," Jack said, and backed away from the group.

PART 2

FAE

37

J ack crouched down and placed a single finger on the wet granite. He whispered something and drew what looked like a small, counterclockwise spiral. Behind his finger, the ground began to glow with a bright, emerald-green shimmer which traced the exact path his finger took. Within this light, ruby-red crystals seemed to float in and out of existence. A soft musical note trickled out of the light and wove its way around and through the group. With it, a pungent scent of flowers and spices flooded the air.

The spiral grew and grew as Jack stood and backed away, still making the spiral motion with his hand. When the shape reached nearly five feet in diameter, the growth stopped. Around the brilliant glow, dozens of pearl white mushrooms sprang forth from the stone in an almost perfect circle. They rose to about three inches in height and produced a warm peach light from beneath each cap. Embedded within the cap of every mushroom sat what looked to be a beautiful gemstone, each one a different color than the last.

"I will travel through first," Jack said. "I will only be a moment. Please remain where you are."

And with that, Jack stepped over the circle of mushrooms and vanished. The effect was like watching someone stroll into a vertical pool of liquid light.

Becky covered her mouth. "It's beautiful."

Michael snapped his fingers. "Stargate!"

Becky turned and smiled. "Right?! It did look like that when he walked through!"

Melissa wrapped her arm around her sister's waist and laid her head on Becky's shoulder. "Just wait."

Thorn and Nanook sat nearby, each of their heads cocked in the direction Jack had disappeared, their ears up. A second later, the elf stepped out of the circle and walked towards the group.

"We are safe. It is roughly the same time there as it is here, so it will be dark. Please remember what I said: once we are through, follow me closely. For now, please hold one another's hands as we pass through the window," Jack said.

Jack reached over, took Melissa's hand, and Michael's as well. Michael noted how warm, almost hot the elf's hand was and wondered if summoning the portal had somehow affected him physically. Becky grabbed Melissa's other hand, and the little chain of friends walked towards the faerie ring.

Jack nodded to the dogs. "Thorn, if you would be so kind?"

Thorn stood, followed by Nanook, and walked towards the circle. Without hesitating, he leapt over the mushrooms and vanished, Nanook a split second behind. Michael grinned; he loved those two.

"All right, then," Jack said, and led the group into the circle. "I will continue walking ahead. Even if you cannot see where you are going at first, please continue to move forward. This is important. Just walk forward until we are clear."

A warm pressure engulfed everyone. To Michael, it felt as if he'd walked right into an enormous block of recently spun cotton candy. Becky felt as if she'd floated smack dab into a cloud of warm feathers. Melissa, accustomed to the trip, felt the same as she had before: as if she'd jumped into a bottomless pool of sun-drenched flower petals; even the scent matched the feeling of it. There was a flash of light; almost everyone's ears popped; the sound of far-off music, like a flute, floated nearby; and then there was nothing. Complete darkness and total silence fell over them. Then, almost at once, things came into focus.

"Is everyone all right?" Jack asked. His voice was low, almost a whisper. He'd come to a stop now.

Each member of the group muttered something in the way of an affirmative and let go of one another's hands. Even the dogs seemed to understand, wagging their tails while shuffling and sniffing about. Michael relaxed; he had looked for Thorn and Nanook first. Once he spotted them, he took in the new surroundings.

"We're not in Kansas anymore, that's for sure," he said.

"This way, please," Jack said, and began walking.

It was nighttime, they were in a forest, and to the group's left, an enormous rock face climbed hundreds of feet almost straight up. Something up there was glowing, something green.

Michael leaned toward Jack. "Is that the Emerald Seat?"

"Yes."

On the other side of the trail, a huge row of wooden bookshelves stretched as far as the group could see until it disappeared into the dark. Here and there the shelving parted as another trail branched off in a new direction. Books of every size, shape, and color were crammed together. No space was left empty. The shelves themselves looked to have grown along the side of the trail, as opposed to having been placed. Michael noted how various-sized roots merged seamlessly with the wooden structures and sometimes wrapped up and around an entire bookshelf. Green, yellow, and even purple vines climbed the sides, tops, and in some cases, the front of each piece, yet nothing obstructed one's view of the books nestled on each shelf.

A cascade of moonlight fell through the treetops, illuminating various patches of forest in shimmering, blueish-silver pools. It was the brightest moonlight Michael had ever seen, literally hurting his eyes—and it took him several attempts to focus. The moon itself peeked in and out of existence through the tree canopy, and looked far different than anything the vampire had ever seen. It was not the silver orb he was used too. For starters, it was enormous—easily five times the circumference of even the largest harvest moon Michael had ever seen. And it wasn't a silvery white, or even gray like he was accustomed to; this moon was bluish-green, almost like the pictures of Earth from the moon's surface. There were clouds, what looked to be continents, and vast oceans up there, so there had to be an atmosphere! Unless.

"Is that…is that Earth?" Michael whispered.

Jack looked up and smiled. "No. That is Grafell, our moon."

"It looks like Earth."

"In a way, yes."

"Do people live—"

"Michael, I apologize. I must concentrate."

"Yeah, sorry, man," Michael said.

The group continued to walk, the dogs darting ahead from time to time, but never far enough that Jack seemed concerned, so Michael resisted the urge to call after them. The path they followed was littered in leaves of all color, some even a metallic silver or gold. You could see your reflection in them as you walked by. The purple and blue leaves were Michael's favorites. Several varieties of the blue leaves resembled glass, transparent in nature and so delicate that the vampire wondered how they'd fallen from above and survived intact. Jack had to stop Michael once and remind him not to touch anything when curiosity got the better of him. He'd reached to pick up one of the beautiful leaves but found Jack's hand on his shoulder almost instantly.

"Some things are not as they seem here, Michael," the elf said.

Michael apologized again and offered an innocent grin. His friend smiled back.

Jack stayed close to Melissa the entire time, and Michael remained by Becky's side as they walked. Jack whispered that they didn't have far to go, then asked everyone to refrain from speaking for now until he made clear it was safe to do so. To Michael, the elf appeared calm on the outside, but somewhere just behind that demeanor, on the verge of panic—as if Jack was going to scream for them to run from an unseen terror in the shadows. It was disconcerting, but to the best of his knowledge, Becky wasn't picking up on it, nor Melissa. They just walked along, mouths open, gazing about, eyes wide.

A bird of some sort called out from the forest beyond the bookshelves, and farther away, a similar call replied. The cliff face on the group's left veered away, and before long, the path was lined by bookshelves on either side. The effect was mesmerizing, but Michael wasn't comfortable without being able to see into the forest due to the literary hallway. There could be anything or anyone on the other side of any bookcases, and no one on the trail would be the wiser. It was a perfect barricade between the path and the forest, but also an equally perfect blind for a predator to use. All a stalker needed to do was mind the spaces where occasional trails appeared to branch off from time to time. Easy enough to do if one wished. Jack appeared unconcerned.

After what Michael felt was at least a half-mile or so, he had to put his hands in his pockets as a deterrent to touching anything—a trick his parents used on him and his brother when they were little and wanted to keep their tiny hands from touching or grabbing at anything that seemed interesting. Michael used the ploy now because he no longer trusted himself in this new wonderland of sorts. A beautiful chrome-colored leaf; a book's spine which appeared to be constructed from pink glass; a glowing mushroom; a brilliantly-cut gemstone; insects which flashed multitudes of colors...the farther they traveled, the more magnificent things appeared.

"This should do," Jack said, and stopped.

Michael and Becky collided with Jack and Melissa, each lost in their own thoughts and wonderment. Jack approached one of the bookshelves to their right, and scanned the volumes one at a time. He picked up dozens of books, a minuscule one here, an enormous leather-bound behemoth there, and flipped through their pages while mumbling to himself. He replaced one after the other on the shelf, and repeated the process all over again. After several minutes, he found whatever it was he was searching for. He removed a small, red, leather-bound book, fanned through the pages, glanced back up at the bookcase, and whispered. He replaced the volume and backed away.

Before anyone could ask what Jack was doing, the bookcase swung open as if on a giant invisible hinge. Behind it, a new path, this one paved in brightly lit stones, stretched off into an almost pitch-black forest.

"This way, please." Jack motioned for the group to follow.

Thorn and Nanook were the first to step onto the new path, followed by Jack and Melissa, while Michael and Becky brought up the rear. When they stepped through the little opening, Becky took Michael's hand. He glanced over at her, surprised, but the way she squeezed it made him think she needed a little reassurance. He squeezed back.

Once they were through, Jack turned and walked back towards the bookcase. He touched the wood, and as soon as he did, the case swung closed and vanished. Not only did the bookcase disappear, there were no other bookcases anywhere in sight. Instead, the path they were now on extended well off into the distance as if it had never intersected with another trail in the first place.

Darkness surrounded the group; the only light came from small, silvery pools cast by the moon above, and the trail itself. The path's multicolored stones emitted their own light. Each one glowed as if it were lit from within somehow. The red stones glowed red; the blue, blue; yellow, yellow; and so on down the spectrum.

"We are far safer here," Jack said. "And we are very close to our destination now. But please know, while this area is less traveled than the Emerald Trail"—Jack nodded in the direction from which they'd come— "we must still be on guard. That being said, we can talk, and we can certainly slow our pace if need be." He nodded at Becky. "Daylight won't be for some time yet, and we should arrive at Erendroll just in time."

"Erendroll?" Melissa asked.

"Yes. I considered taking you to my home, to my parents' kingdom of Kyth. It is well guarded, and secure. My parents are powerful figures in Kyth in their own right, and I will send word home as soon as I am sure you are all safe—not until then. But it is the first place I thought of taking you, and for those reasons precisely, we are now traveling to a far different place, somewhere I have no connection with whatsoever. Erendroll was once a powerful city, built and ruled by elves. Alas, it has been abandoned for a millennium. I believe we will be safe there, for a time."

Jack motioned for the group to follow, and continued down the path. Nanook and Thorn raced further ahead this time, as if they understood what Jack had said about this area being safer.

"It's so much darker here," Becky said.

"The trees here are some of the largest I've seen," Jack said. "As well as the tallest. There are trees further in the wood that are so large, their circumference could easily hold several homes the size of Michael's." Jack stopped then, and cleared his throat. "They...they block out a fair amount of moonlight, even daylight. That is why there is so very little vegetation on the ground—not enough light makes it through the canopy. Hence the lambent lane."

"The what?" Michael asked.

Jack stopped and tapped his foot on the stones beneath everyone's feet. "Lambent lanes are constructed with glow stones. They are similar to the gems the Dren surrendered earlier tonight, but are instead simple, uncut rocks. They glow for thousands of years and produce no heat whatsoever. They are perfect for lighting dark areas, and even better for guiding travelers through forests such as this."

"Lambent lanes," Becky said. "They're beautiful."

Jack smiled. "They are that."

The group continued on. Michael found himself mesmerized by the path, having to pull his eyes away from the multicolored glow stones every few minutes. It was because of this that he failed to notice the pair of eyes now tracking his every move from the shadows beyond.

38

"You don't think Elm will know where we are going?" Becky asked.

Jack's pace slowed. "From what you relayed to me, Elm was sent for us. As far as we know, this is the first time any of us has ever encountered her. I have certainly never met a Dren named Elm before, and again, I highly doubt any of you have. So, while Elm knew our whereabouts to begin with, something we have to assume she was told, everything we do from now onwards is new to her, a mystery. She's hunting us, and by giving us a head start, she knows we will do our best to evade her. But by giving us this time, she will expect us to act in certain ways. Most prey will seek shelter or safety when fleeing a predator. They will seek familiar surroundings, where they might have the upper hand. Intelligent prey would most likely avoid plunging headfirst towards even more danger if they could avoid it."

"Hence, coming here," Becky said.

"Precisely. As a hunter, she will attempt to track us via whatever means she has at her disposal. The Dren are renowned for this. And dragons? Dragons are amazing hunters, and especially adept at tracking. That being said, our trail ends just outside of Michael's home," Jack paused again. It was obvious to everyone now that speaking of Michael's house was very uncomfortable for him. "And now that his home is... well, now that...." Jack tried to clear his throat and choked.

"Jack," Michael said. "It's okay, man. Seriously."

Jack swallowed hard. "Thank you, Michael. As I was saying, our trail ends. The dragon could track us through the air, but only if Elm goes back on her word and begins hunting us within the next few hours or so. I can not imagine a Dren to do so, however. Their word, once given, is extremely important to them. They would rather die than go against it."

"You said the dragon—I can't believe I'm saying that, actually—but the *dragon* could track us through the air?" Michael glanced back over his shoulder as he asked.

Jack nodded. "Yes, though with the storm, it would prove difficult. Even dragons can not control the wind or the weather with ease."

"They can control the weather?" Melissa asked.

Jack nodded. "Yes, though it is rare. So our scent will dissipate to the point of obscurity in very short order, at which point they will no doubt employ a kind of radial search pattern, spiraling outward in ever-larger circles until they find something, *if* they find anything at all. The window I opened atop the Emerald Seat will be detectable for a time—that is unavoidable—but unless they hurry, or are extremely lucky, even that will be near impossible to find. Again, if they did discover it, there's no way they could possibly discern *where* I opened a window *to*. The last thing I would imagine they should think would be me taking you into Fae in the first place, much less to an exact mirror location."

"Mirror? You mean, you went from what you called the Emerald Seat, to the Emerald Seat here?" Michael asked. "I thought I saw something glowing up there!"

"Precisely. Mirror locations are by far the most common way to traverse the expanse between the two realms. But I could have opened the window to any number of places from there. Why would I open it to the exact same place in Fae, a mirror location, as it were? Elm would know that I possess the abilities to open portals and direct them to various locations. Most elves know these things. I would imagine she would consider opening a path to its exact mirror to be careless. And now that we find ourselves here, should someone track us to the exact trail tome, there's no way of telling which bridge we chose. I handled quite a few volumes, and read through dozens of locations."

"Trail tome—is that what the book was? The one you read from?" Melissa asked.

"Exactly. Each volume we passed contained countless pages to countless locations. All one must do to travel, or to reveal a path, is to find the tome you desire, locate the directions within it, and read the name of the location to the tome aloud. If the tome has not been moved too far from its shelf, the bookcase will open to reveal the way."

"So the bookcase just, swings open, and there it is?" Becky asked. "And if you'd picked a different book, or a different location from that same book and read the name, the bookcase would have revealed a different location?"

"That is correct. And now that we have left that particular area, should we wish to return, one method we could choose would be to locate a trail tome leading back. And I know where many of those exist. That particular path is very popular in this part of the realm. Many tomes lead back to it, as it is also one of the largest trails."

"It's too bad we don't have something like that back home," Michael said. "I mean, I might have gotten out of the house more these last few years!"

Jack glanced over his shoulder. "Who's to say that you don't? There are numerous magical artifacts in your world, and quite a few individuals with the proper knowledge and skills to utilize them."

The group continued along the path for a time, while a constant barrage of questions peppered Jack. To his credit, he seemed genuinely happy to receive them, and eager to answer when he could. The further they went, the more wildlife began to appear—mostly insects, from what Michael saw. Some of the same lightning bugs he'd seen before glided about, as well as various types of moths and butterflies; most of flying creatures glowed with their own beautiful light. Michael wondered if Jack and the girls could see how colorful they were, or if perhaps only he could detect the dazzling array of colors. Most of the insects would flitter about, never quite close enough for anyone to touch. One particular type of butterfly left a small trail of what Michael nicknamed Tinkerbell dust. The sparkling shimmer would last just moments, but it was beautiful—and that Becky could see.

Michael noticed one of the creatures, a pink and blue butterfly, struggling to stay aloft. When he looked closer, he saw that one of the wings appeared to have something attached to it, something like a sliver of pine needle or shard of wood...several somethings, in fact. The rapid flittering made it difficult to make out, but after s few seconds Michael discovered exactly what the objects were. The little butterfly had tiny arrows embedded in its wing! It had been shot!

Michael shook his head. This place was certainly strange; there was no doubt about that. The idea that out there in the dark were miniature beings, firing miniature arrows, from miniature bows, hunting tiny glowing insects? Well, that was disconcerting.

From time to time, the injured butterfly would fall to the ground, and just as Michael drew near, it would flutter up and struggle in the same direction as the group. Michael was about to say something when the creature fell to the path again, this time right in front of Michael's boot. He stopped, reached down, and picked it up, careful not to injure it further.

Becky let out a shriek, which spun Jack and Melissa around. Thorn and Nanook stopped dead and raced back towards the scream.

Michael was gone.

39

"Wake up! Wake up, wake up, wake up! WAKE...UP!"

Michael shook his head and did his best to clear his vision.

"Wake up, you! Wake up!"

Something brushed Michael's nose, then tickled his chin. He reached to swat whatever it was, but found his arms bound tight to his sides. In fact, his legs were bound as well, and as hard as he might try, Michael couldn't move much beyond his head, and even that was difficult.

"What...?" Michael asked. His voice came out groggy, rough, like sandpaper on a sidewalk.

"HE WAKES!"

Michael blinked his eyes over and over again in an effort to clear them. All he could see were dark shadows, and even those were muddled, blurry shapes. He coughed, cleared his throat, and tried again.

"What's"—another dry cough—"happening?"

"MUSIC!" a high-pitched voice shouted.

Michael squeezed his eyes tight, then opened them as wide as he could. He was surrounded by trees. Huge black behemoths, much larger than what had lined the lambent lane, stretched on as far as he could see, and as high as his neck would allow him to look. The glowing trail he'd been on was nowhere to be seen. Whatever bound him held him tight, keeping even his head quite immobile. Soft chimes and what

197

sounded like wind instruments began to percolate into existence, and with the music, blurry, colorful lights began to shimmer all about. A small, glowing figure darted across Michael's vision, then raced back again.

"MORE MUSIC!" the same little voice commanded.

As instructed, more and more music began to fill the air. As it did, additional lights began to blink to life.

"Hello?" Michael asked. His voice was back, but his throat still felt like he'd swallowed hot sand.

"FOOD!" the little mystery voice called out.

"What is happening? Where…?"

A soft breeze snaked through the trees, and as it did, Michael's vision cleared even more. Either that, or the breeze took a hazy fog or blanket of smoke with it; he couldn't be sure. But Michael gasped as his sight returned, because hundreds of tiny winged figures came into focus. They darted from one place to the next and then back again. Minuscule, winged, humanoid beings, each wearing a variety of garb festooned with vibrant colors, accents, and flair, dotted the air and ground before him. Some wore swords, while other had bows and quivers of arrows fastened about their person.

One particular figure wore two swords on his back and what looked to be a dagger on his belt. His hair was blond, unkempt, and streaked with purple. His ears were pointed as well as pierced all the way up to the tips. At least a half-dozen brightly colored earrings glistened and sparkled on each ear. His clothing was a myriad of colors and boisterous designs, and his eyes, from what Michael could tell, were solid orbs of glowing burgundy light.

"DRINK!" the tiny figure shouted.

Michael was about to say something else when he noticed

another figure, a much larger person, tied to a tree several yards away and facing him. It was a man, and he looked unconscious. He wore a kind of brass-colored metal armor dotted here and there with elaborate engravings and decorative black paint. An enormous sword hung from his side, and as best Michael could tell, a type of firearm sat in a leather holster on the man's opposite hip. As he looked closer, there was something odd about the man's heat signature. Even where the man wore no armor, the signature demanded Michael's full attention. There was none. The man wasn't unconscious. The man was dead.

40

"What happened? Where's Michael?" Jack asked.

"I don't, I don't know!" Becky said. Her eyes darted into the trees and then back to the trail. "There was this, like this wind, and a...a weird snapping sound, like a 'pop!', and he just disappeared! I...I looked over at the sound and he just, just vanished!" Becky said, and snapped her fingers.

Melissa looked skyward. "Did he maybe fly—"

"NO! He just...he just POOF! Gone!"

Jack knelt down and studied the ground. "He didn't fly," he said, and looked off into the trees.

"Well, where the hell did he go?" Becky asked.

Thorn began barking, followed by Nanook. Both dogs stared off into the forest in the same direction Jack was looking. Thorn growled, and the hair on his back climbed on end.

Melissa crouched between the two dogs. "It's okay, guys," she said, and placed her hands on each dog's head, rubbing their fur. They looked up at her, and Thorn began to whine. Nanook licked Melissa's chin. "It's okay, right, Jack?"

"I think he was taken," Jack said. He stood and directed his gaze skyward. "And if he was, I do not have much time to find him."

"Why? What's that even mean? Who took him?" Becky asked.

Jack looked at the sisters and sighed. "I am not concerned with *who* took Michael. Well, not exactly. I am concerned with the imminent daylight. And even here, in these woods, there will be enough of it to harm him or worse."

"Worse? You mean it could kill him?" Melissa asked.

Jack nodded. "From what I know of vampires, sunlight, even a small amount, is quite deadly."

"Well, fuck that! Let's go!" Becky said. "Where do we, like, where do we go? Who the hell took him?"

"I would imagine pixies," Jack said, holding up a tiny arrow between his thumb and forefinger.

The sisters leaned in and inspected the tiny projectile.

"What the hell, Jack?" Becky asked.

"Pixies are known to abduct travelers. I just...I had no idea they were found in these woods."

"What do we do? Where did they take him?" Melissa asked.

Jack turned back towards the forest. He studied the trees and the shadows for a moment and then knelt back to the path. He inspected the ground again, and then glanced at each dog. They were sniffing the air and staring at the exact same location. Jack closed his eyes for a minute, then shook his head.

"He's not far, if what I am seeing is indeed Michael."

"What?" Becky asked. "How are we supposed—"

"But..." Jack said, "I think these two are fairly sure that who I'm seeing *is* Michael." Jack turned and nodded toward Thorn and Nanook.

The dogs glanced over at Jack, then redirected their attention back towards the dark forest. Thorn began to growl just low enough to detect.

"Then let's go! Let's just follow them," Melissa said, and ruffled each dog's fur.

Jack shook his head. "I'm not sure that's the best course of —"

"Don't worry about us, Jack," Becky said. "Let's go!"

Jack stood up and faced the girls. "No."

Melissa stood up, and Becky took a step towards the elf.

Jack shook his head. "It's too dangerous. I will have a better chance at finding Michael if I am not concerned with the two of you. I will escort you to Erendroll, and then proceed from there with Thorn and Nanook. Please listen to me."

"Jack...." Melissa said.

"No. You do not understand," Jack said. "I cannot—"

"We don't *need* to understand," Becky said. "What we *need* to do is get Michael before that sun comes up! So you can either come along or not, but I'm following these two," she said, and clapped her hands at the dogs. "Let's go, guys! Go get Michael! Go, go, go!"

Thorn and Nanook bolted from the path and into the shadows. Becky jogged behind them, clutching her arm tight to her stomach. Melissa followed not far behind.

"I...!" Jack said, then ran after the group.

41

"FIRE!" the tiny figure shouted.

Michael turned his head away as an enormous mountain of flames erupted in the center of the clearing. The fire clawed its way at least thirty to forty feet into the air, and everywhere he looked, miniature glowing beings zipped to and fro in an excited frenzy. Michael wondered how most of them hadn't spontaneously combusted in the wave of heat which tumbled and rolled out of the flames.

Michael cleared his throat again. "Hello?"

The figure he'd watched shout most of the orders paused and turned towards him.

"Greetings!" the pixie said, and made a bow while floating just feet from Michael's nose.

"Umm, greetings back," Michael said, "I, uh...I seem to be—"

"WINE! Our quarry wakes!"

Hundreds of the tiny beings swirled about the clearing. As they did, goblets, tankards, steins, mugs, and bottles of every shape and color materialized. Shelves appeared on the trees, and dozens of miniature tables floated in midair, while larger tables, the size Michael could use, appeared out of nowhere and balanced themselves on the ground. When they did, glasses, goblets, and various other drinking utensils settled on them. The smell of wine and burning wood flooded the air in an intoxicating wave.

Michael tried to move again, straining against whatever invisible bindings held him in place. Try as he might, the only thing he could move was his head, and even that was a difficult endeavor.

"Do you, umm, would you mind helping me get out of, of whatever it is that's—"

"FOOD!" the same pixie shouted.

Michael recoiled a bit at the shout. The tiny figure's voice was surprisingly loud when he wanted it to be.

"FOOD! SWEETS!" the figure said, and clapped his tiny hands.

Again, Michael watched as a magical display of wonderful foods began to appear and arrange themselves on the tables alongside the varied containers of wine. Everything from breads, cheeses, cakes, fruits, meats, and more were conjured into existence out of nowhere. Those smells were far stronger than the wine, fire, and the strange forest. Michael's stomach growled despite what he normally ate. It wasn't that he couldn't eat just like he'd always done, but he never seemed to get much nourishment from normal, everyday food anymore. He could enjoy it, but for taste and smell alone, it seemed. Blood was what nourished him these days. That being said, the spread before him was something out of a movie. He redirected his attention to the figure before him.

"Hi!" Michael said in an attempt to recapture the little man's attention. "Yeah, could you like, help me out here, please?"

The tiny creature turned his gaze back to Michael and glided closer to the vampire's face. "I am Invyl," he said. "What brings you to our province, elf?"

"Elf?" Michael said. "No, I'm not an...my name is Michael,

and I am not an elf. I am here to—"

"You are an elf," Invyl said.

Michael shook his head as best he could. "Nope, I'm not an elf. I think you have me confused with—"

"You're an elf, Michael."

"I'm not an—"

"Why?"

"What? Why, what?"

"Why would you deny being an elf?"

"Because I'm not an elf!"

"You're an elf," Invyl said. "You're a handsome, kind, and powerful elf."

"I'm not a...thank you. But I'm not an elf! I think you're getting me confused with Jack, or someone else maybe, but—"

"Jack?"

"Yes, Jack! The other member of my group! *He's* an elf."

"And so are you."

"What? No, I'm—"

"Elves are rare here anymore. Why are you here, Michael?"

"I'm not.... Okay." Michael paused and took a deep breath. "Look. I am here with my friends—"

"The other elves."

Michael shook his head. "The other elf, Jack, yes. The girls are not—"

"They are beautiful!"

"I agree, but they—"

"Their skin. It is so dark, so stunning."

"Yes, it is. They are very—"

"Elves are always so beautiful. And strong!"

"I'm not sure what's happening here, lil' guy," Michael said.

"You are our guest!"

"I need to get back to my friends, Anvyl."

"Invyl."

"Invyl, sorry. I need to get back—"

"It's Brimmish."

"Huh?"

"Invyl. It's Brimmish."

"Invyl, Anvil, Advil, whatever your name is, man, I need to get back to my friends, *please*."

"The other elves?"

"Oh, my God."

42

Thorn and Nanook would pause, wait for the group to catch up, charge back into the forest, and the entire routine would begin again. Jack whispered how important it was to stay as silent as possible, and that when they got closer, and he told them to stop, that they must stop without question. The girls had agreed to that, content to be involved in the effort to find Michael and not relegated to the sidelines. They'd been running now for almost ten minutes.

"I can carry you," Jack said as he jogged beside the girls. "I can carry you both if you need assistance."

Melissa shook her head. "I'm okay, thank you, I feel, great! It's kinda...weird." She was breathing hard, but looked fine.

Becky shook her head likewise, but remained silent, and the group continued on. Thorn and Nanook would almost run far enough ahead to lose sight of the group, but would always pause as if they knew just how far to go. They did that without ever looking back. Jack noted how silent the dogs were as well: no barks, no howls, no whining. They weren't even panting. The only noises they made were the sounds of their feet racing through the leaves and branches, and even then, he watched as they avoided stepping on anything that could make too much noise. He told himself to remember their behavior when he spoke to Michael later, assuming they could find him. Assuming they could save him. Jack hadn't told the girls what he'd seen, and what he saw frightened him.

The group carried on until Becky stumbled to one knee. A

grimace of pain etched itself onto her face, and she clutched her arm to her chest. Nanook and Thorn stopped several yards away and waited in silence.

Jack knelt down and placed a hand on Becky's shoulder. "Please, let me help you," he said. His voice was soft, low, caring.

Melissa also knelt down, and took Becky's chin in her hand. "Your arm?"

Becky nodded and whispered a "yes" through clenched teeth. Tears spilled out of her eyes and down her cheeks. "Think the drugs are wearing off. Sorry."

"Shut up," Melissa said, and kissed her sister on the forehead.

Jack placed both hands on Becky's arm and closed his eyes. Again, a soft glow radiated from beneath his palms, and Becky's entire body relaxed. She sighed, and then took a slow, measured breath. She leaned over and kissed Jack on the cheek.

"You're like a walking, talking bottle of pain relief, only cuter," she said.

"Easy, bitch," Melissa said, and winked at her sister.

Jack just nodded and continued concentrating on Becky's arm. A minute later, he stood, took off his shirt, and tore it into one long ribbon.

"Please hold this," he said, handing the shirt to Melissa.

Jack walked over to one of the trees and looked up.

"Wait here," the elf said, and flew up into the shadows.

"Jesus, Smurf, you didn't tell me he was so damned ripped!"

Melissa grinned. "Yeah, I don't think the drugs have worn off. Besides, I didn't tell you all kinds of things!" She chuckled, and Becky smiled.

Jack reappeared and landed next to the women. In his hands, he held three small pine cones—only these were unlike any pine cones the sisters had ever seen. They were bright blue, with silver-tipped barbs at the end of each scale.

"Your arm is broken, Becky," Jack said. "I've been able to dull the pain substantially, but I am not yet able to mend the bones properly. I need to rest and gather my strength in order to do that. But"—he began tying what was left of his shirt in several places—"I can help you with this."

He placed the shirt, which was now a large loop, over Becky's head, guided her arm into the crook of the loop, and pulled the entire sling snug. "This will help keep your arm from moving as much, and these"—Jack held up the pine cones —"these will also help with the pain."

Jack pulled apart one of the cones and gave it a shake. Tiny, metallic-looking seeds fluttered into his hand, and he gave one to Becky; the rest he handed to Melissa. "Place that under your tongue until you can no longer taste it. Then, do so again as long as you need to. It will help. Melissa, please place the rest of these in your pockets," Jack instructed while removing seeds from the remaining pine cones.

Becky did as she was told, and to her surprise, her arm began to feel far better within moments, even better than whatever it was Jack had done to her. The seed tasted sweet, almost like brown sugar.

Jack summoned a new shirt, and when Becky was back on her feet, they proceeded towards the dogs, who still waited in silence.

"We must hurry," Jack said when the dogs sprinted off. He pointed up.

What little sky they could see was no longer black. It was a dull purple.

43

"I'm not an elf!" Michael said again. He almost shouted, but until he knew a little more about these tiny people, he remained as civil as he could considering the situation.

"Elves are noble, brave, and kind," Invyl said.

"Okay, so yeah, so if I agree with you, if I agree to being an elf, will you let me go?"

Invyl grinned. "But you are an elf! Very few beings could have seen what you saw, and fewer still would have tried to help!"

"Invyl. I'm going to be one hundred percent honest with you here, buddy," Michael said, "I literally have no idea what you're talking about! Like, not a clue, man."

"So modest."

"What? No, I really don't—"

"Like an elf."

"Dude!"

Invyl clapped his hands and whistled. A pink and blue butterfly, similar to the one Michael had seen on the lambent lane earlier, fluttered over to them. Its antenna were curled around something, which Invyl took. He nodded to the creature, whereupon it glided away.

"Is that...." Michael said, and stopped. "That's the butterfly you shot! That's the same—"

"Illusion!" Invyl said. "No harm was done."

"No harm? It had your arrows stuck in its wing!"

"In a way. All illusion! Only an elf would have noticed such a small creature in need of help, and only an elf would have offered aid!" Invyl turned in the air and faced the armor-clad corpse standing across the clearing. "HE"—Invyl drew one of his swords and pointed—"...HE was not an elf."

Michael looked past the little pixie and inspected the body again. As he did, thousands of minuscule arrows began to come into focus. Wherever there was exposed skin, gaps in the man's armor, or even softer material like leather or cloth, thousands upon thousands of arrows were lodged fletching-deep. But that couldn't have been the cause of the man's demise. It didn't matter how many arrows that size he'd been hit with. He'd seen pictures of people and their unfortunate run-ins with cacti online, and those had been far, far worse! Unless....

"Poison! The very best kind!" Invyl said. It was as if he read Michael's mind.

"You killed that guy? You poisoned him because he wasn't an elf?"

Invyl smiled. His little glowing eyes shined brighter. "In a way, yes."

Michael struggled against whatever it was holding him, putting everything he had into it. Beads of sweat broke out on his forehead, and his hands and feet began to go numb. It was useless. Whatever bound him, however he was held, he was powerless against it. The more he struggled, the harder he tried, the stronger the invisible bonds.

"Invyl," Michael said, panting from the attempt to free himself. "Look, buddy. I'm not sure, like, at all, what you want from me. But I really, really, really, need to get back to my friends! They're in danger. One of them is sick, and the other is hurt! Do you understand?"

"We Pixies are happy to help the elves!" Invyl said.

Michael looked back at the dead man. "Pixies? Okay. Will you let me go if I tell you that I'm an elf?"

Invyl grinned. "We will set you free with the utmost haste!"

Michael sighed and glanced up through the canopy far above. He couldn't see much sky, but what he could see was brighter than he'd seen it thus far. Daylight was coming. In fact, it looked like it was already here. Michael cursed under his breath.

"Okay. Look. I REALLY need you to let me go. I can't be out here much longer, and like I said, my friends are in trouble—"

"We can help! We always help the elves!"

"BUT I AM NOT AN ELF!"

Invyl fluttered back, and every single pixie in the clearing stopped mid-action. Each turned towards Michael and stared. Even the fire seemed to stop burning, the flames frozen still.

"Look, I didn't...I didn't mean to...."

Invyl's little grin vanished. His colorful hair changed to a solid, well-kept, closely-trimmed blond. The jewelry he wore, including the many earrings, all vanished, and his whimsical clothing transformed into sleek black leather armor.

"You are no elf."

"That's what I've been trying to tell you!"

Invyl's glowing eyes narrowed to small burgundy slits. He glided back towards Michael and drew both of his swords.

44

Jack stopped. Thorn and Nanook had also halted; both dogs now crouched low to the ground. Just ahead, maybe thirty yards or so, a warm glow reached out from the otherwise dark forest. Long, wavering fingers of light stretched towards the group, and faint sounds drifted along with them. A muffled voice here, the sound of an instrument there; someone, or someones were there, and from the dogs' demeanor, it seemed as if Michael could be amongst those someones.

Jack leaned over and pressed himself near the two women. "Please. I implore you this time. Please wait here," he said, and looked at them.

Becky nodded, and Melissa gave Jack a thumbs-up. They remained silent. Jack inspected Becky's sling for a split second, rose several inches from the ground, and floated over to Nanook and Thorn.

He landed near the dogs, careful not to make a sound. "What do you smell?"

Thorn looked up at the elf and gave a single wag of his tail. Nanook licked Jack's hand.

"That's what I thought," Jack said and gave the two dogs a smile. "You understand me, yes?" he asked. The dogs returned his look, their eyes focused on his. "Good. I am going to climb higher into one of the trees to get a better look. Nanook, please position yourself to the east and remain hidden. Thorn, go west and do the same. If I need you, well, you will likely know before I do."

The dogs didn't hesitate; each crept away in near-perfect silence. Jack made another note to tell Michael how impressed he was with them, and that he should learn to speak with them in a more effective way.

Jack glided up into the canopy and made his way towards the circle of light. It wasn't long before he spotted the armored individual hanging several feet from the ground by forces unseen. The man was clearly dead, thousands of minuscule arrows embedded in his flesh and deep into his armor in places.

"Pixies, indeed," Jack murmured, and circled around to get a better look.

Michael was on the opposite site of the clearing; he, too, hung suspended in midair. An enormous fire burned bright in the center of the camp, and countless containers of food and drink littered the area. Hundreds of pixies flittered here and there.

Besides being obviously bound against his will, Michael appeared fine. There were no signs of injury, no spells were attached to him, and his aura looked strong, though it flickered just a bit, likely from the approaching daylight. Jack had to free him before dawn, and he needed to act fast in order to get Michael to Erendroll before the morning light. He had no idea why the pixies had taken Michael, but he didn't have the time to try and solve that riddle, either. While small and innocent in appearance, pixies were powerful beings. Alone, a pixie was someone to be cautious around, but in a group the size of this one, they could be considerable opponents if they chose to be. Even dragons were rumored to avoid conflict with the tiny beings.

Jack summoned his sword and whispered to the glowing blade. Its usual blue light faded away, and the metal took on an almost transparent appearance, making it difficult to see.

Jack whispered something else, and he, too, faded from sight. Thorn and Nanook were in position. They took on the appearance of tightly wound springs ready to explode for their master's sake.

Jack positioned himself and summoned a ball of wind, which he held in his opposite hand. The contents of the sphere twisted and spun in a wild and violent motion, yet contained within an invisible shell. It wasn't a particularly damaging spell, but if you weren't expecting it, a well-directed shot could catch just about anyone by surprise, much less beings as small and lightweight as the pixies. It wouldn't harm them, but it would certainly keep them busy while Jack rescued his friend. If all went to plan, there would be no need to involve Nanook and Thorn.

Jack looked back down at the dogs, and his breath caught in his chest. Nanook hung suspended in a tight cocoon of sparkling silver mesh, and Thorn dangled in a likewise trap on the opposite side of the clearing. Jack turned to race into the camp and was struck in the neck by two tiny arrows.

45

Michael took a deep breath. "Look, I'm sorry if—"

Invyl stopped and smiled. "You are no elf, but you are no enemy, either."

"Huh? No, no, I am no enemy."

Invyl swung both of his swords, slashing them at the air. As soon as he did, whatever bindings that held Michael evaporated, and the vampire fell to the ground. He landed on his feet and regained his balance.

"We do not easily call one a friend here in the Stygiancopse. Very, very few, in fact," Invyl said. "Most strangers prove to be dangerous. Most are deceitful. And most mean us, our kind, or our home, harm."

Michael nodded. "Well, I certainly don't mean any of you any harm! Or this place."

"No, you do not; that is clear now. Even when presented with a choice to lie in order to save yourself, you chose to speak the truth, unlike most," Invyl said, and motioned again to the hanging corpse. "It is one thing to lie; it is quite another to do so in order to hide one's true nature. That warrior's heart was black. His lies could not hide this. He had slain many an innocent soul and would have continued to do so if he had not met us. Like you, we tested him. You passed. He did not."

"So this was all...this was some kind of test?"

Invyl nodded. "There are very few of us remaining, from

what we understand. We pixies are forced to be very careful with those we allow to cross our paths, or travel our lands. And we must take responsibility for those we do encounter."

"And you thought we were intruding on your land?"

"Well, not precisely. Our companions"—Invyl pointed to one of the many glowing butterflies drifting about the camp —"will sometimes encounter someone or something they might not understand, or are concerned with. Should this happen, they will begin a small test."

"The arrows stuck in that little guy's wings, you mean?"

"Precisely. Very few could detect that, fewer would care, and even fewer would attempt to help. If one does, some answers are provided immediately!"

"Answers?"

Invyl smiled. "Kindness towards creatures great and small, especially those of a different species, is a sign of goodness."

"So if I'd ignored the butterfly?"

"Well, she would have absconded with you regardless! You mention your group? She was obviously unsure about you, but certain about them. Why that was, I do not know, but if you had ignored her, she would have brought you here anyway. She would have wanted us to discern the nature of your heart, and whether evil resided there. We cannot release evil in any form once we've discovered it, you understand. If we did, we would be partially responsible for any further harm inflicted on others by said person or persons. He, for instance, was evil. You are not. Sometimes discovering one's true nature takes an enormous amount of time! Other times, with certain individuals like yourself, we can detect the truth in short order. A very simple way to do this is to offer someone the opportunity to lie in order for gain, regardless of what that reward might be, whether it be riches or otherwise." Invyl waved his swords again, and the body opposite them vanished in a shower of flashes and black dust. "We knew you were no elf."

Michael was about to say something more when Jack crashed through the trees, bounced off of one of the many tables, and landed on the ground with a thud. Michael leapt back, and most of the pixies retreated several feet.

Jack's eyes fluttered open, and he looked up at Michael, who was by that point leaning down and reaching for him.

"JACK!"

"I am here to rescue you!" the elf said. He raised his hand; a tiny breeze whispered through the camp, and his eyes rolled back in his head.

"JACK! Hey!" Michael said, and patted the elf's cheek.

"Oh, no," Invyl said.

Michael turned to see a shocked expression on the pixie's face. Before he could say anything else, Thorn and Nanook floated into the clearing, suspended by two silver nets. They squirmed and growled and snapped at the netting while several pixies floated nearby, apparently guiding the dogs through the air.

Michael scrambled back to his feet. "Guys!"

Jack bolted upright and grabbed Michael by the pants leg. "We must flee! The women will be worried!" he said, and pulled Michael back down to the ground. "TO THE CIDERY! AT ONCE!"

"To the what?"

"BOLD ROCK AWAITS!" Jack cried. His eyes rolled back in his head again, and he collapsed to the ground.

"Oh, my," Invyl said.

Michael turned to the pixie. "What's happening? What did you do to my friend? My dogs!"

Invyl raced to Jack and saw his neck. "Your friend must have tracked you, and our sentries must have found him. You have my deepest apology. They are not harmed."

Michael looked back at Jack and the dogs. Of course they would have come looking for him. Jack must have made the women wait behind where they'd remain safe; it was the only explanation Michael could think of regarding their absence. "Your sentries?"

As soon as they were mentioned, several new pixies shot down from the trees and landed on Jack's chest. They appeared to be dressed in foliage and wood, which dissolved into beautiful armor that sparkled in the firelight. Gold metal plate covered all but their heads, and each chest-piece was inlaid with hundreds of sparkling gemstones. They carried swords which they wore at their sides and bows which were strung to their backs. Each held a minuscule crossbow complete with silver metal bolt at the ready.

"An intruder, my Prince!" one of the pixies said, and stomped her foot on Jack's chest. She was just taller than her companions and had long blonde hair, which she wore in a single braid tucked away behind her. It was clear that she was important in this new group; Michael guessed she was the commander.

One of the other sentries stepped forward and pointed towards Nanook and Thorn. "And his beasts! We shall dine well tonight, my Prince!"

"THE HELL!" Michael said.

"You have done well, my friends!" Invyl said. "But I fear we have made a grave error. Release them at once."

The sentries looked shocked.

"My Prince?" the leader said. She stepped forward and motioned to Jack's chin. "He was armed with both sword and spell! The beasts were lying in wait for him to act! Surely they would have devoured half our number before we were able to vanquish them. They are unnaturally strong. Look at their eyes, my Prince! They have an unusual glow the likes of which I have never seen. Surely they are dangerous."

"Those are *my* dogs, not his!" Michael snapped. "And they're not dangerous! Well, they can be, but they wouldn't harm any of you unless you hurt them first, or threatened them! You know, like RIGHT NOW!"

Invyl glided over to the sentries and stepped down onto Jack's chest. "Yori, you are a talented Warden, and your soldiers have done well. But alas, we have made a mistake. Michael is no enemy. Nor are his friends."

Yori's eyes narrowed. She, too, had the same burgundy-colored orbs as Invyl, and they glowed just as the other pixies did—only now they were growing brighter. Her jaw clenched, and she spoke through her teeth. "This one, this...*thing*,"—she glared up at Michael—"is strange. And you say it speaks only the truth? And its heart?"

Invyl smiled. "It appears so, Yori. His name is Michael, and his heart is clean. Even when Michael thought that lies could set him free, he chose the truth and an uncertain fate."

Yori spat on Jack's chest.

Invyl continued unfazed. "I sense no ill intent in him. I see kindness bound within layers of despair, but goodness resides deep within those bonds."

Yori stared at Invyl for a long moment, then turned back to her fellow sentries. They spoke in hushed tones and animated gestures. Invyl watched them without saying another word. After a minute or so, she turned back and cleared her throat.

"My Prince, we will obey your command. I have only one request. That is to ask a simple question of this...of...our *guest*," she spat the last word as if it were made of bile.

Invyl turned to Michael. "If you are inclined to accept?"

Michael looked back at Yori and sighed. "Look, I don't know what is going on here, and I understand less of what's happening right now! All I know is that I stopped to help a butterfly, and ended up being kidnapped by a bunch of Lilliputians! I also know that I need to get my friend over there, my dogs, and my tired ass the hell out of here, and soon!" He looked down at Yori. "So if you have a question, then fire away, bitch."

Yori's face reddened, her jaw tightened, and her eyes turned a shade of crimson. She snarled and flew up from Jack's chest, stopping inches from Michael's face. "My question is this. If you are no elf, then what *are* you?"

46

Michael held up a single index finger, pressed it against Yori's chest plate, and pushed her an arm's length away. The angry expression on the little woman's face was worth the slight, especially when Michael noted how hard she was gripping her sword's hilt, her tiny little knuckles glowing white. Yet as angry as she seemed, Yori remained at the distance Michael had pushed her.

"You wanna know what I am?" Michael looked around the group, and then to his unconscious friend and captive dogs. "You caught me off guard back there. I'll give you that. But you know what, you should be a lot more careful about—"

Michael stopped himself. As much as he wanted to see the expression on Yori's face after he did what he wanted to do, the last thing he needed was anyone knowing that he was a vampire.

"Careful about who…." He stopped again and sighed. "Dammit, you know what? I'm not an elf, like I've been saying. But I can't tell you *what* I am. If I did, it would put not just me and my friends in more danger, it could very well mean trouble or *worse* for all of you! And I'm not doing that. I *won't* do that," he said. "I can tell you who I am, and that's someone with two more friends alone out there in these woods, and I need to get back to them and make sure they're safe! I also need to take my other friend here with me. And those guys, they're my friends, too!" Michael pointed at the dogs, who still looked most displeased. "I'm just a guy trying to help his friends," Michael said. He looked back up at the much brighter sky and winced.

"And I need to do it *soon!*"

Yori remained silent, but the expression on her face had softened. Invyl whispered something to the remaining sentries, and they sped off in different directions.

"And we will assist you, Michael," Invyl said. He looked at Yori, who glanced at Michael, nodded at Invyl, and sped off towards Thorn and Nanook.

Invyl clapped his hands. "This is Michael! He is no enemy! I suspect he could very well become a friend, and we will help him! There are two more of Michael's friends in the copse; please bring them here post-haste!"

Michael watched as a flurry of motion erupted around the camp. Hundreds upon hundreds of tiny glowing figures swarmed everywhere, and a massive amount disappeared into the forest.

"Thank you, Invyl," Michael said.

Invyl smiled and nodded. He walked over to Jack's chin and appeared to whisper something. Jack's eyes fluttered open, and he stared at the canopy of limbs and leaves far above. Invyl floated up and towards Michael.

"Pixies?" Jack asked from the forest floor. He coughed several times.

Michael walked over to his friend and looked down. He smiled and held out his hand. "Welcome back, buddy!"

Jack looked up at Michael and then directed his attention to Invyl floating nearby. He grinned. "I thought so. I never was very good at figuring out their magic." Jack reached up and took Michael's hand.

"This place is really weird," Michael said as he pulled Jack to his feet. "Like, really, really weird."

"My apologies, master Elf," Invyl said.

Jack turned to Invyl and bowed low. "No apology needed, Invyl."

Invyl looked confused and flew closer to Jack's face. "Do we know one another?"

Jack smiled. "I am afraid we have never met, but I make it my business to know of the royalty who rule the borders of my lands. I suspected this might be you, but couldn't be sure. I am relieved to know the truth, if I'm honest."

Invyl's jaw dropped. "You...you are—"

Jack held up a hand and motioned for Invyl to stop. "There is no need for that here, Invyl. As I said, this is your land, not mine. I am honored to meet you."

A tear rolled down Invyl's cheek, and he brushed it away with a quick swipe of his hand. Michael noticed and glanced at Jack, who looked back and shook his head in a manner which told the vampire "later."

"Oh, my God!" a voice said across the clearing.

Jack, Michael, and Invyl all turned to see Melissa and Becky floating down to the ground, hundreds of pixies surrounding them.

"Hey, guys," Michael said, smiling. "We havin' fun yet?"

The two sisters turned and began walking in slow, measured steps towards the rest of their group, their eyes darting all about at the camp's many sights. The rest of the pixies floated nearby.

A loud growl erupted from where Nanook and Thorn were. Michael glanced over and saw both dogs now standing free of their bonds, Thorn snarling at Yori, who had her crossbow drawn.

"You shoot my dog, and I'm gunna let him eat you!" Michael said.

Yori turned and glared at Michael. She darted up into the foliage and disappeared.

"Come on, guys," Michael said, and snapped his fingers.

The dogs trotted over, Nanook sidestepping and finding Melissa's side.

"What's happening? Is this where you were taking us?" Melissa asked.

"Who...?" Becky started, the question dying in her throat.

"Guys, this is Invyl. Invyl, these are my friends," Michael said.

Invyl bowed, and smiled. "Welcome. Michael tells me you are in need of assistance?"

"We are trying to reach Erendroll before dawn, Invyl," Jack said.

Invyl glanced skyward. "I'm afraid we have delayed you beyond that point."

Michael looked up, and this time the light stabbed at him. He crumpled to one knee and let out a moan while pressing the palms of his hands onto his eyes. "Jesus."

Invyl darted to Michael's side. "Michael! What is it?"

"I, uh...I need to get inside. I just. I need to get inside."

Becky knelt down and placed her hand on Michael's back. "We're going to get you somewhere safe."

"Can you help us reach the city, Invyl? Quickly?" Jack asked. "Michael cannot be caught in the open. In the sunlight."

Invyl looked up, nodded, and raced back up into the air. "We will take our new friends to Erendroll! Prepare yourselves!"

The pixies floating about began to swarm around the camp. Every single scrap of food, bottle of wine, table, and utensil vanished in an instant. Then, without warning, they began to land on the group themselves, the dogs included.

"Umm—" Michael said.

"At your command, master Elf," Invyl said.

Jack nodded. "We must reach the safety of a building, somewhere, anywhere that we can shield Michael from the light."

Invyl nodded and, without question, turned to face the rest of the party. "We will escort them to the Moon Glow Inn, as it is closest to the border of our copse. Do you understand?"

A chorus of tiny voices echoed about the camp, and Invyl turned back to Jack. "When you are ready."

Jack smiled. "We are ready, thank you, Invyl."

"What exactly are we—" Michael started, and was interrupted as he was thrust forward at speeds the likes of which he'd never experienced.

"OH, MY GOD!" Becky screamed from somewhere to Michael's right.

The sound of Melissa laughing echoed from somewhere just ahead. Everywhere Michael turned to look, all he could see was a blur, a dark gray blur. Then, just as suddenly as it had begun, the group stopped.

"I'm going to be sick," Becky said from somewhere.

The group had stopped several hundred yards from the edge of the forest. Beyond the enormous trees, the light was intense. It was far later in the day than anyone had guessed due to the natural darkness within the deep woods. Several hundred yards beyond the edge of the trees, an enormous city stretched out for miles. Michael turned his eyes away and pinched them shut. A wave of dizziness struck him, and he fell back to one knee.

"It is very bright," Invyl said. "Should we proceed?"

Michael tried to open his eyes again and couldn't.

Jack walked over and placed a hand on Michael's shoulder. "Would clothing help? Can we cover you?"

Michael felt as if his eyes were on fire and he was kneeling in front of a volcano. "I dunno, man. I've only ever been caught out in the daylight once, and that was in the winter. It was like I didn't have any clothing on at all. Took me days to see at all, and weeks to see colors again."

Jack sighed and looked back out into the clearing.

"Is there, is there anywhere else we can go? Anywhere here?" Becky asked.

"Yeah, back in the trees where it was darker, maybe we can hide him?" Melissa asked.

"We can protect him," a tiny voice said from behind the group. Yori glided over to Michael and placed a tiny hand on the back of the vampire's neck. "I'm afraid he would not survive that distance if what I suspect is true," she said, and pointed to the ever-growing daylight and the city beyond.

"You mean—" Invyl started.

"Yes," Yori said without needing Invyl to finish his sentence.

"To Droll!" Invyl said.

"INVYL, NO!!!" Jack shouted.

Without warning, the group was whisked away.

47

The trip this time lasted several dizzying minutes, and when the journey ended, the sounds of retching followed.

"Everyone okay?" Michael asked. Then he, too, vomited.

It took several long minutes, but everyone recovered from the twisting, turning flight, though each person now knelt on all fours, content to be on the ground and glad to be stationary. Jack was the first to regain his balance and take in their new surroundings.

"Invyl..." he started, and had to steady himself. He took a deep, slow breath, and continued. "...we cannot be here. This could endanger you more than you know."

The group stood inside the entrance to an enormous cave, well away from the pools of sunlight now cascading through the tree canopy outside. Two gargantuan, sapphire-encrusted spires stretched from floor to ceiling, towering at least a hundred feet in total. On their surface, millions of brilliantly polished gemstones sparkled. The cavern was saturated with pixies.

"There is no danger here," Invyl said. "I assure you."

Jack sighed. "Invyl, we are being hunted."

"Whoever hunts you cannot come here," Invyl said. "None can enter Droll without our permission."

Jack walked over to where the tiny pixie floated and lowered his voice. "Invyl. You are most kind. And to bring us here, to your home, is..." Jack paused and looked up at the spires. "Invyl. A dragon hunts us."

The pixie's eyes widened, and his mouth fell open.

Jack nodded. "Now you understand why we cannot stay here. You place yourself in grave danger by helping us, by bringing us to this place. I cannot allow it."

Melissa was on her feet now, as was Becky. The dogs continued to lie on the ground and pant. Michael, his vision returning, limped over to Jack and Invyl. The pixie looked at the group for a moment, then lowered his head.

"Dragons are most powerful creatures," the pixie said. "But even a dragon would find it very difficult to come here, master Elf," Invyl smiled. "And we Brimmish know a thing or two about dragons. We created them, after all."

"You guys made dragons?" Michael asked.

Invyl grinned. "Millennium upon millennium ago. Now come! You may rest here. You are safe."

"Smurf, you okay?" Becky asked.

Melissa nodded and smiled. "I'm just still dizzy." She brushed back her hair and took a deep, measured breath. "Isn't this amazing? I told you this place was amazing."

Becky wrapped her arm around her sister, and hugged her. "It's...it's something!"

"I need to sit down, guys," Michael said.

Jack realized Michael was looking far less stable than he should. He glanced out into the forest and then back at Invyl. "We accept your invitation, Prince, and we thank you. We will leave you at dusk. We cannot risk you and your people. I won't allow it."

Invyl smiled and bowed again. "Please, follow me."

The tiny pixie clapped his hands, and all about the immense cavern, thousands of candles sprung to life. Several fires began to burn, and more pixies came into focus. The cavern walls were dark gray, almost black, with bright gold and silver veins running everywhere. The ceiling of the cave was covered in multicolored stalactites, some dozens of feet across. Invyl motioned to a cluster of pixies, who flew over and hovered near him. They spoke for a moment, and Invyl nodded as the group sped off into the cavern. One small figure dressed all in orange fluttered up to Becky, hovered around her injured arm, then raced off again.

While the cavern's ceiling was covered in stalactites and glowing fauna, the floor looked to be highly polished wood. Thorn and Nanook slipped here and there on it, but otherwise kept up with the group. Each dog was still drooling after the intense pixie-travel, and both dogs' fur looked about as unkempt as it could get. Leaves and small twigs were tangled in it, and their paws were covered in dirt and grime.

The cave's ceiling sloped ever downward as the group continued. Now that they were further along and the sunlight was well behind them, Michael began to feel better. Not only did the light hurt him, it played havoc with his strength—another one of the reasons he was so careful to avoid it. Bursting into flames simply because you couldn't muster the energy to take a half-dozen steps or less was a frightening concept. In fact, he'd almost had to dig a hole and climb into it to wait out the daylight once. He'd lost track of time while out on the trail with the dogs, and found himself flying as fast as he could towards the house. The first thing that had happened was his ability to fly vanished. After he crashed to the earth, he found himself barely able to run, and by the time he reached his back yard, he could barely put one foot in front of the other. Thorn and Nanook had practically dragged him up the steps and into the house. He was blind for a week after that, suffered serious burns, and never, ever lost track of time outdoors again.

The orange-clad pixie who'd inspected Becky's arm re-appeared and floated just in front of her face. "If I may?" the lit-tle woman asked. She held up an extremely tiny vial of what looked to be glowing purple liquid. "It will heal your arm."

Becky nodded and lifted her elbow. The sling kept it close to her chest, and the tiny pixie hovered just over it. She uncorked the vial, and a small drop of the liquid fell onto her wrist where the skin was exposed.

"Thank you," Becky said.

The little pixie smiled and sped away, disappearing into the throngs of other tiny figures flying about the cavern.

"I wish we could live here," Melissa said.

Becky glanced over at her sister. Melissa had a tired, glossy look in her eyes, and her skin was ashen; it worried Becky. She was about to say something when her arm began to tingle—first on the spot where the pixie had placed the liquid, and then up her entire arm, which felt as if it might float up and away.

"That's so weird," Becky said, and wiggled the fingers on her injured arm.

Melissa looked over as they walked. "Is it working?"

"It sure *feels* like it's doing something."

Becky's arm was soon covered in goosebumps and then, just as quickly as it had started, the strange sensation vanished. When it did, the same little pixie reappeared. She fluttered about Becky's arm, a serious look on her face. Then, after a mo-ment, she smiled.

"That was far faster than I expected!" the little woman said. Her voice was so small, Becky had to lean in to hear her. "Are you an elf?" the pixie asked.

"An elf?" Becky repeated, and laughed. "Oh no. I'm a Virginian through and through!"

"A Virgin?"

Melissa burst into gales of laughter.

"Hey!" Becky said, but she was chuckling. "No, not a virgin, I am a Virginian. Virginia is where I am from."

The pixie smiled. "I have never heard of Virginia. I would like to see it!"

"I would like to show it to you," Becky said. "Thank you for that, by the way," she added, pointing at the the vial the pixie still held.

"You are most welcome. I am Mott."

"Becky. And this is Melissa, but you can call her Smurf."

"Hi!" Melissa said.

Mott smiled, made a kind of curtsy, and raced back off into the cave.

The group walked on for another several minutes and rounded a corner. Here, seven ornate arches stretched across seven separate tunnels.

"You will find you can rest here," Invyl said, pointing to the furthest tunnel on the group's immediate right, "These mines used to be inhabited by beings much like you. They left behind wonderful rooms that I am sure you will each find acceptable."

"Thank you, Invyl," Michael said. "I don't think I've ever been kidnapped and taken hostage by a nicer group of people!"

Invyl chuckled, and bowed to the group. "Should you need anything, please do not hesitate to ask," he said, and flew back in the direction from which they'd come.

The group stood there for a minute in silence, each gazing about, everyone in awe of their new surroundings, even Jack. What appeared to be thousands of tiny pixies glided to and fro, engaged in whatever it was pixies engaged in. At one point, three small deer bounded by and disappeared down one of the seven tunnels. Several pixies spotted them but paid little attention.

"Well, I don't know about you guys," Michael said, breaking the silence, "but I need to sleep. Like, really, really bad."

Becky nodded. "Yeah, my legs are toast."

"Are you sure we'll be okay here, Jack?" Melissa asked. "I mean, the pixies won't be in any danger, will they?"

Jack shook his head. "If Invyl says we are safe, then I cannot question him—though I would feel more comfortable if we could depart soon."

Everyone nodded, and they began walking down the tunnel Invyl had indicated for them. It was long, warmer than the area they'd just left, and lined with torches which burned bright orange. Before long, arched wooden doors began to appear on both sides of the group, each recessed into the stone wall of the cave, a single metal doorknob fixed to each. Becky tried the first, and sure enough, just as the pixie had promised, a bedroom, complete with already burning fire and candles, waited beyond the doorway.

"We'll take this one," Becky said. "Oh, but first...." She removed her backpack and unfastened the top. She rummaged about for a second and retrieved the small blue cooler containing Michael's blood. "You might need this," she grinned, then winced as she moved her injured arm.

Michael grabbed the cooler. "Thank you. You okay?"

"Yeah, it's a lot better, but it still stings, thanks."

Michael nodded.

"See you in a bit," Melissa said, and walked over to kiss Jack on the cheek.

The sisters walked into the bedroom, and before they could close the door, Nanook and Thorn followed.

"Guys, no, leave them alone, come on…" Michael said.

The dogs turned in unison, looked back at Michael, then at the women, and completely ignored their owner.

"I guess that settles that!" Melissa said. "It's okay, we'll take care of them."

"Wow, way to show the love, guys," Michael said. He mouthed a "thank you" to the girls and continued down the hallway to the next door.

The next room was very similar to the first: large bed, fireplace, table, and burning candles.

"You take this one," Jack said.

Michael exhaled, and limped into the room. "Thanks, man."

Jack nodded. "I'm sorry for all of this, Michael. I truly am."

"This isn't your fault, Jack. Now enough of that shit. Go get some sleep, dude. It's been a long, weird night. We can talk more later. When I know I can speak in complete sentences."

Jack smiled, and Michael grinned back.

"Good night, Jack."

"You mean day?" the elf replied, and winked. "Good night, Michael."

Michael closed the door, and Jack made his way down the hall to his own bedroom.

48

Becky walked over to the bed and pressed down on the mattress. It was not only soft, it was warm. The bed was large enough that four or more grown adults could sleep in it, and still have room for more. Melissa had already found a chair and plopped down, while the dogs curled up in front of the fireplace atop a comfy-looking rug, their eyes already closed; small snores soon followed.

"Helluva night," Becky said.

Melissa nodded. "Helluva night."

The girls began stripping off their clothes and tossing them into a dirty heap in the corner. Dirt, mud, and various other stains covered everything, their socks bearing the worst of it all. When Becky unfastened the belt holding her knife at the small of her back, she walked it over to the bed and shoved it beneath one of the pillows.

"Do you always sleep with that thing?" Melissa asked.

"I do now, Smurf."

The sisters finished removing their soiled clothing. They moved in slow, tired motions until all they wore were their sports bras and underwear. Scrapes, scuffs, and the beginnings of several respectable bruises were visible on each woman, from head to toe.

"I would murder someone in cold blood for a shower right now," Becky said.

"Right?"

"Oh my God, Smurf! Look!"

Becky pointed across the room. On a long shelf, built snug into the wall, various fruits, cheeses, and breads waited for them. The sisters looked at one another, giggled, and raced over, their bare feet making small slapping noises.

Through a mouthful of sticky-bun, Melissa smiled. "Betcha never thought your crazy sister would drag you off to Middle-Earth, huh?"

Becky swallowed several large gulps of wine straight from the bottle. "I can honestly say this, Smurf"—she took another swig of wine—"hell, no. Like, NOPE! Like, big hella NOPE!"

Melissa spit out her pastry, and the two were soon lost in fits of giggles. When they regained most of their composure, they hauled as much food as they could carry over to the bed and snuggled up under the covers. They tried to give the dogs some bread, even cheese, but they were already sound asleep. One hunk of cheese landed not two inches from Nanook's nose, and she never even opened an eye to investigate. No doubt she was soon dreaming of it instead.

"Smurf, do you remember what happened back at Michael's house? I mean, after the big-ass monster and that bitch showed up?"

Melissa took another bite of cheese and stared off into space for a second.

Becky placed a hand on her sister's knee. "It's okay if—"

"I remember helping Jack and Michael...and poor Thorn. I remember he was cut and bleeding, so we ran around looking for something to put over him." Melissa tore a piece of bread from one of the loaves and took a small bite. "And I, did I get sick? I remember feeling sick and then...then I was on the couch, and you guys were all around me."

Tears filled Becky's eyes. "Smurf...."

Melissa reached over and brushed the hair out of Becky's face.

"Smurf, I think you had a stroke, little girl."

Melissa's eyes widened, and she swallowed hard. "I don't feel like I...I mean, I don't think...." Her chin trembled, and she, too, began to cry.

Becky leaned over and hugged her sister tight. "Do you remember anything with Michael?"

Melissa shook her head. "No."

Becky cleared her throat and wiped her eyes. "He gave you some of his blood, Smurf. We thought maybe he could help you. That his blood could help you."

Melissa looked at Becky and then at the dogs. "Like he did for them?"

"Yeah, kinda, yes."

"And I drank it?"

Becky nodded, and more tears fell onto the blankets in her lap. "You did, and then you slept for a bit. When you woke up you, you looked so much better and, and you seemed okay, and.... *Are* you okay, Smurf? I didn't know what to do! None of us did."

Melissa reached over and wiped the tears away from Becky's cheeks. "I'm okay, sis! Whatever he did seems to have worked. I mean, I don't feel like I had...like I had a...you think I had a stroke?"

"You couldn't talk, you collapsed, and then you started convulsing.... It was scary. I was so scared, Smurf!"

"I'm okay. And I feel fine! I'm tired, but I feel okay—*okay*?"

"You're not mad?"

"Why would I be mad?"

Becky shrugged. "I dunno—we fed you some strange dude's blood? Some weird vampire kid?"

Melissa smiled. "Michael's older than us, goofy!"

"You know what I mean though. I mean—we straight up had you drinking blood from a guys wrist!"

Melissa nodded. "Under any other circumstance, I would think that that was crazy. Stupid even. But...."

Becky sighed. "...yeah."

"I'm just glad he was willing to help me, you know? I mean, we just met the guy," Melissa said. "But he's really nice. I like him."

Becky smiled and took another bite of her cheese. After a minute, she took a deep breath. "And he's so stupid hot..." she said with her mouth full.

"Beck!" Melissa said, and slapped her sister's shoulder. "Bad cougar! Bad slutty cougar!"

Becky lunged over and hugged her sister tight. "I can't lose you, Smurf!"

"I'm not going anywhere yet," Melissa said.

"Good! Because I'm going to make Michael turn you into a damned vampire if I have to! I don't care! I just can't lose you, Smurf!"

"You won't," Melissa said into her sister's shoulder. She squeezed tighter. "...cougar."

The girls broke into another fit of laughter.

49

Michael lay naked on the bed. His entire body hurt, and if he'd had any other clothes with him, he would have tossed his entire outfit into the fireplace. The arrow wounds were nearly healed, but they left behind shadows of pain that radiated to almost every extremity. His head was pounding, and his hands shook to the point where he'd almost dropped the first bag of blood he drank.

The blood helped, and even though there wasn't really much of it, Michael had consumed an entire bag. He'd have to find more later. How he'd do that, he wasn't sure, and it worried him. The more he used his abilities, the more blood it took to recover. Vampirism was strange in that the less blood he had, the harder it became to rest fully. Recovery from wounds, or even just fatigue, was directly related to blood. He'd certainly heal without it, but it was a long, arduous process, and until he had blood, he couldn't sleep. Not a wink.

Michael stared at the ceiling and marveled at several carvings there. The entire room looked as if it had been chiseled out of stone and then decorated by exceptionally skilled artists. Everywhere he looked, figures of men, beasts, landscapes, flora, and even constellations were expertly carved into the walls and ceiling. The floor was polished to such a degree that it was almost mirror-like. Whoever built this place took great care in doing so, and clearly took pride in their work. Some of the carvings looked so real, so lifelike, that Michael swore they moved from time to time—especially the carvings of birds. For all he knew, they did.

The incident with the pixies had been strange, very strange. Invyl made it sound like abducting travelers was a common practice. And the bit about "testing" them made Michael pretty uncomfortable. He'd almost lied to the pixie when he started to get worried that he might not get back to Jack and the girls. What would have happened then? What would have happened if he HAD said he was an elf?

Then again, he somewhat understood it.

He likened it to airport screenings. The whole purpose of your visit, how long do you plan to stay, background checks, all that jazz. But there'd been the dead guy! Michael was pretty sure he'd never seen a corpse hanging on the wall of an airport terminal. Days ago, when he'd met Jack, the elf had told him he'd been able to "sense" Michael's heart, or intentions, his, how did he put it, his goodness? Michael wondered if that were true of all the beings here. Could they all sense a person's true nature? Could they all sense if a person was a good guy, a bad guy, or just a, you know, a normal guy? Was that the real reason Invyl and the other pixies hadn't turned him into a vampire pincushion?

Michael was in the midst of these thoughts when he drifted off to sleep.

50

Jack inspected the room and marveled at the artistry carved into the walls—clearly elvish, and obviously ancient. He'd heard of the infamous sapphire spires standing sentinel at the entrance to the fabled Droll, but had never seen them. He'd seen paintings and drawings of the place, but never imagined he would see the actual thing. Droll had been the home to many elves for quite some time. Then, for reasons unknown, the elves had left and built New Droll, or Erendroll as they eventually called it. The city even boasted replicas of the giant sapphire spires.

Invyl was surprised at the news his guests were being hunted, and by a dragon at that, but he'd accepted them into his home regardless. This both worried and fascinated Jack. He knew little of pixies, but one thing he did know of was their fierce loyalty to all things innocent and, in particular, to kind souls. Invyl had clearly taken a liking to Michael, which not only reinforced Jack's own assumptions about the vampire, but also assured him that maybe his concern over the pixies' intentions was unwarranted. They'd tried to help, and they'd even gone so far as to bring Jack and his friends into their home. Jack had never heard tell of such a thing before.

He walked over to the room's fireplace and stared into the flames. He held a glass of wine in one hand and an apple in the other; both hands trembled. The last few days had taken quite a toll on him, not just physically, but mentally as well. It was the mental side of things that concerned him most. He could always rest to recoup lost physical energy and basic mental faculties, but his intellectual reserves, the part of his mind that tapped into his conjuring and divination capabilities, took more than just a nap or two. His ability to access what Michael and the others referred to as magic was tied directly to his mental capacity, and the more he used, the more of a toll it took on all aspects of his being. In effect, the more power he summoned, the weaker it, and he, became. Jack knew of several instances where an elf had used so much of their mental fortitude that they had died from the effort. With everything that had happened over the last several days, he needed to make sure he prioritized resting and recharging here in Droll.

Jack finished his glass of wine, set it on the mantel above the fire, and took another bite of the apple. The fruit was delicious, and the wine spectacular. He was thankful for it. The night had been long, and he suffered quite a few injuries, some severe enough that he was still unhealed.

He walked over to the bed, sat at its foot, and removed his boots. He groaned and winced as he did. His shoulder pained him more than anything else, but he hoped a good night's, or day's in this case, sleep would rectify that.

When he lay back on the bed, Jack smiled. It was far more comfortable than he imagined it would be. Why he'd thought that, he hadn't a clue, and he was glad to be wrong. His thoughts turned to Melissa and Becky: two very human women now surrounded by very inhuman beings, in a very otherworldly place. There were so many things here they couldn't possibly understand, so many beings who could harm them, or worse. So many dangers. So many marvels both horrifying and wonderful. He questioned his decision to bring them here. But again, he was far more comfortable here himself, and more powerful. If he was to protect them, this was the place to do it.

"Not that you have a stellar record thus far," he said to the ceiling.

He'd had his fair share of losses this past night. First the Dren surprised him. They could have killed him if they had so chosen. And then the dragon—that shocked him—and finally the pixies! They, too, had taken him by surprise. He was certainly finding himself on the losing end of more encounters than not.

He just needed to rest, to regroup, to think clearly.

Who was hunting them? Why were they targeted? Jack had no enemies. His family was not at war with anyone to the best of his knowledge. So who was hunting them? He'd been spared; but why? He and Melissa were both spared, just the two of them from what he understood. Michael had certainly been targeted for death. Pine had meant to kill Becky. And if this Elm was accompanied by a dragon, someone very powerful must have sent them, and for a reason Jack could not fathom. Dragons do not hunt indiscriminately, and they certainly are not known to hunt innocent beings. Jack might not really know Michael all that well, and he'd certainly not known him for very long, but he was clearly a good person, and nowhere near worthy of a dragon's attention. Not in that way.

So who had sent them? What had been said about Michael and Becky? Jack ran scenario after scenario through his head, finally landing on his parents. If anyone could help him, if anyone could defend themselves from the likes of a dragon, it was them. They were ancient, possibly older than the dragon which hunted them now. And Melissa was in no shape to be thrown into this odd puzzle, none whatsoever. She did not have much time. Jack desperately needed to find a cure for her disease.

Melissa had reacted well to Michael's blood, and Jack wondered if more of it might cure her ailment altogether. The dogs healed amazingly well when they ingested some of it. Perhaps there was another way to help the woman he was so in love with, a way that didn't involve her becoming a vampire like Michael. Though, if she was, if she became a vampire, Jack would have far more time with Melissa than he would if she remained mortal...if she remained such a fragile human. A blink of an eye was all they had. Just like that, just as soon as it began, human lives ended. It was unfair of him to think that, but think it he did.

Jack sighed, gripped one of the glowing gems the Dren had given him, and began his ritual of meditation. He drifted off to sleep as more and more questions crept into his subconscious.

51

Michael was dreaming of donuts and chocolate milk. Soft, warm, icing-drenched donuts, and rich, creamy chocolate milk. Why he was dreaming of this, he didn't have a clue. He hadn't had a donut or sip of chocolate milk in years—decades, even. When Michael tried to make sense of the dream, he came up with nothing. But he enjoyed the sweet chocolate coating his lips and tongue. It even smelled good—amazing, even— and he wanted more.

He could control most dreams now. That was one thing about being a vampire that Michael really did enjoy: his dreams were incredible. Not just vivid; his dreams were spectacular in that he always understood that he was dreaming. Whenever he drifted off to sleep, and whenever he began to dream, Michael understood within moments what was going on. It was exhilarating! He could do anything he wanted, make anything happen, be anyone, see anyone, be anywhere at any time. And inevitably he saw his family. He'd spend Christmas morning with them, or Thanksgiving dinner; he'd go trick-or-treating with his younger brother Kyle—all kinds of things. And they were so real! So real that Michael had the ability to force himself to believe in them while he was dreaming, to surrender, become one with the dream, to believe everything that was happening there was truly happening for real. But tonight he was dreaming of donuts and chocolate milk; why or how that had started baffled him.

"You're a vampire…" a voice said from beside the bed.

Michael was halfway through another chocolate-dipped

donut when he bolted upright.

Standing by the side of the bed was a tall, blonde, maroon-eyed woman. She wore so little clothing that at first Michael thought she was nude. The firelight behind her spilled through her attire as if the fabric was unable to restrict light at all. She was stunning.

"Who...?"

"You're a vampire, are you not?" the woman asked, and took a small step towards the bed.

"I, uh...." Michael cleared his throat and looked around the room. The candles had been snuffed out, and the fire was burning much lower now. "Who are you? How did...?"

"You know who I am," she said.

Michael looked closer. She was more than beautiful; she was gorgeous in a way he never thought possible. It didn't hurt that she was all but nude, the light from the fire caressing her smooth, perfect skin and playing fascinating tricks with various curves and features.

"I don't think I do," Michael said. "I think I'd—"

"I am Yori," the woman said.

Michael's eyes widened, and his mouth fell open. "Yori? Little pixie Yori? The little Yori who wanted me dead back there, Yori?"

The woman nodded.

"But you...you're—"

"You are a vampire, yes?" Yori said. This time she sat on the bed next to Michael.

Michael looked down and was grateful he'd managed to pull the covers over him after he'd drifted off. "Look, I don't...uh, you know, umm…I don't think I—"

Yori leaned in and kissed Michael on the mouth. She pressed into him hard and moaned while she did. Michael kissed her back. Her lips tasted like vanilla, and he pulled her closer, wanting to taste more. The two embraced for another moment, then Yori pulled away.

"Vampires are thought to be extinct," she said. Her eyes, solid maroon with no apparent iris or pupil, seemed to narrow in on him, focused, very focused.

Michael cleared his throat and tried to slow his heart before it broke free of his ribcage. "Ummm… I don't really know how to answer that. I don't think I *should* answer that, actually."

Yori grinned and leaned in for another kiss. Michael stopped her.

"How umm, how did you…." he motioned up and down towards the pixie.

"We can change form whenever it suits us." She ran her hand up Michael's thigh. "Size can be important sometimes."

Michael's heart crashed around in his chest at a dizzying speed. His breath caught in his throat, and his hands began to tremble. God, she was beautiful.

"I, uhh—" Michael said.

Yori stopped and leaned back. She looked hard at Michael, staring deep into his eyes, and then she smiled. "You're a virgin. Or might as well be."

"What? No, I'm not, I mean… I—"

"You might have been with a boy or a girl, but you've never been with a man or a woman, have you?" Yori asked. She ran her tongue over her teeth and grinned while biting her lower lip. "I will not hurt you."

"Hurt me? No, no, that's not what I was...what.... What I was going to say was, I don't think we should. I mean, we just. Like...." Michael stopped and sighed.

Yori tossed her head back and laughed. "You are frightened! You need not be. I will be gentle, unless...unless you would have me otherwise?"

Michael tried to swallow and found it almost impossible. He cleared his throat, and shook his swimming head. "I, uhh, I'm not sure we should do this."

Yori cocked her head to the side and smiled even more. She sat there for a moment looking Michael over, and he could almost feel her eyes on his bare chest, his stomach, his arms, his....

"I am making you uncomfortable," Yori said. She continued to smile, then bit her lower lip again.

"Well, I wouldn't say that, it's just—"

Yori turned her head and stared at the door. Her smile grew even larger, and her eyebrows rose. "The other woman? The girl with the injured arm!"

Michael felt his face flush, which was rare. "Umm...."

Yori laughed again; her voice was as beautiful as she was. It stabbed at Michael's heart and stomach.

The pixie leaned in close enough to press her lips to Michael's ear. "Perhaps she could join us?"

Michael gasped and pulled his covers up to his chin. "I...!"

Yori laughed long and hard at that. "I am making a joke, Michael," the pixie said and stood. "It is clear you have feelings for another, which saddens me. And this is also why I made a small joke at your expense; you must forgive me."

Michael just nodded. He thought if he tried to speak, his heart might actually explode.

Yori leaned over and kissed Michael on the cheek, and then his neck. "She is lucky. But should you find yourselves...incompatible...." Yori turned towards the bedroom door. She lingered in front of the fireplace for a moment and grinned as Michael tried to avert his eyes. "...should you find yourselves incompatible, seek me out. I have never had a vampire in my bed. Much less, such an"—she paused—"an inexperienced lover. I can teach you many, many things, Michael."

Michael nodded. "O-okay...."

There was a flash of green light, and Yori returned to her normal size, complete with gold, gem-encrusted armor. The pixie flew towards the door and dove beneath it, where the wood hung an inch or so from the ground.

Michael sighed and collapsed back onto his pillows. "What just happened?"

52

Nanook whimpered once, followed by Thorn. Melissa cracked her eyes, only to be greeted by two furry faces just inches from her nose. Both dogs began wagging their tails, and Melissa smiled.

"Hello," Melissa said, her voice cracking.

Both dogs pranced about, Nanook pacing back and forth from the bedroom door to the bed.

Becky moaned. "They probably need to go out," she said. Her face was still smashed onto her pillow; an enormous wine-colored drool mark stained the fabric. She never opened her eyes and was snoring again within seconds.

Melissa reached out and scratched each dog behind the ears. She wasn't sure how long they'd been asleep, but it felt like ages, and she felt better than she had in a long time.

"Gimme a second, guys."

Nanook and Thorn sat down and continued to wag their tails. Melissa noted how much cleaner the two looked, as if they'd been bathed and brushed while she and Becky had slept. Maybe she'd just imagined how dirty they'd been last night.

Melissa climbed out from beneath the covers and walked to where her clothes should have been piled on the floor. Everything was gone.

She was about to say something when she noticed new

identical outfits folded on the shelf which had contained the food and drink the women had attacked earlier. The plates, bowls, and goblets, along with everything else, had vanished, and only a single bowl containing grapes and apples remained. Two small loaves of bread sat near a large bowl of what appeared to be butter, along with a jar of dark amber honey. The new clothing was folded into two separate piles, and directly beneath each, two pairs of boots, also identical, sat on the floor. There was no sign of their original clothing. Next to each pile sat rose-colored glass basins of water, washcloths already soaking at the bottom and colorful flower petals floating on the surface. In the corner of the room, two water bowls sat on the floor, half their contents gone. She felt a pang of guilt for not thinking of that the night before, but the dogs hadn't even seemed interested in food earlier, just sleep.

Melissa walked over, removed what little clothing she had on, and gave herself a quick wash. The water was warm and smelled heavenly. When she was done, the fire dried her in short order while she inspected the clothing. There were undergarments, for which she whispered a quiet "*Thank God,*" and she began putting everything on. She was surprised at how well everything fit, almost as if it had all been tailored just for her. The pants were a dark brown brushed leather. A bra, very similar to the sports bra she'd been wearing, was next. It, too, fit perfectly; in fact, it was so comfortable that Melissa grinned as she adjusted herself in it. The shirt was an incredibly lightweight emerald green fabric, soft and silky in appearance and texture. The sleeves were mid-length, and the neckline plunged a bit further than she liked, but it was amazing.

She sat down on the floor and pulled the boots on over her pants legs. They were tall boots, reaching just below her knees, and reddish-brown in color. They were also laceless, but just like everything else, they fit astonishingly well.

When she stood up, Melissa looked down and smiled. These

new clothes were not only comfortable, she looked pretty good in them, too! She wished she had a mirror.

"You guys ready?"

Thorn and Nanook jumped up and raced to the bedroom door. Melissa grinned, glanced back at her sister who was still fast asleep, and walked over to the door. She opened it just enough so the dogs could get out and she could squeeze through. She shut the giant door and followed Nanook and Thorn.

"Stay close, guys."

The dogs slowed and took up a pace on either side of Melissa. She walked back in the direction she remembered coming and took time to inspect their surroundings a little more. It was obvious that they were in a cave, but it would be unfair to call it just that. The walls were still still rough and uneven—tool marks could be seen now and then, and the ceiling had a similar look—but every few feet a tapestry hung, or a rug had been thrown. Paintings and drawings, some so small that Melissa couldn't quite make them out, decorated the walls. Candles burned on small shelves carved into the rock, and small sconces drifted through the air, casting warm light wherever they went. Most of the light here seemed to come from glowing stones scattered throughout the cave. They were embedded in the floor, the walls, and even along the ceiling, and they looked identical to the ones Jack had explained on the lambent lane. Melissa's favorite colors were the peach and dark purple ones.

"Hello!" a tiny voice said from nearby.

Melissa turned to her right and saw a tiny male figure floating there. It was the first time she noticed that the pixies had wings! They were almost completely transparent, like dragonfly wings, and striking from the amount of colors that shimmered on them.

"Hi!" Melissa said.

The little pixie smiled and waved his little hand. "My name is Blaze. It's the hair," he said, and pointed to his fiery red hair —not orange, not auburn. The pixie had crimson red hair.

"I can see why! My name is Melissa."

"It is a pleasure to meet you, Melissa. We were told you might sleep this long."

"Oh yeah? How long were we asleep? Is anyone else awake?"

Blaze shook his head. "Oh no, you are the first to wake, or at least, you're the first to leave your room!"

"Ahh."

"I assume you are leading these two somewhere where they can, well, relieve themselves?" Blaze asked.

Melissa grinned. "I am."

"They do look as if they need it," Blaze said, smiling. "Come! I will show you the way that is best."

"That would be great, thank you, Blaze."

The pixie nodded and motioned to a corridor leading north.

"So tell me, Blaze, this is your home? There seem to be a lot of rooms large enough for people, you know, my uh, my size?"

"That is true! Long ago this was once an elven home. When they left to build what became known as New Droll, or Eren-droll, we moved in! From what I understand, the elves actually suggested it, and, well, we protect the secrets which still reside within these walls. We are guardians as well as residents here now."

"Ahh...magical secrets, huh?" Melissa asked, winking at the pixie.

"Very much so, miss," Blaze answered, and his little maroon eyes sparkled.

A minute later, the two entered an enormous round room. All manner of plants, giant trees, and foliage grew here. Countless insects and birds glided about, and several small, furry creatures scampered to and fro. Melissa craned her neck and marveled at how high the walls climbed, at least a hundred feet or more. There was no ceiling here, only open, starlit sky.

"Oh wow!" she said. "You were right about us sleeping for a while! It's nighttime already?"

"It is, miss, though the sun just recently set."

"This place is beautiful!"

"Thank you! This is one of our many gardens. Your furry companions may come here anytime they, you know"—Blaze chuckled—"to, well, *fertilize* the area."

Melissa laughed. "You hear that, guys? Go nuts!" she said, and motioned the dogs on towards the immense indoor forest.

Nanook and Thorn raced off into the shrubbery and disappeared amongst the trees and flowers. After a moment, several excited barks and yips echoed out of the garden.

"You may leave them here with me if you would like. I will see that they are returned to you," Blaze said. "I sense they may be hungry as well. There is quite a bit of game here in the glade; they are welcome to hunt if need be."

Melissa raised her eyebrows and took a breath. "Well, I don't know if...I guess that's okay? They're not really my dogs, they're Michael's."

Blaze looked back in the direction the dogs had raced. "Well, they certainly consider you family!" he said.

"Yeah? How can you tell?"

255

Blaze smiled. "They look on you fondly. And one, the female, speaks your name even now."

"She what?"

"She speaks your name, miss. Can you not hear it?"

Melissa chuckled. "I guess not, Blaze. But I like that they like me! I like them, too!"

"Where are you from, miss?"

Melissa sighed and chuckled. "Far, far from here. I live near the ocean in a place called Virginia Beach."

"I love the ocean," Blaze said. "I've seen several, and I am always astounded at their beauty."

"It sure is pretty."

"Are all who come from there...." Blaze stopped, and an almost embarrassed expression crossed his face. "What I mean to say is, does everyone look like you in this, Virginia Beach?"

"Look like me?"

"Your...skin, miss. It is so much darker than I've ever seen. It is so very beautiful."

Melissa smiled. "Thank you, Blaze! No, not everyone looks like my sister and I, though a lot do! There are all kinds of beautiful people there. Some with brown skin like mine, some with skin like yours, some with darker complexions, and some in between! The beach is a nice melting pot of races."

Blaze seemed to consider that for a moment, and eventually smiled. "Yes, I would very much like to see this place! Perhaps I can pay you a visit someday?"

Melissa nodded. "That would be wonderful, Blaze. My doors are always open to you."

"Thank you, miss!"

"You can call me Melissa, Blaze."

"Then Melissa I shall call you!"

"There you are!" a tiny voice said from the garden. "I was wondering where you'd gotten off to! Our guests finally woke, I see."

A new pixie flew up to Blaze and Melissa. He wore similar clothing as Blaze, but also wore a sword, a bow strapped to his back, and a small quiver full of arrows on his hip. "I am Stin, miss."

"My name is Melissa. It is nice to meet you, Stin."

Stin smiled, leaned over and kissed Blaze on the cheek, took his hand, and turned towards the garden. "I see your companions are enjoying our glade?"

Melissa turned back towards the trees. "They seem to be, yes! I was telling Blaze here how beautiful this place is."

Stin smiled. "We are grateful to call this our home," he said. "Blaze and I live just there!" Stin pointed skyward.

For the first time since they arrived in this portion of the cave, Melissa noticed thousands of tiny glowing windows dotting the cavern walls, and just as many minuscule doors next to them. They spiraled all the way around the garden, stretching up and up towards the open sky above.

"Oh my! You must have a wonderful view!" Melissa said.

Stin and Blaze both nodded. "Would you like to see our home?" Stin asked.

Blaze nodded. "Perhaps we can have some tea? It's a wonderful night for it!"

Melissa looked back up to the tiny doors and windows high above. "I would love to guys, I just don't—"

Before Melissa could finish her sentence, everything around her fell away into almost complete darkness. A split second later, she was back, only now she was hovering mid-air, and to her right floated Blaze and Stin. She was now the same size as the two pixies, and somehow flying!

"I love tea!" Blaze said, and took Melissa's hand. Stin took the other.

53

Jack sat up, wiped beads of sweat from his forehead, and scanned the empty room. The fire burned low, and every candle was now cold. How long had he slept? Was it nighttime yet? Had Elm's grace period ended, and if so, was she actively hunting them now?

Jack took several deep breaths and calmed himself. As he did, he moved his arm and inspected the spot where the arrow had struck him. A tiny scar remained, but other than that, he seemed to have healed. That meant he'd slept for at least several hours. He opened the hand he'd used to hold the glowing gem all night. His hand ached, and to Jack's surprise, the gem no longer shined. Instead, its entire surface was jet black and lined with thousands of minuscule fractures. A moment later, the gem disintegrated into a fine mist and vanished. Jack knew he'd drained himself over the last few days, but to such a degree that his body would draw so much power from an otherwise indestructible artifact stunned and worried him.

As he climbed out of the bed, he saw that the pixies had not only cleaned his clothing, they had replaced several pieces of it. He'd heard tales of pixie hospitality—they were legendary —but until now, Jack had never had the pleasure of experiencing it. The stories held up so far.

As he dressed, Jack found himself wondering about Melissa. Had she slept well? Had she regained some of her strength? Was the vampiric blood still coursing through her veins, and if so, was it still helping her? And if it was, how much longer would it go on doing so?

"Thank you, Michael," Jack said as he pulled on his boots.

Jack wondered if Michael had slept well, and if his wounds had healed. The vampire had taken quite a beating in the last twenty-four hours, not to mention he had lost his home, been swept away to a strange land, and promptly been kidnapped by beings he had no clue even existed. Jack wondered how the vampire was holding up mentally as well as physically. A pang of guilt rose in the elf's stomach and jolted him. He'd have Michael's home rebuilt as soon as possible.

Jack tore a piece of warm bread from a small loaf that had been placed on the nightstand and took a bite. Just as he expected, it was delicious. Jack looked around the room, made certain he had all of his belongings, and left. He needed to check on Melissa.

"We were beginning to debate whether or not we should wake you," Invyl said as soon as Jack entered the hallway.

"Hello, Invyl," Jack said. "How long were we asleep?"

The pixie smiled. "The sun set not long ago. Your friend should be safe outside of Droll now."

"That long?" Jack said, and began walking towards Melissa's room. Invyl floated alongside.

"You must have been very tired," the pixie said. "Not to mention your injuries. We took the liberty of cleaning and repairing your clothing. We also bathed and groomed the dogs. They are extraordinary creatures, I must confess! Though their language is quite strange. Regardless, I hope that is acceptable?"

"It is, and thank you very much, Invyl."

"Do you require any further aid? Your shoulder was damaged quite badly from what I was told."

"I believe I am healed, Invyl. You are very kind, thank you. One of our group, Rebecca...her arm is in need of attention."

"Yes, we noticed that. Mott, a very good friend of mine, did administer a healing draught to her arm, though it still requires aid. I presume you would like to check in on your friends, then?"

"Yes, please."

Invyl nodded. "The woman called Melissa has taken Thorn and Nanook to one of our glades; it is not far from here. Her sister still sleeps, as does the"—Invyl cleared his throat—"vampire."

Jack stopped and turned; Invyl returned his gaze.

"Invyl...."

"Your secret is safe with us," Invyl said. "I do not know who hunts you, nor why. But I do know kind hearts when I feel them. They are far, far harder to hide than dark or stained ones. Your companion Michael has one of the kindest hearts I have ever felt."

Jack made a small bow to the pixie, and Invyl bowed back.

Invyl clapped his hands once. "Besides! Things can be so boring here at times! It has been a pleasure sharing a small amount of your adventure with you!"

Jack laughed. "I am glad I have met you, Invyl."

"Likewise."

Jack sighed. "But I must warn you...I do not know who hunts us, or the extent to which they will go to succeed. I am worried what might happen to those whom we encounter, and worse, to those who give us aid. Please, Invyl, for your sake as well as the others here, I implore you, speak of our passing to no one. Mention the vampire to none."

"I give you my word," the pixie said.

"And I give you my word that when this is over, should we prevail, I will return to this place to express my gratitude."

Invyl smiled. "That is not necessary, Jack. Just promise to come back and tell us all about it!"

"I promise."

"Now, where to?"

"I should see to Rebecca. Her arm requires my attention now that I have regained my strength."

Invyl nodded. "This way, my friend."

54

Blaze and Stin guided Melissa up above the trees within the glade and towards one of the small wooden doors nestled into the rock face. They seemed to carry her along, much as they'd carried them all through the forest earlier. Apparently, all they had to do was touch you, and then off you'd go with whatever pixie held you, wherever that pixie wanted you to go! It was a helpless feeling, but considering her current situation, Melissa was quite fine being flown skyward to a magical home in order to have a nice cup of tea with two magical pixies in a magical cave overlooking a magical indoor forest.

When they reached the door, Melissa noticed a tiny balcony just below the set of windows next to it. There were several chairs, three small tables, and two minuscule potted plants growing there. The door was carved out of wood that had either been stained a wonderful shade of burgundy, or was naturally that color; she didn't know which.

"Here we are!" Stin said, and ushered Melissa and Blaze inside.

Melissa glided into the home and was set down in a slow, gentle motion. Her feet landed on a beautiful green carpet with gold tassels running along two of its borders. Blaze followed, and Stin closed the door.

"Welcome to our home!" Blaze said.

Melissa inspected her new surroundings, a huge smile spreading across her cheeks. A fire burned to her left, and two plush chairs rested before it. A small table sat between them, holding two silver steins. Beyond the living room, another long wooden table, this one stained a wonderful shade of blue, stretched off into another room. It was surrounded by dozens of what looked to be well-used chairs. Two rose-colored glass bowls filled with what looked like small white berries sat at either end of the table. A kitchen lay beyond that, complete with wood-burning stove and an island littered with fresh herbs and vegetables.

"Do you enjoy honey or cream in your tea?" Blaze asked as he made his way into the kitchen.

Melissa had to clear her throat before she could answer. Her brain was being bombarded with so many new images, ideas, sights, and sounds that she was finding it hard to speak. The mere fact she was standing in what amounted to a dollhouse carved into the side of a cave wall was enough to give her pause.

"I..." Melissa paused. "Both, please."

"Exactly how I enjoy it," Stin said. "Please! Come outside, it's a lovely evening to sit on the terrace."

Melissa followed Stin outside while Blaze rummaged around in the kitchen. The view was breathtaking in that it *literally* took Melissa's breath away, and she had to grab the railing until her heart quit fluttering and her head stopped spinning. Before and below them, an endless void dropped away. They were so high up that Melissa couldn't see the ground she'd just moments before been standing on—only a hazy green. Several of the trees here reached even higher than the pixies' home; from Melissa's new perspective, they seemed so immense that her mind was having a difficult time making sense of their enormity.

"Are you all right, miss?" Stin asked.

Melissa realized she was gripping the metal railing quite

hard and glanced over at the pixie. "I never really thought I was afraid of heights. I guess maybe I am."

Stin smiled and placed a warm hand on Melissa's shoulder. "No harm will come to you, I promise. You will not fall; in fact, you couldn't fall if you wanted to! Blaze and I would not allow it."

Melissa chuckled. "Thank you, Stin."

Blaze walked out onto the terrace, three steaming mugs of tea floating just in front of him. One glided right to Melissa, the other to Stin. Melissa reached out and took the mug; the tea smelled divine.

"Such service!" she said, smiling at Blaze. "Thank you!"

"It is my pleasure!" Blaze said, "It is not often that we allow those who are not from here to visit. The least we could do is offer you a cup of tea. It's made from dried akala berries and silver-tips!"

"He's so tea-obsessed," Stin said, and winked at Blaze.

"Tea is life, Stin! You should know that. It's how we met!"

The three sat down, and Melissa took a sip. She was amazed at how sweet and wonderful the concoction was. "It's very, very good! Like a raspberry vanilla tea. Thank you again!"

Stin and Blaze both smiled and sipped from their mugs.

"Have you lived together for very long?" Melissa asked.

Stin chuckled, and Blaze smiled.

"I would say the first century or two were somewhat...erratic," Stin said.

Blaze raised his eyebrows. "Agreed."

"But for the last few decades, I would say that things have settled into a rather comfortable norm."

"Wow!" Melissa said, "That's so, so long."

The pixies both looked at Melissa, confused.

Melissa cleared her throat. "I mean. I guess….Well, you see, I've never met anyone who's lived that long, much less been together anywhere near that amount of time. It's very impressive."

The pixies looked at one another and then back at Melissa.

"How old are you, miss? If you don't mind us asking," Blaze said.

Stin slapped the other pixie on the shoulder. "Blaze! That is not very polite in some societies!"

Melissa smiled. "It's okay. I'm twenty-eight next month!"

Blaze spit out his tea, and Stin threw his head back and laughed.

"I knew it! She's mortal, you silly thing!" Stin said.

Blaze coughed and wiped his chin. "Mortal! I am so sorry!"

"For what?" Melissa asked. "It's okay."

Blaze shook his head. "No, I mean…for not seeing that earlier. Being mortal must, well, it must be so very difficult! We do not meet very many"—Blaze looked uncomfortable with the word—"mortals like you. Actually, I think you might be my first!"

Melissa reached over and patted Blaze on the knee. "It's okay, Blaze. I'm pretty used to it by now! I haven't met very many immortals."

"We mustn't keep you then!" Blaze said, and stood.

"It's okay, Blaze, I can finish my tea," Melissa said.

Stin took Blaze's hand and pulled him back down to his

chair. "Blaze, you are embarrassing yourself."

Blaze sat back down and took another sip of his tea. "What is it like, miss? To be so, well, so fragile?"

Stin slapped Blaze on the shoulder again. "Blaze! You are so unfiltered at times. You do know that, don't you?"

"I'm sorry," Blaze said, and stared down into his tea.

Melissa thought about that for a moment. "It's okay Blaze. To be honest, I wish I wasn't so fragile sometimes. I don't mean immortal, or, maybe that's the wrong word to describe your kind. I mean, I wish I was healthier. I have a—" Melissa stopped to wipe away a tear before it could spill from her eye. She took a deep breath and continued. "I have a disease. It's not a very nice one, and there's not really much I can do about it. The doctors do what they can, and give me all kinds of medicines, but, well, it's hard. I'm not sure I have much time left, if I'm honest." Melissa looked up and noticed the pixies' eyes were watering. "...don't, guys. I didn't tell you that to upset you! You asked what's it's like, and I thought that was the best way I could answer you. Do you understand?"

Blaze nodded and swallowed hard. "I think so, miss."

Melissa offered the pixie a smile. "I think that being human, or being mortal, just means you have to make the most of what little time you do have, you know? Live each day to its fullest! Celebrate the things you can—like this tea! Or like meeting the two of you! I could live to be a thousand, and I wouldn't trade *that* for anything! I can say I met two new friends today!"

Blaze and Stin maintained their composure for several seconds, then burst into ugly sobs.

Melissa set down her tea and reached over to comfort both pixies. "Guys, guys, it's okay!"

"You are so brave!" Stin said between hiccups and sobs.

"So, so brave! And kind," Blaze said while wiping his nose.

"Thank you," Melissa said. "But guys, really, don't feel sorry for me, okay?"

It took a while, but the pixies regained most of their composure.

Stin took a deep breath and another long drink of his tea. His face was red and swollen when he looked back up. "So tell us, Melissa. What brings you here?"

"That is something I have been very curious about myself," Blaze said. His face was just as swollen as Stin's, if not more so. "There's talk everywhere of the visitors, of you, but none appear to know much about you."

Melissa sat back and began telling the two pixies all about the events which had led her, Becky, Jack, and Michael to this fantastic place.

55

Michael opened his eyes and scanned the room. He was alone this time. When he didn't see the dogs, his heart began to race, but he recalled them opting to stay with the girls for the night and relaxed. He was so used to seeing them as soon as he woke up each night that their absence startled him quite a bit. That made him curious as to the time.

"Alexa, what—" Michael sighed. "...dammit."

Michael climbed across and out of the bed. The floor was warm, which surprised him considering it the fire was so low. He scanned the room for his clothes and noticed they'd been replaced by garments very different in appearance from his own. Michael walked over to the shelves and picked up the shirt folded there. It was a billowy, long-sleeved design, open at the neck and so black that the fabric seemed to absorb some of the light striking it. The cloth felt smooth, almost silk-like, but weighed quite a bit more. The pants were black as well, and they appeared to be a type of leather. Michael held them up and took note of the reinforced knees and backside. There was a strange veining on the pants which looked almost as if tiny plants had grown up from the bottom of each leg, all the way to the waist, and rested somewhere just below the surface of the material. The effect was beautiful.

A pair of boots sat on the floor beneath the clothing. They were tall—Michael guessed they would come to just below his knees—cuffed at the top, and also deep black in color. A black leather belt, black gloves, a kind of sleeveless vest—also black —and a beautiful knife, complete with black leather sheath, completed the set.

"I'm going to look like a ninja," Michael said, and grinned.

Michael got dressed and was so impressed with the fit and feel of his new clothes that he almost forgot how much black he was now wearing...*almost*. The boots might have been his favorite new item; they were not only comfortable, they were almost silent as he walked around the room. Unless he tried to make noise, the footwear was deathly quiet.

"Yup. Ninja."

The knife was a thing of beauty, and Michael wasn't surprised at all to find the blade, all six or seven inches of it, was also black. The edge was razor sharp and shaved his forearm with ease. The handle was a black stained wood with a diamond pattern etched into its face that made gripping the knife easy and it slipping in his hand unlikely. Michael had no training whatsoever with bladed weapons, but if he needed to, he was positive he would be able to figure something out. Maybe he'd ask Jack for some lessons; the elf had a damn sword, after all. And didn't Becky have a pretty scary-looking knife? Michael was positive he remembered seeing her brandishing one, and she'd looked like she knew how to use it. Maybe he'd ask her?

Michael hesitated about putting on the vest, but when he noticed all of the hidden pockets on the inside, he thought better of it. He even slipped on the gloves, though he couldn't imagine why he'd wear them. Still, better to wear them at least here so as not to offend whoever it was that had left them for him. It took Michael a minute to figure out what to do with the knife. The sheath had a small leather belt attached to it, but nothing large enough to go around his waist. He was about to stuff the blade into one of his pockets, or into the back of his pants, when he thought to try the strap on his leg. Sure enough, the sheath fit perfectly around his calf, the blade's handle just visible below the cuff of his right boot.

Michael wondered where the rest of his clothes had gone, but didn't really care. They were ripped and torn to no end, and if the pixies had tossed them out, then so be it. He might miss that t-shirt, though—a Ramones shirt he'd had since he was a teenager. Michael grabbed the little blue cooler he'd placed on one of the shelves and opened the lid. The ice inside had long melted, and the last two bags of blood floated in the water. They were still cool to the touch, but he'd have to drink them soon. A small pang of fear reached out and stabbed at Michael for a minute. He'd have to find more blood eventually. That could be a problem.

Michael closed the cooler, scanned the area for anything he might have forgotten, and went in search of his dogs and his new friends. He wondered what time it was as he left.

56

"Becky?"

Becky stirred beneath the covers and moaned.

Jack sat down on the edge of the bed and placed a hand on what he guessed to be the lump's shoulder. "Rebecca?"

Becky bolted upright, her blade pressed against Jack's throat before she realized what was happening.

The elf held up his hands and smiled. "I am sorry that I startled you."

Becky blinked and focused in on Jack's face. "Jesus, Jack! What...I could have killed you!"

Jack smiled. "You are very adept with that blade; I believe you could have. I am sorry to wake you. We did try the door for several minutes."

"We?"

"Invyl was here. When he saw you were still sleeping, he left in search of Melissa."

Becky lowered her knife and scanned the room. She and Jack were alone, and the door was shut again. A vague memory of Melissa taking the dogs out earlier floated out of the haze. When she looked back at Jack, she noticed he was looking away as they spoke. That was when Becky realized she was sitting there topless.

Becky sighed and drew the covers back over her breasts.

"Sorry, you startled me. I didn't think to get dressed before fending off my attacker."

Jack chuckled and stood up. He walked over to the fire and kicked one of the smoldering logs with the tip of his boot. The flames danced back to life. "I am here to help you with your arm, if that is all right?"

"You can look now, Jack," Becky said.

Jack turned; Becky had propped her back against the headboard and drawn the blankets up. "Does it still pain you?" he asked.

Becky moved her arm and was about to say something, when she gasped and drew in a quick, sharp hiss.

"I take that as a yes," Jack said with a concerned look.

Becky clenched her teeth, her jaw rippling, "Yeah, I think I slept on it. I know I rolled over on it a couple of times. Woke Melissa up more than once, but she just rubbed my head and wiped away the tears until I fell back asleep each time."

"She has a kind heart."

Becky studied the elf for a moment. "Yes, she does. You be careful with it."

Jack looked her in the eyes and nodded. "I intend to," he said. "I swear it."

Becky grinned and patted Jack on the thigh. When she did, she hissed again, and pinched her eyes shut for a moment.

"I am sorry I could not offer you more assistance before you slept," Jack said.

Becky nodded. "It's okay. It was just a long night."

"That it was," Jack said, and knelt onto the floor next to the bed. He motioned to her injured arm. "If I may?"

273

Becky held out her arm. A large bruise and a considerable amount of swelling had taken up residence overnight. "Is this going to hurt?"

"Not at all," Jack said, placing his hands above and below Becky's injury. As before, a warm golden light flooded from the elf's palms.

Becky closed her eyes and sighed. "Oh, my God." A second later, her entire body relaxed, and Becky slumped down into the pillows. "Oh, my God, that feels sooooo good."

As the light grew brighter, so did the warmth. Along with the heat, Becky noticed the sensation of tingles, almost like electric feathers being brushed across her skin. The feathers passed, and a feeling much like being massaged settled in. Jack closed his eyes, and as soon as he did, Becky felt her entire arm beginning to grow warmer, then cold, then warm and back to cold again for a minute or so. The sensation spread to her entire body; it felt incredible.

"That should be much better now," Jack said, and removed his hands.

Becky opened her eyes and looked down. The first thing she noticed was the blanket had fallen away again, and Jack was averting his gaze for a second time. She covered herself and smiled. "That was amazing Jack; thank you so much," she said. She wiggled her fingers and extended her arm. The pain was gone, as were the bruise and the swelling.

"You are most welcome," Jack said, and stood. "I will leave you to get dressed. I'm afraid we need to depart very soon, as we can not remain here much longer."

"Sure thing. Do you know where Melissa is?"

"Yes, she is not far from here. Apparently she took the dogs to a kind of garden, according to Invyl. He has gone to look for her now, and I am on my way there as well. Would you like to accompany me?"

"Yeah, that would be great. I just need to get dressed."

"I will wait for you outside."

Becky laughed. "Jack, you don't have to do that. You can just, you know, avert your gaze."

"I..." Jack started, and then stopped. He shifted his feet and stared into the fire.

"You're cute," Becky said, and climbed out of the bed. "You're dating my sister. I'm not going to hit on you, goofball."

"Thank you. I mean...I don't know what...." Jack stopped and cleared his throat.

Becky laughed at that. She enjoyed making Jack squirm a bit. And to be honest, she didn't mind flirting with him just a little. It had been a long time since she'd been anywhere near naked with a man in the immediate vicinity.

"The pixies have replaced your clothing," Jack said, pointing to the wall and shelves across the room. "I believe they also left you items to bathe with."

Becky walked over to the clothing and smiled. "Wow!" She stripped down and gave herself a little duck bath. The water was warm and smelled amazing. She glanced over at Jack and felt a little bad for making him uncomfortable, but not enough to ask him to leave. He might be her sister's new beau, but she wasn't above a little innocent flustering. She really liked that he had averted his gaze and seemed so uncomfortable. Not because it boosted her confidence, but because it reaffirmed his obviously dedication to her little sister. A lesser man might have snuck a peek, *or worse*. It wouldn't have been the first time.

"Wanna get my back?" Becky asked.

"Rebecca—"

"Jack, I'm kidding! I'm just messing with you."

The elf said nothing, and Becky felt bad.

"I'm sorry, Jack. I'm just having a little fun at your expense. Plus, if you'd agreed, I would have kicked your ass for cheating on my sister."

Jack chuckled. "Ahh."

"Friends?" Becky asked.

"Of course."

Becky got dressed, marveling at the clothing and how well it fit. When she was done, she noticed a new knife had been placed nearby, complete with a double sheath and straps.

"I'm decent," Becky said. "Can you, uh, can you help me with this?" Becky asked and held up the gear.

Jack turned and inspected the sheath. "Ahh, that is very nice!"

The pixies had left not only a new knife for Becky, but it sat in a sheath that would hold two knives in a "X" pattern at the small of her back, hilts down for quick access. Jack showed Becky how the straps were fastened and how to adjust everything. He walked over to the bed, retrieved the other knife, and slid it into the empty sheath, where it snapped in place. It fit as if the sheath had been custom designed for it, and for all Jack knew, it probably had. The pixies were incredibly adept with their magic.

"This..." Jack said, holding up the old sheath Becky had worn, "...could be used later if you find the new ones uncomfortable, or unnecessary."

Becky reached behind her and drew both blades. The new knife was almost identical to her MK3, though just a bit longer, and double-sided. The handles were also very similar.

"Ooooh, I like this!" she said, smiling.

Jack smiled back. "Let's hope you don't have to use them."

"What's the fun in that?" Becky asked, adding a wink.

Jack smiled.

Becky put the knives away. She tiptoed up and kissed Jack on the cheek. "Thank you for my new arm, Jack. You're a good guy. I'm glad you and Melissa found each other."

"I am, too, Becky," Jack said. "And you are a very good sister."

Becky smiled. "Look, before we go, can we talk for a second?"

"Of course."

Becky took a deep breath. "Do you think you can help Smurf?"

Jack's eyes dropped to the floor. "I do not know, Becky. But I hope so. I was not anticipating this, whatever *this* is, happening to us. That is my main concern at the moment."

"I know, I know. I don't think any one of us was ready for whatever that was all about. I know I wasn't ready for any of this! What I meant was..." Becky lifted Jack's chin and looked into his eyes. "What I meant was, why Michael? Didn't you say you two just met? So why him?"

Jack looked Becky directly in the eyes. "Have you ever wondered if some things just happen because they are meant to happen? I do not mean fate, or, well, maybe I do. But that some things, some events just occur because they are meant to?"

"I guess, sure. My ex sprained his ankle on the morning

he was slated to deploy on a mission in Afghanistan. He got benched. The helicopter he was supposed to be on was shot down later that same day. Everyone onboard died. He lived."

"I am sorry, Becky. And you do understand," Jack said.

Becky wiped away a tear. "Yes."

"I believe I encountered Michael for a reason. I believe we met so that I could discover a way to help Melissa. Vampires are so, so rare, you understand. Some say they are even extinct. And what occurs the very night I see Melissa again? For the first time in over a year? A vampire literally flies out of the sky to say hello."

"Fate," Becky said.

"Fate."

"And you think that, what, his blood might be able to help her?"

"It certainly stopped or at least helped with whatever was happening the other night."

"Yeah." Becky wiped away another tear and looked up at Jack. "What if it doesn't help her, though? What if she has more of his blood and just, she just keeps getting sick?"

Jack placed his hands on Becky's shoulders. "I do not know."

Becky sat there for a moment, silent. Her eyes darted back and forth as if she was thinking of a million things at once, and after a minute more, she fell into Jack's arms, burying her face in his chest. She began to sob. "She's too good of a person to die, Jack. She's too, she's just too damn…."

Jack hugged Becky back. "I know. I also know that vampires do not appear to fall ill, ever."

Becky pulled away and stared up at Jack. "What do you mean?"

Jack sighed again and shook his head. "I do not know if Michael can help her, but if he can, if his blood alone does not cure her," Jack paused and cleared his throat, "turning her might prove to be the answer."

"Into a vampire, you mean?"

"Yes. Becky, I know that is not—"

"Great! Let's turn her into a vampire! I don't care! If that helps her, if that cures her, then I say get rid of the garlic, toss the holy water, and get Michael to turn her!"

Jack was caught off guard, and his expression showed it. "I... I did not think you would react this way."

"She's my sister, Jack. I'd do anything for her—or to her, in this case! Do you think he will? I mean, can he? Michael? Can he turn her?"

"He does not know," Jack said. "He has never attempted it before, and he could not remember exactly what was done to him. He is very young."

"So you talked about it?"

"Briefly."

"But was he at least willing to think about it? Maybe try?"

"I believe he is, and I believe I know how it is done," Jack said. "There is much more to discuss, however. There are"—Jack paused—"for the time being, Melissa appears to have reacted very well to Michael's blood. So I think we should focus on who is hunting us, and why, for now. We cannot help Melissa if we are not here to do so."

Becky nodded. "Right, right. Thank you, Jack. I mean it, thank you for everything. And you're right. I do believe that sometimes things happen for a reason."

Jack nodded. "Do not thank me yet. I still have no idea why we have been targeted, or by whom."

"Well, thank you anyway. And yes, let's go do some hunting of our own! I owe that green bitch and her dragon some payback."

Becky grabbed her backpack as well as Melissa's, which Jack took. "Should we see if Michael's up yet?"

Jack smiled. "Yes. After you," he said, and motioned to the door.

As they left the room, a sick feeling curled up in Jack's stomach. He found himself wondering why he withheld the information that the process of turning Melissa might very well end her already fragile life—likely *would* kill her, in fact, at least from what he understood of the process. It wasn't like him to keep something like that secret, and it nauseated him.

57

Michael opened his door just before Becky could knock on it. "Boo!" he said, grinning.

Becky jumped back and smiled. "Well, hello, Princess Bride," she said, scanning Michael from head to toe.

"Huh? Ohhhh, I get it," Michael said. "I was going for more of a ninja kinda look!" He held up his hands in a mock martial artist pose.

Becky shook her head. "Nope, Princess Bride for sure. All you need is a sword and a mask."

Michael laughed. "I guess I can live with that. Hi, Jack."

Jack nodded. "Michael, I take it you slept well? Have you recovered?"

"I think so; little stiff, but otherwise, I'm good. You guys?"

Jack nodded, and Becky moved her arm about.

"Think so," Becky said. "Fastest I've ever had a broken bone heal."

"Had a lot of broken bones, huh?" Michael asked.

"Eleven, last time I counted."

Michael's eyes widened. "Seriously?"

"Yup."

"Wow, impressive! So what's the plan? You guys even know what time it is?"

"I was going to ask you," Becky said. "Our phones died yesterday."

"It is just past sunset," Jack said. "We were going to find Melissa and the dogs. She took them out earlier, and Invyl says they are in a garden of sorts not far from here."

"Come along, Westley!" Becky said, and headed down the hallway.

"Yeah, so I guess that's gunna stick?"

Becky laughed. "Oh, yeah."

Jack leaned over to Michael as they followed Becky down the hall. "Who is the princess bride?"

Michael laughed. "If we get out of this thing alive, I'll show you."

The three made their way down the hallway, slowing just enough to occasionally inspect the paintings and artwork adorning the walls. Michael didn't remember any of it, and barely recalled much of the giant cave they now found themselves in. Music floated through the air, as did the scent of flowers and the occasional spice. The air was cool but not cold, and the light from all of the candles and floating sconces was warm and cheerful.

"It's too bad we can't just hide here, ya know? Or at least stay here while we try to figure this whole thing out," Michael mused.

"I was thinking the same thing," Becky said. "I keep thinking I'm dreaming, or that I'm in some sort of elaborate theme park or something!"

Jack leaned back over to Michael. "What is a theme park?"

The vampire chuckled. "Man, I have so many awesome things to show you when we get back home." He clapped the elf on the back.

"You guys are awake!" a voice said from just ahead.

Jack and Michael looked up as Becky jogged down the hallway and hugged Melissa. Thorn and Nanook trotted over to Michael, and three pixies floated nearby.

"Wow! Look at you," Becky said, giving Melissa and her new attire a once-over.

"Twinsies!" Melissa laughed. "And Michael, whoa, you look —"

"As you wish," Becky interrupted.

Melissa covered her mouth and giggled. "Oh, my God! He does!"

"Yeah, yeah," Michael said.

"Hello, Melissa. How are you feeling?" Jack asked.

Melissa walked over to Jack, gave him a hug, and reached for his hand. "I feel wonderful. I just had tea with my new friends! Blaze, Stin, this is Jack, Michael, and my lovely sister Becky."

"A pleasure to meet you," Blaze said.

"Greetings," Stin said, and made a little bow.

"It seems your companions thoroughly enjoyed the garden," Invyl said, floating down to Thorn and Nanook. He pried a small leaf from Nanook's hair and let it fall to the ground. "I wasn't sure they were going to come back out, if I'm honest!"

Michael reached down and rubbed each dog's head. "They love the woods, that's for sure. Thanks for looking out for for them," he said, as much to the girls as to Invyl. "Oh, and thank you for the new clothes! Mine were pretty banged up."

"Yes, thank you!" Melissa and Becky said in unison.

"New?" Invyl asked. "Oh no, they are not new; those are your old clothes! We just…improved them, or rather, coaxed them into their proper forms—their natural forms for this place."

Michael looked back down at his solid black attire. "I'm not sure I understand any of that, man, but I do appreciate it!"

Invyl nodded. "Think of it as allowing something to be whatever that something wishes to be, or feels as if it should be."

Michael smiled. "Yeah, nope. But I'll take your word for it!"

"I'm afraid we must be going, Invyl. Your hospitality was most generous," Jack said. "I will not forget it."

"You are most welcome," Invyl said. "And I must apologize again for earlier, Michael. For your abduction. There are times when our trials are a bit, how do I describe them…?"

"Terrifying?" Michael said, winking at the pixie.

"Yeah, that's kinda what I was going to say," Becky said. She, too, was smiling.

Invyl smiled back and bowed again. "Well, I am glad we met, regardless of the circumstances. Such encounters are so very rare for us. Most do not end quite as pleasantly."

Blaze and Stin fluttered up to Melissa. Each pixie was now dressed head to toe in armor, and both carried a sword and bow, as well as quiver of arrows.

"We have discussed this with Invyl," Blaze said.

"And with one another," Stin said.

"Where our friend Melissa and her family go, so shall we," Blaze said.

"Your enemies are now our enemies," Stin said.

Jack smiled and held up his hand. "You are very kind, but—"

Blaze landed on Melissa's left shoulder. "Your enemies are

now ours."

"We will not accept a refusal, master Elf," Stin said.

Jack stammered and looked at Invyl.

Invyl shrugged. "I have never once been able to talk these two out of anything. I won't pretend to attempt so now," he said, and smiled. "Besides, they are quite powerful warriors in their own right. I suspect they will prove valuable in whatever fight lies before you."

"Awesome!" Michael exclaimed. He clapped Jack on the back again. "Pixie power! I love it!"

58

Thorn and Nanook raced passed the sapphire spires and stopped at the trailhead leading off into the dark forest beyond.

"Thank you again, Invyl," Michael said. "I'm glad you kidnapped me, man!"

Invyl laughed. "We've never abducted a kinder soul."

What amounted to several thousand pixies had escorted the group to the mouth of Droll, and they now hovered about as everyone said their goodbyes. Graffell shone bright through the otherwise black night, casting a strange pinkish hue on everything beyond the forest and just into the mouth of the cavern. It was enough light that even Melissa and Becky could see quite well.

Melissa turned to Invyl, Blaze and Stin floating nearby. "I really hope we can come back and visit."

"Me, too!" Becky said. "And thank you for my new knife! It's amazing."

Michael reached down and retrieved his blade from the sheath on his leg. "Yeah, ditto on that, man. This thing is awesome!"

Invyl smiled. "It was our pleasure."

Jack reached into his pocket and withdrew one of the glowing gems the Dren had left him after their attack. He extended his hand and offered it to Invyl, who had to use both hands to accept the gift.

Invyl's eyes grew wide, and his mouth dropped open for a moment. "Jack, this is far too valuable."

Jack raised a hand in protest. "A small pittance for your friendship, Invyl. I hope this serves you well."

Invyl looked back up to the group and nodded. "You are most kind. This will grow for a thousand years, and a thousand years beyond that."

Blaze and Stin waved their goodbyes along with everyone else. The group made their way into the forest and soon disappeared into the shadows, the dogs leading the way. Each pixie began to glow, and each grew brighter the further into the shadows the group walked—something Becky and Melissa thanked them for.

After a minute, Michael turned back to get one more look at the pixies and their home, and just as before when he'd looked backwards after Jack had used the magical bookcase, nothing remained—only a dark path snaking its way through the trees. Even the mountain was gone.

Michael shook his head. "I'm not sure I'll get used to this place anytime soon."

When Becky looked over at him, he motioned behind them. He chuckled as Becky saw the same thing and gasped.

"Where are we going now, Jack?" Melissa asked.

"I feel that Erendroll will be safe for everyone. From there, I can go in search of answers. We need to—"

"Wait, you're going to leave us there?" Melissa asked.

Jack sighed. "Melissa, we have barely been here a day, and look what has already happened."

"Dude, that butterfly wasn't my fault," Michael said.

Jack glanced over his shoulder. "No, it was not. I only meant that—"

"And besides!" Becky said. "Look what happened! We got a place to rest, some new clothes, and made some new friends!"

Jack stopped and turned to the group. "I am afraid—" He stopped. "I am afraid I am unable to protect you here. What happened earlier could have just as easily proven deadly, or worse."

"Jack," Melissa said, and placed a hand on the elf's arm. "It's not your job to protect us. We're in this together, remember?"

"He is right, though, miss," Blaze said.

"I have to agree," Stin said. "This is no place for mortals."

Jack nodded. "Thank you both."

"That being said," Stin continued, "...there is strength in numbers."

"I hate to pick sides here," Michael said. "But I agree with Jack. Yeah, I could have gotten us in a bit of trouble back there, and he's right, it worked out. But this place is nuts! I mean, until yesterday, I thought I was pretty much invincible! And those little guys?" Michael pointed at the pixies. "Those guys strung me up like a piñata and there was like, literally nothing I could do about it. And that was just because I picked up a butterfly with an arrow in its wing! I mean, they knocked poor Jack here for a loop, too, not to mention, they strung up Thorn and Nanook along with you guys, and they did all that like it was just another day at the office!"

"Guys, we don't have time for this," Becky said. "And I mean that literally. No one knows what time it actually is, and if we're going to get somewhere safe before morning, then we need to keep going. We can discuss who's protecting who and all of that shit after we've found somewhere to hole up!"

"Your sister makes a good point," Stin said.

"Thanks, little guy."

Stin nodded.

"I agree," Jack said, looking up. "I believe we will have more than enough time to reach the city before dawn."

Nanook and Thorn both barked from further ahead on the trail, and the group carried on. Behind them, deep in the shadows, another figure followed along.

59

The trees were now just as tall and just as dark as they'd been when the group first entered the forest via the trail tome. Becky craned her neck skyward as they walked and wondered aloud exactly how tall they were.

"How tall are the redwoods back home?" Becky asked.

"I think they're two, three hundred feet tall?" Melissa replied.

"Hyperion is like three hundred and eighty feet tall!" Michael said. Both sisters turned in his direction. "It's the name they gave the tallest tree in Redwood National Park."

The sisters stared.

"I watch a lot of documentaries."

"Check out the big brain on Brad!" Becky said.

Michael grinned. "You like that flick?"

Becky nodded. "Who doesn't?"

"Nice."

"Some of these trees reach well into the clouds on certain days, if I remember correctly," Jack said. "Though they grow in a much deeper section of the forest. They can be very dangerous."

"How so?" Melissa said.

"If they fall, they crash into numerous other trees. Their

roots are quite large as well, and their limbs are as big around as some of the trees you see now. You can hear them break, or fall, for quite a long distance."

"We have a home in some of the tallest," Blaze said.

"The Sentinel allows us passage there, as we tend to the trees' needs on a regular basis," Stin said.

Jack glanced over at the two pixies flying nearby. "You've seen Sentinel?"

"We have," Blaze said. "Invyl spent years just trying to approach her."

"Not an easy task," Blaze said.

Stin nodded. "True. She injured him more than once until he was finally able to learn her language. After that, she welcomed us."

"She even grew one of our cities!" Blaze said.

"Who is this Sentinel person?" Melissa asked.

"Sentinel is no person," Blaze replied.

"Sentinel is rumored to be the largest tree known to exist," Jack said.

"Well, she has spoken of even larger," Stin said. "Far larger, and far older."

Jack looked back at the pixies. "Surely you jest?"

The pixies shook their heads.

"Far larger," Blaze said.

"You're talking about a tree?" Michael asked. "A talking tree?"

"You DID bring me to Middle-earth, Smurf!" Becky called ahead to her sister.

Melissa laughed. "I guess I did!"

"Would you believe me if I told you that Tolkien has been here before?" Jack asked.

Melissa stopped dead. So did Becky and Michael.

"Who?" Blaze asked.

"ARE YOU SERIOUS?" Michael asked.

"WAS ALL THAT REAL? I mean, the ring and all?" Becky asked. "HOBBITS?"

Jack began to laugh. "No, no. I am sorry, but that was far too easy."

"Dude!" Becky said, and punched Jack in the arm.

"I apologize," the elf said, but he continued to chuckle.

Stin turned to Blaze. "Tolkien?"

Blaze just shrugged.

"Yeah, not cool, man!" Michael said. "I wanted to live in the Shire when I was a kid."

Jack continued to laugh and proceeded along the trail. "My apologies, I very much needed to laugh."

The group walked for another several minutes before Jack stopped everyone and looked skyward. The trees were so tall here, and the canopy so thick, that no amount of sky could be seen.

"One moment." Jack flew up into the canopy and disappeared.

"Yeah, be right back." Michael followed Jack.

When he broke through the last of the limbs and leaves, Michael gasped. The sky was not just filled with stars—it was positively brimming with them. The forest of trees below looked like an angry dark ocean, rolling and churning in the night, but it was beautiful at the same time. Millions of glowing insects—or for all that Michael could tell, beings like the pixies—glided about above the trees. Sometimes they would flicker, or flash, and sometimes they would pulse in a slow, rhythmic pattern. Some did not flash at all, but maintained a constant warm glow. There were green, yellow, orange, pink, and even blue lights drifting about everywhere. Occasionally one or more would dive back below the canopy, and some would race out. It was mesmerizing.

"There," Jack said.

Michael turned and saw his friend pointing in the opposite direction. Not far from where they now found themselves stood an enormous city. Buildings both large and small stretched on and on until it looked as if they continued right into the side of a distant mountain; not up and over, but *into*. No window was lit, no light flickered along the streets, and shadows covered everything. Here and there a tree sprouted through a rooftop. In one instance, several trees held a huge section of building nearly fifty feet in the air, while the rest sat broken on the ground where it had been originally intended to remain.

Michael noted the stillness throughout the city. He half-expected to see some sort of movement, someone walking along a path, an animal moving between the buildings, even a stray dog or two weaving in and around the streets, maybe deer. But nothing moved there at all.

"It looks haunted," Michael said.

"I was thinking the same thing."

"Wait, what? Really? I was kinda joking, man!"

"It seems unnaturally still. Would you agree?"

"Yeah, man, it's just...it looks really creepy. That's where we're going?"

"Yes."

"Well, it doesn't look too far off, maybe twenty, thirty minutes of hiking? Should we just fly everyone there?"

"I think we should conserve our strength," Jack said.

"Okay. Do you want me to scout ahead? See if I can—"

"Wait," Jack said.

"Dude, I won't touch anything this time, I prom—"

Jack dove back into the trees a split second before one of the girls screamed.

60

Michael raced behind Jack, crashing through the branches in an effort to catch up. He hit the ground with an enormous amount of force, throwing dirt and debris into the air, and then spun in all directions. "What is it?"

Jack stood next to the sisters, his arms spread out, forcing them behind him. Blaze and Stin were gone, as were Thorn and Nanook.

"Thorn just charged off into the trees," Melissa said.

Becky had both knives in her hands and was spinning around looking for signs of whatever had scared the dogs. "They bolted! They just, they both bolted. The little guys charged after them."

"Which direction did they go?" Jack asked. "I see nothing."

"THORN! NANOOK!" Michael yelled. He was greeted by silence. "GUYS!"

"I see nothing," Jack said again.

"I'm going," Michael declared, and started off into the trees.

"Michael, wait." Jack pointed.

Something was moving in the shadows. Michael turned towards whatever it was and crouched, ready to act. Thorn bounded into sight, and Nanook followed.

"Guys!" Michael shouted. "What the hell?"

Blaze and Stin appeared behind the dogs and raced back to

the group.

"We are being followed," Stin said. The pixie was breathing hard.

"Whoever it was"—Blaze took a breath—"was fast."

Stin nodded. "Very…fast."

"Are you all right?" Jack asked.

The pixies both nodded and continued to try and catch their breath.

"I am sorry we could not catch them," Blaze said.

Michael crouched down and ruffled the hair on each dog's head. "Good job, guys."

The dogs wagged their tails and turned back to the shadowy trees.

"Remember what I was saying about flying everyone into the city?" Michael said.

Jack nodded. "I think you might be right."

"Okay, then, let's do this," Michael said. He turned to Becky. "You ready for another Air Uber?"

Becky walked over to Michael and took off her backpack. Michael slipped it over one of his shoulders, and Becky put her arms around his neck. "Thank you. If it gets us out of these woods, I'm all for it. This place is creepy," she said.

"You ain't seen nuthin' yet," Michael said.

"What?"

"Just don't thank me yet."

Jack put Melissa's backpack on and scooped her off the ground. "It is not far. Blaze and Stin, can you remain here with Nanook and Thorn until we return?"

"There is no need," Stin said. He landed on the back of Nanook's neck, grabbed two handfuls of hair, and whispered into the dog's ear. Nanook began wagging her tail.

Blaze landed on Thorn and did the same. "We will follow you."

Jack nodded and leapt into the air. Melissa squealed and closed her eyes. Michael followed and watched as the dogs each took several strides and leapt into the air, the pixies secure on their backs.

"You guys okay?" Michael called down to the dogs. Thorn and Nanook both looked in his direction and wagged their tails as they climbed into the sky. Michael swore that if dogs could smile, they were doing it now. Michael turned his head closer to Becky's ear. "What about you? You okay this time?"

"Sure hurts a lot less! Not to mention the lack of rain."

"Five stars, remember?" Michael said. "It's not easy arranging good weather like this!"

Jack cleared the treetops a moment later, as did Michael. They turned toward Erendroll and raced towards the city. Blaze, Stin, and the dogs followed close behind.

"Oh, my God," Becky said above the sound of the racing wind. "Is that where we're going?"

"Seems like it," Michael said.

"It looks so...."

"Yeah, I told you not to thank me yet."

Becky watched as the city grew closer and closer. The buildings looked strange, not just old, and overgrown with various vines and plants, but *strange*—as if the buildings had been grown out of either stone itself, or a mixture of wood and stone, instead of being built by hand. She'd certainly never seen anything like it before.

As they flew above the first of the smaller buildings, Becky noted how dark, how alone and quiet the city seemed. She hugged Michael a little harder. Michael noticed the hug, and felt Becky's heart begin to race a little more than it already had been. He could even smell the adrenalin that began pumping through her system.

"I'm not going to let anything happen to you guys," Michael said. "Okay? Jack and I are way more prepared now than before."

Becky nodded and kissed Michael on the cheek. Michael's heart began to race, too.

61

Jack found the building he was looking for and began a slow descent. As they drew closer to the ground, he scanned the area and saw no immediate cause for alarm. He'd been here years and years before, and even then the city had seemed a little strange. Nothing really disconcerting, just strange—but he'd also explored the city in the daytime.

"No one lives here anymore?" Melissa asked as Jack set her down.

"Not for a very long time, no."

Michael and Becky landed a moment later, followed by Blaze, Stin, and the dogs. Once on the ground, the pixies flew up and towards the building Jack pointed out. It was a tall structure, and what appeared to have once been bright red tiles covered the roof, which came to multiple points at various locations. At its tallest, the structure was seven, possibly eight stories high, and at one end, the remains of a stable could be seen. The walls were a mixture of stone and wood. The wood looked as if it had been grown and the stone laid within its branches as it grew. It was beautiful in a bizarre and puzzling way.

"I remember when this place was so alive, so wonderful," Blaze said.

Michael set Becky down and made sure she was okay. He handed over her backpack and walked over to the dogs. "You guys okay? Little better this time?" The dogs wagged.

"Yeah, I'm not so sure this is less creepy, guys," Becky stated, wrapping her arms around Melissa.

"This was once a vibrant city full of wonderful people," Jack said. "I do not think it is a place to be feared. Mourned, maybe, but not feared."

"Where did everyone go?" Melissa asked. "It looks like everyone just got up and left."

"The Jotunn," Blaze said.

"The Joe what?" Michael asked.

Stin pointed off to the snowcapped mountains in the north. "The elves built their city all the way to the Blue Mountains. They did not know the Jotunn called them home, and when the elves carved into the heart of the mountain, the Jotunn attacked."

"Instead of risking a war they did not mean to start, the elves surrendered Erendroll to the Jotunn," Jack added. "The Jotunn accepted, but never moved into the city which had been left to them. They simply let it waste away, content to let the land reclaim it."

"So are we, like, are we trespassing?" Michael asked.

"No one has seen nor heard from the Jotunn for millennia," Blaze said. "Not even the pixies who have called the Stygian Copse our home since before the elves lived here. None of us have seen the Jotunn since that period."

"Some say they left the area not long after Erendroll was abandoned," Stin said.

"So to answer your question Michael, I believe we are safe. I do not think anyone calls this place home, or even lays claim to it any longer," Jack said.

"Yeah, well, it's still creepy," Becky said.

Michael nodded. "I'm with her."

"Well, creepy or not, let's find a place to hole up before the sun rises. Somewhere Michael can go, and where we can all get some sleep later," Melissa said.

Jack walked over to the door of the building and pressed on its enormous wooden frame. It swung open without a sound, and a small, dust-burdened gust of wind spilled out, where it dissipated around the group.

"Yeah, that wasn't spooky at all," Michael said.

Stin and Blaze began to glow much brighter. Everyone moved forward. Michael glanced at the dogs, and noted they were crouching just a bit, their ears flattened.

"Jack," Michael said. "Do you think maybe, ya know, maybe you and I should check it out first?"

"I'm not staying out here," Becky said.

"Yeah, me either," Melissa said, and grabbed Jack's arm.

Jack smiled. "I sense no danger here."

"Whatever you say, man." Michael shrugged and stepped into the building.

The first room was immense. The ceiling was easily twenty to thirty feet high, and all along the walls stood bookshelf after bookshelf. Thousands of dust- and mold-covered books lined the shelves, and all about the floor rested dozens of desks and chairs. In the very center of the room, a large, round fireplace stood; a stone chimney hovered above it, stretching up through and out of the ceiling. The chimney, too, was covered in very full bookshelves.

"It's a library!" Melissa exclaimed, a huge smile spreading across her face. "That makes me feel so much better!"

"Someone's never seen *Ghostbusters*," Michael said.

"Says the vampire," Becky said, and punched Michael in the shoulder.

"Touchè."

62

Jack took Blaze, Stin, and the dogs to search the remainder of the building while Michael and the women got a fire burning with several wooden chairs Michael tore apart. When the group returned, Jack shared that the rest of the building was filled with rooms positively overflowing with books. Remarkably, more than half were still readable, though a good portion had deteriorated beyond hope; some had even disintegrated to the point that only their covers remained.

They also reported that there were several interior rooms in the building, so Michael could take his pick when the sun rose. Unfortunately, there were no beds to be found, but at least he wouldn't burn alive in his sleep.

The pixies had also scouted the immediate area and found no sign that anyone had followed them, or even been able to. Blaze and Stin set about laying several traps, which they promised would alert the group to anyone or anything approaching their location, whether on the ground *or* in the air. Blaze even made sure that should anything attempt to burrow beneath their wards, it or they would discover quite a nasty surprise. Jack was impressed with how well the two pixies wove their magic and how adept they were at setting traps. It was no surprise the other pixies had ambushed the group so effectively yesterday; watching Blaze and Stin confirmed that Jack and his friends had stood no chance. It was both impressive and disconcerting.

"I hoped this was the same building," Jack said as he swung his sword down on another ancient chair. The wood exploded. "My brother and I found this place long ago as children, but we were never brave enough to venture inside. We looked through that window there," he said, indicating a blue stained-glass window to his right. "After returning home, we learned that this building was once called the Red Library. Likely named so after the tiling on the roof, at least, to the best of our knowledge. There is supposed to be a Black Library in the city as well."

Michael tossed another chair leg on the fire. The wood was so old and so dry that it burned to ash in minutes, and had no odor at all. "Why were you hoping this was the same place?"

"We need to know more about who might be hunting us. Specifically, I would like to know more about the Dren. Little is known about them, so I was hoping a library built so long ago might contain information we have not seen in quite some time, or was thought lost to time. Not to mention, there perhaps is long-lost documentation on the vampires and their strange disappearance."

"Guys, I need to sit down for a bit, if that's okay," Melissa said after tossing another piece of wood into the flames.

Jack stopped what he was doing and walked over to where Melissa stood. "Of course. Wait here. We found a few comfortable-looking chairs earlier. I cannot promise the material will not disintegrate beneath you, but it is worth a try!"

"Thank you, Jack."

"Where?" Becky asked.

"Just upstairs. Allow me a moment," Jack said.

"I'll help."

Jack nodded, and he and Becky went off in search of more comfortable seating.

"How are you doing?" Michael asked Melissa as he sat down

beside her.

"I'm okay," Melissa said. She smiled. "I just get so tired these days. Par for the course, I guess."

Michael nodded. "My, uh, my little brother had asthma. When we were kids, he always had a hard time playing with us, especially in the winter. I used to watch him suck on his inhaler like three, four times an hour on the really bad days. He'd get the shakes, you know, from all the medicine? It would just suck it right out of him. BUT, he always came around! You just need to rest a little bit, that's all. Chill out, and you'll come around, too."

Melissa leaned her head on Michael's shoulder. "Thank you. You're really a nice guy, you know that?"

"Awww, shucks, little lady."

Melissa laughed. "I mean it. You don't even know us, and you're off on this crazy...whatever it is with us."

"Don't mention it; my calendar was wiiiide open!"

Melissa laughed again.

Michael patted Melissa on the back. "So where are your little bodyguards, anyway? I think they kidnapped my dogs."

"I think they're outside scouting around. Jack said something about setting wards or some such? I know Blaze mentioned teaching Thorn and Nanook how to sniff shadows? I kinda sorta didn't understand it."

"Setting wards and sniffing shadows, huh? Yeah, you got me," Michael said. "What's the story with you three, anyway? I mean, where the heck did you find Frick and Frack?"

Melissa chuckled. "I met Blaze when I woke up to take the dogs out to you know, do their business."

"Thanks for that, by the way."

"Sure! I like your dogs a lot."

"Me, too."

"Anyway, Blaze, he showed me the garden they have. I wish you guys could have seen it! When I say garden, I mean, like, they have an entire forest in that cave!" Melissa waved her arms in a giant circle over her head. "It was enormous! That's where Stin was, and the next thing I know, they're inviting me into their home for a cup of tea!"

"Into their home? Aren't you a little...*big* to make a house call with them?"

"I know, right? They, like, they shrunk me down to their size and flew me up to their home! It was so cute!"

"Shrunk you down? Really? Was it weird? Like *Honey, I Shrunk The Kids* weird?"

Melissa laughed. "You know, there weren't any giant ants or anything, and when we went inside, it was just, like, normal, you know? Everything was normal size."

"Wow. And tea? They made you tea?"

"They did! I can't remember the name of it, but it was delicious. And we sat out on their little balcony, drank tea, and talked. It was lovely! They asked how we'd ended up here, so I told them the whole story!"

"Wait"—Michael bolted to his feet—"did you tell them about me? That I was a vampire?"

Melissa looked up. "I...I did, is that...it's okay, right? I mean, they weren't all that surprised, really. I, just...I guess they were a little bit, but, they kinda just took it in stride, you know?"

"Melissa, I...I don't think. I'm not—"

"The pixies all know, Michael," Jack said from the back of the room. He and Becky were making their way down a set of stairs with a reddish-brown couch. "I think they deduced it in short order."

"Are you sure?" Michael asked.

"Invyl seemed to know," Jack said.

"Okay, okay...." Michael looked back down at Melissa. "Sorry. I just, I wasn't sure if we should, well, if it would be okay or not to tell people."

"I'm sorry if I—"

"You didn't! It's okay. I just, I was worried that telling people might make it easier for whoever the hell is after us to track us down, you know? Apparently there aren't a lot of vampires running around these days, even here."

"Oh...yeah, that makes sense. I'm sorry," Melissa said.

Michael touched Melissa's shoulder. "It's okay. Like Jack said, I guess they all figured it out anyway."

"They did," Jack said, and sat his end of the strange-looking couch down near the fire. Becky dropped her end, and a cloud of dust erupted from the surface.

"It's not the Ritz, but it looks comfortable," Becky said. She pressed down on the faded cushions. "Feels okay." She began brushing off the dust and grime, and waved Melissa over.

"Come here, Smurf." She patted the back of the couch. "Give it a go."

Michael reached out his hand and helped Melissa to her feet.

"You guys don't need to worry about me. I'm fine, I promise!" Melissa protested. She did, however, accept Jack's hand as he guided her to the couch.

Michael noticed Melissa's heat signature ripple just slightly as she sat down on the new furniture, and he also took note of her ankles. For some reason they seemed a bit warmer then anything else. He assumed she was just breaking in her new boots and thought nothing more of it.

"Wow, it's pretty nice, actually!" Melissa said, leaning back.

Becky smiled above her and began rubbing her sister's head. "Good! Rest here a bit. There are several more of these upstairs, so Jack and I will go get 'em. Can you?" Becky asked, looking up at Michael while pointing down at her sister.

Michael nodded. "Of course."

"Guys, you don't—"

"Shut it, Smurf!" Becky said, and dragged Jack away to get more comfortable seating.

63

Michael broke apart another piece of furniture and tossed the scraps into the fire. "Are you warm enough?"

Melissa nodded. "I am, thank you."

"Wanna hear something weird?" Michael asked as he sat back down.

"Ooo! Gossip!" Melissa said, and rubbed her hands together.

Michael chuckled. "I guess it's a little juicy. You know that, that one pixie? The chick with the bitchy attitude?"

"Oh, the one back in the woods? The one who wanted to kill us?"

"Yup, that's the one! She, uh, well she came into my room yesterday, while I was asleep."

"Oh, yeah?"

"Yeah, and she was like, she was our size! You know how you said Frick and Frack shrunk you down to their size? Well, I guess they can grow to ours if they wanna!"

"Really? What did she want?"

"It was weird! She was, well she was flirting with me. I mean, she...don't tell the others, but she was, like, practically naked."

Melissa sat forward. "Are you serious?"

"Totally! She was dressed in this like, little transparent

getup! And she full-on kissed me! It was so weird!"

Melissa laughed. "Sup' playa!"

"Playa? No! I'm not! Really!" Michael protested, but he started laughing, too.

"Well, was she pretty? I couldn't really tell back in the woods."

"Oh, my God, she was…yeah, she's uh, she's pretty, all right!"

"Did you guys, you know?"

"Oh no, no, no, I umm…." Michael recalled what Yori had said about Becky. "I uh, I told her I was um, you know, tired."

Melissa cocked her head to the side, her eyes narrowed. "Tired? Really?"

"Yeah, um, I didn't know what to say! But yeah, isn't that kinda strange?"

"Well, you're not so bad-looking, you know."

"Ha, thanks."

"I'm serious! And you did kinda, well, you sort of told her off back there when she was all up in your grill."

"Huh? I don't get what that has to do with anything."

"That can be hot sometimes."

"What? She was pissing me off!"

"Yeah, and you didn't back down! You kinda let her have it a little. That can be hot sometimes. I'm not saying arguing with a woman is a sure-fire way to get laid, but you stood your ground, and I suspect she realized she was, you know, over-reacting a little."

"You're saying she knew she was being a bitch?"

"Women always know when they're being a bitch. It's our

superpower."

"So, wait—you're saying if a woman is being bitchy, I should just call her out on it?"

"No! Not at all."

"I don't understand...."

Melissa laughed. "And you *never* will."

"What?"

Melissa was giggling hard now. "Best not to try and understand. But, trust me, I bet that's why she paid you a little booty call."

"Okay, now I'm totally confused."

"Don't worry, you did the right thing."

Michael shook his head. "I don't even know what I did!"

"And that's what makes you so damn cute."

Michael sighed. "You women need to seriously come with instruction manuals, you know that, right?"

Melissa continued to laugh. "Not enough paper in the world, cutie. Sorry."

"So tell me," Michael said. "What's the story with you two? I mean you and Jack?"

"He didn't tell you?"

"Not really, no. I mean, he said he met you last year out at Humpback, but that was kinda it."

"Ahh. So yeah, I was spending a few weeks hiking through Virginia. One of those, you know, soul-searching adventures. Bad breakup and all that."

"Gotcha."

"So it was late. I decided to camp up near Humpback, and one night I just decided to go see if I could spot any shooting stars. I like to hike at night. I overheat easily, and it's cooler then. Anyway, I figured the rocks were a good place to chill out for a bit, and they're not that far from the campsites. So I took a little blanket, grabbed my head lantern, and found an area to chill for a few hours."

"And that's when you met Jack?"

"Yep! I was just kind of laying there, and up walks this crazy hot...well, you've seen him!" Melissa said, and laughed. "Up walks this guy, and he's all polite and, smooth, and...well, he's just all...JACK! So we spent the whole night chatting, and that's when I decided to hang around there for a few more days. I think it was the third day or so when I found out who he REALLY was, you know. He took me to this amazing little lake, and we saw a unicorn, and...well, isn't that, like, every little girl's fantasy?"

Michael chuckled. "You tell me! Clearly I can't figure you guys out."

"Well, even if they say no, it really is every little girl's dream to meet a prince, or princess, and see a unicorn. Trust me on that one!"

"Gotcha. Guess I need to get a unicorn, huh?"

Melissa smiled. "No, you've got a couple fur-babies! They'll always do in a pinch."

"Noted."

"So, yeah, I told him I'd be back this way in a year, and we agreed to see what would happen then!"

"Yeah, I heard that part. I gotta say, isn't that a little, ya know, made for Hollywood?"

"I know, right?"

"Well, I guess it worked out for you."

Melissa's smile faded, and she looked down at the floor. "Kinda, yeah. That's when, that's when all of the complications started, you know, with the whole…" she motioned to her entire body. "I almost didn't come back. But the more I thought about it, the more I couldn't bear not to. And Becky, well, Becky being Becky, she came along."

"And she knew about Jack? I mean, that he was an elf?"

"Well, kinda? I mean, I eventually told her, and I swore he was who he said he was. But it's one of those things, you know? One of those, you kinda gotta see it to believe it, things? She thought he was some kind of stalker or something. Jack tell you she pulled a freakin' knife on him the first night?"

Michael laughed."He did, actually!"

"That's Becky for you. She's always been a little overly protective of me. I guess it didn't help that she and her boyfriend had broken up. Kinda."

"Yeah? What, umm, how uh, how kinda?"

Melissa studied Michael for a moment. "Well, Luke, he is, or he was, Special Forces, you know, SEALS?"

"Like, Seal Team Six and shit?"

"Exactly like that."

"Damn!"

"Yeah, anyway, he's been through some rough times. A lot of that happened while they were together." Melissa sighed and took a deep breath. "I guess he just brought a lot back with him, you know? Like, how do you *not*? It wasn't a great time for them. They did the whole therapy thing, and I guess eventually they decided it would be best if...well, they're better friends than they ever were partners. It's actually worked out kinda well, but there's still a lot of...hurt...there, you know?"

"That sucks."

"Yeah. But it's all for the best. They keep in touch. He's an instructor at BUDS now. They get online and play that game, what is it, that uh...anyway, they play some game on the Xbox together all the time."

"Your sister's a gamer?"

"Oh, my God, you have no idea. She owns like every single console out there. She's addicted."

"Who's addicted? To what?" Becky asked from across the room.

Michael stood as Becky and Jack returned with another piece of furniture and met them at the base of the stairs to help.

"I was just telling Michael that you're addicted to video games."

Becky smiled. "Damn straight!"

The three brought over the new chair. It was very similar to the first, though mold seemed to be creeping up three of the legs. They dusted it off, Michael gave it a try, and when the furniture didn't collapse under his weight, Becky and Jack went in search of more.

Michael added more wood to the fire and tried out the new chair. It was surprisingly comfortable, and he wondered how something like this could have possibly survived for as long as Jack said the city had been abandoned.

"Magic furniture," Michael said.

"Huh?"

"Magic furniture. How else can you explain all of this stuff still standing, or not being piles of dust after all of these years?"

Melissa smiled. "I guess you're right."

"So about your, um…you don't mind if I ask about your, what is it again?"

"Sickle cell?"

"Yeah, sickle cell."

"It's genetic, I guess. Becky doesn't have it, and neither do my parents. But I guess my mom's mom had it? I've been on medicine my whole life. It never really became a problem until this year; well, not a *real* problem anyway, nothing like… it kinda decided to get all aggressive this year."

"I'm sorry. Seriously, that sucks."

"Thanks. I just wish—" Melissa's voice cracked. "I just wish Becky didn't have to worry, you know?"

"Yeah. Is there, I mean"—Michael cleared his throat —"there's nothing they can do?"

Melissa shook her head. "Not anymore, I mean they treat the symptoms, and I swallow all the pills. I've had about a zillion transfusions. It's just, I guess there's not much else they can really do beyond that."

Michael sighed. "That sucks."

"Yeah. I just don't want to…. The strokes, I'm afraid of the strokes. That's one of the things that can happen, ya know? A blockage in the brain. You can get these, like, these clots all over the place. I think that scares me more than anything. I mean, give me a heart attack, or, I don't know, take me out quick! But don't turn me into a vegetable first, know what I mean?"

"Jesus...." Michael looked up at the girl as she wiped away several tears threatening to spill down her cheeks. He cleared his throat. "Melissa...what if, I mean, what if I could help you? Like, I don't know if I can, or if I can even do anything for you, but...but what if? What if I could make you better? Fix it?"

"Like the blood you gave me?"

"Yeah, like that, only. What if...like, what if that was permanent?"

"You mean if I was like you."

Michael nodded. "Exactly. I mean, don't get me wrong, I get it! I didn't ask for this to happen to me, and believe me when I tell you, it can really, I mean REALLY suck sometimes! And, I'll be honest, I don't even know if I can...if I can, like, turn you. I have no clue about that shit, but, well, *what if*?"

Tears spilled from Melissa's eyes now. "I think this is the part where I tell you how I've lived a good life, how I'm ready to go, and how one lifetime is enough and all that shit? Right?" she said. She was crying now, but also smiling.

Michael grinned. "I mean, that's what would happen in the movies! They'd drag that shit out. But not before me spouting clichéd shit like, "*I love you too much to condemn you!*" or "*This is no gift! It's a curse!*" and all that other gothy, angsty, and lazy trope-ish bullshit."

Melissa laughed and ran her hand across her nose. "Well, yeah, fuck that! I don't want to die. If you are willing to, to do that, I'm not going to sit here and pretend I'd have to think about it, Michael."

Michael stood up. "Hell, yeah! Fuck death!"

Melissa laughed harder. "Yeah, fuck death!"

He and Melissa laughed and laughed until a confused Jack

and Becky came back into the room carrying a third couch.

64

Blaze watched the ghost for another full minute before getting Stin's attention and whispering into his ear. "That's the third one I've seen."

"Three? I saw one over by the fountain, maybe two, I couldn't get a good look," Stin replied. "I think Thorn might have spotted one as well."

Blaze studied the dead as they roamed the city block. "Why so many?"

"Maybe we're just lucky?" Stin said. "I've never heard of ghosts residing in Erendroll. Not like this, anyway."

Nanook and Thorn trotted over to the two pixies and stared at a ghost roaming in and out of the small building across the street. The specter appeared to pay their little group no attention. It just drifted through the building's walls, would vanish inside for a moment, and then circle back and emerge on the street again.

"Can you make out any features?" Stin asked.

Blaze flew several feet towards the apparition and paused. "I think it's an elf. A male, perhaps?"

"I believe you're right."

Blaze shook his head again. "It's very strange! Why *are* there so many?"

"I've heard they are attracted to death," Stin said. "Some say they can predict it."

The pixies glanced at one another.

"Should we try to communicate with them?" Blaze asked.

Stin flew up next to Blaze and studied the spirit further. "I doubt we could. I've never had much luck getting one to even see me, much less hear me. You?"

"None whatsoever. Though to be honest, I've only ever tried two, maybe three times. I think there's something about being related?"

Stin nodded. "I've heard that as well. I believe it best to ignore them. I doubt they can see us anyway. And it was certainly no ghost that followed us in the Stygian Copse."

"Agreed."

Stin motioned back towards the library. "More wards?"

Blaze nodded. "More wards, indeed."

Thorn and Nanook followed the pixies back towards the Library, stopping only when instructed to, and waiting patiently while one of the pixies wove another ward, or set another trap. Thorn continued to watch the ghost across the street. It certainly wasn't the first spirit he'd seen, but he didn't like that this one kept looking at the group when the pixies weren't watching. It made the hair on his neck and all down his spine stand on end. No, he didn't like that one bit.

65

Becky rummaged through her pack and sighed. "I knew I should have grabbed a few more apples or something. I totally forgot."

Jack snapped his fingers, and a small table full of fruit, bread, and cheese appeared.

"Seriously, how do you do that?" Becky asked. "Can you just make anything you want appear?"

"Yeah, man, how does that work?" Michael asked.

Jack smiled. "It is not very difficult. Perhaps one day I can teach you? And to answer your question, Becky, no, I cannot simply summon anything I would like. That food, for instance, and even the table, already exists. I just brought them here, or rather made them accessible. Whenever I travel, I arrange certain items to be available at all times. In some cases, I have entire rooms full of various things available to me. All of these items are currently in my home. The food is prepared daily. For instance, I knew fruit would be available on that particular table, but I did not know what kind. And that table as well as the bowls, well, they are not really here, they are still in my home. We only perceive them to be here, with us, now. As soon as you take something from that table, only *then* is it actually here."

Michael shook his head, "Yeah, nope. I just don't get magic, I guess."

Jack laughed. "It is all very simple, really. And it is not

magic; it is more what you would call, physics? Anyone can do something like that; it is only a matter of learning how. I am sure your phones, if taken back in time, not even one or two hundred years into the past, would seem like magic to whoever saw them, yes?"

"Yeah, but a piece of machinery isn't magical food or floating candles appearing out of nowhere!" Becky said.

Jack smiled. "No, no, of course not. But that loaf of bread was made by someone, baked in an oven built by someone. That table was crafted by someone else. The apple grew on a tree before being plucked by yet another person, and they were all placed on that table by even more hands. I only made it available to us—and even that is something each one of you could do with the proper education, the proper knowledge and understanding. It would be like calling a friend via one of your devices. You know the friend will likely be on the other end of that call, but you do not know where. When they speak to you, perhaps you then hear the ocean on their end? Perhaps the sound of animals? And now, those are available to you as well! It is all very similar."

"You're saying we can all use magic?" Michael said.

"For lack of a better description, yes."

Michael sat back. "Hmm."

"Excuse me for a moment," Jack said. "I need to contact someone."

The elf stood, walked across the room, and stepped outside.

Becky sliced a piece of apple and handed it to Melissa, then offered Michael another slice. "Can you? I mean, do you still?"

"Do I eat?" Michael asked, and accepted the slice of apple. "I can. I just don't seem to get a lot out of normal food anymore. But I still like to eat. I mean, Doritos, Ben & Jerry's, hello?"

Melissa smiled. "I love Doritos."

"I know, right?" Michael said. "I'd smack a kitten for some Americone Dream right now."

Melissa sighed. "Or some Chunky Monkey!"

"Mmm, ice cream. Ugh, just stop. So what were you two laughing so hard about earlier?" Becky asked.

Michael looked at Melissa, who put a hand on Becky's knee.

"I was telling Michael about the anemia."

"That it sucks dick?" Becky asked.

"Pretty much," Michael said.

"...and how Michael's blood helped the other night. And if..." Melissa took another deep breath. "God, I hate crying, you know? Why do I cry so much?!"

Becky leaned over and hugged her sister. "It's okay, Smurf."

Melissa hugged Becky back and wiped away a tear before it could escape. "And we talked about, you know, if being a vampire might...if...." This time, the tears came.

Michael leaned forward. "If maybe turning your sister, I guess that's what you call it, if she was a vampire, like me, if that might make her better, or at least, you know, kick the sickle cell's ass?"

Becky wiped away her own tears. "And?"

"Well, I don't really know," Michael said. "I don't know a whole lot about it, to be honest. Like I said, I've only ever even met one other vampire, and that bitch, well, she kinda left me hanging after she did what she did. Pretty much told me fuck-all about it."

Jack returned, and behind him Blaze, Stin, and the dogs followed.

"No one will get close to us until we allow it," Blaze said.

"Well, at least they won't get close without us *knowing* about it, and not without a few nasty surprises, that is!" Stin said.

"Awesome, guys, thank you," Michael said. "These two keep you company?"

Thorn and Nanook pranced over to Michael and laid down at his feet.

"They did. I like them very much!" Blaze said.

"Yes, they are extremely intelligent!" Stin said.

"Good, good," Michael said and crouched down to scratch the dogs' heads. Nanook licked Michael's hand.

Becky gestured at Jack. "You make your call?"

Jack looked confused for a moment, then chuckled, "Yes, I reached out to my brother. He should be here soon."

"Is your brother older or younger than you?" Michael asked.

"He is the eldest of us."

"What's his name?" Melissa asked.

"Frost."

Michael laughed. "No, really."

Jack looked confused. "I do not understand."

"You're telling us you have a brother named Frost?" Becky asked, grinning.

"Yes. I fail to see—"

Michael fell backwards and crashed into a chair, which broke apart under his weight. He laughed hard enough that the dogs immediately began to lick his face, their tails wagging hard. "You have a brother named Frost? You're both elves. Jack and Frost. Jack Frost?"

Becky and Melissa were both now laughing as well. Blaze and Stin looked just as confused as Jack.

"I do not understand," Jack said.

At that, the three laughed even harder.

"Oh, my God, I'm going to pee," Becky gasped.

66

When everyone regained some semblance of composure, Michael did his best to explain to Jack why they'd all lost it for no apparent reason. While the elf understood there was a reference, he failed to see the humor in it, but did not seemed to be offended.

"So when does, uh, Old Man Winter get here, anyway?" Becky said, stifling a giggle. "Can he help us?"

"He should arrive soon. I gave him instructions on how to best avoid the wards. And yes, I believe he will be able to assist us. He has had more dealings with the Dren than I, and he is far more powerful than I am. He should be able to shed some light on their motivations, or at least help us gain some insight as to why this might be happening," Jack said. "Meanwhile, I would like to begin searching these books. Would you mind if I helped you all do the same?"

Michael cocked his head. "Huh?"

Jack reached up to one of the shelves circling the chimney above the fire and retrieved a book from the lowest shelf. "Come," he said to Michael, and walked behind Melissa and Becky. He opened the book to the first page, leaned down, rested one arm on the back of the couch where they sat, and with his other, held the book out between and in front of the two sisters so they could all see the pages. Michael walked over to where Jack stood and peered over the sisters' shoulders.

The words and letters on the pages were alien to everyone

but Jack, so he translated them to the group. "Herein lies the song of Vry," Jack said. "This is appears to be an epic poem. What I want to do is help you all understand how to read some of the languages and writings we might encounter here."

"Dude, I sucked at Spanish in school," Michael said. "I don't think I'm—"

Jack chuckled. "No, this will be different. This is elvish, an old elvish tongue, to be precise. Do this for me. Look at the first two lines of this page. Do not try to decipher the lettering, or pronounce anything. Just look at each word closely as I tell you what it is. Repeat every single word, precisely how I say it. Understand?"

Everyone agreed, and Jack nodded. "Blaze? Stin? Do you know how to read old Elvish?"

"We do!" Blaze said. "Though my pronunciation is not very good."

"I am somewhat proficient in it," Stin said. "Would you mind if we read along regardless?"

"Of course not," Jack said, and the two pixies flew over and landed on Melissa's shoulders—Stin on the left, Blaze on the right.

"All right then, just focus on each word, and repeat after me. It should not take long."

Jack cleared his throat, and just before he began to read, the hand he used to hold the book began to glow a soft, almost lavender color. The pages themselves began to glow as well, only *they* emitted a soft green light. Jack read each word in a slow, deliberate manner. Everyone repeated what he said, and followed along just as Jack instructed.

"Before the first cry, of the first babe, within the first forest, long stood Vry." "None now live who remember the first stone laid there, or by what hand which laid it."

By the time Jack finished the last word of the second sentence, everyone could see and understand the words as clearly as if they had written them.

"Oh, my God, that's awesome!" Becky said. She continued to read. "*Those who recall the beauty therein, and the peoples who called Vry home....* Oh, my God, I can read it! Can you guys read it?" she asked, looking from Michael to Melissa and back again.

"I can!" Michael said.

"So can I! That's beautiful," Melissa said.

"Far more clear," Stin said.

"Yes, much better. Thank you, master elf!" Blaze said.

Michael clapped Jack on the back. "Dude! Where were you in my freakin' high school Spanish class?"

"I know, right?" Becky agreed.

Jack smiled and handed the book to Melissa. "I am glad to help. Perhaps now, we might be able to sort through the books here in a far more efficient and expedient manner! I want to find anything I can on the Dren, and on dragons."

"That is so weird..." Becky mused as she continued to read the book. "It's like one of those optical illusions, you know, the ones where if you stare long enough, they move or form a picture?"

"Totally," Michael said.

Melissa coughed. Blood speckled the pages. "Oh, no."

Becky leaned over. "Smurf?"

67

Melissa tried to wipe the specks of blood from the page, whereupon they smeared into tiny crimson raindrops. "Oh, no...."

Becky pulled the book from Melissa's hands in a slow, gentle manner. "Smurf, it's okay, let me look at you."

Melissa looked up, her eyes filling with tears. "I'm sorry," she started—and two rivers of blood began pouring from her nose.

Jack raced around to the front of the small couch and knelt down in front of Melissa. Blaze and Stin flew up and looked on from a distance, concern washing over their faces.

"Here," Jack said, and handed Becky a small piece of blue fabric.

"It's okay, baby girl," Becky said and wiped the blood away from her sister's lip and chin. "It's okay."

Michael placed a hand on Becky's shoulder. "Is there anything I can do?"

Becky reached up and touched the vampire's fingers. "She'll be okay. Won't you, Smurf?"

Melissa nodded and gave a thumbs up.

"Why don't you just put your head in my lap for a few minutes, okay?" Becky said.

Melissa turned over and laid back as she was told, tears streaming down the sides of her face, Jack's small handkerchief pressed against her nose.

"Just rest," Jack said.

Becky looked up, and Michael locked eyes with her. He nodded, and tapped Jack on the shoulder. The elf looked up, and Michael motioned for him to follow. The two walked off towards the staircase at the far end of the room, and Blaze and Stin fluttered down and began gently pulling the hair from Melissa's face, each singing a quiet little tune.

When they were out of earshot, Michael leaned close to Jack. "I gotta do something, man. I've already talked to Melissa a little bit about it."

Jack nodded. "I spoke with Becky earlier."

"Yeah? What did she say?"

Jack glanced back at the two sisters and then at Michael. "She wants us to do whatever we can. Whatever it takes. But I would expect nothing less from her. She loves her sister very much. We did not discuss the dangers, nor did we address how little you or I even knew of the act."

Michael took a deep breath. "Do you think maybe Frick and Frack over there can do anything?"

Jack shook his head. "I do not believe so. I think part of the reason they are traveling with Melissa is they feel somewhat sorry for her. I'm certain they can sense the overwhelming innocence, the goodness in her. And I somehow doubt they would not have already tried to help if they thought in any small way they could."

"Well, shit...."

"Shit, indeed."

Michael cursed again under his breath. "You mentioned people dying? Something about the weak or sick not surviving the, the whatever? The process?"

Jack looked back over at Melissa. "I read that the very young, the very old, the sick, weak, or gravely injured may not survive, yes."

"And you didn't really talk to Becky about that."

"No."

"Any reason why not?"

The elf turned and looked at Michael. "I was afraid."

Michael sighed and clapped Jack's shoulder. "I get it, man."

A single tear rolled down Jack's cheek and fell to the floor.

Becky screamed, "SMURF!"

Michael and Jack turned to see Melissa convulsing on the couch, Becky holding her head.

68

Michael and Jack raced over. Michael held Melissa's legs, while Jack placed his hands on her shoulders.

"We gotta turn her on her side," Becky said.

Everyone shifted and turned Melissa onto her left side, facing the edge of the couch.

Becky pointed to her backpack. "Get something between her teeth."

Blaze raced down to the pack, drew his tiny sword, sliced through one of the straps, and raced it up to Becky.

Becky grabbed the nylon strip, folding it over on itself. She then worked it into Melissa's mouth, and resumed holding her head.

"I can calm her!" Stin said. "If you think it would help?"

Becky looked up at the pixie and nodded. Stin began to wave his hands in the air in front of him. Tiny trails of light flashed all around the pixie and then glided towards Melissa. After several seconds, millions of glowing particles surrounded the thrashing girl, and the convulsions began to subside. Melissa choked and clawed at the air, causing Jack to grab her wrists in an effort to restrain her.

"It's okay, baby girl. It's okay, Smurf," Becky said.

Melissa cried out and screamed, though the sound came out strained and twisted.

"Oh, my God," Becky said, and began to sob. "It's okay, Smurf, it's okay, it's okay...."

Michael didn't even ask. He drew his new knife, sliced into his wrist, and reached for the nylon strap in Melissa's mouth. No one objected. Blood poured over her lips and covered her chin. Michael leaned down and whispered in her ear, "You gotta drink this, kid. Remember what we were saying earlier? Fuck death, okay? Fuck. Death!"

Melissa's eyes shot open for a moment, and she tried to look up, but the convulsions continued, and her eyelids fluttered.

"You gotta drink, Smurf," Becky said.

Michael grabbed Melissa's mouth and pried it open even further. Blood poured in, and Melissa coughed. "Fuck death, kiddo! Remember?"

Melissa's eyes opened again, and she looked up at Michael. She moaned something, and then managed to swallow. A second later the convulsions slowed even more, and she pressed her lips tight to Michael's wrist and drank.

"There ya go! There ya go!" Michael said.

A moment later, the convulsions stopped, and Melissa fell away, breathing hard.

Jack brushed the hair from her forehead and leaned in. "Melissa?"

"Smurf? You back with us, baby girl?" Becky said.

Blaze swooped down, and a wave of light poured out of him. Jack, Michael, and Becky squinted and turned their heads, but Melissa took a slow, deep breath and relaxed. Stin glided down, and he, too, began to glow. Together, the pixies conjured enough light that the entire room appeared as if a small sun had taken up residence.

After a few minutes, the pixies' light faded, and Melissa's eyes fluttered open. She coughed once and looked up at the group. "Is everyone okay?" she asked.

The group sighed collectively, and Michael rolled backwards onto the floor. "Oh, thank God."

An explosion erupted outside, followed by an intense flash of orange light, and someone crashed through the closest window in a tidal wave of shattered glass.

69

Michael, Jack, and the pixies were on top of the figure, a man, before the glass settled to the ground. Jack lifted him into the air with one arm, his sword snapping into existence in his other hand. Michael grabbed at one of the intruder's arms from behind, and the figure reached up to the hand that held him by the throat.

"Pixies?" the stranger asked, choking. He offered a strained smile.

"FROST?" Jack exclaimed, and let go.

"WHAT? WHO?" Michael asked, still holding on.

"It's okay. You can let him go," Jack said. "This is my brother, Frost."

Michael dropped the man, who landed in a heap and began to cough. He was tall like Jack, only instead of long blonde hair, he had dark curly hair, and his shoulders were more broad. He was of a slightly larger build, and appeared to be at least an inch or two taller than his younger brother. His eyes were bright green.

"You said there were wards," Frost said, and cleared his throat. "You didn't tell me there were so many, or that they were the work of pixies. That could have come in handy, Jack."

Jack reached down and helped his brother to his feet. "I apologize," he said, and walked back towards Becky and Melissa, who were both sitting upright. The dogs were snarling beside them, and Becky's knives were drawn.

Frost turned to face Michael and the pixies. "Bad timing?" he asked.

Michael held out a hand. "Yeah, kinda. Sorry about that."

Frost reached out and shook Michael's hand, and Michael walked back to the girls, leaving Frost alone with the pixies.

"You are the brother?" Blaze asked, sliding his tiny golden sword back into its sheath with a tiny clack.

Frost made a small bow. "None other," he said, and brushed several shards of broken glass out of his hair.

"Are you all right?" Stin asked. "The wards can have"—he paused—"...lingering effects."

Frost nodded and continued to brush himself off. "My ears are ringing quite a bit, but I don't think any real harm was done."

Stin nodded.

"...not that the ward was ineffective, mind you!" Frost added.

Both pixies smiled.

Frost dusted himself off and tore away a long white cape which hung down to his calves. There were scorch marks all over it, and holes, some as large as a fist, dotted its surface. "Well, so much for that," he said and tossed the cape onto the ground. "Not very fashionable these days anyway."

"Our apologies," Blaze said. "If you will forgive us," he added, and the two pixies flew back to Melissa.

Frost pulled a piece of glass out of his sleeve and followed. "I guess where entrances are concerned, that wasn't the most graceful," he said when he reached the couch where the sisters sat. "Please accept my apologies. You must be Melissa." Frost held out a gloved hand.

Melissa reached up and shook Frost's hand. "Hello."

Jack knelt down to Melissa, took her chin, and looked hard into her eyes. "How are you feeling?"

"A little dizzy, but okay," Melissa said. The blood had absorbed into her skin as before, and no sign of the trauma remained.

"Good, good."

Melissa looked back up at everyone. "Did I, did I have a seizure? It felt like, like I went numb. Like I couldn't feel...." She trailed off and leaned into Becky.

Becky slid her knives behind her and hugged her sister. "You're okay, Smurf."

"Everyone, this is my brother, Frost. He has come to help," Jack said. He motioned around the group. "Michael, Becky, Melissa, Blaze, Stin, and finally, Thorn and Nanook."

Frost nodded to each one and smiled. "My apologies again regarding, well, *that*," Frost said, motioning to the smashed window and the debris. "I am not well versed in pixie wards, I'm afraid."

"We will repair the wards now," Stin said, and he and Blaze flew off towards the broken window and back outside. Almost immediately, small flashes of light and tiny electric sounds began as the two set to work.

Thorn and Nanook each gave Frost a small sniff, then raced over to the smashed window and leapt through to join the pixies.

"Jack tells us you might be able to shed some light on who's attacking us, and why?" Michael asked.

Frost turned to Michael and shook his head. "Not without

knowing more. I only just learned of your plight," Frost turned to his brother. "You mentioned Dren? And what's this about a dragon? Were you serious about that?"

"Unfortunately," Jack said.

70

Everyone filled Frost in as best they could for the next hour. He asked an occasional question from time to time, but otherwise just listened. Frost seemed very impressed with Michael's abilities, and just as concerned with Melissa's ailment, though he marveled at how well she now appeared to be having just endured an episode.

The pixies returned and told everyone about the ghosts outside. The brothers took the information in stride, but the sisters and even Michael were full of questions. Elves, pixies, and dragons were far more acceptable than the news of ghosts haunting the area. Michael, for one, had raced to the windows multiple times in an effort to see them, but the ghosts appeared content to remain hidden for now. The pixies went back to work on the wards, complaining about there never being too many protective spells for any given occasion. The dogs followed.

"I don't know if this will help you," Frost said, and removed a small silver bracelet from his pocket. "When Jack mentioned you were ill, our mother created this. She hopes it brings you some comfort." He held the piece of jewelry out so Melissa could see it. "If I may?"

Melissa held out her hand, and Frost fastened the small, unassuming chain to her wrist. "Thank you," she said, and offered Frost a smile.

"Again, I am not certain it will help, but we hope it does in some small way."

"That's very nice of her."

Jack looked at the bracelet and then at his brother. "Rose tear?"

Frost nodded. "She is far better with moonstone, but did not have any quality pieces available. She sent word for some."

Jack nodded. "Thank you."

"Now, back to these Dren that attacked you. You mentioned a name? Elm? Do you recall any others?" Frost asked.

"I think one was named Pine," Becky said. "There was another one, but I can't remember his name, Rex, or Tracks, or something."

"Wasn't it Trex?" Melissa asked.

"Yeah, maybe that was it, Trex," Becky agreed.

Frost shook his head. "I'm afraid I do not know these Dren, or at least, I've never met them. But if the one calling herself Elm was traveling with a Dragon, *that* will certainly make things easier. Can you describe her or that particular dragon in more detail?"

Michael stepped into the middle of the group. "Yeah, umm, Melissa, you tell Frost here all you can about that, and don't forget to tell him exactly what she said to you! Remember, the bit about 'if you survive' and all that stuff? I need to borrow your sister and Jack for a few minutes outside, if that's okay? I'm a little worried about those crazy wards the pixies are so good at, you know, like, if we had to get out of here in a hurry, how we might do that and not blow ourselves up!"

"I do not think—" Jack started.

Michael cut the elf off. "...humor me, man."

Becky stood to accompany Jack and Michael, while Frost sat

down on the couch next to Melissa.

"Elm said something about you *surviving* her hunt?" Frost asked.

Melissa nodded, and proceeded to recount her exchange with the Dren, while Michael led Jack and Becky out of the library and onto the small road just outside.

When they were clear, Michael turned and looked at Becky. "So yeah, not to uh, get sidetracked or anything, but what are we going to do about your sister? Was that another stroke? Or, or…I don't know! I'm just worried I won't be able to keep helping her like that, like, what if she's just getting weaker?" Michael turned to Jack. "And what you said a while ago? About the weak, or the old, not surviving the process of being turned? So what if…what if she's just getting weaker? Or what if we can't pull her through another episode like that? I mean, that was what? Twenty-four hours after the last one? I mean —"

Becky placed a hand on Michael's shoulder. "Michael."

"But really! What if I can't—"

"MICHAEL," Becky said again.

Michael took a deep breath. "Sorry, I just…I'm just worried. You know, what if I can't help her again? I don't know what the pixies did in there, but…."

Becky hugged Michael hard enough to knock the wind out of him, then pulled away just as quick. "I know, I know. I think we're all feeling the same way."

"I am concerned that she grows weaker as well," Jack said. "Michael's blood certainly seems to help, but for a limited amount of time, it appears."

Becky turned to the elf. "What was that about the weak and old?"

Michael glanced at Jack. "How much did you tell her?"

Becky stared at the elf. "Yeah, Jack, how much did you tell me?"

Jack looked Becky in the eyes. "I do not know much about vampirism, as I mentioned before. But one thing I did discover about the process of creating a vampire was the need for a healthy individual. Preferably an individual who is not very young or old where humans were concerned. But...there is always a risk, especially with weakened or injured individuals. The process can prove"—Jack looked at his feet and sighed—"the process can be fatal, Rebecca."

Becky swallowed hard and looked back at Michael. He nodded. "Well, so can this fucking disease," she said. "Does, does she know it might—" Becky's voice cracked, and she took a second to compose herself. "Does she know it might kill her?"

Michael shook his head. "No. We didn't really get that far."

"But you're, you're willing to try?" Becky asked.

Michael nodded.

Becky smiled. "I'll talk to her. See what she wants to do." Becky looked at the pixies hard at work across the courtyard, then back at Michael and Jack. "And you guys think there's no other options? Are you sure?"

"I'm not sure if there are or not," Michael said. "But I don't think that's the point right now, ya know?"

"I agree," Jack said.

Becky nodded. "Okay."

"And Michael is right. Even if there is something else, another way to help, I am not certain there is enough time," Jack said.

"I just think...." Michael sighed and looked back at the library. "I just think that the longer we wait, the less chance she has."

Becky looked up at Michael. "And you're sure about this? I mean, are *you* okay with this?"

"I was going to ask you the same thing! I mean, I don't want to see her get any worse, and I sure don't want to make things any worse than they already are! You know, like...." Michael dropped his head and paced back and forth for a second. Becky and Jack let him. "I just don't want to hurt her, guys."

This time it was Jack who placed a hand on Michael's shoulder. "I am not sure you could, my friend."

Becky nodded and wiped away several tears.

Michael took a deep breath. "Okay, then. So, so, we uh, we're doing this thing! I think maybe she should rest first, you know? Try and regain a little bit of her strength? Try and get her some decent sleep? Maybe you guys can talk a little more?" Michael said to Becky. "I mean, I talked to her a bit earlier. She convinced me she was willing to do whatever it took. Maybe you could just, I don't know, just check in? Make sure she's okay with it?"

"I'll talk to her some more," Becky said. "And thank you."

Michael nodded.

"I agree about letting her rest," Jack said. "Maybe there is something Frost and I, perhaps even the pixies can do to help her sleep, possibly even rest well enough to regain some of her strength before...well, before tomorrow night."

"So we're all in agreement, then. This needs to happen, and happen soon, right?" Michael asked.

Becky and Jack nodded.

Michael took a deep breath. "Okay, then. Good. Good, good,

good." He sighed. "...shit."

"I'm going to go back in, make sure Smurf is okay, try and fill Frost in on anything she might miss," Becky said. She started to walk back towards the door, stopped, turned around, walked back, and kissed both Michael and Jack on the cheek. "Thank you both."

"I will join you," Jack said.

"Actually, can you hang back for a sec, man?" Michael asked. "I wanna run something by you."

"Certainly."

"Don't be too long, guys," Becky said, and headed back into the library.

Jack turned to Michael. "Are you all right?"

"You gotta promise me something, man," Michael said. His hands were shaking again, and his voice trembled just a bit. "After, uh, after we do this thing, no matter what happens, you gotta promise me you'll watch me. Have Frick and Frack over there tie me up for a few days if you have to, but, I can't...I can't risk doing anything like what happened before. You know, the last time I drained someone like that. When I...when I might have hurt all those people."

"I promise. I will ensure that you are watched, and yes, if need be, cared for and restrained," Jack said.

"Thanks, man. I didn't wanna, you know, talk about that in front of Becky. She's got enough on her plate, ya know?"

Jack nodded. "You are a good man, Michael."

"Thanks, buddy. I'm gunna hang out here for a bit, if that's okay. Need to kinda clear my head before we do this. Besides, I wanna make sure the pixies don't blow up my dogs."

Jack smiled and walked back into the library.

Michael looked up at the sky. The night was nearly over, and far to the east, the sun was beginning to rise. Maybe no one else could see it yet, but he could; a faint purple glow peeked over the horizon. Michael thought back to Melissa. He couldn't get the image of her staring up at him during the last seizure, the fear in her eyes, the pain. He hated what was hurting her and wished it was something he could control, something he could fight physically. He'd beat the ever-loving hell out of something like that, and the fact that he couldn't just pissed him off.

"Fuck."

Melissa lying there, staring up at him, flashed across Michael's vision again, and was followed almost immediately by the memory of what had happened the last time he'd taken that much from a person. The news flashes on the television, the stories in the papers, the pictures of those who'd gone missing. Michael recalled the dreams he'd had about those faces. Horrible, nauseating dreams. Knowing that he'd likely murdered those people after killing the Hill kid had made him sick to his stomach then and wasn't doing wonders for his stomach now.

Michael walked over and leaned against one of the library walls. "Fuck."

He threw up.

71

Frost listened to everyone's stories and agreed with Jack that learning more about the Dren might be the best course of action at that point. He was also very excited that they were in an ancient library surrounded by books that might contain knowledge of the Dren, and possibly even the dragon that accompanied Elm. Blaze and Stin placed more wards in the surrounding areas and informed the group that only those present could trespass over or even near them and remain safe. The wildlife in the area was also safe, but anyone else? Well, they would be in for several nasty surprises.

When the first rays of sunlight began to reach up and over the horizon, Michael had gone off in search of an interior room where he could browse through whatever books he found and then get some much-needed sleep. He drank a small bit of blood from the cooler; the ice had long since melted, but the water sloshing around the bags was still cool, and the meal did rejuvenate him a bit. Becky and Melissa had also gone off to get some sleep, again accompanied by Thorn and Nanook. Jack, Frost, and the pixies continued browsing the books throughout the library.

Michael cleared the least dusty space on the floor and stacked several books there in order to make an impromptu pillow. He rolled his vest up on top of the little stack and set about inspecting the rest of the room. Michael didn't need light, which was nice, so he investigated the books surrounding him. Every single wall was covered in volume after volume, floor to ceiling. One particular shelf drew Michael's attention first: a row containing just over a dozen books, all bound in similar green and black leather. The books were chained to the shelf as if they might decide to slip away if untethered. The chains holding each book in place were nearly two feet long and, upon closer inspection, appeared as more of a suggestion not to take the books.

Medicine, Geography, Herbalism, Blacksmithing, and more Geography made up the majority of the contents here—nothing about Dren or dragons, at least not yet, anyway. One of the chained books fell to pieces when Michael opened it, its pages fluttering down to the floor and covering the tiny room in a wash of ancient paper. Michael crawled around for a minute retrieving the errant pages, and in doing so recognized the volume to be something along the lines of a recipe book. If he understood the writing, the most well-read and worn of the books was literally full of recipe after recipe for alcohol. From wine, to beer, to mead, those and other alcoholic beverages filled the manual.

Michael chuckled. "Figures you'd be the most popular book! You're well-loved enough," he said, and stuffed the loose pages back into the bindings.

One recipe for what looked to be honey mead referenced a kind of silver honey from little silver bees known as Sterling Stings. Two wonderfully detailed drawings of the honey and the bees sat below the recipe. The artist had even used metallic paint to illustrate that when he said "Silver Mead" and "Silver Bees" he really meant silver! An illustration of the mead looked like a stein filled with mercury, and promised to be some of the best-tasting mead ever imbibed—and apparently the silver bees' honeycomb, prepared in a specific way, could be used to heal burns and staunch blood flow. According to the book's description of the bees, long before this recipe was written down, the bees' corpses were used as a kind of currency. Michael folded that recipe and stuffed it deep into one of his pockets. If he ever found silver bees and silver honey, he'd know what kind of drink to start making!

Eventually, Michael did find a book on dragons. It wasn't chained to a shelf like the first books he'd investigated, so he laid down and began flipping the pages in the dark. Beautiful drawings of the animals, complete with names, apparent lineages, and even the languages each spoke filled page after page. Michael was shocked to realize that dragons spoke multiple tongues and even had a language all their own that no one had yet deciphered. Why he was so surprised made him literally laugh out loud. So dragons could speak? So what? With everything else he'd seen and heard in the last two days, there really shouldn't be much that surprised him at all anymore. Ghosts, pixies, elves, magical bookcase trails, glowing rocks, trees taller than most of the buildings he'd ever seen—trees that talked, no less—and so on, and so on. These were just the tip of what he guessed was an enormous bizarre iceberg floating in an equally strange and magical sea.

Michael did his best to recall the description of the dragon the sisters had given them. They'd mentioned it had metallic blue scales, and something about white horns, or claws, or white something. There were several dragons in the book that came close to matching those features, and Michael dog-eared each page in order to show the pictures to his friends after everyone had gotten some sleep. He felt bad about the dog ears, but not enough to stop doing it.

One of the dragons named Vellrex looked like he could be a match. Vellrex had been old even when this tome had been written, and apparently, he was adept in sorcery.

Michael sighed. "Great...a dragon-wizard," he said. "Sure, why not?"

Michael felt the sun outside and began to lose his fight with fatigue. Ever since becoming a vampire, he could always tell when the sun was up. Even sequestered in a dark room, sometimes several floors below ground, he could *always* tell. It was as if he could feel its warmth through the walls, the ceilings, the earth itself. And with it, always, came a fatigue he was almost powerless to fight unless he was starved for blood. Michael yawned and closed his eyes.

The idea that he could be killing his new friend in a few hours flooded into Michael's mind just as he began to drift off. It promised a series of tortured nightmares he was sure to endure. The last thing he pictured was a sobbing Becky standing over her lifeless little sister, while a grief-stricken Jack stood nearby, his eyes locked on Michael's.

Outside, with the coming sun, figures closed in on the library.

72

Melissa's head was propped up on Becky's lap, and Becky ran her hand through her sister's hair. Nanook and Thorn, in turn, rested their heads on Melissa's lap. They'd dusted off a nice little spot on the floor of another windowless room and made themselves as comfortable as they could. The dogs certainly didn't seem to mind, so long as while Melissa was getting her head rubbed, so were they.

Becky sighed. "I *really* liked that pixie bed."

"You sounded like you sure enjoyed it, Snuffalupagus."

Becky laughed. "Hey! So I'm a deep sleeper, what can I say?"

"And drool monster."

"Okay, now. Did you take your pills?"

"Yes, Mom."

"Hey, you know I gotta ask."

"I know, I know," Melissa said. "So Frost is nice," she added, and glanced up at Becky. "Cute, too!"

Becky smiled. "They sure don't look like brothers, though, do they? Jack and his long, blond hair and blue eyes, Frost and his short, curly, dark hair and green eyes. Jack and his Captain America jaw, Frost and his big ol' Thor shoulders."

"You read too many comics. You do realize that, right?"

"Says the girl who fell in love with a sword-wielding elf on a mountaintop, in the middle of the night."

"Touché. But you do read too many comics."

Becky smiled. "I do."

Melissa poked her sister in the ribs. "So Frost has green eyes, does he?"

Becky chuckled. "Oh, my God, they're so green!"

The sisters laughed, and Melissa rolled over onto her side, while Becky began to rub her shoulder. Thorn grumbled at being disturbed, and Nanook just walked over and curled up next to him.

"You think Mom and Dad are worried?"

"They know we're in and out of cell range all the time, Smurf. Besides, you know Dad," Becky laughed. "I'm sure he's *totally* fine!"

Both sisters giggled at that.

"We'll get back, and the National Guard will be all over Humpback."

"Oh God, you're right," Becky said. "I bet he calls the D.O.D. and has 'em re-task a satellite to look for us if we don't check in soon."

"If?" Melissa said. "He's probably had a satellite on us since we left the city!"

"We're probably on a milk carton by now. I mean, it has been over twenty-four hours, God forbid!"

The girls laughed harder, and poked more fun at their father for a while. Jack and Frost had summoned quite a few floating candles for the sisters' little room, and despite the dust-covered books and faded carpet, the space was quite cozy. The candles put off a nice bit of heat as well, and the crisp snap hovering about had dissipated in short order. Stin and Blaze had somehow managed to make tea again, and both women found their canteens completely full of the stuff. Blaze promised it would help them each sleep and that the tea would ease Melissa's recent headache. It was true, and it was delicious.

"Your two little bodyguards are quite smitten with you," Becky said, and took a sip from her canteen.

"And with each other! Did you notice that?" Melissa asked.

"I did! I wonder what the story is there? We'll have to ask them all about it when this, whatever all of this shit is, is finally over."

"I love Blaze's little head of hair."

"Oh, my God, I know! He looks like a little flying golden matchstick!"

"He does!" Melissa giggled.

Becky ran her hand through Melissa's hair again, leaned down, and kissed her on the cheek. "I love you, Smurf."

"I love you, too, sis."

Becky wiped away a tear before it had a chance to fall, and took a deep breath. "So about Michael, and...with what's been happening to you lately...."

Melissa rolled back over and looked up at her sister. "We kind of talked about it."

"Yeah? He mentioned the two of you had a little chat. What, umm, what all did he say, really?"

"He offered to try and help me. To, you know, to make me like him. A vampire."

"Yeah, he was pretty worried back there. We all were. He's a good guy."

"I like him," Melissa said.

"Enough to trust him?"

Melissa nodded. "I do. Even Jack seems to really like him. And I trust Jack's opinion, too. What do you think? About all of it?"

Becky leaned her head back onto the wall and stared out into space. "Honestly Smurf, all of"—she waved her hands in the air—"this. This is all crazy! But I don't care, you know? I don't care if tomorrow morning you and I wake up in the tent, and all of this turns out to be some weird, crazy dream. A product of bad Pop-Tarts and freeze-dried bacon and beans. I don't care. What I do care about is you. I want you to be okay! I'd do anything to make you better, Smurf, you know that. I mean, we're sitting here having a discussion about turning you into a damned vampire to make you better! A vampire! What the hell? So, yeah. I'd do anything for you, no matter how crazy it was. I mean, look around! You don't get crazier and more bat-shit than this!"

Melissa laughed. "Tell me how you *really* feel," she said.

Becky looked back down at her sister and grinned. "I think you'd make the coolest vampire on the block, kiddo. Especially if you never had to worry about being sick again, you know?"

Melissa blew a little kiss to her sister and rolled back onto her side to face the room again. "I wonder what it's like?"

Becky began to tell Melissa about the dangers Michael and Jack had mentioned—and stopped herself. She just couldn't do it, and it made her angry, sad, and confused all at the same time. Her sister deserved to know the risks, but she just couldn't bring herself to tell her. Maybe she was being selfish, maybe she was just being intentionally naïve, and maybe she was just scared. Whatever she was, it didn't matter, because she couldn't do it. She'd avoided THAT conversation for a year, and she wasn't going to have it now, not the night before Melissa might be cured. Right or wrong, she just wasn't doing that.

"I'm sure it will be fine," Becky said. "I bet it's awesome. You'll be like a female Blade!"

Becky laughed. "Waaaaaay too many comic books."

"Yeah, I know," Becky said. "Now shut it and get some sleep, okay?"

"K." Melissa closed her eyes and then reached up and squeezed Becky's hand. "Do you think vampires can have babies?"

Becky swallowed hard as a sudden stab of pain tore its way into her chest. "I don't know, Smurf. Get some sleep, baby girl," she said, then began to cry as softly and quietly as she could.

73

Frost shook his head, placed an immense leather-bound tome back on a shelf, and turned to his brother. "That does it for this cabinet. Nothing about Dren, or even dragons. And certainly no mention of vampires anywhere. But if you want to know about lost gem mines, some far-fetched chemistry, or even several different hidden lakes, I can help you there. You?"

Jack shook his head. "I found two which mention the Dren. Nothing about vampires or vampirism at all. It appears the Dren were once enslaved."

Frost walked over to Jack and looked at the books he'd gone through. "Enslaved? By whom?"

"Elves, it seems."

Frost made a disgusted sound. "What all did it say?"

"Nothing, really; it was mentioned in passing. The other book just mentioned lands held by Dren, which we already know about. Beyond that, nothing."

"There must be thousands of books here," a tiny voice said from above.

Jack and Frost looked up. Blaze and Stin hovered near a banister on the second floor.

"I would wager hundreds of thousands, if every room is as full as these," Stin said.

"There are two rooms on this level that were locked quite well. We unlocked them, but we found only more books inside," Blaze said.

"Nothing on these Dren," Stin said.

Blaze nodded. "We did find several books on dragons, however."

As soon as the pixie mentioned the books, three large volumes floated out past the guardrail and landed on a table next to the brothers.

"Those are the volumes. One appears to have been spell-sealed. I would caution you about any attempt to open it until we have a closer look," Stin said.

"We are off to search the higher levels," Blaze said.

"Thank you both," Jack called up, and the two pixies vanished back towards the rest of the library.

"Handy having them around," Frost said. "Why are they here again?"

"They seem to have taken a liking to Melissa," Jack said.

Frost smiled. "I can see why! She's beautiful."

Jack smiled, too. "Very."

"She has a warm heart, a kind innocence about her," Frost said, picking up another book. "I wish there was more we could do."

"Thank you. Tell me again what our parents said."

"Oh, you mean after they stopped lamenting about you falling in love with a mortal and the fact you'd discovered a living vampire?"

"I know, I know...."

"Our father almost ordered an invasion of Northern Orknayvar when he heard about the Dren."

Jack looked up, and his mouth fell open. "Are you serious?"

"Very. Mother calmed him down before he started a war, but yes, Jack, he didn't take the news of his youngest son being attacked very well. Mother just, well, she's Mother. I've never really been able to tell what she's thinking, but she was upset."

"I just don't understand why!" Jack said. "Why are they hunting us?" He threw a book across the room where it crashed to the floor and skidded to a dusty stop, several pages fluttering to the ground.

Frost pulled his brother around, grabbed him by both shoulders, and shook him hard. "Enough of that! Do you understand? Pull yourself together!"

The brothers stared at one another for a moment, and then burst into gales of laughter. Jack collapsed onto a chair and wiped away several tears. "I thought you were going to slap me there for a moment!"

"You know, I thought about it?" Frost said between chuckles. "It is good to see you again, Jack. It's been far too long."

"Agreed."

Frost held out his hand and pulled Jack back to his feet. "Now, what say we find out who is after my baby brother, shall we?"

"Also agreed."

The two resumed pulling book after book from the shelves.

"Tell me again how you met the vampire?"

"His name is Michael, and believe it or not, he lives near the Emerald Seat on the other side of the veil. He saw me visiting the area for several nights and thought perhaps I, too, was a vampire."

"Really?"

"He did. Well it makes some sense when you think on it from his perspective. Knowing nothing of elves, or Fae, nothing of the windows between worlds, and literally thinking he might be the only vampire in existence. One night he sees someone just appear and then disappear, followed by a second night, and then a third, and so on. So he came to pay me a visit."

"Well, that must have been a surprise for him."

"It was."

"And tell me, baby brother, why would you tell him who or what you really are? What possessed you?"

Jack was quiet for a moment and then looked back at Frost. "You know, I have no real idea? He just seemed so...so innocent, and so very lonely. I don't want to say it was pity, but I did feel sorry for him. He's very young."

Frost smiled and rubbed the arm Michael had grabbed earlier. "He's also strong, I'll give him that."

"You should have seen him fight the Dren, brother. It was impressive, to say the least."

"Do tell."

"He killed each one that was sent for him. If I'm correct, he mentioned at least five attacking him at his home."

"He killed them?"

Jack nodded. "Every single one of them. And then he killed the one attacking the girls mere moments after I arrived."

Frost looked surprised. "And you say he is young?"

"Very."

"And he managed to survive a coordinated attack, and then

kill yet another of the Dren who threatened you and the sisters?"

"Yes."

"And now you hope he can cure the poor girl?"

"I hope he can save her, yes."

Frost sighed. "Jack, I will only say this once, so you must permit me to do it. You know there are reasons our interactions with mortals are kept so short, and are so rare. Even our hearts, as long as they may beat, are fragile things, brother. Their time is just so, so brief."

Jack smiled at Frost and nodded. "I think that's why their lives burn so bright."

"You always were a romantic, I'll give you that. But the shades here, even they sense it. You've noticed them watching, have you not?"

Jack turned to one of the windows. The morning sun was just beginning to shine outside. "Do you mean the spirits here?"

"I do. Have you seen them?"

"I have not."

"They see us Jack. They see *her*. Shades are attracted to death, impending death; they know when it lingers nearby. They are drawn to it, hoping that when it arrives, they, too, may be set free of the bonds which continue to hold them here."

"I've heard the stories, Frost. And since when did you become such an expert on ghosts?"

"Since I lost Mereth."

Jack lowered his head. "I'm sorry. She was a lovely soul."

"Thank you."

"I know you mean well, brother," Jack said. "I love you for it. I do. But know that I am well aware of who and what Melissa is. I did not care that she was mortal when we first met, and now, even though she is dying, I do not regret loving her."

"You are most definitely a romantic," Frost said, and offered his brother another smile. "I will say no more about it. Forgive me, but I had to speak."

"I know."

A ray of sunshine flooded into the room, and with it came the sound of wards being triggered in the street.

74

Michael was thrown into a wall, or was it the ceiling? He couldn't tell; all he knew for certain was that something inside him snapped, likely another rib, and he bit down hard on his cheek, filling his mouth with warm, salty blood.

"What the fuck?"

He scrambled to his feet, raced over to the door, ripped it open, and was immediately blinded.

Michael screamed, slammed the door, and fell to his knees, blinking his eyes and rubbing at them in an effort to see again. His left arm stung, and his face was scorched. Sunlight.

"HELP!"

The sound of another explosion ripped through the room, and books flew from the shelves on every wall, pelting Michael from all directions.

"Jesus! Help! Jack? Anyone!"

Thorn barked from nearby. So did Nanook. Muffled screams worked their way into the room, and Michael's vision began to clear. Everything was blurry, but he could see again. He crawled over to the door, shielded his face, squinted his eyes as best he could, and pulled the door open a fraction of an inch. Light poured into the room, and Michael slammed the door shut again as his face and hand began to burn.

"Fuck, fuck, fuck!"

He dove back to where he'd been sleeping and began to

rummage through the scattered books. He found his gloves, pulled them on, and rolled down his shirt sleeves. After that, he pulled his vest back on and stared at the door again. He glanced at the wall behind him and tried to remember where that led. If he was right, it led to another windowless room, and just beyond that, Becky and Melissa were holed up, as well as the dogs.

"Okay, okay, okay, okay, okay...."

Michael began tearing at the remaining books on that wall, tossing them to the floor behind him. When he found the wood behind them, he tore through it, and into the wall behind that.

75

Becky cradled Melissa in her arms, both knives drawn and at the ready. Thorn and Nanook crouched in front of the door, teeth bared, hackles raised.

Melissa held her sister. "What's happening?"

Another explosion rocked the entire room, and the candles winked out, plunging them into darkness.

"I don't know, Smurf, I—" Becky stopped as the black pixie blade she'd been given began to glow. It was a soft amber glow at first, and then it grew into a bright orange light, enough for whoever held the blade to see by in the dark.

"We gotta get to Jack," Becky said. "Or Michael."

Melissa buried her face in Becky's chest. "I'm scared!"

Someone shouted from downstairs, and another explosion shook the room.

"Smurf, we gotta go! Now!"

Just then, a hand punched through the wall above the two. Books and debris pelted the sisters, and a large section of the wall disappeared with a loud crunch. Becky pushed Melissa away from the intruder and raised her knives towards the growing hole in the wall.

76

Frost was thrown backwards into several chairs and eventually another bookcase. He rolled over almost immediately and jumped back to his feet; two large swords materialized in his hands, their blades solid black. He dove towards the enormous hole which now existed where the library's east wall once stood.

Frost yelled. "JACK! Down!"

Jack ducked as his brother flew overhead, slashing down at an enormous figure climbing through the wreckage and into the library. A severed arm bounced down the crumbled stone and slid to a stop at Jack's feet. The injured Dren screamed until Frost severed his head a split second later.

"Up, up, up!" a tiny voice yelled from above.

The brothers looked up to see Blaze, sword drawn, motioning to the two. The brothers leapt into the air and landed on the balcony overlooking the first floor. The pixies floated nearby, each already summoning a spell. As soon as Jack and Frost were clear, the entire bottom floor erupted into bright blue flame, and the destroyed wall shot back into place and cemented itself together.

"How did they find us?" Jack asked.

"I don't know," Frost said, pulling a large shard of wood from his shoulder; blood poured down his arm.

Two explosions erupted outside, and the sound of trees crashing to the ground reverberated through the library.

Everything shook.

"Those were the wards we set at the forest edge!" Blaze said.

"There must be *many* of them," Stin said.

Jack pointed his blade across the enormous foyer towards the staircase beyond. "We have to get to the girls."

One of the giant windows exploded into the library below, sending glass flying everywhere. A single tiny figure darted into the room and began looking about.

Stin yelled down at the new arrival, "WARDEN?"

Yori looked up and raced to the group above. "There are hundreds of them," she said.

"How did you find us?" Blaze asked.

"IT WAS YOU!" Stin said before Yori could reply. "You were following us back in the Stygian Copse!"

"Why are you here, Yori?" Jack asked.

The pixie looked over at Jack and made a small bow. "I followed you from Droll. I was mistaken about you and your friends before. Forgive me. I followed you to make amends. I thought it best to remain hidden should someone else be tracking you. Until now, none were. None at all."

Another concussive blast shook the building, and curtains of dust fell from the rafters above.

"Well, your presence is welcome, Warden," Frost said.

Yori nodded to the elf and turned to Blaze and Stin. "Your wards: are any of them deadly?"

"Some. Most are not, but they will be effective enough. Why?" Stin asked.

"Because they brought a dragon."

77

Michael pulled away another section of wall and stopped when he saw Becky lunging forward, knives drawn. He caught her hand just before her blade pierced deep into his forearm.

"It's me! It's me! Hey!"

Becky gasped. "Oh, thank God!"

Michael ripped away one more section of wall and climbed through the hole. Thorn and Nanook raced over and jumped up to greet him. Michael rubbed each dog's head and turned back to the sisters.

"What the hell is happening?"

Another blast shook the room, and Becky fell against the wall, Michael grabbing at her to keep her steady. Melissa let out a small scream from the floor.

"We don't know! We were going to come find you," Becky said.

Michael pointed over the the small amount of light pouring in from beneath the door. "I can't go out there. I tried, almost went blind doing it, hence the…" Michael pointed back to the hole he'd ripped into the wall. "Whatever's happening, I'm sure Jack and Frost are on top of it, not to mention the pixies. I assume the blasts we're hearing are their booby traps or whatever," Michael said.

On cue, two more explosions went off outside; the sound of several screams and shouts followed.

"Yeah, that's gotta be them," Becky said.

"We need to go help!" Melissa said.

"Smurf, I don't know."

"Yeah, we don't even know what's going—"

A cavernous roar reverberated through the building, each person feeling it in their chest more than hearing it.

"What. The. Hell?" Michael asked.

"Oh, my God, it's them," Melissa gasped. "The dragon! It's them!"

The roar erupted again, and this time the entire building shook.

78

The ceiling above Frost, Jack, and the pixies, as well as every floor and room above that, exploded up and away in a deafening cacophony of violence and noise. Debris fell everywhere, and the group dove for cover amidst the deluge. A huge, nightmarish claw reached over the ruined wall of the library, followed by an enormous scaled head. The dragon looked at the group and roared again.

Yori, now the size of Jack and Frost, launched three arrows at the dragon's eye from the flat of her back. The beast lowered its head, and the arrows bounced harmlessly away. Yori rolled backwards as the dragon snapped at the floor where she'd just been, and Frost swung both swords at the monster's neck. The blades skipped across the metallic blue scales, leaving bright glowing trails behind but nothing more. Jack swung his own blade and just missed the dragon's eye as the beast reared up and out of reach.

Frost yelled at the pixies, "FLY!"

Yori leapt over the balcony while Blaze and Stin raced out over the room below and towards the staircase beyond. The dragon looked back down at the elves, tore away another huge section of wall, and disappeared over the broken stones. Elm landed on the balcony between the two, smiled at each man, and drew two glasslike swords.

79

The room where Michael had just been erupted in light, which shot through the hole he'd torn through the wall. Michael closed his eyes and dove out of the way while grabbing Becky and Melissa in his arms. Thorn and Nanook leapt through the opening, and the sound of horrible fighting followed.

"Guys!" Michael yelled and looked towards the light. He immediately fell to his knees, hands pressed against his eyelids, and screamed.

Becky raced to the hole and saw two male Dren swinging their bows at each dog, too close to fire their weapons. The entire eastern wall of the room was gone, and two giant hooks were now embedded in the floor of the room. Nanook had one of the Dren by the arm and was whipping her body back and forth, tearing at the man's armor, and, by the sounds of it, the man's flesh beneath that. Thorn was circling the other Dren, launching in and out of the man's reach while snapping at his legs.

The Dren dealing with Nanook dropped his bow and pulled a long silver dagger from a sheath on his belt.

"Michael! To your left!" Becky shouted, and leapt through the hole in the wall.

Michael felt to his left and found a kneeling Melissa there. He grabbed her and hugged her in both arms."Tell me what you see!"

"They're in your room!" Melissa said.

Becky did her best to remember everything she'd been taught about close-quarter knife fighting and tried to adapt that to wielding two blades instead of one. Her sudden appearance took the Dren dealing with Nanook by surprise, and she slashed at the man's face, then at his hand when he thrust the dagger in her direction, now ignoring a still-thrashing Nanook. Her second strike landed home, and the man yelled and dropped his knife. Becky kicked it away and strafed to her left to put the closest Dren between her and the other man, who was now glaring at her as well.

Becky glanced back through the wall. "GET HER OUT OF HERE!"

Michael clenched his eyes as tight as he could, grabbed hold of Melissa, and plunged out into the sunlit hallway.

80

Michael's left shoulder exploded in pain as he collided with the opposite wall outside the doorway. He didn't let it stop him; instead, he grabbed Melissa's hand, spun her around, and picked her up in his arms.

"Hold on," Michael ordered. He raced further into the building towards what little shadow he could see behind his half-closed eyes. "Tell me where!"

"Left! Turn left!"

Michael did as he was told, opened one eye just enough to see more, and sped down a new, much darker hallway, Melissa held tight in his arms. Another explosion shook the building, and several doors along the new passage burst open, shards of wood blasting into the hallway along with cascades of daylight. Michael closed his eyes and barreled into a door on his right and crashing to the floor, dropping Melissa as he did. The two were plunged into darkness, and Michael crawled over, slamming the door shut.

"Are you okay?" Melissa asked as she crawled towards her friend.

Michael rubbed his eyes. "I'll be okay," he said between gasps for air.

The room was larger than the previous two, and just as before, filled with books and bookcases. Three rows of shelving ran the length of the room, and Michael raced down the far aisle, pulling Melissa along behind him. When they reached the end, they found themselves in a dark corner of books from floor to ceiling. Michael began tearing the books from the shelves, tossing them onto the floor.

When he had an entire section of bookcase cleared, he turned to Melissa. "Here, get in here," he said.

Melissa crouched down and curled up into the space. Michael shoved the pile of books in her direction with one boot. "Try and stack these up around you," he said, and ran back down the row. He returned a second later with a dust-filled carpet and tossed it over the pile of books and Melissa. "Try and hide as best as you can. I'll be back."

Melissa did as she was told, and covered herself and the books. Michael glanced back over his shoulder as he left. The poor girl looked like a pile of dusty debris, nothing more. Michael went one step further and reached up to pull an entire bookshelf over into the aisle.

"That's just me," he yelled as the books and shelving crashed over, further hiding his friend.

Michael took a deep breath, flung open the door, and raced back out into the sun-drenched hallway, straight into a towering Dren.

81

Blaze swooped down onto the head of the first Dren who burst through the library doors. He planted the tip of his blade deep into the man's hood and shouted the name of a spell he knew well. The Dren's entire body went rigid, and he collapsed face first to the floor, where he remained. Blaze flew back up, sword raised, and waited for his next target.

Stin fired through the broken window at a Dren just outside of the Library. He thought it must have been the ninth arrow he'd hit her with so far, and she was still standing; he was impressed. Stin glanced down at his quiver just as more arrows materialized, and he grinned. The Dren he was firing at had stepped on one of the wards and was now frozen in place, unable to move anything below the waist. The last arrow stuck the woman's neck, just as the others had, but this one seemed to do the trick. The woman's eyes fluttered for a second, then rolled back into her head, whereupon she tumbled over, setting off yet another ward. There was a bright flash, and the Dren was catapulted up through the air and out of sight. The sound of a sickening thud from the roof not far from where Stin now hovered told him where the woman finally landed. A shower of dust into the library from the rafters above confirmed it.

Yori shouted from somewhere behind the pixie. "Stin! Move!"

Stin flew to his right just as a giant set of black iron hooks burst through the window, a green transparent chain trailing behind. The hooks smashed through several chairs and desks and slid to a heavy stop. A second later, the chain went taut, and the hooks raced back in the direction from which they'd come, pulling everything in their path with them—including the entire wall Stin had already repaired once.

Yori scooped Stin out of the air with one hand and rolled away from the falling timbers and stones that came crashing down.

Stin looked up from Yori's palm. "Now I know why you enjoy changing sizes so often!"

Yori grinned, offered Stin a wink, and flew back up onto the balcony where Elm had just landed, leaving Stin and Blaze to deal with the invaders on the ground floor.

Another Dren raced into the room, and just as before, Blaze made quick work of him; he was amassing an impressive pile of attackers at this point. Stin returned fire out of the library and wondered just how many Dren were descending on them. From his viewpoint, he counted at least a hundred.

"You'll need more," Stin said, and smiled as his tiny arrows found their marks, and Dren after Dren collapsed.

82

"Why do you hunt my brother?" Frost asked as he circled behind the enormous figure.

Elm looked down at Frost. She towered over the elf by at least a foot and a half. "I cannot reveal that to you, Frost, second son of Laendrill, son of Kalleth."

"You know our parents," Jack said. "Then you know what you risk here."

Elm turned to Jack. "I do. But some risks are worth the dangers they carry, are they not? You should know this well."

"Know that I call these elves friend, woman," Yori said, pointing her golden sword towards Elm's throat.

Elm glanced at the pixie. "I would gladly do the same under different circumstances, Warden."

Yori nodded.

"Then why are you doing this?" Jack asked. "Your men confessed that there was no honor in this!"

Elm glanced back at Jack and sighed. "I will tell you the same thing I told your poor love, and her brave sister. Should you survive this, seek out those who sent me. I am not the threat."

"Do not do this," Jack said. "I beg of you. If you know of my love, then if not for us, for the girl's sake! For Melissa's sake."

Elm lowered her swords "*I* am not doing this. Remember

that, Jack, son of Laendrill, son of Kalleth. Alas"—Elm raised her swords again—"shall we?"

Frost lunged at Elm, both of his swords slashing deep into the Dren's armor just below the knees. Elm rolled forward, swung one of her swords, and stopped Yori's golden blade just before it struck her neck. Jack parried to his left as Elm's other blade raced towards his chest; the two swords clashed against one another, and a strange sound reverberated through the room. Jack felt a surge of electricity shoot up his arm and into his shoulder. Elm's blades were enchanted. From the look on Yori's face, the pixie had realized the same.

Yori flew up and over Elm, slashing downwards, only to be met with one of the Dren's blades colliding hard with her chest plate. The air in the pixie's lungs exploded, and Yori crashed onto the ground, her left wing torn almost in two, blood pumping from the shredded veins.

Jack avoided several of Elm's strikes, only to find himself being driven backwards towards open air. Frost lunged at the Dren's back, finding nothing as Elm rolled to her left and then leapt back to her feet.

Frost drew a large gun from his belt. "Dodge this," he said, and fired several shots at the woman.

Elm's armor sparked to life as huge bullets ricocheted in various directions. A small, thin line of blood appeared on her cheek, and her eyes locked on Frost's.

"A coward's weapon?" Elm asked, and swung one of her swords towards the elf.

"A brother defending his family's weapon," Frost replied, and parried Elm's attack, firing several more rounds at the Dren. None found their mark, and Frost cursed through clenched teeth.

Elm spun just as Jack slashed in her direction and missed. In the same motion, the woman launched three crimson knives through the air, two piercing the wall behind Frost, the third burying itself in Frost's chest. He stumbled backwards; Yori caught him and guided the wounded elf to the ground as he coughed up a frightening amount of blood. Yori drew her crossbow, dove *towards* Elm, and fired.

The Dren batted the metal bolt from the air and met Yori's blade with both of her own. The strange metal on glass sound erupted from the swords, and Yori let out a scream.

83

Becky grimaced as the first Dren she'd cut looked down at the horrific wound she'd just delivered. "I got a shitload more where that came from, asshole," she snarled.

Nanook was no longer attached to the man's wrist, and instead was now engaged in a similar tactic as Thorn. She darted in and around the Dren's legs, snapping and tearing at the man's boots whenever she could get close. The armor meant she was doing no real damage, but it did throw the towering invader off balance enough for Becky to deal with him.

Thorn, on the other hand, had managed to draw blood from the Dren he was fighting. The dog had gotten through the man's armor in just the right place below the knee, and sunk his teeth in deep. When the Dren drew his sword to slash down at the dog, Thorn bolted out of reach and continued to circle.

"Come on, fucker," Becky said, and slashed at the man's arm again.

The Dren managed to pull his sword this time and slash simultaneously in Becky's direction. Becky ducked beneath the attack and lunged forward, shoulder first, into the man's crotch. She stabbed upwards, hoping to find the magic spot, and sunk the MK3's blade in hilt deep. Her hand was showered in warmth, and Becky rolled backwards. When she looked up, the Dren had dropped his sword and held both hands between his legs. A second later he collapsed to his knees, a fountain of blood pooling at his feet.

"Gotcha," Becky said.

Nanook jumped onto the man's back and sunk her teeth into his neck. Becky heard bone snap, and the Dren went limp, fell to the floor, and remained there. The other man roared, and slashed at Nanook with his sword. She dodged the attack and lunged, puncturing the man's wrist. Thorn latched onto the man's other arm, and Becky charged forward, sinking both blades into the man's right inner thigh. Again, a thick geyser of blood soaked her hands as well as her arms and face.

Becky leapt away, wiped the blood from her eyes, and watched as the man collapsed to one knee. He looked up at Becky, back down to his thigh, and smiled. Becky knew she had killed him, and he seemed to know it as well. The Dren nodded to Becky as his eyes rolled back in their sockets, his eyelids fluttering shut. The dogs let go as he collapsed backwards, and Becky's legs gave out beneath her. She hit the floor hard, and looked up to see Thorn and Nanook staring at her.

From the other room, behind the giant hole in the wall, another Dren looked in on the scene of carnage.

84

Michael gasped as the Dren he'd collided with grabbed him by the throat and pinned him to the wall. The light pouring into the hallway scorched Michael's eyes and burned at his face and neck. He screamed while reaching out and clawing for anything he could find. He found the Dren's arm and squeezed as hard as he could. The Dren let out a surprised yell as Michael felt bones snap and erupt from the man's arm just below the elbow. Michael didn't stop; eyes clenched shut, he pulled the man's arm away from his throat and struck out with his other fist. It felt like he collided with metal, and the sound of a sword skittering away down the hall confirmed Michael's suspicion.

"Mother fu—" Michael said, and struck out again. This time, his fist landed on the man's body, and the Dren backed away, gasping for air.

Despite the pain, Michael opened his eyes, saw the man's blurry shape just feet from him, and dove forward, reaching for the Dren's throat.

"HERE!" the Dren shouted.

Michael lunged towards the sound and found his fingers deep in the Dren's mouth. The Dren bit down, and Michael grabbed the man's lower jaw. With one quick snap, Michael ripped the man's jaw from his head, tongue and all. A horrible gurgling sound filled Michael's ears, and he dove back in the direction he'd come, slamming the door shut again.

"Jesus Christ!" he yelled, and crashed to the floor.

"Michael?" Melissa shouted from her hiding place.

"They're everywhere! Just stay where you—"

Another of the horrifying roars rocked the building as a huge section of wall and ceiling peeled away into the blinding light. Michael heard Melissa scream and stumbled towards the sound, only to be slammed to the ground, pinned beneath something heavy, something Michael could not move. Another scream came from just ahead. He pushed hard into the ground, trying to lift himself and whatever held him down.

"MELISSA!"

Michael opened his eyes and screamed again as hot, molten light bored into them. His arms gave out, and more alien objects fell onto his back, arms, and head. The weight grew worse and worse, driving the air from the vampire's lungs in a slow, steady stream. Michael gasped and struggled to inhale; the last sounds he heard before passing out were his ribs cracking beneath the weight of whatever was crushing him to death. His final thought was of poor Melissa.

85

Frost groaned as he pulled the blade from his ribs, its red glass now covered in blood. His head was swimming, and he spit more blood onto the floor. It was very difficult to breathe, and all he wanted to do was lie back and close his eyes.

Jack glanced towards his brother. "FROST!"

Elm swung her swords in Jack's direction and corrected as one missed and the other was stopped by his blue sword. Yori slashed down at Elm's legs and rolled just as the Dren's sword stopped her attack. A tiny arrow wizzed through Elm's hair, and she turned to see a pixie firing in her direction in rapid procession. She dodged another arrow and pulled her hood up while turning her back towards Stin and his assault. The little arrows began to bounce from Elm's armor, one after the other.

"Jack! Down!"

Jack turned to see Frost back on his feet. He ducked just as Frost threw Elm's own blade back in her direction. The Dren spun and swatted the knife up into the air with her sword; as it fell, she slammed one sword point down into the wooden floor, caught the falling knife, spun, and launched it towards the stream of arrows pelting her from behind. The arrows stopped, and Elm retrieved her blade just as Jack smashed his sword into the woman's leg. The armor held, and Elm batted Jack's sword from his hand with the butt of her own. Jack cried out as the bones in his wrist snapped, and Elm kicked him up and over the banister.

Jack spun in the air, dazed, and smashed to the ground

below, his head bouncing off of one of the tables. Darkness overtook him.

86

Becky stared up at the Dren looking down at her. The man's beard, a dark blue, shimmered in the light, which poured in from the open door behind him. He smiled, and held out a hand to help Becky to her feet. Thorn and Nanook growled but did not lunge at the man.

"Your sister needs your help, warrior," Pine said.

Becky clambered backwards and clutched the arm Pine had so easily broken just two nights ago. "What the fuck?"

Pine glanced at the two dogs. "I mean you no harm," he said. Thorn and Nanook stopped growling, but their hackles remained up.

"I've come to right the wrongs done to you by my clan," Pine said. "I swear to you, I mean you no harm."

Becky pulled herself off the ground and held her knives out in front of her. Another Dren burst through the door to her left and was immediately pinned to a bookcase by a large red arrow through his neck. Becky spun around to see Pine lowering his bow.

"I told you. I am here to help. I should have never agreed to follow Elm," Pine said, and held his hand back out to Becky.

Becky looked back at the the dying man and the giant arrow holding him in place. "Why the fuck should I trust you?"

"If you recall, I stopped my attack at your camp when we first met. Do you remember my words before the vampire attacked me?"

"What? No! I was too busy not being murdered, asshole!"

Pine sighed. "I will hunt you no more, though it likely means my own death. That is what I said to you then, and I meant it. I mean this now: I am here to help you. If you do not trust me, I understand, but your sister still needs your help. There is no time for this, that I promise as well," he said, and held his hand out once again.

Becky shook her head. "Do you know where Melissa is?"

"I believe the vampire took her towards the west of the building."

"Shit..." Becky said, sheathed one of her blades, and grabbed Pine's hand.

Pine helped Becky through the hole in the wall while Thorn and Nanook followed. Another Dren raced by, and Pine shoved Becky behind him. "Wait here."

Pine walked over to the door, peered out in both directions, drew his bow, and fired another shot. From further down the hallway a short cry of pain rang out, and then silence. Pine turned and motioned Becky to follow.

87

Frost collapsed to one knee just as Elm's two swords collided with both of his. Again the strange, painful enchantment raced into Frost's arms and pierced his chest. Yori kicked out at Elm and caught the Dren in the small of her back. Elm stumbled forward, turned, and swung one of her blades at the woman. Yori ducked, and an intense fire erupted along her spine as both of her iridescent wings fluttered to the ground, severed at their base. The pixie screamed and collapsed.

Frost stabbed at Elm's turned back and was almost surprised when his blade dug deep into the Dren's armor just below the ribs. Elm gasped, rolled forward, and stumbled to her feet. Yori, still screaming, charged towards the giant woman, and launched her shoulder into the Dren's hip. The two spiraled over the balcony and crashed onto the floor below, not far from where Jack lay unconscious.

Elm landed on her side, the pixie on top of her. Yori's head smacked the ground, and the Warden rolled over, motionless. Elm struggled to her feet just as Frost dove from the balcony, both swords raised. Elm sidestepped, and brought the hilt of her swords down onto the elf's spine, sending him crashing through one of the few remaining tables. Frost hit the ground hard and moved no more.

PART 3

HOME

88

Michael gasped for air and tried to open his eyes, but found they were being held shut. He tried to move and couldn't. Something touched his face, and when he tried to flinch away, found he was unable to move his head as well.

"Michael? Don't move, okay? You're hurt. We're trying to help you."

Michael's chest was on fire, while the rest of his body felt as if it were numb, or had fallen asleep and was just waking up. The strange sensation of pins and needles was starting to set in, beginning with his feet and hands. Something wet touched his lips, and Michael tried to open his mouth; he was so, so thirsty.

"It's okay, Michael, just try and swallow."

Michael did, and coughed immediately. His chest exploded in waves of agony, and he screamed.

"I'm sorry, I know it hurts, but try and drink, okay?"

The voice was familiar, and Michael tried again to open his eyes again. He failed.

"Beck—" was all he managed to choke out before he coughed again.

More liquid flowed into his mouth. It was warm, salty, and...it was blood. Michael swallowed; this time he didn't cough.

"Becky?"

"There he is," Becky said, and brushed Michael's hair from his eyes. "Don't talk, okay? Just drink. You're going to be all right."

Michael relaxed, swallowed several more gulps of blood, and sighed as the pain in his chest and the feeling in his extremities began to return.

Becky looked up at Pine. "Get me some water."

Pine nodded and raced from the room.

"Michael, your eyes are full of dried blood. Don't try to open them yet, okay? I'm going to wash them clean."

Becky felt a little lightheaded and pulled her arm away from the vampire's mouth. Her breath caught in her chest as she saw his elongated canine teeth for the first time.

"Melissa?" Michael asked, and coughed again.

Becky placed a hand on Michael's cheek. "She's fine. Don't talk, okay?" Becky cut a strip of her blouse away and wrapped it tight around her wrist. She jumped and swatted at the shirt when it began to vibrate, and the cloth she'd just cut away grew back over the next several seconds.

"Shit! So, uh, so our clothes repair themselves now, I guess?" she said, and tried to smile down at her very injured friend.

Pine raced back into the room and handed Becky a blue leather bag. It sloshed when she took it and uncorked the top. She nodded to the Dren, who nodded back.

"Michael, I'm going to pour some water onto your eyelids, okay? Don't worry. Keep your eyes shut."

Becky proceeded to wipe away as much of the dried blood as she could and smiled when Michael finally did open his eyes. "Welcome back."

Michael stared up at a starlit sky behind the splintered wreckage of what was once a roof and wondered how long he'd been unconscious. Then the giant Dren staring down at him behind Becky came into focus. Michael gasped and immediately began to scramble to his feet, only to be held down by Becky and then by Pine.

"DREN!"

Becky took Michael's face in her hands and pulled his gaze back to her own. "Michael, it's okay! It's okay! Look at me!"

Michael tore his eyes from the Dren and focused on Becky.

"He's here to help. He's the one who found you! Got you out from under all of those beams. It's okay! Michael! Look at me! It's okay!"

"She speaks the truth, vampire," Pine said. "I mean you no harm."

Becky relaxed her grip on Michael. "I'm sorry, I didn't even think."

Michael relaxed.

89

Yori cradled Jack's head in her lap, her hands on his temples, a low green light pulsing beneath the pixie's fingers. Frost held his hands on Jack's chest, and he, too, worked a spell to bring his brother back around, as well as heal whatever wounds he could detect.

"Does it hurt?" Frost asked, glancing over at Yori. "Your back?"

"Yes," the pixie said, and continued to concentrate on Jack.

"I will do what I can when we finish here," Frost said. He was covered in dirt, shards of splintered wood, and glass, while rivers of dried blood caked the side of his face, neck, chest, and arm.

"I've had worse," the pixie said.

Frost smiled. "You were amazing. I fear none of us would have survived that fight without your aid. I am in your debt. *We* are in your debt."

Yori opened her eyes and offered Frost a slight smile. Jack took a large breath, and his eyes fluttered open.

Jack focused first on Yori, and then on his brother. "Melissa?"

Yori stopped what she was doing, ran her hands around to the back of Jack's head and then to his shoulders, and guided him into a sitting position. Frost leaned forward and helped, taking his brother's hands in his own. Jack winced and clenched his teeth.

"You need to focus on yourself for a moment," Frost said.

Yori glanced up at Frost and sighed. "He should know."

"Know what?" Jack asked, spitting blood onto the floor. "Where is Melissa? Frost?"

Frost sighed and looked Jack in the eyes. "She's gone, Jack. She's gone."

90

Michael took several deep breaths and winced as his ribs knitted themselves back together. It hurt. It hurt a lot. He was sure he'd broken every single rib, both front and back. He wanted to vomit from the pain, but the idea of doing that, and the pain that would follow, helped him resist the urge.

"How?" was all Michael managed before a coughing fit threatened to consume him again.

"They just stopped," Becky said. "All of a sudden. They just stopped and left."

"They found what they were looking for, I'm afraid," Pine said, and crouched down to offer Michael another sip of water, which the vampire accepted.

Michael took a sip, coughed, and took another drink. "What?"

Becky looked at Pine and then down at Michael. Tears welled up in her eyes, and she took one of Michael's hands. "They took Smurf," she said. "They took my little sister."

Michael's eyes widened, and he struggled to his feet against both Becky's and Pine's protests.

"Which way?" Michael said and coughed again. Blood sprayed the floor before him, and he wiped his mouth with one sleeve.

"They opened windows. We will need tracking spells to follow them," Pine said.

"Can you walk?" Becky asked.

Michael nodded but threw one arm around her. "Where's Jack?"

"He's downstairs," Becky said. "He fought Elm with Frost and Yori."

"Yori's here?"

Becky nodded. "She showed up right when the Dren attacked. Jack's hurt. They're all hurt, but Jack was still unconscious when we found you."

Michael coughed and pointed to the doorway. Pine reached over and took his other arm, and the three made their way out and into the wreckage of a hallway.

"Dogs?" Michael asked.

"They're fine, they're downstairs," Becky said. "They're pretty badass in a fight."

Michael nodded. The hallway was littered with debris. The eastern wall was simply gone, as was a huge portion of the ceiling and whatever rooms had existed above it. Countless books were scattered everywhere, and countless more pages fluttered about in the evening breeze. As the three made their way to the stairs, the sounds of their boots crushing the spines and pages of the books was a sad one. The library itself creaked and groaned. Every few seconds another beam would fall, and once what sounded like a section of roof collapsing into the building caused Michael to jump. The pain in his back made him regret it.

When they reached the stairway, Michael gasped at the destruction below. The entire eastern face of the library lay in ruin on the city street. No furniture remained intact, and even the giant chimney in the center of the room had been blown to bits. Below, Yori, her human size again, was helping Jack to his feet while Frost held the elf's arm. The three looked as bad as Michael felt; Frost looked even worse with the dried blood caking him. Thorn and Nanook sat on the far side of the room, staring down at something, their ears laid flat. They glanced up once at Michael as he started down the stairs, then returned their attention to what was on the floor.

91

Blaze cradled Stin in his arms while rocking back and forth, a small song drifting from his trembling lips. Tears poured from his eyes, his chest heaving as he cried. Stin was gone. A huge gash had nearly severed the pixie in two. The red-bladed knife which had struck him was buried deep in the stone above. Stin still held his tiny bow, an arrow nocked in the string, never to be fired.

"Oh, Stin..." Becky said as they reached the bottom of the stairs.

Michael collapsed to his knees between Thorn and Nanook, who nuzzled into him and whimpered. "Dammit..." he said, and coughed again.

Jack, Frost, and Yori joined the rest of the group and stood in silence behind Blaze and Stin's lifeless body.

"I'm so, so sorry," Becky said and knelt down. She reached out and touched Stin on the arm with a light, delicate finger.

Blaze looked up at everyone and then back down to his love. "When they die, where do they go?" he asked.

Yori reverted back to her smaller size and walked over to where Blaze sat on the ground. She knelt down beside Stin, reached over, and closed the pixie's eyes.

"We don't go anywhere," she said, and leaned over to kiss Blaze on the cheek. "They remain here," she added, and touched Blaze's chest, just above the heart, "...and they remain here," she said, and motioned to the air around them. "They will always be with us. No one ever truly dies when there are those who live to still remember them. And even then, they remain. Stin is still *here,* Blaze. He is now, and always will be with you, with us, with everyone."

Blaze looked up and smiled at Yori. "Thank you."

Everyone, even Pine who knelt to one knee, expressed their condolences to Blaze, and Yori set about preparing a small funeral pyre for the little body. Michael tried to talk to Blaze, but each time he did, he found himself beginning to cry and could not muster the words. Instead, he limped outside and destroyed the first thing he came across: a stone statue of a lion nearly as tall as himself. Michael ripped it apart and cursed into the night.

92

Yori and Blaze led a small ceremony for Stin and cremated their friend. Everyone stood by quietly as the pixie vanished into flame and smoke, drifting up and away into the night sky. Thorn and Nanook lay near the fire and whimpered. Michael was nowhere to be found.

Frost, Jack, and Becky regrouped inside what was left of the library, and began discussing how to track the Dren. Pine offered his assistance whenever possible.

Jack looked up at the Dren. "You said you followed them here? How?"

Pine tossed a huge piece of wood into a second fire Frost had built. He turned back to the group. "After our first encounter two nights ago, I dedicated myself to assisting you. I would have arrived earlier, but my wounds were severe. The vampire threw me from quite a height."

Becky spat into the fire. "Obviously not high enough."

Pine smiled. "No, thankfully," he said, sitting down on the floor. "When I found Elm, they were looking for you every-where. Even Vellrex was searching."

"The dragon?" Frost asked.

Pine nodded. "I was shocked to learn that Elm had given you one day to prepare. That was very strange indeed. When I rejoined the clan, I informed them of Trex's death, and pro-ceeded to do what I could to help you all from where I was. I stayed, listened, even searched, but I was still hurt, and fell behind almost hourly. I hoped to learn of your location and to reach you before Elm and her forces. I was too slow. Please forgive me."

"Why? Why help us?" Frost asked.

"There is no honor in what Elm does. You are innocents. You have done us no wrong, pose no threat. You are no more a danger to us than a shadow is to its creator," Pine said. He glanced at Becky. "And you are brave, strong, admirable."

"So who exactly is this bitch?" Becky asked.

Pine looked up and then out at the brothers. "Elm is the oldest of us. She is our queen."

Jack walked over to the fire and stared into the flames. "But why is she doing this? Why did they take Melissa? Who precisely is behind this? Who can command a queen?"

"I do not know who Elm follows. She told us all that she had no choice, but that once this thing was done, once this was finished, the Dren would be free of all who once held power over us."

"Where would they have gone? Do you have any idea where they would take my sister?" Becky asked.

Pine shook his head. "No. None were told anything beyond what we were here to do. Kill the vampire, kill you"—he nodded at Becky—"spare the elves, kill anyone else we found standing with you, and to bring the girl, Melissa, to Elm unharmed."

"Unharmed?" Jack asked.

"Yes."

Frost stood and winced as he did. "Is there something about Melissa I don't know?" he asked the group. "Aside from her involvement with my brother, is there something else? Anything?"

Jack threw up his hands and shook his head. "Nothing!"

Becky shook her head as well. "All I know is she met you and all of this, this insanity began!" she said, and kicked a pile of debris; wood and stone flew across the room. "She meets you"—she stabbed a finger at Jack—"falls head over heels for your fucking bullshit, gets sick, and now people are out to kill her family and friends and take her off to God knows where! That about sum it up for you, Frost?"

"Rebecca—" Jack said.

"No! No, you stay the hell away from me, Keebler!" Becky said, tears streaming down her cheeks, a knife now held tight in one hand. "Melissa's just a naïve little girl who wouldn't hurt a fucking fly! She's sick, dying, scared, and now some giant blue-haired cunt takes her away? Why? And now she's all alone, and that is all YOUR fault, asshole!" She jabbed a finger towards Jack. "If she had never met you, who knows! Maybe she wouldn't even be as sick as she is!" Becky tried to say more, stumbled about her words, cursed again, and ran out of the room, disappearing into the dark streets.

Jack collapsed to his knees and put his fist through the library's stone floor.

93

Yori put her arm around Blaze and handed him the tiny leather pouch with two leather straps containing Stin's ashes. They were still warm."You must wear this close to your heart, young one."

Blaze looked down at the little pouch and kissed it. "You were the better of us," he said, and tied the pouch around his neck. "Thank you, master Warden."

Yori nodded. "We have fought side by side now, young Blaze. We have lost a kindred spirit together. You will call me by my name henceforth. Do you understand? Not Warden. I am Yori. An equal should refer to their equal by name. More importantly, friends."

Blaze turned and hugged her hard. When she winced, Blaze took a step back and apologized.

"Let me help you, Yori," he said.

Yori reached out and touched his arm. "I will be fine. This is not the first time a pixie has had her wings clipped. They do grow back, you know."

Blaze smiled. "Please let me; I need to stay busy. You understand that, yes?"

Yori nodded and turned her back to Blaze. Blaze touched the open wounds and closed his eyes. Almost immediately, a blinding flash of light erupted from Blaze's hands, and Yori gasped. Two beautiful wings unfurled from Yori's back and began to flutter. Yori dropped to one knee and took a deep breath. Blaze grabbed her arm and helped her back to her feet.

"How did...?" Yori asked between deep gasps for air. "That should have..." she panted, "...that should have taken weeks to complete."

Blaze smiled. "Are you in pain?"

Yori shook her head. "No, no, I.... That was so, so powerful."

"Rage and grief are powerful emotions," Blaze said. "Channeled into something productive, there's no limit to what one can accomplish. Even regrowing a friend's lost wings."

Yori smiled, fluttered up several inches into the air, and hugged Blaze. "I am proud to call you friend."

Blaze hugged Yori back. "I as well. Besides, I need you at your best so you can help me kill Elm."

94

Michael hovered high above the library and stared at the soft glow of the fires inside. His ribs were better now, and his spine hurt less; even the persistent cough was gone. He'd watched poor Stin's ceremony and swore to avenge the little guy. He'd really started to like those two, and seeing poor Blaze so grief-stricken pissed Michael off, badly. He also listened in on Pine's story and the questions everyone threw his way.

Michael still wasn't convinced Pine was on their side. Nor was Michael convinced he wouldn't just fly down there, grab the giant man, and finish the job he'd obviously botched at Humpback in the first place. He wanted to kill someone, and he wanted to do it soon; he needed it. Melissa was his responsibility, and he'd failed her. The whole reason he was even here was to help the poor girl, to save her, and he'd failed. He failed everyone. He failed her, he failed Jack, he failed poor Becky, and he failed himself. If Melissa wasn't dead already, she would be soon. There was no hope she'd survive another episode like before, whether he was there to try and help or not. He needed to get to her, and get to her soon. The faster he was able to try and turn her, the better chance she had at seeing tomorrow— and the night was coming to an end.

Becky sprinted from the library and dashed down a dark side street. Michael followed her and flew down when she collapsed to the ground in a small alleyway.

"Becky?" Michael asked as he landed near the sobbing woman.

Becky looked up, cried out, and raced over into Michael's arms, slamming into him hard. He hugged her back, and the two stood there for a long while, neither saying a thing. Michael closed his eyes and swore he'd make this right. He'd get Melissa back to her sister. He'd save her from the disease trying to kill her, and he'd make sure she and Jack had a shot at happily ever after.

Becky wiped her cheeks and looked up to Michael. She didn't say anything, she just grabbed his collar, pulled him down and kissed him hard. Michael's heart began to race, and he kissed her back, lifting her from the ground.

"I'll get her back," Michael said when the two finally stopped. "I promise you, I'll get her back."

Becky smiled and kissed Michael again. "*We'll* get her back. Emphasis on we."

Michael grinned. "Deal."

"Deal."

"You ready to go back in there?" Michael asked.

"I kinda said some pretty shitty things, especially to Jack."

"Yeah, I heard. I wouldn't worry about it. Seriously."

"You keeping an eye on me, vampire?"

"At this point, I'll always keep an eye on you."

Becky laughed. "Oh, yeah?"

"That sounded a lot more creepy than I meant."

Becky grinned, pulled Michael back down, and kissed him again. "We get out of this alive, and I'll show you something *really* worth keeping an eye on."

Michael grinned, and Becky slapped him on the behind, hard.

95

Thorn and Nanook looked up as Michael and Becky walked back into the library. The dogs pranced over to them, and Michael rubbed their heads. "I'll get you two something to eat here in a second."

"Allow me," Jack said. He snapped his fingers, and two enormous steaks appeared in front of the dogs. They each took one and padded away, already drooling.

"Thanks, buddy," Michael said, and hugged Jack.

"It's the least I can do," Jack said.

Becky cleared her throat. "I'm sorry for what I—"

Jack shook his head and hugged Becky before she could finish. "Don't. There is no need."

Becky cried a little, and even Jack wept.

"So what's the plan?" Michael asked.

Jack stepped back from Becky and turned to Frost and Pine, who sat near the fire. "Let's figure that out together."

"Not without us," Blaze said. He and Yori flew over to Becky.

"We will find your sister," Yori said.

"And we will get her to safety," Blaze added.

"Thank you both."

The two pixies both made small bows, and the group rejoined Pine and Frost by the fire.

"Sorry about…" Becky said, pointing in the direction she'd run earlier.

"Do not apologize," Frost said. "It's been one hell of a day."

"You will never need to apologize to me for anything," Pine said. He made a low, formal bow. "I pledge my bow to you and your family. I owe you and your line that much."

Becky nodded at the giant Dren. "Thank you."

Michael looked at Pine and smiled. "No hard feelings?"

Pine smiled back. "None. Perhaps we can…test our skills against one another some other time?"

"Well, you go get a few friends, maybe two or three, better yet, seven or eight, and let me know when you're all ready, okay?" Michael said.

Pine laughed at that. His voice, a low, strong rumble, echoed about the ruined library. "I like you, Vampire."

"Yori! Your wings!" Frost exclaimed.

Yori pointed at Blaze. "My friend is very skilled at healing."

Blaze smiled, fluttered down to a tiny rock, and sat by the fire.

Yori clapped her hands, and an immense green light flashed before her. Everyone blinked, and when they looked back, Yori stood there just as tall as Michael.

"Can all of you do that whenever you want?" Michael asked, glancing at Blaze and back again.

"No," Yori said, sitting down. "Not without considerable practice."

Michael nodded, and he and Becky both sat down, followed by everyone else.

"So," Michael said. "How do we go about getting our girl back?"

96

"Jack, Yori," Frost started, and stood back up. "Sorry, I think better on my feet," he added. He began circling the group. "Do you recall what Elm said while we were fighting?"

"You mean while she was kicking your ass?" Becky asked.

Michael stifled a chuckle. Frost, Jack, and Yori all looked over at Becky. Pine just smiled.

"Sorry, bad joke," she said, and offered the three a small grin. "I'm nervous. I crack stupid, badly timed jokes when I'm nervous."

Frost continued. "What she said when she referred to me by name?"

"She called you *Frost, second son of Laendrill, son of Kalleth,*" Jack said.

"Precisely!" Frost said.

Michael shrugged. "I don't get it."

"Me neither," Becky said.

"I'm not my mother's second son. I'm the oldest of the two. I'm her first," Frost said.

"Unless that's a particular difference in the Dren vernacular?" Jack asked. He turned to Pine. "Would you refer to the oldest as first, second, third, etcetera, as new children were born?"

Pine shook his head. "No. First born are first born, second

son or daughter, and so on."

Jack looked back up at Frost. "Are you sure?"

Frost nodded. "And she referred to you as *son of Laendrill*, not second son. Why?"

"Maybe she was just confused? Maybe she doesn't actually know you guys all that well? What does any of that matter?" Becky asked.

"Because Elm does not make mistakes," Pine said. "And she knows everything there is to know about her prey. She would not have misspoken."

"Then she wasn't making any sense," Michael said. "I'm with Becky, so fucking what?"

"What if she knows something that we don't?" Frost said. "And she warned us, several times, remember? First you!" Frost said, and pointed at Becky. "She told you to seek out those who sent her, did she not?"

Becky nodded. "Yeah, and she said it wasn't her doing this. Whatever the hell that meant. Sure felt like she was the one doing it when she almost strangled me."

"She said the same thing to us! She warned that she was *not* the enemy," Frost said. "That she was not the threat. Why would she say those things? And if she knows us so well, why would she make a mistake about our lineage?"

"What if she didn't?" Michael asked. "What if you guys have another brother, or sister?"

Frost and Jack both looked at one another and then into the fire, each lost in their own thoughts for the moment.

Michael continued. "If Elm is willing to tell us to find out who sent her, and she's showing us more of her hand, then who's to say she really doesn't want us to get to the bottom of it?"

"She would not betray the trust of whoever sent her," Pine said.

"Unless she resented being tasked with it!" Michael said. "What if she was being forced?"

"I cannot think of anyone powerful enough or brave enough to force Elm's hand," Pine said.

"Yeah, but what *if*? I mean—explain her actions?"

Pine shook his head. "I cannot."

"And why not kill us all when she had the chance? What did you say earlier?" Michael asked. "That your orders were to kill me, kill her"—he pointed at Becky—"and kill anyone else helping us?"

"Yes."

"So why let us live? I mean, she had us right where she wanted us! Why just take Melissa and leave?" Michael asked.

Pine now stood. "You appeared dead, that much is certain," he said, and looked at Michael. "Even I thought so when we found you. No one should have survived that. You are far stronger than we imagined."

"Yeah, but Yori? Becky? Blaze?" Michael asked.

Pine looked around at the three members of the group Michael had named. "I guarded Becky and hid her from the rest, even when the hunting party were collecting their dead. As for the pixies, I do not know."

"The last thing I recall was attacking Elm," Yori said. "We fell, and I lost consciousness."

"I saw her fall," Frost said. "But even before Elm incapacitated me, I did not think Yori was badly injured; unconscious, certainly, but gravely injured, no."

"Maybe the little guy just hid?" Michael said, and looked at Blaze.

Blaze looked up from the pebble he now sat on, "No. I watched Stin fall and raced to him. I did not need to hide; the Dren simply ignored me after that. I do not know why. I did not observe them further from that point. I am sorry."

"Don't apologize, Blaze," Becky said.

The pixie looked up and nodded.

"So why leave anyone alive?" Frost asked. "And why, what did you say, Michael? Show us her hand?"

"Yeah, seems weird, right?" Michael asked.

"And how did they know where we were?" Jack asked. "There is no possible way Elm could have directed so many of her forces to us so quickly."

Pine shook his head. "What I know is there was a grace period, as Elm promised there would be. After that, we all searched and found nothing. Even Vellrex was unable to locate you."

Michael jumped to his feet. "I thought you said Vellrex earlier! You did you say Vellrex, right?"

Pine nodded.

"I read something about him! I knew it was him!" Michael said. "He's in...." Michael's voice trailed off. "He was in the book I set aside. Whole damn room's gone now. We'll never find it."

"We don't need to," Jack said. "Tell us of Vellrex, Pine."

"The dragon has been with Elm for as long as anyone can remember. Tales tell he was raised by Elm," Pine said. "I don't

411

know much more, only that he is an excellent tracker, can see spirits, and has been known to cast spells from time to time. I believe it is how he hunts."

"Could he have found us?" Jack asked.

"No. We found the trail tome you used, but deciphering which destination you selected would have taken weeks, months even. Not hours."

"So how did you all get here? How did you find us?" Frost asked.

"Elm. She gathered our party, opened a window, and this is where it led. How she knew, or how she was given the information, or by whom, I know not," Pine said.

"Fucking riddles in the dark," Becky said, and laid back onto the floor.

"Who else knew you were here?" Yori asked.

"Besides you, and literally everyone back at Pixie Central?" Michael asked.

Yori glared at Michael. "You would not have been betrayed by us."

Michael nodded. "No, no, no...I know, I was—" he stopped, and turned to Frost.

Frost looked back at Michael, and the elf's eyes widened.

Michael took a breath. "Oh, shit."

97

Jack stood and looked at his brother. "Where did you come here from?"

Frost was staring into the fire now.

"Frost!" Becky said.

Frost looked up and then back at Jack. "Home."

"Oh, no," Michael said. "The uh, the shit about your family, the, the, what did you say, the first, second, and third, son and crap. Elm doesn't make mistakes! Remember? She was giving us hints! Clues!"

Jack summoned his sword, which snapped into existence. He yelled and swung it down onto a giant wooden beam. The wood exploded. "You came from home? Who else knew we were here before you left?"

Frost sank to his knees. "Mother."

Jack shook his head. "No, no, no, she—"

"Laendrill," Pine said, his voice low. "But why?"

"Are you saying your mother is behind all of this?" Becky asked.

Jack's sword vanished, and he circled back to Frost. "How? How did you come here?"

Frost looked up. "I opened a ring."

Jack cursed.

"What cause would your mother have?" Blaze asked. He was now hovering eye level with Jack.

"I don't…" Jack said, then took a measured breath. "I don't know."

Frost stood and looked across the fire at Jack. "They couldn't find you using the trail tome."

"So Jack calls you," Michael said, and motioned to Frost. "Tells you where we are. You come this way, and good ol' Mom phones Elm. Elm jets over here and waits until dawn when she knew I'd be screwed in the sunlight. She rips the fucking building apart with her damn dragon to make sure I'm out of the fight, kicks all of our asses, and then bolts with Melissa! Sound about right?"

Everyone was looking at Michael now.

"Occam's Razor, guys. Simplest explanation is usually the right fucking one!"

"What the hell?" Becky asked.

"But why would she do that?" Pine asked. "To her own children?"

"Spare the elves, right? Isn't that what you said?" Michael asked.

Pine nodded.

Michael turned to Frost and Jack. "Don't hurt her kids," he said and pointed at them. "Take Melissa, her youngest son's lover, and kill everyone else." Michael looked over at Becky.

Becky looked from Michael to the brothers. "What the fuck?"

"It doesn't make sense. Why would she do that?" Frost asked.

"WHO KNOWS!" Michael shouted, and threw his hands in the air. "You got a better explanation for what the fuck just happened?"

Frost's jaw clenched, and he took a step towards Michael.

Michael pointed at the elf. "Don't. I kicked Hagrid's ass over there," he said, pointing to Pine. "I'll *really* fuck you up."

Becky slapped Michael's arm down and stepped between him and Frost. "Both of you knock it off! We need to figure this shit out!" she said. "And I'll kick both of your asses if you start that bullshit again!"

Michael took a deep breath, and after a pause, he nodded at Frost. Frost, in turn, nodded back.

"Jesus," Becky said. She turned to Pine and asked, "Did that timeline line up for you?"

Pine looked at Michael. "It sounded very close, yes. And we did wait until morning before beginning the attack."

"And you think Elm had no clue where we were, right up until she opened a, whatever you call it?" Becky asked.

"A window. And yes, I'm certain," Pine said.

"I'm sold," Becky said, looking at Jack.

Jack shook his head. "I just don't understand why?"

"Melissa doesn't have time for this," Michael said. "So let's go ask Mom what the hell is going on!"

98

Becky rummaged through the wreckage that had been hers and Melissa's room. She shuffled around on all fours, tossing debris this way and that, stopping occasionally to inspect something. Shards of wood, stone, books, and scattered pages covered everything, making the job difficult.

"Got it," Michael said. He held up a small orange bottle. "This all there is?"

Becky took Melissa's medicine and kissed Michael on the cheek. "Yeah, that's it. She should have taken this hours ago."

"Okay, let's get back down there."

"Hang on a second," Becky said. "Look, I know I've said it a hundred times, so here's a hundred and one: thank you."

"Becky, it's no problem."

"But...."

"Uh-oh."

"But if something happens to me—"

"Nothing's going to happen to you."

Becky pressed a finger to Michael's lips. "...if something happens to me, you gotta promise something, okay?"

Michael nodded.

"You gotta take care of Smurf, okay? Promise me that. I mean, you turn her, okay? Make her...make her like you, okay?

Promise me."

Michael nodded again.

"Say it."

"I promise."

Becky wrapped her arms around Michael's neck and kissed him again. Michael kissed back and swore to himself that he would make sure Becky and Melissa were safe. He wasn't going to fail again.

"God, you're a good kisser," Becky said. She grinned.

"I could say the same thing about you."

"You better!"

"You're a good kisser."

Becky smiled, gave Michael a peck on the cheek, and then slapped his ass. "Come on, rambler, let's get ramblin'!"

Michael followed Becky out of the room and back down to the first floor, where almost everyone else was waiting.

"Frost and I agree that we should go alone," Jack said. "If any of this is true, it could be far more dangerous than anything we've encountered."

"Well, you and Frost can kiss my ass," Becky said as she descended the wobbly staircase.

Jack sighed. "Becky, this is our home, our mother, we—"

"And Melissa is *my* sister. We're going with you!"

"I agree with the warrior," Yori said, inclining her head toward Becky. "If your mother truly is behind all of this, and Elm is aiding her, then you will need all of the assistance you can get."

"And I will see Elm punished," Blaze said.

"They're right, Jack," Frost said. "They have a right to be there. Even if we're wrong, they should come. For all we know, Elm could return to this place."

"Guys, we don't have time for this," Michael said. "*Melissa* doesn't have time for any of this."

Jack sighed.

"I have them," Pine said from behind the group. He walked back into the library with Thorn and Nanook at his side.

"Oh, yes, one moment," Blaze said. He flew over to the dogs, ran his hand along each one separately, then clapped his hands together. Dazzling gold and silver armor began to materialize on each dog. Perfectly-fitted plate mail and chainmail began to appear, first on Thorn, then Nanook. A moment later, the dogs were outfitted almost entirely; even their tails sported magnificent armor. From the way the dogs reacted, and the frenzy with which each wagged, it appeared as if the armor weighed very little, if anything at all.

"Oh, my God! That's awesome!" Michael exclaimed. He crouched down, and Nanook and Thorn raced over and bar-reled into him. "You guys look so damn cool!" He ran his hand over the armor; it felt cool to the touch and seemed to vibrate under his fingers. "Just don't go testing it, okay? No. More. Arrows!"

Blaze glided over to Michael and held out his hand. Michael held out his hand likewise, and Blaze dropped a small golden whistle into his palm. Immediately, the whistle grew in size, and Michael held it aloft.

Blaze smiled. "That will remove the armor, and likewise summon it whenever needed."

"Thank you," Michael said. He smiled at the pixie. "You're a cool little dude, you know that?"

Blaze smiled. "I will train Nanook and Thorn how to summon the armor themselves at a later time."

Michael's jaw dropped. "Um."

"And these are for the rest of you," Blaze said. He flew from one person to the next and gave each a small gem. These, too, grew in size in each person's grip until the gemstones were an inch or so in diameter. "Should you find yourself in danger, simply throw the bringing stone to your feet with some force. It will take you to Droll, where Invyl will be able to help you."

Everyone thanked Blaze and tucked their gift away.

"I'm taking us into the courtyard," Jack said. "Frost and I will go first and guide you all from there."

Jack knelt down and began to draw a large circle with the tip of his finger. As before, a deep green light sprang up from the lines his finger drew, followed by peach-colored glowing mushrooms. When he was done, he looked around the group.

"I am sorry this has happened to all of you," Jack said. "I cannot begin to understand it. But...if what we believe is determined to be true, I owe you each a debt that I fear can never be paid."

"We..." Frost said. "If this is in fact the work of our mother, then we...*we* owe you all an unimaginable debt."

"Let's just go get our girl back, okay?" Michael said. "We can play the blame game later." He turned to Frost. "And, uh, no hard feelings? Heat of the moment and whatever?"

"No hard feelings," Frost said, and smiled at Michael. "I admire your tenacity. We will be good friends."

"Same thing goes for you, big guy," Michael said, and punched Pine in the arm. It was like punching stone.

Pine made a small bow and smiled.

Jack stepped into the faerie ring and disappeared. Frost followed close behind.

Becky grabbed Michael's hand and stepped forward. The portal vanished before her foot crossed the threshold, and the group was left alone in the ruins.

99

Becky cursed. "Son of a bitch, I knew it!"

"What just happened?" Michael asked. "What the—"

"Too dangerous, remember!" Becky said.

"They are very noble," Pine said. "Foolish, but noble."

Blaze flew down to where the faerie ring had vanished. "Noble or not, I suspected they might try that," he said. He touched the ground and flew back up and out of the way. The same ring reappeared almost instantly. Blaze smiled and turned to the group. "The stones I gave you are practically useless; forgive me."

Yori laughed. "I was wondering what a *bringing* stone was."

Blaze grinned. "There's no such thing, I'm afraid. But what I did hand you is a wonderful way to track someone!"

"You tricked them?" Michael asked.

Blaze nodded. "I was afraid they might attempt to confront the dangers ahead alone. I ensured they did not. After you," he said, and motioned for Becky and Michael to continue through the portal.

Pine laughed. "Clever pixie. Very clever!"

Becky grabbed Michael's hand again, and they stepped into the faerie ring. The same warm pressure as before engulfed the two. A flash of light, the sound of distant music, and eventually nothing. Then, almost at once, a beautiful courtyard came into focus, as did Frost and Jack no more than five feet away.

Becky marched forward and socked Jack in the jaw. He fell to the ground, and Becky stood over him, fists clenched. "You ever try and sacrifice yourself for us again, and I will kill you!" she said, then held out her hand.

Jack rubbed his jaw, accepted Becky's hand, and stood up. Before he could say anything, she hugged him.

"We're in this together, idiot!" Becky said, and looked up into the elf's eyes. She kissed him on the cheek. "No fucking heroics!"

Jack wiped away a tear, and squeezed Becky back. "Forgive me."

The rest of the group appeared, and the portal vanished.

Pine knelt down and placed his hands on his knees. "Strange window," he said.

"Much different than Dren incantations, I'm afraid," Blaze said. "You will recover momentarily."

Yori walked over to Michael and nodded towards an enormous marble staircase. Two armor-clad men stared back at the group. One was now gripping a sword at his waist.

Frost raised his hand towards the guards. "I bring Prince Jack and guests of the house. Send word to our father that we have returned."

The two guards looked at one another and then back at the group below.

"Your father has left the kingdom at the Queen's request, my lord," one of the men said. "Shall we inform your mother?"

"That will not be necessary," Jack said. "We will take food and wine in the water garden. Please see that refreshments are prepared; our friends are tired and seek rest. And where might our mother be?"

The guard, still holding his sword, replied, "She is entertaining guests in the north wing, my lord. A private affair, I am afraid."

"Thank you," Jack said. "Please see to the refreshments, and send word to have rooms prepared."

"As you wish, my lord," the guards said in unison and disappeared down a long hallway.

Frost turned to Jack. "Guests."

"Private affair," Jack replied.

"Okay, so now what?" Michael asked.

"Follow us; please stay close. Say nothing," Frost said. His flamboyant, almost cavalier demeanor was gone.

The brothers led the group up a giant staircase and into an extensive marble hallway. Every few feet stood a silver door, each with a small stained-glass window at eye level and a delightfully-colored glass doorknob. The doors were recessed in the walls on both sides of the hall, directly across from one another, and ran the entire length.

Michael stared up at the domed ceiling and noted that every few yards, giant iron spikes jutted out just below the marble. One of the doors in front of the group opened, and an armed guard stepped out. When he spotted the group approaching, he stood against the wall and saluted until everyone had passed. The man's silver helmet covered his entire face; even the eyes were hidden behind the metal. How the guard could see was a mystery, but when they passed, he did look down as two large, fully armored dogs strolled by, tails wagging.

The hallway ended in another courtyard, this one several hundred feet across. Surrounding the enclosure were four large archways, presumably leading north, south, east, and west. A white marble path led to each, forming a perfect cross which intersected with another path that followed along the circular yard. The tunnels extending past each arch looked similar, if not identical. Jack led the group straight across, pausing only once to whisper to Frost. Frost glanced skyward and then around but continued walking.

Michael leaned over to Becky. "Pretty quiet for such a big place."

Becky nodded. "I've got a bad feeling about this."

Michael chuckled. "*Star Wars*? Really?"

Frost turned his head and made it clear the two should stop talking. When the group entered the second tunnel, the only difference here was the doors. They were still metal, but unlike the silver doors behind them, these were a light, blue-tinged metal. The stained-glass windows in the doors were also slightly different. Each was composed of various shades of red and no other color. The handles on the doors were also red, and to Michael resembled giant rubies. He had to resist the urge to reach out and touch one.

At the tunnel's end, the group entered a majestic forest. To their immediate left and right, towering, white, perfectly smooth walls stretched so high into the night sky that not even Michael could see where they ended. The trees here were all silver as well; their bark shimmered and sparkled as the group approached. The path they now found themselves on was comprised of loose, beautifully-carved gemstones. Rubies, diamonds, sapphires, emeralds, citrine, and more covered the path like one would use gravel anywhere else. Becky gasped and almost stepped off the path until she realized everyone else save Michael walked along as if it were perfectly normal. She glanced up at Michael, who looked back, his eyes as wide as hers. He mouthed a profanity, and she nodded right back.

All through the area, tall metal torches were driven into the ground; foot-high flames climbed from each. They burned bright, which made the path, as well as the shining silver trees, sparkle and glitter even more. It was a dazzling effect, and almost overwhelming, which Michael imagined was the intent. Even the leaves which would occasionally float down to the ground were spectacular—each a different shade of transparent color, almost like glass. Michael and Becky walked right into Pine and Yori when the brothers stopped the group.

"Our mother is in there," Jack said, pointing to a small glass building several yards away. The windows were translucent, and only shadows could be seen within.

"Let us go first this time," Frost said.

"Please," Jack added. "I implore you. Even her sons are not allowed into meetings such as this appears to be. Her guards might react without thinking if we approach with guests in tow."

Everyone nodded that they understood. Frost and Jack proceeded forward, and the group waited.

100

"Yeah. I have definitely got a bad feeling about this," Becky said.

Michael nodded. "Me, too."

The brothers walked down the path towards the glass building, pausing just outside the door. They appeared to speak for a moment, and then together, they opened the two doors leading into the structure and stepped inside.

"I do not like this," Yori said. The words came out in a hiss.

Pine shook his head. "Nor I."

Michael turned to say something and noticed Blaze was gone. So were his dogs. "Shit. Shit, shit, shit...."

Everyone looked up, and Michael pointed to where the pixie and his dogs *should* have been.

"Oh, no," Becky said. She spun around, searching the forest.

Everyone did the same, and no one saw a thing. Blaze, Thorn, and Nanook were gone.

"Should we search for them?" Pine asked.

Yori was already hovering several feet above the group, turning in all directions. "I see nothing."

"WHERE IS SHE?" a voice shouted from the glass structure.

"That was Jack," Michael said. "I'm going!"

Becky was already moving before Michael could tell her to

wait. Pine and Yori fanned out in opposite directions, each with bows drawn, arrows pointing towards the glass doors several yards away. Michael lowered himself back to the ground, grabbed Becky's hand, and marched forward.

"NO!" another voice shouted.

A loud explosion rang out, and a brilliant red flash of light erupted out of the glass walls; with it, the windows vaporized into tiny sparkling projectiles. Michael leapt in front of Becky, shielding her as best he could from the incoming shrapnel. Sharp, burning fire struck him from head to foot, and the blast shoved him to the ground, Becky beneath him, their ears ringing.

A second explosion shook the ground, and Michael rolled over to see Elm swinging her swords at a tall, armor-clad woman. Frost and Jack lay crumpled on the floor of the now ruined building.

Michael looked over at a dazed Becky. "Are you okay? Becky? ARE YOU OKAY?"

Becky looked over, blinked several times, and gasped for air. After a moment, she scrambled to her feet. "I'm good!"

"I'm going!" Michael said, and raced towards the building.

Becky drew her knives and sprinted forward. To her left, Yori was firing arrow after arrow into the building; Pine was doing the same from her right. Blaze and the dogs were still missing.

Michael crashed into Elm with as much speed and force as he could muster over the short distance. The giant woman was catapulted into the air, and before she struck the ground, Michael hit her again, this time carrying her up into the tree-limbs high above.

Elm shouted, and Michael pulled her face close to his as they rose. He shouted back, "My name is Inigo Montoya! You killed my pixie! PREPARE TO DIE!"

Limbs exploded everywhere as Michael tore up into the trees, the Dren held tight in his arms. Elm drew back one of her swords and stabbed at the vampire's mid-section. Michael let go of the woman, catching her wrist as she began to fall and the sword missed its mark. He then twisted his entire body, and threw Elm as hard as he could towards a giant silver tree. Elm crashed into the wood where she tumbled back towards the ground some hundred feet below. Michael sped after her.

Becky raced through the open latticework of the little building and slid towards the two unconscious brothers. The other woman, undoubtedly their mother, sprinted out of the structure in the direction Michael had carried Elm.

Becky slapped the elf on the cheek. "Jack!"

Behind Becky, Thorn appeared and leapt through the air, racing in the direction Michael had carried Elm, his teeth bared, his armor shining bright. Nanook slid to a stop next to Becky, shoving her snout into Jack's face and licking at his nose and mouth.

Jack began to stir, and when he did, Nanook tore off in the direction Thorn had run.

"Becky," Jack said, and opened his eyes.

Becky was already crawling over to Frost, who was beginning to move. Yori dropped to the ground beside Frost, reached down, grabbed his arm and yanked him to his feet. "Get up, elf."

Frost ran his arm across his eyes and stared at Becky and the pixie. "Where's Jack?"

"Here," Jack said, his blue sword snapping into view. He shook his head and began scanning the area.

Frost nodded at his brother and summoned his own black swords.

"What happened?" Becky asked.

Jack turned to Becky, his face a mask of rage. "Our mother," he said, then charged in the direction Laendrill had fled. Yori flew after him.

"The vampire is in trouble," Pine said from just outside the building. His face was bloodied, and shards of glass glistened alongside the shining blue hairs of his beard.

Frost and Becky looked in the direction Pine pointed, and saw two distant figures grappling in the trees. Pine aimed an arrow and fired.

Michael gasped as one of Elm's hands wrapped around his throat, and the two crashed back towards the ground.

Elm jerked her head to the right and, without warning, she released Michael's neck as an enormous red arrow sliced through the air where her arm had just been. They struck the ground then: Michael on his feet, Elm on her back. The earth shook, and Michael dove towards the woman. Elm rolled backwards, sliced up through the air with one of her swords and connected with one of Michael's gloved hands. The pain was staggering, but to Michael's surprise, the material deflected the sword's edge. Blue sparks flew in all direction from the impact, and Elm's eyes widened. Michael's hand went numb, but he punched Elm square in the face with it regardless. The Dren stumbled backwards and dropped to a knee, the sword she'd tried to use on Michael now shattered.

Michael was panting. "We haven't met yet," he said and sucked in another breath, "...not really anyway," he continued. He moved towards her. "You killed my friend. And you owe me a new house, bitch."

Elm climbed back to her feet and smiled at the approaching vampire. "You are as strong as Pine described," she said, and wiped away a trickle of blood from the side of her mouth. "I wonder if you are as intelligent?"

Michael dove to his left as Elm swung her remaining sword, spun, and grabbed at his throat. He was too slow this time, and the Dren's hand closed around his neck again. She turned and slammed Michael into a tree several feet above the ground.

Elm swatted away Michael's attempts to remove her hand, and leaned in close to his face. "Go to your friend, vampire," Elm said. Before she could say more, she spun around—still holding Michael by the throat—snatched an arrow from the air, and threw it back with matching speed in the same direction it had come. She then carried Michael to the opposite side of the tree and held him against the trunk. More arrows sped by.

"She needs you now, vampire. You will find her in the south wing behind a silver door with a yellow handle. There is not much time. Yellow handle, vampire!"

Michael gasped as Elm threw him several yards in the direction of the tunnel they'd come through.

The Dren turned to leave, and there, not ten feet away, hovered Blaze, his golden sword pulsing with a strange green light, Thorn and Nanook growling beneath him.

101

Becky crashed into Pine as the giant Dren stopped dead. "What are you—"

"Look," Pine said, lowering his bow and pointing into the trees.

Becky followed his finger and there, glowing in the dark, hovered Blaze. Elm, sword drawn, stood several feet away, facing the pixie.

Becky turned back to Pine. "SHOOT HER!"

Pine looked down and shook his head. "No. This is the pixie's prize now, not ours."

Becky looked back toward Blaze and cursed. "But he's so...."

Pine touched Becky on the shoulder and turned her towards him. "His anger far outweighs his size, girl. And this is his fight now, not ours. Do you understand?"

Becky cursed again and noticed the arrow sticking out of Pine's shoulder for the first time—one of his *own* arrows. "Are you all right?!?"

Pine reached up and yanked the arrow free. Blood trickled down his armor, but he smiled. "I've never been struck by the same arrow I fired," he said.

Becky shook her head and turned back towards the shattered building. Jack was charging through the trees, Yori and Frost not far behind. "Where's Michael?" she asked.

Pine scanned the forest and then pointed towards the tunnel. "There," he said. Michael was sprinting down the hallway. "I go where you go."

Becky nodded, and the two ran after Michael. As they drew closer to the tunnel, the doors began to open, and a sea of armed guards poured out.

102

Michael picked up speed, knocking guards out of his path as he ran. One of the men swung at the black blur which had just raced by, then turned to see a towering Dren at the other end of the tunnel.

Michael flew across the courtyard and into the the passageway lined with silver doors. "Yellow handle, yellow handle, yellow—" He found the door and shoved against it. It was locked. Michael took a step back and sped towards the door, slamming his entire weight against it. The metal buckled in the frame, and the door burst from its hinges. Michael stumbled into the room.

"Melissa?"

The room was small, not what he was expecting at all. It was a bedroom, and there, in the center of a large bed, lay Melissa. Her eyes were closed, her hands folded on her chest, in them a small bouquet of flowers. She'd been dressed in a long blue gown and blue slippers, and her heat signature was all but gone. Michael raced over and reached towards her.

"Hey, kiddo," he said. His voice cracked, and it hurt to talk. "Melissa?" he touched her cheek in a soft, gentle motion. It was cold.

Michael began to shake, his face burning as the blood rushed into his head.

"Hey, kiddo!" he said again. "You still in there?" A tear fell from Michael's eye and landed on the bedspread. "Come on,

Smurf."

Melissa didn't move. Michael stood up and turned away from the bed, clenching his fists. He was going to kill his friends' mother, then he would kill Elm, and then he would kill anyone else that was responsible for all of this. He yelled towards the open door and slammed his fist into one of the bedposts. It exploded into the room.

"Hi," a weak voice said from the bed.

Michael spun, and Melissa smiled up at him. "Kiddo!" Michael dove onto the bed and crawled over to her, scooped her up, and cradled her in his arms. "Oh, my God!"

Melissa hugged Michael back. "Are we there yet?" she asked.

Michael looked down, confused.

"Joke," Melissa said. "This trip sucks."

Michael laughed and squeezed her again. "I'm totally leaving a negative review online, that's for sure."

Melissa giggled, and Michael pulled himself away to look down at her. "Are you okay? Did they hurt you? Can you walk?" he asked.

Melissa shook her head and laid back down on the pillows. "I just need to sleep a little, I think."

A worried look crossed Michael's face, and he lowered his friend back down onto the bed. Her heat signature had improved, but it was still weak, still low. Michael noticed one of Melissa's pupils was completely dilated, and his heart skipped a beat. He didn't know much about strokes, but he knew enough to recognize a possible sign. Elm was right. There wasn't much time.

"Hey, kiddo?" Michael asked, his voice low, soft.

Melissa looked up at him, raised a hand and touched the side of his face, and closed her eyes. Michael touched her on the shoulder and leaned down.

"Smurf?" Melissa's eyes opened back up. "Fuck death. Remember that, kiddo? Fuck death."

A tear spilled out of Melissa's right eye.

"Don't be afraid, okay?" Michael said.

Melissa smiled.

"All right, then," Michael said. "Fuck death. Just keep thinking that, okay? Fuck death."

Michael took a deep breath and tried to calm his nerves. He extended his teeth and bit into Melissa's neck as gently and carefully as he could.

103

Laendrill turned to face Frost, Jack, and Yori. She glanced once more in Elm's direction, and then back at her sons. "You don't understand," she said, her swords vanishing.

"Then explain it!" Jack said.

Yori drew her bow and aimed the arrow at the elf queen's left eye. "Lie and die, queen."

Laendrill glared at the pixie. "Careful, child."

Frost took a step towards his mother. "You used me to get to them. Why? EXPLAIN THIS!"

Laendrill looked back at Frost and Jack. "Family," she said. She sighed and sank to the ground. "You should have known your sister, your oldest brother. They were so, so beautiful," she said. Tears began to spill from her eyes.

"You…" Frost said, and stopped.

"Father, you and father, you had more children?" Jack asked.

Yori lowered her bow, but kept a hand on the string and the arrow nocked there.

Laendrill looked up. Her usual stunning features, her perfectly flowing blonde hair, her deep brown eyes, even her skin seemed to take on a suddenly tired, aged look, as if a shadow of time had fallen over her, and with it the pain and weariness of countless years.

"Not Kalleth, no," Laendrill said. "I was married long, long before I met your father. When I was far younger, far more naïve, in a land far from here. His name was Johnathan, and he was magnificent. We had two perfect children; we lived in a perfect little world. And it was shattered overnight."

Jack crouched down, reached out, and touched his mother's arm. "Why? Why all of this?" he asked.

Laendrill looked her son in the eyes. "Because of a vampire."

104

"My name is Blaze."

Elm nodded. "I am Elm, daughter of Cypress."

"You stole a part of my heart, Elm, daughter of Cypress," Blaze said. His sword hummed; the eerie green light surrounding the blade pulsed.

Thorn and Nanook began to circle left and right of Elm, careful not to draw too close.

Elm glanced at the dogs, lowered her head, and stared at the ground. "The other pixie."

"His name was Stin."

Elm looked back up and nodded "I will not forget it," she said. Elm glanced down at her remaining sword, then back at the pixie. She tossed the blade to the ground. "Stin was a skilled and brave warrior. I did not mean—"

"He was my life!"

The ground erupted. Dark, wet earth and debris filled the air alongside stunning flashes of intense light and heat. Brilliant golden chains snaked up into the air and wrapped themselves around Elm's feet, legs, and torso, ripping the Dren to her knees. She cried out, straining against the shining links in vain, while the chains tightened with her every move.

Elm screamed and groaned amidst her efforts to continue speaking. "I am"—something in the woman's body cracked, and Elm gasped, her eyes now wide—"sorry for your loss," she said. Her body began to convulse as waves of agony rippled across her face. "I wish you"—she choked for a breath—"... you to know that"—another sickening crack, another scream —"that before I die. Know, that I am sorry." Elm's eyes focused through the torment, and found Blaze's. "I hope to know your lover, your Stin, in the next life. I hope to make amends, should I meet him."

Blaze tightened the fist holding his sword, and his entire body trembled. The chains began to glow even brighter, and tendrils of black smoke now twisted and turned around the strange metal. Elm cried out as she was pulled closer and closer to the ground.

"I am sorry, Blaze."

The pixie glanced down at the small pouch containing what was left of his lover and then back at the woman who had murdered him. Stin, who loved tea as much as Blaze. Stin, who showed Blaze that he never needed to fear being alone. Stin, who loved animals, loved to sing, loved to laugh. Stin, who would never hold Blaze's hand again. Stin, who made the world a better place, was now gone forever. And now, would never care for the animals in the glade again, never sing, never laugh, never dance, never love again.

The green light enveloping the pixie's golden sword faded, and Blaze slide the weapon back into its scabbard. He took a deep breath, wiped his eyes, and glided towards Elm. The chains vanished in a wisp of dark amber mist. As he glided forward, he removed Stin's ashes from around his neck. He reached inside the little bag, took a small amount of what remained of his companion, and let the ash fall over the Dren. Elm closed her eyes, and tears began to flow down her cheeks, leaving behind streaks where the ash now settled.

After a moment, Elm looked up at Blaze, her face now covered in ash and streaked with glistening trails of pain and regret. "You do me a great honor, Blaze. I do not deserve it."

Blaze glided closer, leaned forward, and kissed Elm's forehead through the ash of his lover. "He is a part of you now, Elm, as am I. Forever."

Elm collapsed the rest of the way to the ground, sobbing. Blaze glided away and vanished into the forest.

Thorn and Nanook looked at Elm, studied her for a moment, then turned and raced in the direction Michael had gone.

105

Michael swallowed one last mouthful of Melissa's blood. While he drank, he had begun to feel the girl's heart, hear it in his ears, feel it in his chest. The sensation was almost overwhelming. At the first sign of Melissa's pulse slowing, her breaths coming in longer, more labored gasps, he stopped and pulled away. Her eyes were closed again, and her breathing shallow.

Michael leaned back down to her ear and whispered, "Fuck death, kiddo."

He pulled the knife from his boot, slashed his wrist, and held it to Melissa's mouth. She reached up the second the blood touched her lips and held on.

"There ya go, Smurf!"

Two armor-clad soldiers, swords drawn, burst into the room and were immediately ripped back out and tossed like dolls down the hallway by Pine.

Becky raced into the room a second later. "Smurf?"

"She's okay, she's okay," Michael said. "I, I think, I...." His head was swimming.

Pine ducked through the doorway, picked up the smashed metal door, and wedged it back into place as best he could. "I will guard the entrance."

Becky crawled across the bed to her sister and looked over at Michael. "Did you?"

Michael nodded. "I don't know if...."

Becky leaned across her sister and kissed Michael on the cheek, then reached down and ran her hand through Melissa's hair. "I'm here, Smurf, I'm here."

Melissa continued to drink, and Michael struggled to slow his heart as it tried to claw out of his chest. His head was spinning now, and his ribcage felt like it was going to explode. He gripped the bedpost and squeezed. The wood cracked in his grip.

106

"I don't understand," Jack said. "What vampire?"

Laendrill climbed back to her feet. The strange shadow which had covered her face vanished, and she appeared as she always did: strong, majestic, beautiful. "Marian. That was your sister's name. She fell secretly in love, you see. Her father and I had no idea. It seems your brother, Eric, knew about the affair; he and Marian were always so close. She might have been able to keep something from her father, even her mother, but it would have been impossible for her to keep a secret from Eric. And he her. They were as close as the two of you," the queen smiled and looked at her sons. "Marian had fallen in love with a vampire"—Laendrill spat the word when she said it—"and was soon with child, an elven vampire child."

"There are no such beings," Yori said.

Laendrill looked over at the pixie. "No, not any more," she said, turning back to Frost and Jack.

"Your brother tried to convince them to reveal the relationship, the child, at least to Johnathan and I. Balthazar, the child's father, refused. He and Eric fought." Laendrill looked up and sighed. "Your brother was a skilled fighter. I taught him well," she said, and stared off into space for a moment.

"The vampire had no chance of surviving. Horrified at what her brother had done, Marian fled to Balthazar's family. His father, Edward, killed her when he learned of his only son's death." Laendrill looked back at her children. "Edward traveled west into our kingdom, and he murdered everyone that stood in his path. Your brother, your father, everyone."

"And your mother slaughtered *him* in return," a voice said.

Everyone turned as Elm walked towards the group. "And then made a vow to me," the Dren continued. "That she would free my people evermore if we did but one thing."

"Destroy the rest of the vampires," Jack said.

Elm nodded. "We were a slave race. Property of the elves from time immemorial."

"And you agreed to it," Frost said.

"What would you *not* do for your entire race? Is there anything, boy? Anything you would refuse in order to save every man, woman, and child from slavery?"

Frost took a step towards the Dren. "I would not slaughter another race!"

Elm sighed. "This from the lips of a child that has never known slavery. Be careful what you say, boy. There are things in this world that you will never understand until you have lived them."

"Michael," Jack said. "You found out about Melissa, and when I learned she was dying, you what? You had me followed?"

"I followed you myself," Laendrill said, "Never again will I fail my children! A mortal? A dying mortal? And then, what, what did you think, that your new friend, a *vampire,* could save her? Better to let her die a mortal, and my son grieve an untainted love."

Jack's sword appeared in his hand. Frost turned and grabbed his brother's wrist. The two locked eyes.

Jack ripped his hand from Frost's grip. "And father? OUR father? Did he know?"

"Kalleth knows nothing of any of this," Laendrill said.

"And then what?" Frost asked.

"Your mother found me," Elm said. "She informed me that we had failed, that a vampire still lived, and that our agreement was nullified until said vow was kept. We were to end the vampire and those around Melissa. From there, Melissa would likely blame her sister's death on you, Jack, on the strange world you had exposed her to, and she would die alone, leaving you to move on with your life in time."

The sword in Jack's hand vanished. "Or what? What, Elm? Our mother would enslave your people again? It is a different time! We live in a different world!"

Elm shook her head. "I could not risk refusing her," she said, and looked back up at Laendrill. "But…I could plant seeds."

Laendrill glared at the Dren.

"Seeds which I could watch grow. Seeds which could lead you to the truth." Elm looked back down at Jack, and a sad, mournful look washed over her face. "And so they did, and so I have."

107

Michael's head was pounding. Melissa continued to drink until he finally had to pull away. The thumping stopped, and he collapsed back onto the bed, breathing hard.

Becky crawled over to him and took his face in her hands. "Hey! You okay?"

Michael focused on Becky's face. "I think so?"

Becky smiled and turned back to Melissa. The girl was breathing normally again, and the color had come back to her face. No blood was present on her lips anywhere.

"She looks much better," Pine said from the doorway. "But I am worried. I do not understand where the rest of the guards are?"

Michael sat up, swung his legs over the edge of the bed, and collapsed into a heap on the ground. "Remember? They said something about the king leaving?" he said from his back. "Maybe he took a ton of people with him? Maybe there's just not a lot of people here in the first place? I need a cider. Like, really, really, bad."

There was a whimper at the door, and Pine pulled it open just a fraction. Thorn and Nanook barreled in and raced to Michael, whereupon they proceeded to lick his face repeatedly.

"Guys!" Michael said, and ruffled their heads, their armor clinking and clanking as he did.

"Smurf?" Becky said from the bed.

Melissa's breathing had slowed again, and the color had drained from her face. Michael gripped the edge of the mattress and pulled himself up from the floor. Pine came over and helped him onto the bed, then returned to the door.

"Hey, kiddo?" Michael said.

Melissa gasped for air and began to convulse.

108

Jack walked over to his mother and locked eyes with her. His hands shook, and his voice trembled through clenched jaws. "You are no longer my mother. I am no longer your son. You will leave my father's kingdom. And you will never return." He took another step closer. "If you do, I *will* kill you."

"Jack," Frost said.

Jack turned and stared at his brother. "What would you have me do?" His voice was now a loud mixture of rage, despair, and confusion.

Frost began to say something, and looked away.

Laendrill smiled at Jack. "You may be my son, child," she said, and her hand shot forward and grabbed Jack by the shirt. She picked him up easily. "But never presume to threaten me."

Elm fired three quick arrows at the queen and sprinted forward. Frost had already summoned his blades, but stood his ground, and Yori launched her own arrow. Laendrill swatted them all, never once taking her eyes off of Jack's.

Elm dove towards the queen and was thrown aside by an unseen force. The Dren crashed into a tree and slumped to the ground. Laendrill returned Jack to the ground, swatted two more of Yori's arrows away, and looked at Frost. Frost, swords still in hand, stood motionless, his eyes wide, his mouth open. The queen smiled, and vanished in a swirl of light and shadow.

The three stood quiet for a moment, then joined Elm, who was already climbing back to her feet.

"She is gone, then?" Elm asked as she gripped her side.

"She fled. Like a coward," Yori said.

Elm turned to the pixie and smiled. "Brave words from such a young spirit."

"I need to find Melissa," Jack said.

Elm turned to the brothers. "She is there." The Dren pointed back towards the tunnel, where several dozen guards were stumbling out, looking confused and battered. "Look for the silver door with the yellow handle."

Jack nodded at Elm. "Thank you."

"Before you go," Elm said, "Understand that I will hunt you no more. And I am sorry for what happened here. There was no honor in it, and I fear I will never regain my own." Elm bowed low and limped back into the forest.

"Let's go, Jack," Frost said, and the three made their way back towards the castle and their friends.

109

Melissa was barely breathing by the time Jack, Yori, and Frost made their way to the room where Melissa had been kept. When it was clear she was not going to survive, Michael raced from the room. Frost, Yori, and Pine followed.

"You did everything you could, Michael," Yori said when they were further down the hall. "You should not blame yourself for this."

"Tell that to Melissa and Becky," Michael said.

"She may yet live, my friend," Pine said.

"The Dren speaks the truth, Michael," Frost added. "For now, I ask for your help."

Michael looked at the elf and shook his head. "I'm not sure that's the best move, man."

Frost smiled and placed a hand on Michael's shoulder. "I will be the judge of that. I need your help in assisting me with the injured soldiers. I need all of your help, please."

Across the courtyard, a dozen or more soldiers had stumbled out of the hallway where Pine and Becky had fought through their ranks. Some of them lay on the grass, motionless.

"Your self-pity serves no one, vampire," Yori said, and began walking towards the injured.

"Jesus," Michael said. He paused, then nodded at Frost and Pine.

Pine looked down at Michael. "I, too, am responsible for this. I, too, feel your grief."

Michael nodded, and they followed Frost and Yori towards the injured soldiers.

Yori proved to be just as skilled as Frost when healing the wounded. She made her way from one elf to the next, repairing whatever damage she could, and offering words of support when needed. Pine, too, was skilled, though he did not appear to possess the same magical abilities as the pixie and the elf. He did, however, have several ointments and draughts, which he administered here and there. Upon helping each soldier, the Dren would apologize, and ask for forgiveness.

Michael was contemplating sharing some of his blood with an unconscious young elf when Becky came running into the courtyard, calling for him.

110

Michael sat on his brand-new deck. The wood was so new that the entire back of the house smelled like a lumberyard. He sipped on a cold cider—this one, a Bold Rock Peach. Below, the dogs romped around in the moonlight, taking turns tackling one another and generally getting as dirty as possible. The house was back to its old self, but even better. An army of elves and pixies had made sure of that. There were all kinds of special features, too, some high-tech, others magical. The magic ones he'd yet to really figure out, but they promised to be nice when he did!

"I like the Granny Smith better," Becky said from her own glider.

"Yeah? The peach is growing on me," Michael said.

"I agree with Becky," Jack said. "Miss Smith makes a far better cider."

"No, it's not..." Michael started, then chuckled. "Never mind."

Melissa crashed into the top of a tall pine on the far side of the lawn and sprawled on the ground below, where Nanook and Thorn proceeded to lick her face repeatedly. It had taken several days, and more than one close call, but she had pulled through the transformation, much to everyone's surprise and relief.

"Comin' in hot!" Michael called down.

"You okay, Smurf?" Becky asked.

Melissa stopped giggling long enough to give the group a single thumbs-up from the pile of fur engulfing her, then continued playing with the dogs.

"Gotta work on sticking that landing," Michael said. "Took me months. I'm still shocked at how quick she picked up the flying bit!"

"She's always been a quick learner," Becky said.

"To flying!" Jack said, and raised his cider.

Becky leaned over and whispered in Michael's ear. "He's hilarious when he's drunk."

Michael laughed. "Right?" He raised his bottle. "To flying!"

Becky raised her bottle, and the three took another sip, content to enjoy the rest of the summer night.

The End

(SNEAK PEEK)

The FATE series continues!

HERITAGE

Fate: Book 2

By
DAVID S. SHOCKLEY II

1

The man struggled. He twisted, pulled, and fought as hard as he could, but it was useless. The woman attacking him was the strongest person he'd ever encountered—the strongest THING he'd ever encountered. He'd tried to hit her, but found only empty space when he swung. He'd tried to kick her, and the one time he managed to connect, he screamed as his shin, ankle, and toes cracked in several places. It was as if he had tried to drop-kick an anvil.

He tried throwing a couple of elbows, only to yelp again as more of his bones splintered upon impact. He couldn't move or see much of her now, but he could feel her, and what he felt mirrored what it must be like to find oneself embraced by a car accident: pinned motionless by unyielding metal and sharp, fiery objects.

He tried to move again, and failed; the panic coursing through his veins flooded into what was left of his consciousness. He cried out, because while the pain in his neck was excruciating, the agony gripping his spine and crushing his ribs was growing worse. Elizabeth heard the whimper; she reached up with one hand and covered the man's mouth. She never once removed her teeth and lips from his neck. It wouldn't take much longer.

The man's struggles flagged and faded, until finally they stopped altogether. His body convulsed several times, another whimper spilled out of his throat, and he went limp.

Elizabeth withdrew her teeth, pulled back, and licked her lips. They tasted of warm salt. She held the body at arm's length, cocked her head to the side, mimicking the corpse, and stared into its eyes; there was nothing there, not anymore. No fear, no horror, no soul.

A single tear slipped down the body's cooling cheek, and Elizabeth smiled.

"Thank you," she said.

She licked the corpse's throat, studied its empty gaze once more, and let go. The body fell for several hundred feet and collided with the water with a sickening finality. Even from so far up, the vampire heard the splash. It was a nice sound: solid, complete, finished.

Elizabeth licked her lips again and flew back towards the lights of the oceanfront boardwalk. The buzz that enveloped her after a kill was always a good one: dangerous, but also divine, and this one...this one made her happy. In the beginning, she'd had quite a hard time controlling herself after a hunt and feeding like the one she'd just enjoyed, but she'd learned, and now she *used* the wild energy, the almost sexual frenzy that erupted within her after taking prey. The boy she'd just killed had a friend, who was no doubt wondering where his accomplice had gone. Elizabeth was intent on educating him.

~

Peabody's Nightclub was packed. It was almost always that way on Friday nights during tourist season. The club had been around since the early 90's, so even the locals still came here despite avoiding the rest of the oceanfront below 45th Street during the summer. There weren't many places left that were older than twenty, thirty years, so generally speaking, the city's residents avoided "the strip." There were countless other places a local could go for music, drinks, and the company of single others—spots that didn't reek of the annoying and aggravating atmosphere drenching the Virginia Beach strip from early June through late August.

The locals knew the good places well and did their best to keep them secret from the hordes invading the city each summer. The internet had made that harder and harder to do over the years, but there were ways around that. Ways of keeping the tourists at bay.

Despite its lack of charm during tourist season, though, the strip was a wonderful place to hunt. A lot of predators used it. And a few of them were better hunters than most.

Elizabeth strolled past the extensive, overheated, and somewhat desperate line of patrons waiting to get into the club and its hopefully cooler air. She flashed a smile at the bouncers checking IDs and made her way through the glass doors behind them, much to the chagrin of several curious and attracted onlookers. The giants guarding the entrance just nodded and grinned as she passed. One of the behemoths glanced over his shoulder and couldn't help admiring her figure; he was positive her body was perfect, flawless—almost too exquisite, and painfully so. He swallowed hard, pulled at the crotch of his black jeans, and looked back down at the ID he held in his now trembling hand. His chest hurt, and other areas were throbbing as well. It was going to be a long night.

Vampires had spent most of the last century cowering behind their closed and well-hidden doors. But now, ever since word had seeped out that they were no longer being hunted, most had shed the security of the dark alleyways and forgotten parts of the city. Elizabeth knew of maybe six other vampires in the area, and all but one was now venturing forth and testing the waters again. A little dip here, a fang or two there. Elizabeth was enjoying it; after so long living in isolated fear, it was…well, it was amazing.

The music was loud, the temperature in the club over eighty, despite the building's extensive air handling system. Partygoers were shedding clothing left and right. Blasts of cold fog enveloped the dance floor every few songs, and each time they did, the throng was reinvigorated. Glistening bodies writhed and danced to the music erupting from the speakers, while a DJ with long purple dreads bobbed her head on the elevated stage. Behind her, various lasers and intense swirling lights flashed and strobed out over and into the undulating crowd.

Elizabeth pulled off her little white blouse and abandoned it to the sweat- and grime-covered floor. She'd buy another; that one had blood on it now, anyway. By the time the night was over, the hundreds of partygoers would have trampled it and its dark red evidence into gross, sticky oblivion. The staff would toss whatever was left of it into the trash tomorrow, and not long after that, the blouse containing the murdered boy's blood would be forever lost.

Elizabeth wove her way into the sea of bodies in a silver-sequined bikini top and formfitting black leather pants. Her dark hair cascaded over her shoulders and down her back; there was still a bit of blood in it. She spied the man whose friend she'd just killed dancing with a petite blonde. The girl was clearly drunk—probably drugged like the last one, really —but she wasn't stumbling yet.

Elizabeth moved in. One more snack before retiring for the evening. One less monster in the world.

The vampire glided up to the couple and smiled over the girl's head. The man couldn't help but notice her; Elizabeth didn't even need to use her thrall. She would later, of course, but for now she had his attention, and why not? Elizabeth was the most gorgeous woman there. She was the *only* woman in the sea of young girls: tall, sexy, and confident, a feature just as attractive as anything else.

The boy was a tall kid, too, probably 6'1", 6'2", in his early twenties, very fit, with a haircut that screamed military. He smiled over his prey at Elizabeth and moved to sidestep the little blonde. Elizabeth looked down at the girl and willed her to find a friend, call for a ride, and go home. She added a little fear, and leaned down to the blonde's ear.

"Don't ever let a guy you just met hand you an open drink again. *Ever*. And stay away from the clubs for the rest of the summer. Study, learn to knit, draw, whatever," Elizabeth murmured.

The thrall slammed into the girl's subconscious like a wave of stone and pure intent. She stumbled a little, looked up at the beautiful vampire, blinked several times, and drifted away.

The vampire turned her attention back to the other predator. "Hello, cutie," she said over the music.

The boy tore his eyes from the girl he'd drugged and, after a moment, smiled at his new target. "Hi yourself," the dead man called back.

ABOUT THE AUTHOR

David S. Shockley

 David Shockley has been writing novels for over two decades, or most of his adult life. His works universally reflect such themes as the strength of family - regardless of its makeup - personal conviction, and the courage to find good in the world, wherever and in whomever it resides. He loves sports and music, is a fanatical movie enthusiast, cotton candy addict, and has never met a roller coaster or thrill ride he didn't like. He was a 2010 national karate champion in kata as well as silver medalist in kumite for his age-group. His favorite bands include The Ramones, Great Big Sea and Creedence Clearwater Revival. His favorite authors include Jack London, William Shakespeare, Elmore Leonard and Stephen King. He currently lives in Virginia and has spent most of his life in and around the ocean. His love of longboarding has been a great source of fun and relaxation since he was a kid. He encourages everyone he meets to try it at least once.

BOOKS BY THIS AUTHOR

The Elves

Jimmy Peterson is sick. Very sick. Living within the children's ward at St. Joseph's Hospital at the height of World War II, Jimmy suspects that his illness is far worse than anyone will admit, especially to him. But Jimmy knows better: endless medications, constant pains and wracking coughs are the unfortunate realities of his days. One wakeful night in the ward, he receives an unexpected visit from none other than Santa Claus. Saint Nick invites Jimmy on an adventure, one which will grant him a brief respite from the illness that plagues him. Of course Jimmy accepts and within moments finds himself sitting wide-eyed in Santa's sleigh, soaring through snowy skies behind eight flying reindeer.

When they arrive at the North Pole, Jimmy meets an assortment of extraordinary characters, all of whom are eager to introduce him to the many marvels of their home. Each encounter is more astonishing than the last, from cooking classes with elves to mice that talk to the endless wonders of Santa's workshops. He enjoys every magical moment, relishing the contrast to life in a children's ward, with its frightened patients, unsavory medicines and desperate parents. Despite his delight, Jimmy constantly struggles to conquer the fear that wells up inside him when he faces the reality of returning to the ward. More than his own pain, Jimmy dreads the impact his illness will have on his family if his health continues to decline.

This Dog's Afterlife

Do you ever wonder what your dogs are thinking? How they feel? What they're dreaming about as they run, whimper, bark, and growl in their sleep? Who or what they're playing with when they romp around all by themselves? What they're looking at when all you see is a blank wall or an empty doorway? Will we see them again after they've gone? Are they still here watching over us – helping, perhaps even snuggling with us like they used to? What if they wrote and sent you a story from the great beyond?

This Dog's Afterlife answers those questions. Tucker, the canine narrator, takes the reader on an adventure starting from the most unlikely of places: the last day of his life. At that moment, he realizes that the end is really just a new beginning. Tucker encounters many new wonders and finds he has much to learn. Fortunately, he has help in the form of his father, Rocket, and a cast of canine characters who show him the ropes. Along the way, he learns that some souls don't immediately move on to the afterlife, but instead, find themselves adrift. Those souls can be found and helped, but it's a delicate and dangerous task. When he tries to rescue the lost soul of a young boy, Tucker realizes that even after death, sorrow is a very real, very tangible thing, and that there are still fears to overcome and hard choices to be made.

Shell: A Short Story

Richard was going to kill himself tonight. There were just a few things that needed to happen first.

Today was the twenty-second day since his wife Rebekah, daughter Penny, and unborn child Emma were murdered...so today was not only the day that Richard was going to kill himself. Today was also the day Richard would kill the thing that had murdered his family.

He only had to wait a few more hours.

Push: A Short Story

Jeff just discovered something. Something impossible. Something crazy. Something really, really weird. Jeff just discovered that he's magical. Magical, mystical, and downright miraculous! But weird...really, really weird. And gross. Yeah, it's a little gross.

Back

What if you were given the chance to relive your life?
With all of the memories you have now
Able to change anything you wanted
What if once you got that chance, all you wanted was to come back?
What if you couldn't?

BACK opens with everyman Mike Johnson waking up the morning after Easter to discover that he has returned from his comfortable married existence to his life as a twelve-year-old boy. No warning, no wishes, no angel needing his wings – just instant Star Wars pajamas and elementary school. The story centers on Mike's struggle to accept his new situation and understand why he's there, all while trying to cope with being an adult in a child's body and without continuous access to coffee.

Lineage: Fate: Book 1

Three decades.

For three decades, Michael has been on his own. Self-imposed exile - his only option - has been lonely. Necessary? Yes. Lonely? Absolutely.

But tonight?

Tonight everything changes.

Up until tonight, Michael thought involuntarily becoming a vampire would be the wildest thing to ever happen to him.

Nope.

Not even close.

Made in the USA
Columbia, SC
22 November 2020